Sis, hope you enjoy this read, is a sequel to *Once Upon a Nightmare* — remember, it ended in a dream — this isn't —

Luv Ya
Bill

Ded Reckoning

William F. Lee

William F. Lee

Ded Reckoning

Copyright © 2012, by William F Lee.
Cover Copyright © 2012 by Sunbury Press, Inc.
Cover image "Atrani" by Lawrence von Knorr – used with permission.

NOTE: This is a work of fiction. Names, characters, places and incidents are the product of the author's imagination or are used fictitiously, and any resemblance to actual persons, living or dead, business establishments, events or locales is entirely coincidental.

All rights reserved, including the right to reproduce this book or portions thereof in any form whatsoever. For information contact Sunbury Press, Inc., Subsidiary Rights Dept., 50-A W. Main St., Mechanicsburg, PA 17055 USA or legal@sunburypress.com.

For information about special discounts for bulk purchases, please contact Sunbury Press, Inc. Wholesale Dept. at (717) 254-7274 or orders@sunburypress.com.

To request one of our authors for speaking engagements or book signings, please contact Sunbury Press, Inc. Publicity Dept. at publicity@sunburypress.com.

FIRST SUNBURY PRESS EDITION
Printed in the United States of America
October 2012

Trade Paperback ISBN: 978-1-62006-131-2
Mobipocket format (Kindle) ISBN: 978-1- 62006-132-6
ePub format (Nook) ISBN: 978-1-62006-133-9

Published by:
Sunbury Press
Mechanicsburg, PA
www.sunburypress.com

Mechanicsburg, Pennsylvania   USA

Also by William F. Lee

The Bottom of the List

The Boys in Blue White Dress

The Light Side of Damnation

Once Upon a Nightmare

Home is a Long Time Ago

Acknowledgments

I thank the efficient and accommodating folks of Sunbury Press. As in the past, they make it happen. Larry Knorr, thank you for your confidence and aggressive spirit. To Allyson Gard, my Sunbury editor, a job well done once again. I repeat, and quote, "Your words have supported those who stumbled." The process has been prompt and pleasant.

A very special thanks to Mary Hughes who once again assisted me on this journey. She was again figuratively at my side each step with encouragement and helpful suggestions. Most of all I value her friendship.

Also I thank my "ole" Marine Corps buddy, Bob Reed for his assistance in the initial editing phase. He has helped me before and it is always valued, but not as much as his friendship. That is most important.

And as usual a "thanks" to my compatriot members of The Lesser North Texas Writing Group for their valuable critique and insightful input in the early stages of this novel. A special thanks to the leader and benevolent dictator of the group, Carol Wood.

Most important for me has been the input; the encouragement; the patience; and the love of the single most important person in my life, my wife, Jodi. She is, and has been, my wife; my best pal; my girlfriend; my "luv" for fifty-seven years. It doesn't get any better. I loved her the moment I saw her in Laguna Beach over fifty-seven years ago; have every day since; do now and will forever. Thanks for bearing with me ... my goodness, she has read every script of the six novels six times and every published book three times.

Last, and certainly not least, I thank my readers for their support and excursions through my novels ... and for their continued suggestions and input.

PROLOGUE

*"God be with you, because you'll probably
be alone when it all goes bad."*
A gunfighter's rule.

Samantha kisses him on the cheek and coos over her shoulder on the way to the front door, "I'm leaving, Hunter."

"Sam. Hey, wai..."

"Work to do; places to go; appointments to keep."

Hunter shouts from the kitchen table as he shoves his chair back with his butt and shouts, "And miles to go before we sleep, and miles to go...whatever, before we...we...our brains out," his voice trails off becoming a sigh that transcends into a sly smile.

"I heard that. Was close. That's yet to come. Tonight, Tiger."

Hunter's eyebrows raise, and he smiles as he pads hurriedly to the front door in his bare feet and jockey shorts, leaving his coffee mug and *San Diego Tribune* on the kitchen table. The paper is opened to the Sports Page and the mug is more than half-empty like the '71 Padres season is going. He less than slams, and more than bumps, his left thigh on the sharp wooden corner of the dining room table as he hurtles through the room, then slides to a halt on the tiled front entryway.

"Damn," rubbing the abrasion on his thigh as he reaches the wide-open doorway. Samantha is holding the knob in one hand and her briefcase in the other. Hunter is framed in the doorway for all the world to see with the outside entryway light acting as if it were an overhead theater spot. Sam's amorous gaze holds Hunter as if he were a mannequin in a shop window.

"My, my, my. What jockey shorts do for you. Or better, what you do for them." She pauses, beaming. Actually more a cross between a grin and a feigned hungry snarl. She softly pats and rubs him. "My, my. Scandalous advertisement material."

"Who's doing the vetting now?" Feeling sheepish he grins, remembering his similar jousting remarks yesterday when they first met at Lindberg Field. Then, as if the entire neighborhood could hear he whispers, "Why leave now? We can take up where we left off, or relax in the Jacuzzi, or both. I mean last night was great...one of the best."

"One of the best?"

"Okay. The best, but it's been a..."

"Me too, but I have work to do. So do you." She slips her index finger in the band of his shorts; pulls the elastic out several inches, peeks in, and then lets it snap close. "Don't forget, call Joe. Bye." She brushes his gaping mouth with her glossy pink lips. The entire entryway is not only engulfed in the light but also swallowed up with her scent. Her auburn hair, smelling like spring flowers, bounces on her shoulders as she laughs. It announces her joy for the neighborhood to see and hear. The whole world for that matter.

Before Hunter can say another word, she cavorts down the front walk toward her car on her long athletic legs which are needed to withstand the weight and jouncing of her more than generous breasts. It's the Blue Hour, after the French expression, *l'heure bleue.* It's morning civil twilight. Early by most standards, especially on a month-end Saturday.

As she nears the end of the walk, both she and Hunter hear a shout from the neighboring house. "Good morning, Ms. McGee. Nice day." The neighbor, the contracted Property Manager for Hunter's leased home, is Mrs. Columbo. Teresa, or Dee. She has sing-songed her tiding from half-way down her front walk. Her minx-like smile, difficult to see in the twilight, betrays the lilt in her voice.

Hunter glances at her. Thinks. *Looks sweet; purrs deep; and plays rough.*

Samantha echoes, "Morning, Mrs. Columbo. Nice day." Her words are unenthusiastic and hissed like an angry cat as she pauses for the necessary prudent several moments before she opens the driver's door of her mist-green Pontiac Firebird and slides in.

Hunter mutters, "Psssss. Ouch."

Then he manages to break his stare from Sam's abundant share of the gene pool. Looks again at Mrs. Columbo standing in a loosely fitting sheer summer ankle-length caftan, holding her copy of the *Tribune* teasingly against the front slit of the robe. With her black hair she looks like a geisha girl standing in her oriental garden. Teasing, tormenting or simply embarrassed, nonetheless with claws out. His view in the civil dawn light is enhanced by his neighbor's outside light. Civil twilight, nautical twilight, light or not light, one can't mistake this vision or the intent.

She ain't embarrassed...she's either teasing or tormenting, or both.

He stands stunned by her appearance and the cat-like exchanges and imagery of both women. Two felines, both with fur up on arched backs; spitting; hissing; tails swaying angrily. Hunter smiles, continuing to be mesmerized with his neighbor's morning "look" for a few additional moments. *Damn. I mean, God damn.*

BOOM!

The blast is deafening. The flash of light brings dawn early for a moment. The heat and flames searing hot. Windows shatter on both sides of Hunter's front door. The house across the street loses the three windows facing Arcola Street. The entire right side door of her sleek '68 Firebird and Samantha's upper torso, smash into and splinter the split-rail fencing in Hunter's front yard. Shrapnel-like pieces clatter on his and Dee's roofs. The trunk lid clunks on the asphalt roadway some twenty yards up the hill on Arcola. The hood rattles off the cul-de-sac metal barricade His forehead is creased by flying shrapnel, like the old days in the paddies. Blood begins to ooze into his eyebrows.

Hunter is knocked halfway to his butt. Only his vise-like grip on the front door knob prevents him from going all the way down. The door slams against the wall and the force of his weight now thrusts him back up like a spring-loaded coil. That triggers the front door to whip forward, propelling him onto the outside brick entryway like a F4 Phantom hitting after-burner. The remnants of the car and what's left of Samantha are lost in the firestorm with plumes of thick, smoke spiraling upward like the chimneys of ghastly Auschwitz. Hunter Ardal William Kerrigan's instincts, his training, his experiences, his every fiber reacts exactly as one would expect. One being Joe Zachary, his CIA Handler; others being his numerous combat buddies in Nam; and one for sure being himself, the "Hawk." His initials.

He knows Sam is gone. He sees a man pushing himself off the ground in the weed-ripe mesa below the cul-de-sac at the end of Arcola. The man staggers, turns to look back for several fatal seconds. Then starts walking briskly, but not so much so as to attract unwanted attention. He's in a business suit. Odd. He doesn't belong there, and he's carrying something in his right hand. Not a weapon, or it might be what was his weapon.

As Hunter instinctively starts his run for the man, he glances toward Dee and shouts, "Are you hurt?"

"No. What ..."

"Get inside. Call the police. Don't come out." He leaps over the remaining split-rail fence in the corner of his front yard, and in two bounds hurtles the two foot high metal protector at the end of the cul-de-sac and vanishes down into the mesa below. He's running full out.

The man is still at the same pace and hasn't looked back. Hunter is closing fast. Bare feet. Jockey shorts. Beginning the final glide and swoop, hands like talons.

The troops have said. Joe Zachary will say.

The Hawk is out and flying on ded reckoning, or deduced reckoning, or dead reckoning. However it's spelled. Old, new. Oxford or Webster's. It means ...

Someone else is going to die.

CHAPTER 1

*"Be aggressive enough, quickly enough.
There's no such thing as
'too aggressive' once the fight is on."*
A gunfighter's rule.

The man hears the Hawk's accelerated breathing before the sound of Hunter's bare feet thrashing through the knee-high grass and weeds. Either way, it's much too late. The man quickens his pace and begins a body turn to face who or whatever is swooping down upon him. The momentum of his turn is hastened by Hunter's hand clutching and jerking his shoulder, spinning the fleeing man around as if at the end of a bungee cord. Hunter follows with a jackhammer blow to the man's chest with the heel of his right hand. The blow is directly over the heart and, if desired, can be a killing one by an expert. Hunter is exactly that; however, he wants only to stun and fell the man.

His quarry snaps backward as if his feet are swept from beneath him, landing on his shoulder blades and butt. His slender shoulder line at the edge of the mesa with a forty foot drop to a metal storage building hidden in the canyon's shadow at this July 31st Blue Hour. Hunter straddles his unconscious prey; the man's head drapes backward over the edge of the mini-mesa. He searches through the man's coat and trouser pockets and finds a Walther in a shoulder holster, one electric detonator, a rent-a-car document, and a wallet. Hunter rifles through the billfold, thumb flips through fifteen hundred dollars in hundreds, American. A few extra twenties, and a driver's license. Hunter mumbles, "John Smith. Yeah, right." The rummaging also produces a few credit cards, each with different names. S*tolen. Or provided.*

John Smith stirs as he regains consciousness. Hunter reaches down, grasps him by the knot of his tie, pulls his head up and slaps him several times to hasten his awareness.

The man's eyes open, and he begins to stammer. Hunter growls, "Let's talk, asshole. Who are you?"

Still groggy and gasping for breath, the man begins to reach inside his suit coat with his left hand. Hunter delivers a crushing karate chop to the man's left shoulder, shattering his collar bone and causing the arm to drop to the side. Hunter's blow is the concentrated visualization of the hand, as a blade, going through the target. In this case the fragile collar bone.

Hunter barks in the well-known Drill Instructor lingo. "Speak, maggot." Slaps him twice, the last a back hand. Then snarls, "Who are you and why this shit? Why her? And don't give me any John Smith crap."

The man sucks in some civil twilight humidity, eyes watering with pain, and with a heavy Irish accent, spits, "Fook you."

Hunter growls again, "Wrong answer."

He grabs the man's arm in his hand, lifts it up and lays it on a rock beside John Smith. Smith slowly rolls his head to his right. A look of fearful wonderment drapes across his face. Hunter smashes another chopping blow through the man's forearm. It splinters like balsa wood, and the man's anguished scream can be heard for hundreds of meters. It's a picture compound fracture, bone splitting the skin. The man screeches in pain, writhing on the ground but only from the hips down, unable to move his arms and shoulders.

Smith is not a big man, five-six, seven at best. Dirty blond hair, left long and straight. He is shaven but his suit, tie and shoes cry cheap. He stares at Hunter. Angry eyes reflecting pain, surprise and anticipation in puke-greenish hue. By comparison, Hunter is huge. Six-three with an in-top-condition powerful frame formed like two wedges placed on top of one another. Wide shoulders, tiny waist. Thick hips and thighs, sleek muscular legs. Black, well-trimmed hair and dark eyes, now flashing rage.

Hunter snaps again, "It's goin' to get worse. Who are you and why this? Why her?" He pauses, "Or was it supposed to be me?"

The man sneers in pain. His twisted face scarlet in Shanty-Irish anger. He clinches his teeth in anguish, shakes his head in refusal.

Hunter snarls, "For Samantha," and smashes a driving blow with his fist into the man's nose, splaying and splintering it across the face. Two upper front teeth shatter. Blood gushes from the man's nose and mouth. Just the one painful utterance. Followed now with only loud, anguished whimpering. The blood flow, among other factors, interferes with meaningful conversation.

Hunter, in a deliberate, calm tone, says, "Last chance, Mick. Tell me."

The man, his eyes now registering veritable fear, responds in his thick Irish accent, "Me name is Patrick Shanahan. Paddy. Paid to kill the girl."

"Who paid and why?"

The man hesitates. Hunter snaps, "For Sam again," and takes his right fist with the middle finger knuckle gnarled outward, posturing it as a blunt spike, smashes it into the left eye crushing the man's eyeball. The scream this time is through the gaps where his front teeth were moments ago, blood still spewing from his gums and nose. He cries out, "The Army. The RA."

"The RA?"

The man blinks and with anguished pride, says, "PIRA. Provisional Irish ..."

Hunter finishes, "Republican Army. The friggin' IRA by any name."

"No. It be the PIRA now."

Hunter grits his teeth, "The Army, the RA, PIRA, it's all the same fuckin' thing. The IRA. What the hell are you doing over here? Why my woman? Here with me? You useless piece of shit!"

"Payback for years ago. The lass's father. First 'er mum, then 'im and now 'er."

"Her father? Why? Who ordered it? Who paid you?"

"Don't know. Am a soldier...doin' it for the cause."

Hunter aims his left fist, middle finger knuckle gnarled, at the man's right eye. Shanahan screeches, "Please. 'Ave mercy." His accent more pronounced now. "I don't know names. I just come, follow me orders. Do me job. 'Tis for the cause. Nothing personal." He continues to twist on the sun-baked soil, loose stones and fire-prone grass in the canyons north of Mission Bay. Tears run from the one good eye of the confessor, Paddy Shanahan.

Hunter snarls, "The cause? The Army?" Then slightly louder, "Nothing PERSONAL?" Still louder, "NO NAMES?" Then with a hissing tone more deadly than the sidewinders that dwell in these canyons, "Well, I believe you." Hunter lets out a breath, then says blandly, "But you see, lad, it's personal now. Patrick or Paddy Shanahan, John or Johnny Smith or whatever your name is, you made it personal. You murdered my friend. My woman." Hunter pauses, looks at the lightening sky, growls, "And I can't let you go back, or get word to anyone about me...or talk to your Irish asshole buddies. You've gotta die, lad. But I will recommend a closed casket."

The Irishman, the PIRA soldier is virtually comatose.

Mindful of the mesa's drop-off, Hunter steps over the man, says, "But if someone does come after me, Paddy me lad, they're goin' to die hard." He lifts the smallish man by the neck, with its protruding Adams-apple, and with a violent wrench snaps Shanahan's neck like a dry twig. The Irishman's body goes limp. One heave and he's over the edge of the mesa. Hunter watches him tumble, roll, and bounce to the bottom, arms flailing like loose wires in a hurricane. Patrick Shanahan is but a muffled thud on the concrete slab below, minus one shoe and followed by a stream of loose rocks and floe-like sand. And a few uprooted weeds. The cheap suit is ruined, not much of a loss. The Shanahan clan, if there is one, is one less. A loss to them but not to Hunter. To the PIRA, a KIA, per chance more.

With the sounds of sirens closing, Hunter picks up Shanahan's weapon, wallet, credit cards, license and hurls them down the slope. The electric detonator device follows. He turns and starts picking his way toward his house and the stench of the still smoldering and smoking vehicle.

It's sunrise now. A slight breeze from the northwest isn't cooling these canyons. The humidity already over eighty percent. Hunter is shiny in perspiration. Visibility is easily five or more miles. To the south he can clearly see awakening lights in Mission Bay.

He mutters, "Goin' to be a pretty day for most people." He pauses. Then, as if an oath, "But coyote ugly days coming for some others."

He's more careful in his footfall now than during the chase. However, still in jockey shorts he doesn't allow his bare feet to inhibit some haste. After re-crossing the mesa he starts the seven foot climb up the embankment to Arcola Street as marked SDPD patrol cars, unmarked faded and dented detectives' cars, two fire engines, and an ambulance skid to a halt. Sirens whine down, red and blue lights still flashing as first responders leap forth into a controlled frenzy of methodical action. Distant sirens herald the arrival of others. Only the beach at Tarawa could have been more chaotic, noisy and cluttered.

Hunter mutters, "I'm gonna look just a little suspect here." He pleads to the lightening sky, "Abba, let Bradovich be here."

Hunter climbs over the cul-de-sac barricade and is met by two on-edge uniformed police officers, weapons out and pointing center mass at Hunter. They shout in unison, "HALT. HANDS UP AND OUT FRONT." Followed by one officer, circling to one side and calling out, "GET ON THE GROUND. NOW. GET DOWN, NOW."

With a sigh and frown, Hunter, in bare feet, gingerly halts. Hands go out and up, palms open and forward. He's about to lower himself to the ground in a prone position when he hears, "WHOA. WAIT ONE. HANG ON." A slight pause, then, "What the hell are you doing here...looking like this, Kerrigan?" It's Detective Eugene Bradovich. A former Marine Criminal Investigation Department (CID) agent and friend of Hunter's, now with the San Diego Police Department. Bradovich still has his high and tight Marine haircut but has added a few inches to his once-trim waistline. He's Hunter's height, but softer probably caused from too many fast-food cheeseburgers and as a result of his reputation as a ladies' man.

The two patrolmen remain poised. Arms extended, weapons held with two hands, still pointed center mass. At the ready, until Bradovich steps over, pushes their arms down to their sides. First one, then the other, saying, "Guys, easy. I know this man...damn well." The officers step back, weapons down but still held by both hands, arms forming a triangle in front of them. Tense. Still ready.

Bradovich continues, "Hunter, what the hell is going on?" He half turns and looks at the still burning car. Then the car door and torso hanging on the split rail fence. Turns back to Hunter, "Jesus, Kerrigan, what the hell happened here?"

Hunter says, "Car bombing," pointing at wires leading away. Then, "Brad, let me get inside and put some clothes on. In the meantime, the guy that did this ran down the mesa and jumped over the edge trying to escape. I believe he's dead. He's lying at the bottom by the metal building. He blew the car...wires strung down the barricade here and out onto the mesa." Hunter again pointing to the various spots he's mentioned. He looks to the fence, grimaces and mutters, "Jesus, I was out saying goodbye to her. My date," his eyes flashing watery anger. Then asks, "Let me get dressed? Okay? Then come inside. I rent here now. In that house with all the friggin' shattered windows ... and shrapnel and crap on the roof. Looks like my command bunker."

Before Bradovich can respond, Dee dashes up, sandals flopping, and hugs Hunter. While sobbing, yet still in her contralto, raspy voice and mixed languages, "*Mamma mia! Che macello.* My God." Head turning taking in the terrifying scene continues, "Oh sweet Jesus. Oh, Lord." Then pushes herself a few inches back from Hunter, nonetheless clutching his face with her hands, pleads, "*Stai bene?* Are you okay?"

She holds Hunter, hands cupping his face looking at his forehead and whimpers, "You're bleeding." She stops. Glares at Bradovich who is staring at her in disbelief. Actually, he's ogling. Dee's raven dark hair is unbrushed, touching wildly on her shoulders. She looks as if she has had a euphoric tussle in bed, or got up from a dead sleep with no time to primp. The latter is more the case except for the earlier morning cat-fight routine. She's replaced her sheer robe worn earlier with a halter top, no bra. Her breasts are barely restricted by the halter and are still pressed hard against Hunter's chest. His body unintentionally aides the containment of her own self-contained-underwater-breathing-apparatus. The SCUBA gear occupies all Bradovich's attention. She's also wearing "hot pants" made famous by PSA "stews" which hide little and accentuate her soccer ball butt and slender, shapely legs. In sandals the shape is distinct, let alone what they might look like in heels. Her dark flashing eyes are set in a perfectly sculptured roman-like face. Her complexion is clear, tanned, and Italian. She is to anyone that goes to the movies, a Sophia Loren or Elizabeth Taylor clone.

Dee snaps at Bradovich, "What are you staring at, and who the hell are you?"

"Well, ma'am, in order of the questions, one helluva beautiful woman. Do you have any sisters?" He takes in a breath, "And I'm Detective Bradovich, San Diego PD...at your service, ma'am."

"You wish." Pauses, settles, and in a more raspy tone, "It's about time you got here. I called hours ago. I'm ... and yes I do. Neither of us would waste our ... you took ..."

"Five minutes, ma'am. That's flyin' on a Saturday morning."

"Well, it seems like hours," she snaps. Then in a more civil tone, "Anyway, I made the call. I reported all this." Then cooing to Hunter, "You're not dressed. And you're hurt."

Hunter says, "I'm fine. This is Detective Bradovich."

Dee responds, "I know. We introduced ourselves."

Bradovich injects, "No, I introduced myself. You ..."

"I'm Teresa Columbo. Mrs. Columbo. His neighbor," hugging Hunter again. "And the Property Manager for that...that house," pointing to Hunter's shambles, "and his landlord. In a manner I suppose." She pauses, knowing she is starting to ramble. Bradovich continues to stare. Hunter shrugs. Dee looks at Hunter, then glares at the detective and snaps, "And don't you get any funny ideas. If my husband, Angelo, were alive and here, he'd set you straight. I'm just the Property Manager here, mister." She pauses again, "And neighbor...and a concerned citizen." She takes a deep breath as if to continue.

Bradovich says, "I believe you, ma'am."

Hunter says, "Look, Mrs. Columbo, he's got a lot of work to do." Then looks to Bradovich and says, "Brad, let me get inside, get cleaned up, dressed and assess the damage to the house. Then you come in after getting things moving and resolved here, and we'll talk. Okay?"

Bradovich nods in agreement. Looks at Dee, shakes his head, then holds up his hand, palm out to prevent a comment from her. Says, "You're right. I've got a lot of work to do."

Hunter says, "Great," turns to go and stumbles over Magpie, sitting alertly at Dee's side. The fawn-colored boxer leaps aside but not without a low protective growl.

Dee grabs Hunter's arm, says to Magpie, "Come. Heel." and leads Hunter toward the house, the dog alongside.

Bradovich mutters under his breath, "Wonder which one she's talkin' to," then hollers, "Hunter, I'll be in shortly. Don't go anywhere and don't touch anything out here." Then adds, "That goes for you too, Mrs. Columbo."

Both raise their arms indicating they heard the directive.

Dee whispers to Hunter, "Did you hear what he muttered first?"

"No."

"Good. I don't like him."

"I do. Good man. Saved my life, twice."

"I like that man. Did I tell you that?"

Hunter enters his house, shaking his head, with Dee grasping his hand. Magpie follows making herself at home.

While the jousting between Bradovich, Hunter and Dee has been transpiring, others have gone about their duties. The firemen have extinguished the flames. They and ambulance responders are working gingerly to free Samantha's torso hung on the car door and in the split-rail fence. Others do the same with her remains in the car. Firemen still lay on foam in spots. Police officers are taping off the crime scene and controlling the neighborhood onlookers. Some of the latter are already dressed for the beach; some are in their golf outfits; some in shorts and sloganeer T-shirts; and some housewives in robes with an assortment of peanut butter, jelly and egg stains. This group has been joined by the usual school of piranha, the press. Noisy and nosy and gaining volume.

As Bradovich turns away from Hunter and Dee and surveys the scene on the street, he's confronted by one of his cohorts from the detective department. The plainclothesman announces, "Found him. Or it. Dead. Messed up real bad. Must of been a helluva fall. Seen less damage from jumpers."

"What'd ya mean?"

"The guy is banged up real bad. Neck's more or less pruned. Face is smashed up...like someone that's been in the ring with Rocky Marciano. Got a wallet. Empty." Using his fingers to tick off each item, he recounts the items found strewn along the slope. He adds, "And a new Walther and lot of cash for a guy wearin' a cheap suit. Worse than mine." He laughs at his humor. Pointing to his partner he adds, "Steve's lookin' for the car down in one of the parking lots below." He pauses again, head tilted to one side.

Bradovich mumbles, "And?"

"The ME needs to see this guy, Brad. Here. Where he lays. Somethin's not right."

"Okay. Got it. Get some cops down there to help and get it marked off. And get some people scouring this mesa area. Follow those wires," as he points to them lying on the pavement, near the barricade. This is at the least a car bombing. Possibly a helluva lot more." Bradovich shuffles and kicks the air, "Ah, shit. Nam was easier. Just the guys in black pajamas." Then shrugs, mutters, "And pith-helmets later. Tough little bastards."

The detective stares motionless. Waits. Then gives a "thumbs up" and responds, "On it. And, oh yeah, we found an electric detonator on the slope. A little further down."

"Electric detonator? Sure, why the fuck not. Shit." Shakes his head. "I thought I left this crap behind." Bradovich, shakes his head, shouts, "I'll be up here for a while, then in the house. That one," he points to Hunter's white stucco house with the pale yellow trim. All the houses in this neighborhood are stucco. Different pastels, different colored trim, and all have a red brick fireplace on one side. All the backyards have six-foot wooden fences. He turns, walks over to the coroner who is working with the firemen on the torso on the split-rail fence. It and the remainder in the car are burned beyond recognition. Bradovich can tell the car was a two-door and the remains, a woman. Nothing pretty or sleek about either now. He tells the coroner about the "perp" at the bottom of the hill, adding, "That body is more important than this one." He adds soulfully, "That one at the bottom is the doer. This one is the...the...the done one... or the do-ee." He takes in a breath, gags a bit. The stench from the burned body is catching up with everyone. Bradovich mutters, "Oh cheez-it, what a Saturday morning." Pauses, takes a handkerchief and wipes his brow, then hands. "And hot too."

The coroner looks up, says, "Could be worse. Could be a Santa Ana. Then this stench could carry all the way to the beach. Possibly La Jolla. Damn, what a way to end a month."

The other detective, Steve, is now up top. Bradovich directs him to get some help and start working the crowd and neighborhood for witnesses. Then asks, "Did you find the car?"

"Yep. Pretty easy. Not many cars parked in that place this time of day on a weekend. It's a rental out of Lindbergh. Couple of weeks."

"Okay, call in and impound the car. Get forensics on it." He sighs and begins walking the immediate area.

Dee shuts the door behind them letting go of Hunter's arm. She starts to speak. Hunter puts his hand up, says, "I've got a call to make."

Dee nods, "Good. First, however, you ought to take a quick shower and get the blood off your head, hands, chest, and toss the jockey shorts. Then get dressed." She pauses, "Although if it weren't for the circumstances, I'd prefer you not."

"What?" He frowns. "Jesus, Columbo."

"DeLuca. Never mind. Forget it. Look at yourself. Go get cleaned up and put something on. Then make your call. I have some calls to make as well. Get some window people over here and some industrial-like cleaners in here."

Hunter barks, "Use the one in the kitchen, okay? I'll go get cleaned up."

"Okay." She lets out a breath, then adds in a soft husky tone, "I'll be back in a jiffy to take a look at that gash on your forehead. Go." She mumbles softly as he turns to leave, "John's right. He's clueless."

Hunter strides down the hallway, looking at his hands, arms and chest for the first time. Blood, and not his. Only his on his brow from whatever piece of shrapnel creased him. He mutters, "I've got to talk to Joe. It's goin' to hit the fan real soon and it won't be evenly distributed."

He whispers, "Good Lord. Poor, beautiful, Samantha." Pinches the bridge of his nose, sighs. "Jesus, Mary and Joseph."

Then a tad louder, "What the hell is the IRA doin' here?"

CHAPTER 2

*"In the midst of this chopping sea of civilized life,
such are the clouds and storms and quicksands and
thousand-and-one items to be allowed for,
that a man has to live,
if he would not founder and go to the bottom
and not make his port at all, by (ded) reckoning,
and he must be a great calculator indeed who succeeds."*
Henry David Thoreau

    Showered, Hunter stands in front of his bathroom mirror, towel wrapped around his waist. He leans over and wipes away the steam mist with a few swipes of his forearm. He straightens, stares at his image and thinks of what Thoreau suggested as an approach to life in *Walden*. He also remembers the two hard, miserable years of training he just finished at The Farm in Virginia. Plus the eleven years in the Corps. Some of those in combat, certainly more than enough. Also the hours in the CIA classrooms and labs and the long lonely nights studying. Especially the hour upon hour reviews in those labs of the language tapes in Italian, French, Spanish, German and some Farsi, God only knows why. He spoke most of these fluently while growing up in Europe. No time was spent on his other language fluencies in Mandarin Chinese and Vietnamese. They shouldn't come into play for this assignment. And certainly no time was spent on the little Comanche he learned from his mother although the value of this attribute would have phenomenal code value, as the native Americans "Code Talkers" did in World War Two. And finally, all the soul-searching in the pre-dawn hours at the end brought him to accept this is his life now. As before him the life of his father, a CIA Section Chief, killed in service. His mother, part of that same assassination, like Samantha and her parents. All a different storm cloud, but perhaps from the same eye.

    He mutters softly, "First, my mission. Pisces, or Robert Camack, or Bobby Camack or whatever. It's no different now." He drops the towel, says aloud. "It's the same as it was before. Seek out the enemy and destroy him, and his will to fight. If the IRA-men get in the way during the process, they will die as well." And as he turns to get his clothes he'd laid out on the bed, he bumps into Dee standing in the bathroom doorway.

"Damn, Mrs. Columbo. What the hell are you doing in here? This is my ..."

"Room. Yes, I know. And it's Dee, and I was going to take a look at that ... that, whoa big fella," her coy grin widens. "Ahhh, look at that gash you have on your forehead."

"Well, it's nothing. Stopped bleeding." He quickly steps around her. "Anyway, it's up on my forehead, not down there." She shrugs her shoulders, grins, says nothing and sits on the bed. Then shakes off her sandals with suggestive wiggles of her feet. Standing in front of her he snatches a clean pair of jockey shorts and leaps into them, and hastily follows with a pair of slacks and a T-shirt with the phrase, "Swift, silent, and deadly" stenciled across the chest. Then sits on the end of the bed and pulls on a pair of socks and loafers. Dee slides next to him.

She says, "I'm sorry. I just...never mind. The cut is okay. Looked worse than it is, but I was truly worried about it. I should care for it. Put something on it. Iodine, a bandage." She takes a breath. "Oh, I'm doing it again...going on so. It's a habit that started after my husband, Angelo, went missing, and then ..." She inhales deeply and in her raspy tone says, "I called a handyman friend. He's on the way. He and his buddy will clean up the mess, but they can't fix the windows today. Those will have to wait until Monday. They'll cover them with plastic and tarps in the meantime. I hope that's okay?" She pauses again and allows a coy grin to capture her lips and says, "If the window thing bothers you, you can stay at my place."

"Okay. Thanks...No. No, I mean the windows will be fine. I can stay here. Need to stay here. Now I..."

"Whatever. Go make your call. I have to call my children and let them know I'm okay in case the news has managed to spread across the planet."

"Your kids. Yeah, I should have thought to ask." He pauses. "Oh yeah, I knew that." His eyebrows crinkle, "Geez. Right. They're not home?"

"Children. Kids are baby goats. And no, they're not home. They are visiting their grandparents and great-grandparents in Napa Valley. My folks own a winery there. Nice." She sighs. "It's beautiful there...and great wine. Somehow it always tastes better in that place than when I have a glass or two at home. Oh well, the children will be there for the summer. I hope to be going also, at some point. Darn, I'm doin' it again. Sorry."

"Yeah, you are. Okay, now then, I guess that's good. Their being gone I mean. Well, I gotta call. Now." He gets up from the bed and hustles out of the room, down the hall and carefully steps into his office. Glass shards lay everywhere. He closes the door behind him. Pauses, and smiles. Mutters, "What the hell, the windows are open. Shoot, there are no windows." Goes to the closet, unlocks the door and closes it behind him. The Agency has rigged the closet into a small communication center with a phone, tape machine, recorder, and a small fold-out writing board, and a fold-down seat. Both of the latter fold back up into the wall. He dials the number for Joe Zachary. Joe answers on the first ring. He's at the office, or asylum, however one prefers to think of the CIA complex at Langley. Ruth, Joe's vivacious wife prefers asylum, or on occasion worse. Her pastimes, have been and still are, raising their family, looking beautiful, loving Joe, and arranging dates for Hunter at every opportunity. She's not been successful at the latter. She keeps choosing "nice girls."

Hunter says, "Joe. Hello. Listen, let me speak. We, I, have an event on my hands here. Just happened."

"An event?"

"Yeah, an event. A friggin' disaster. Listen. Let me finish. Samantha is dead. A guy from the IRA just killed her. Car bomb. I got..."

"Sam," blurts Zachary. "For ..."

"Joe, listen. Yeah, Sam is dead." He adds the grim details, then, "I got to him, consequently I have some information, but he didn't survive our conversation."

"My God. How can that be? She's hardly involved."

Hunter reminds Joe, "Well, she is, was involved. She got all my credentials, cards, cover and stuff for me. All set up when I arrived here." He pauses. "As I said, it was an ugly scene. The bomb was...it was...shit, it blew the damn car in half...and her. Damn it was...was like a first-over A4 dropped a thousand pounder then the next one made a napalm drop." Hunter sucks in some air, then back in his icy PRC-10 Company Commander's voice, "Joe. The IRA? That's out of the loop."

Joe interrupts. "Well, not exactly. The IRA is not in 'this' loop. However, this is something entirely different, I suspect. But the prime target, not your termination project, we suspect is using a rogue from PIRA. Samantha McGee was only a trusted contact for us. Plus she's ..." he pauses uncomfortably, "or was, family. But not an agent. Well," he takes another breath, then coldly asks, "Are the police there?"

"Of course. This must be San Diego's Hiroshima. Fortunately, one is an old buddy, friend of mine."

"You have no friends, remember. Have you spoken to him yet?"

"Not really. He's coming in the house, shortly."

"Well, don't speak to him, or anyone. And hang on a minute, don't go away. I've got to make a call or two. Take care of business."

Hunter waits. Opens the closet door and peeks out. Doesn't see Dee. Looks out the window, or what was the window, and sees the activity still going on. The remains have been removed. More cars and more people than before, and he notices Bradovich in a group talking and pointing. Hunter continues to survey the scene until he hears Joe say, "I'm back." Joe informs him that he's sending an asset from the area. "The Feds will be on this like ducks on a June bug. The FBI's SAC from the San Diego office is on the way. Ours will be there; as a result we'll have an Agency representation. The teamwork stuff we all talk about."

The instructions continue. He is not to talk to anyone else other than tell the locals that this is, or will be, a federal case, and that Hunter is to talk to only the Feds. Then they go through a question and answer format about the guy in the canyon. During this exchange, Joe explains that years ago Sam's father was with the CIA and had worked undercover with the Brits in Ireland. Joe adds, "He was Irish through and through; spoke the language, Gaelic, or as they say, 'The Irish.' He looked the part and got inside. Caused a lot of problems for the IRA. He retired, of course. Was out of the service. Then two years ago, when the Provisional IRA broke away, they came looking for him. They have a violent ideology. Killed his wife also. Now Sam." He pauses, "Hell, violent is too tame a label. They've killed about 1,100 British troops and another 600 or so that are civilians of some sort in England, mainland Europe, and some here." Joe pauses, catches his breath and continues. "Any-who, her folks retired and lived in England. London. As a matter of fact in the same general area where your folks lived while you were at Harrow-on-the-Hill going to school. Westbourne Terrace, wasn't it?" He pauses again. Hunter says nothing. Joe goes on. "The PIRA hate hard and carry grudges a long time. Forever it seems. Anyway, there you have it. Except for the other matter."

Joe pauses again, audibly sighs. Hunter remains silent. Then Joe says sternly, "But this can't, cannot, interfere with our mission. Your purpose. This is nothing more than a casualty from long ago. The PIRA as an organization is not involved with Pisces. Understood?"

Hunter says he understands and gives Joe the name of Patrick Shanahan. The credit card names. And the damage report on Shanahan.

Joe says, "Jesus, Hunter, why didn't you just shoot the bastard?"

"I was in my jockey shorts and bare feet. I didn't have the Puppy with me." Hunter is referring to his weapon of choice. It's a new prototype, the M39-WOX-13A, originally designed for Marines, with a silencer (suppressor) kit. The weapon is to become the MK22ModO. Informally it is appropriately called the "Hush Puppy".

Joe drones, "Hunter, always bring a gun. Preferably, bring..."

"I know. Two guns, and bring all my friends who have guns. I know the rule, I was just saying goodbye to Sam after a...never mind."

"Okay, Hunter. Okay. Now then, as I said, your mission has not changed. Pisces killed Hermann Mueller, our guy in Pisa, just yesterday. And he slaughtered some restaurant owner and his entire family who knew Mueller. And something else, I suspect. However, there is a guy named Antonio Rizzo, who worked for the restaurant and may have seen something or knows a lot about Pisces and his henchmen. He may still be around. Probably hiding if Pisces left him alive. Our intel tells us that Pisces has left. Gone. We don't know where. And, as we told you, his real name, at least when he was with us, is Bobby Camack. Robert Camack. He has used Roberto Camack on occasion. He used Roberto Muscarella in Pisa. We know that. That's all we've got on names."

"Joe, do you employ any Comanche's? Besides me."

"What?"

"They always knew where the cavalry was. Never mind, go on with the brief."

"Oh, yeah, and he's vanished. We believe forever. Finished. Kaput. However, he may get edgy when he gets wind of this other matter. And he's got a woman somewhere. A wife. Find her somehow and we'll have him. He's probably headed there."

Hunter interrupts, "We? Are you comin' along?"

"Don't be a wise guy. Go find him and terminate the bastard, but get the info we need first. And, Hunter, I just about forgot. He's got two yahoos you'll probably have to plow under to get to Pisces, or his wife." He pauses. Gets no comment. Says, "Stop in to see me on the way. Take a couple of days to get squared away and settled. Your mind settled. But no more than three."

"Do I keep this place?"

"Yes, and keep the Property Manager. What's her name, Terry Columbo?"

"No, it's Dee...Mrs. Teresa DeLuca Columbo."

"Dee? Dee?"

"Yeah, that's her nickname. The way she introduced herself to me and Sam."

"Sam?"

There is a pause; a silence on the phone. Hunter says, "Joe, you still there? Joe?"

"Yeah. Tell me you're not doin' her. Tell me you didn't do Sam. Tell me."

"No, of course not. Sam was all business. As is Ms. Columbo. Hardly knew, or to be more precise, know them. Just met the both of them yesterday, for Pete's sake."

"Well, that's good, I hope. You know you thoroughly screwed up a couple of Ruth's friends. Remember, you're an operative now, an asset. You don't have any friends. You don't have a private life other than your cover. You're an author."

"Joe, I know all that."

"Yeah, well, remember the rules. This one in particular. 'Be polite. Be professional. Be prepared to kill everyone you meet.' Do you read, Hunter? Don't forget, talk only to the agents out there. Call me if something comes up. Otherwise, I'll see you on Tuesday or Wednesday, Thursday the latest. Remember, Pisces is the kill target. And, remember the total mission." There's a pause. "And try to limit the collateral damage."

CLICK.

"Collateral damage? Shanahan wasn't collateral damage. Sam was, and when I start shootin' anything I hit is the target, not ..."

Bzzzzzzz.

Hunter hangs up, stands, and locks the closet door after stepping out. Tiptoes around and over the broken glass and out of the office, into the hallway and to the dining room. Sees Dee, back to him, leaning on the kitchen counter, talking on the telephone. Mutters, "Oh, man. What a.. a...chassis." Then louder, "Hey, Mrs. Columbo, Dee, I'm done with my call. Have to talk to you."

She turns, nods and puts her index finger in the air signaling one more minute. Says a few more words into the phone, then, "I love you. Tell your sister I said the same thing. Bye. See you soon." Puts the phone back on the holder on the wall and says with a smile, "Children. What's up?"

The smile evaporates, and Hunter hears the reason for it vanishing.

Bradovich says, "Hunter, we need to talk. That guy didn't jump or fall off the canyon. So, don't bullshit me. Now then..."

Steve, one of the other detectives, pops his head in the front door and shouts, "Brad, the Chief is on the radio. Says he needs to talk to you. Like right now. And there are a couple of Feds here. One is FBI. I'm guessin' the other is a Spook."

Bradovich shakes his head. "Okay. On my way." Then turns back to Hunter. "Hunter, ol' friend. I don't know what you've got yourself into but...ahhh, never mind. I'll be right back. If I can." He leaves, crunching glass in the entryway as he goes. Stops, looks around to ensure Steve is gone. Hunter has not moved. Brad says, "Hawk, if you need help somewhere along the line, give me a call...at home." He turns and is out the front door.

Dee comes up to Hunter, running her index finger along the words, "Swift, Silent and Deadly" on his T-Shirt. "What was that all about?"

"We gotta talk."

In the warmth of a mid-afternoon sun, Danny Shanahan looks at his younger brother, Sean. Takes a sip of his pint and says, "I wonder when Paddy will be comin' home? It's been well over a week now."

They sit quietly at a table in the corner of the pub's outdoor patio. Actually, just the sidewalk with tables set out when the weather is grand. The street before them has only a few men walking about since it is near the supper hour. Later, it will be alive with activity, especially here at The Well.

"Don't know, but none too soon for me. They be enough troubles without some of our own."

"Aye, none too soon." They both take a long drink from their pints. Put the glasses down and like they were twins, wipe their mouths with the sleeves of their shirts. Sit back, and gaze out onto the roadway.

Derry to the locals and countrymen, Londonderry to the world, is broiling with troubles and has been for years. It may well be coming to a head. The Shanahan clan has lost three men from the family and one lass in the war. A grandfather and a father; a son or brother; and a young lass, a sister. What is left are the three lads, Paddy, Danny, and Sean and their Ma. And Paddy is off on a job for the cause.

Sean takes another gulp of his draught. Looks at Danny and asks, "Patrick will be back, won't he?"

"Aye, I hope, lad. I hope." He then takes a swallow, his last. "Hell yes, he'll be back. And soon, too. Now, drink up, Sean. It's supper time and we need to be puttin' a foot under us. We have a job tonight for Muldoon. Remember?"

Pisces opens the door to his villa. Calls out, "Gina, I'm home."

Into the foyer, on the run, comes the house mouse, the maid, Gina Pappalardo. She is better looking than her namesake. Gina coos, *"Buon giorno, Signore Catalano."* She continues on in her native Italian. "So good to have you home again. Signora Catalano went down to the beach to swim and relax."

"To shop, but that's fine," he responds in English.

"Just for some fresh fish, Signore. The catch of the day," she responds in the same language.

"I know, and thanks, it's good to be home. I plan on staying much longer this time. Perhaps forever. Could you bring me some Chianti on the veranda? I too want to enjoy the sun. Relax. It's been a long trip."

"Yes, Signore, sir. Sorry. Was business good?"

"Ah, as the English might say, bloody good." He laughs softly. Nods to Gina. "My wine, please." Roberto Catalano strolls through the large tiled living room, onto the veranda. From here he can see down the now shadowed mountain to the town and the sea which is reflecting the reds and oranges of evening twilight. He murmurs, "I have to paint this view. I have the time now." He sits in a large, well-cushioned chaise lounge, first taking off his jacket and tossing it over another chair. Then slips off his shoes, wiggles his toes and finally stretches his arches.

Gina arrives with the Chianti and places the glass on the lounge-side table. She pours a sip. Stands aside while Signore Catalano picks up the glass, sniffs the bouquet, nods in satisfaction and takes a sip. He nods again. Gina finishes her chore, then places the bottle on the table. She pads quietly back toward the house wondering if Roberto will take advantage of this time that the Signora is gone. They often have, but it looks as if not at this moment.

Gina lingers at the door gazing back at Roberto. *Perhaps he is losing interest. I am not as young as I once was. We'll see; it's only his first day, first moment back.*

Pisces watches her leave. Smiles in satisfaction, then looks out over the veranda view and murmurs, "Pisces is dead when Pisces wants to be dead."

Then after a few moments, "And finally, Pisces is dead. To the world. "

But not to her.

He peers at Gina as she shifts and sways her hips as she enters the villa kitchen.

CHAPTER 3

"Always cheat; always win. There ain't no such thing as a fair fight."
A gunfighter's rule

    The two federal agents ring the doorbell and wait at the still open front door. It is ridiculous to be so proper under these circumstances. After all, it's one of their own they've come to see; one of their own they're going to cover up and shield. Emergency vehicles still clog the cul-de-sac as does a neighborhood crowd, including the press. And it's a Saturday. A day already warm and humid made worse by the lingering heat and spun out smoke of the bombed car. Nonetheless these two callers are in business suits, starched white shirts and power ties. Additionally, the handyman and his helper that Dee called are standing behind the agents, half-surveying the damage to the house and waiting to come inside. They are in their business suits: coveralls, San Diego Padre baseball caps, sweat-stained T-shirts and leather tool belt holsters fastened around their waists. Watching this front door dog and pony show is Eugene Bradovich, standing in the street, leaning against his vehicle. He mutters, "Be careful ol' buddy. If you need me, call." Removes his elbows from the roof of the car, leans across the top of the car and adds, "And watch your six, Marine."
    Hunter comes to the door, introduces himself to the two Feds. The FBI Agent shows his credentials and presents himself as Special Agent in Charge (SAC), James "Jim" Ryder. The Spook does the same, simply as Agent John Oboe. Then adds, "My friends call me...never mind, I don't have any friends."
    Hunter replies, "Agent Ryder. Hello. Agent...Agent, ah, what was your...your, ah, never mind. I don't either." He and Oboe exchange icy stares. Then Hunter waves all inside, adding, "C'mon in."

The two handymen push by everyone and go directly to Dee, who is standing in the middle of the living room still in her bra-less halter top and short shorts.

Dee says, "Bobby. Richard."

Richard says, "It's Dick."

Bobby smiles and remarks, "No. That's what you are," and sniggers, then quickly feigning courtesy adds, "To Miss Dee you're Richard." The two clowns laugh. Dee doesn't. Nor do the agents. Hunter glares at the two workmen and takes a step toward Bobby.

Dee cuts him off. Places a hand on Hunter's chest, "Please, leave it be." Then faces the Moe and Curly duo, snaps, "Stop it, you two. Follow me, and I'll show you what needs to be done, which should be apparent. And where to start. And I want it done right, and quickly." Looks at Hunter, shakes her head and rolls her eyes. "Sorry. I'll get them started, then join you three."

Agent Ryder says, "FBI, Special Agent in Charge, James Ryder, ma'am, I'm the..."

"I heard," retorts Dee. "I'm Teresa Columbo, the Property Manager here. I'm responsible to the owner for...oh my, God...oh, Lord. She, uh, Samantha, I mean, Ms. McGee was the owner. I still represent...I'm so sorry but..."

"You're doin' it again, Dee," interrupts Hunter.

Ryder feigns a smile and says, "Well, ma'am, good you heard and we understand your confusion ... and grief." He pauses, "But we won't be needing you to join us. If you and the workmen just stay in those rooms that need repair, we'll be out of your way on the patio. Agent Oboe here," jerking his thumb, "will need to talk to you later. In your place." He looks to Oboe and gets a confirming nod. Then asks, "Next door, isn't it?"

Dee looks to Hunter. Sees him nod. Agent Oboe nods also, but with a sly grin. She pushes Bobby, with Richard in front of him, toward Hunter's office.

Dee half-shouts over her shoulder, "Got the message."

Then several steps along her way, murmurs, "They're all clueless."

Dee and the two handymen disappear into the office. She tugs on the closet door and finds it locked, again.

Hunter and the two agents stride through the living room, go outside to the chairs adjacent to the Jacuzzi on the patio. Only after Agent Oboe surveys the area outside the backyard fencing do they sit.

Hunter asks, "Any bodies? Friends?"

Oboe asks, pointing at Dee's house, "Who lives there? The pretty lil' landlady?"

Hunter says, "The Property Manager, Mrs. Columbo. Yeah."

Oboe says to Ryder, "Let's get this over with, then I'll have a chat with the good Ms. Columbo," smirking at Hunter like a boxer jabbing, hoping to invite an expected roundhouse right. It provokes only an icy stare.

Ryder begins by asking Hunter to tell what he knows, saw, and did this morning. Hunter delivers a more than complete "SitRep". Ryder listens to the situation report without interrupting. Then follows with questions. Akin to an endless oral exam. Agent Oboe listens, watches, and on occasion asks a question himself or clarifies a point for Ryder. The result of this hour-long interrogation is that there will be a cover-up. It will be in the hands of the Feds because Samantha McGee was an individual under contract to the government, and thereby a federal employee. And of course, because it involves the death of a foreign national and because the CIA deems it thus to control the cause, the information and results. What is difficult for Hunter to digest is the seemingly willing cooperation between Ryder and Oboe, particularly since the latter is a wise-ass. This session is a wonderfully executed scam. Nonetheless, Hunter's mind is set on finding and killing Pisces, completing his ultimate mission, and, if lucky along the way, kill a gaggle of passing PIRA. Ryder drones on explaining the agenda and what will be said to the press.

When Agent Ryder finishes he gets up, shakes Hunter's hand, turns and strides through the house and out the front door. Outside he finds the groups have increased in size with the arrival of several more of his own agents. After Ryder has left, Agent Oboe gets in Hunter's face. He grows more "Langley-like," and says, "I've been told to remind you that this is not your business and not involved with your project."

"Joe said that?"

"Yeah." He pauses, staring at Hunter. Nearly a challenge. Then adds, "And, you're not to talk to any officials. To no one. And you are to be on your way by Wednesday, Thursday the latest. Keep in touch with your handler, and visit with him before you depart country." He starts to leave, stops and says, "Oh, by the way. There is no Agent John Oboe. And I wasn't here. Bye, Jarhead."

"Why do you need to talk to Mrs. Columbo? She's just the Property Manager and not part of any of this. Why make it look like she's involved?"

"Because I've been ordered to do it." He does his pause and stare routine again. "You get your job done. I'll do mine. And if I were you, I'd have a plan. Then I would have a backup plan because the first one won't work. Ever hear that, Leatherhead?"

"Yeah, I've heard that. How come we're in the same business, and I've just met you and already hate your bony ass? Ever hear that?"

"Yeah, and it scares me to death. Makes me shake like a cat shi ..."

Hunter's jack-hammer blow with the heel of his hand crashes against Oboe's forehead before he can finish. Oboe is on his back, dazed but not unconscious, next to the pool. His watch hand dangles in the water. Hunter leans over and finishes Oboe's remark, "peach pits on a marble floor. And if we meet again I'm going to kick your ass before we start talkin'." He reaches down and rolls Oboe into the pool and growls, "It's Leatherneck, shit head."

Oboe flops, sputters and splashes in the water like wet long johns on a clothesline on a windy day. He pulls himself out of the pool. No longer looks like the sleek leopard he projected throughout the day. Pushes himself to a squatting position before standing. Once on his feet he shakes his head, clearing the webs. Stares at his clothes, trying to decide how to get dry. He squirms out of his suit coat and slowly wrings it out, pen and sunglasses clattering to the concrete. He can't, or doesn't want to completely recover his composure. He manages a less threatening glare and mutters, "Maybe so. If you see me comin'." He staggers slightly, then turns and leaves calling for Dee as he enters the house from the patio dripping water through the living room. Dee comes to him with a beach towel in hand and leads him from Hunter's house, arm around Oboe's shoulder, soothing him while giving Hunter a scornful look. Magpie sits in the yard, watching. Hunter saunters to the front door and watches as they cross the yard. As they do, Oboe looks back, smiles and winks at Hunter.

Hunter mutters, "Should slit his throat now and get it over with." Pauses, hears Dee call out for Magpie to "come". He sees Magpie gazing at him with what looks like a smile on her face. Hunter shakes his head. "Well, the dog likes me."

Then he turns to locate Moe and Curly, the two handymen, and determine how far along they are. He finds them and sees the two clowns are good at what they do. The plastic sheets cover the windows. Glass shards gone. Holes plugged in the walls. They tell him that they'll be back early Monday morning to put on the cover-up paint and replace the windows. They also report they've cleared off the roof and inspected it. No damage.

Now that he has time, Hunter ambles back into his bedroom to sort out his gear, papers, and clothes. He never unpacked his suitcase nor arranged all the "vitals" Sam had put in place for his mission. The different passports. Information on bank accounts, here and in Geneva. Also a wad of cash in a 8x10 plain brown envelope, clipped closed and scotch taped. Names to use, credit cards. Samantha had already been sent photos in his different disguises, matching the names. Sam had everything ready but she wasn't ready for Shanahan, and evidently had no clue she was being stalked. Hunter pauses, staring at the envelope, mind drifting. *The agency should have known, watched her or at least warned her. Or I should have.*

He murmurs, "Well, shit." Looks across the bed at his image in the full-length closet mirror where not that many hours ago, a completely nude, voluptuous Samantha was teasingly doing the same in front of him. Again, in a murmur, "If I do run into any of those bastards, I'll make it messy, Sam."

Finishing putting everything away, he returns to the front of the house and opens the door. Sees that the mess out front has been cleaned up as good as possible. The asphalt is charred. The section of split rail fencing is not yet replaced and the grass plot between the sidewalk and curbing is scorched. A tow truck is hauling away the remains of Samantha's Pontiac. It follows the ME's wagon. And Sam. And the Irishman. Hunter extends his arm and leans against the doorframe, running his other hand through his cropped hair. *Sam, I'm sorry. Damn sorry. I'll make it up somehow.*

He pushes off the doorframe. Gazes about. The crowd has dispersed, including the press which is strange. He sees a patrolman posted at the end of the cul-de-sac. *Good ol' Bradovich.* One vehicle does remain, parked along the curb outside of Dee's house. The *Bony-ass'* sedan.

In the kitchen, Hunter glances at his watch then pours himself an apricot brandy. A stout one. Says out loud to no one, "It's evening somewhere. Washington. For sure in Ireland. Italy." He ambles out to his patio to sit. Alone. With his thoughts.

Pisces stands and watches as Anna gets out of the spotless and shiny family sedan. A black four-door 1970 Mercedes-Benz 600. The driveway and garage are on the down-slope side of the villa. Bruno is at first holding the car door open, the front door. He offers the lady his hand. She takes it and slinks out of the seat like a cheetah. Their hands touching for a second too long. Bruno then turns to get packages and Anna's bright, multicolored beach bag from the rear seat. He is Pisces' long time driver and bodyguard. The cheetah, Anna, Pisces' wife. Signora Anna Puglisi Catalano. Pisces squints. *What the hell is she doing riding in front? Bruno knows better. Too close. Too friendly. Much too friendly.*

Pisces returns to his spot on the lounge chair, pours another glass of Chianti, and waits for Anna to come out and welcome him home. In a few more minutes than necessary she does, with Bruno trailing behind. Bruno speaks first, "Hello, Bossa. Welcome backa. All wenta well, yes?"

Before Pisces can respond, Anna says in English, "Welcome home, Roberto." Then in Italian which she uses nearly all the time in and around the house with Pisces, and every moment in town, "I have missed you terribly, Roberto. This trip was much too long and you did not call. Look, I have been to the beach." She takes off her sheer screamingly bright red outer beach garment, and spins around displaying her tanned body that's barely tucked in to her scant white bikini. She says, "See, my tan makes me look more Italian than Sicilian. And it is all for you, my love."

Anna is Sicilian. Puglisi an old established name. She is younger by ten years than Roberto Catalano, who is forty-three, and she is holding her figure, tone and complexion as good as any twenty-year old. Dark brown hair and eyes, shapely petite body and however diminutive, generous in portions. And her summer-cloud white teeth are still more so within her bright maraschino red lips. She neither wears nor needs much make-up other than the lipstick and matching polish. She sits down next to Pisces on the lounge chair, leans over, and smothers him with a kiss, leaning into him hence he receives the full pressure of her giving breasts. When she releases him, she says, "Oh, Roberto, I love you so. I do. And I have missed you. Like a canvas misses the brushes of the painter. The strokes. The artistry." She smiles, grazes her index finger across his lips and says, "I will have Gina serve us supper here on the veranda," engagingly smiles again, "And then we will make love. Here or where we choose."

She turns abruptly, says, "Bruno, put those packages in my room. You are done for the day."

Pisces says, in English, "Bruno, do as the Signora says, but then come to my study. I have something I want to discuss with you."

"Yessa, sir." Bruno leaves. Anna departs as well, strutting several paces behind Bruno as if a dog at his heel, into the living room that adjoins the veranda. Gina, eavesdropping from the kitchen doorway, smiles.

Pisces takes a slow sip of his wine and watches the two go. Stares after them for several moments. Glances at Gina just as she ducks from view. He returns his glass to the side table, stands for a moment, then strolls toward his office, hands in pockets. Looks off to the far end to the veranda gate that leads to the garage below. Sees Rocco, his other bodyguard and confidant. Pisces motions him to come.

"It's all under control. We've got it covered. Be on track by Thursday, the latest. And he'll be in here to get an update briefing, the latest intel." Joe Zachary listens for a few more moments to John MacBeer, his boss. Hunter's boss. And the Deputy Director of Operations. MacBeer also served with Hunter's father, Patrick "Corker" Kerrigan, in London. Herman Mueller, Aries by code, also worked for MacBeer. And interestingly enough, so did Robert "Bobby" Camack at one time before Corker uncovered Camack, now Pisces, as a double agent.

Finally, Joe Zachary says, "Yes, sir." And hangs up the phone in his office. It's been a long day. One of many. It's the nature of the business, or the game, depending on one's perspective. And John MacBeer demands that no one leave the office, or the board game, before he does. Joe sighs. He knows the nature of the business, the game, all too well. Plus he knows the nature of the board master, MacBeer.

Joe's mind wanders. He knows Hunter from the Corps. Hell, early on Hunter reported to him. Now again. They're both still Marines. There are no ex-Marines. No matter the era, on duty or not; in uniform or not; once a Marine...always a... He mutters, "Everyone knows that." His thoughts and muttering reminds him of what an Army General once said: "There are only two kinds of people who understand Marines: Marines and the enemy. Everyone else has a second-hand opinion."

Joe locks up his desk, slings his suit coat over his shoulder, and heads out his office door mumbling, "Oh man, this is goin' to get ugly."

In Derry, the Shanahan brothers return home from their task. This one a deadly one. A loyalist, causing problems for the Army, the PIRA, hence the cause, was the target. A warning had been given and not heeded. Two in fact. There was no third, just an ending. It's a much shorter game than American baseball. The man was shot in the back of his head while making love to a buxom lass. Unfortunately, she too became a victim. Danny Shanahan was the shooter; the younger brother, Sean, the "eyes" in front of the quaint inn on the edge of town.

Their worried mother welcomes them home and hugs them as they enter through the back of the cottage and into the kitchen. She scurries, red faced, to pour them some tea. Sean asks, "Any word from Paddy, or from someone who knows?"

"Not a word." She feigns a smile. "Not to worry. Go get cleaned up and be quick about it. I have brewed some tea for me boys. And me grandmother's fine, fine minced-meat tarts for you to munch on with your tea. Hurry now." The two young men leave the kitchen. Their mother shudders, shakes her head, and continues with her chore. One she's done many times before as a young lass for her father, and later for her husband, on many additional dark, worrisome nights for others in her brood.

The woman, older looking than her years, prays in Gaelic or as some say, in the Irish, "Lord, thank ye for bringing me boys home safe. Now bring me Paddy back." Then makes the sign of the cross.

"Safely, Lord. Safely." Blesses herself again.

CHAPTER 4

"The 50-50-90 rule: Anytime you have a 50-50 chance of getting something right, there's a 90% probability you'll get it wrong"

Anon. *Murphy's Other 15 Laws*

Hunter ambles inside from his patio and reheats this morning's now cold tar-thick coffee. He putters around, washes his brandy snifter and slides it on a handy first shelf of the liquor cabinet. The wall phone's shrill ring and its rattling in the cradle startle Hunter. He snatches the receiver, answers with a simple but bad-mannered, "Yes. Speak."

"Hunter? It's Brad. Gene Bradovich. I'm calling from home."

"Yeah, Brad. Didn't I just see you, Marine? Hanging around the ammo dump." Joking, wanting to BS with his Corps buddy, but shouldn't. "Hey, ol' buddy, I'm not supposed to be talking with you unless we're grousing about the Padres or Chargers. And not likely then."

"Yeah, I know the rules. The game." He pauses. "Hawk. I don't know what you're into and shouldn't care except ... I do, and I love you, man. I've been around. The cops here. CID in the Corps. Nam with you. Listen, I can smell paddy shit. Ambush. Here, Nam, anywhere. Something ain't right, buddy. Got that ol' lovin' feelin'."

"Listen, Brad, I'm not supposed to ..."

"No, you listen, friend. I'm here. If you need help, call me, man. I can take the point, or I can take the drag, but I'll cover your six no matter what. Something's not right here, man."

"Brad, I'm fine. Everything is okay."

"Major, I can smell paddy shit a long way off. When the hairs on my arms and neck bristle, something' ain't right." Bradovich exhales a long audible breath, "I owe you, Hawk. Big time. Call. You copy?"

"Roger, I copy. I do." Hunter pauses, turns and props his butt against the counter's edge. "But no sweat. The crap today doesn't involve you or the city. Won't happen again, at least not here. I'm okay. In a way I'm doin' the same old things. Body count and MedEvacs so I'm in my element. Right? "

"Yeah, right. I said my piece. But ya know that booby traps and hand-to-hand ain't the San Diego element. Remember, you call me anytime. I can still hack it. Semper Fi." Then a click. Seconds later a dial tone.

Wish I could, Marine. Can't. Not now. God willing, wind and weather permitting, later.

Hunter hangs up, pauses a moment, moves the few steps back along the kitchen counter and grabs his mug. He stares at the lines of lettering on each side of the mug. On one, "Still a Marine." On the other, "Not as lean but still as mean." Taps the mug twice on the counter top. *I hope.*

He pours himself a cup of the now simmering coffee. The steam twirls upward carrying a strong aroma of coffee beans from someone's mountain, however it looks like sludge. Hunter stares at it and remembers "Black Death", the instant coffee in C-Rations. His mind drifts back. The nights, wet, lonely, with the sounds of the darkness. The static, the rushing sounds, and the wanted and not wanted nothing of the radio's company "tactical net". Then a click, a chest pounding heart beat, the hour-long single second of silence, then the welcome whisper, "Lima Three Alpha in place. Out." Then the wait would begin again and the coffee, the bite of "Black Death", is a bunker's or a fighting hole's teddy bear. It's wonderful. Hunter stares at the mug.

He takes a sip. Follows with, "Ahhh, it hasn't lost its punch." He grimaces, teeth clinched, head shaking. "Whew!" *Perhaps the environment makes the coffee.*

The phone in his office rings. He mutters, "Damn," takes another slug of slow death, sets the mug down on the countertop and hustles to his office. Unlocks the closet, flips down the seat and writing board, closes the closet door and snatches the phone from its holder on the fourth ring. Says, "Yes."

"You're supposed to say the password."

"I forgot it. Actually I don't give a hoot right now."

"Well, dammit, Hunter, it's supposed to be used. It's..."

"Make it Capricorn. I can't remember that other one. This is my birth month, so if I screw up again you can just hum Happy Birthday and I'll catch on."

"Capricorn, huh? That's more than four letters and doesn't start with an "f". Might be difficult for you to..."

"Joe."

"Okay." Zachary sighs. "Capricorn it is. Anyway, just a quick call. Everything's covered. We'll take care of Samantha, her business, and whatever. The locals are covered too. So, take a few days. Work out a plan. Stop here and we'll talk. Finish and cover details, and off you go. This has to be done in a matter of weeks. We'll lose Pisces if we don't. This bastard is slippery, and I sense he's getting ready to disappear forever. MacBeer wants him done. Terminated. Then you and I will take care of the other matter. Got it?"

"Yeah, got it. It's all ded reckoning, Joe. Only one fix and it's old. The remainder are just ports in a storm. But, I'll get it done. See ya Thursday morning. You be ready with the latest Intel. Oh, and Joe, make sure it's better than that F-1 crap you used to feed me in Nam."

"Okay, I will. Geez, you never forget." He laughs. Then, "Now, Hunter, listen. Please don't interrupt for a few minutes. Pay attention and I'll ..."

"This sounds like the beginning of the fan and shit fable."

"Just shut up and listen."

"Wait a sec, let me put on my helmet and flak jacket."

"Dammit, Hunter. Okay. Okay. Now then, you have a new teammate. Ms. Columbo. Well, actually, not in fact new. I probably should have ..."

"What the hell are you saying, Joe? Are you saying that Teresa Columbo is going to be in on this? Are you, nuts?"

"Hunter, I said to shut-up and listen. Now pay attention, dammit. It's a long story. She worked here before she met her husband and came back a short time after he went missing. Actually, been on the job for two years now. She knows more about you than you might think. And, this is important, we need to keep her in the loop." He pauses to allow Hunter to react. To blurt out a profanity. Anything. Joe gets no response, accordingly he continues, "She will be working with you. Will pass herself off as not only your landlady but as your typist and editor. Well, pass herself off is not descriptive. She is a great steno, and writes well." Another pause. More silence. Joe continues, "An author needs help. And she's good at this, and other things."

"What other things?" Hunter exhales audibly. "Never mind. Don't answer that. So, all this shit has been going on behind my back. She is, or was, Sam's backup? Right?"

Zachary hesitates and says, "Not exactly. If anything, more the other way around."

"Well, hell, Joe. I fucked the wrong one. Right?"

"Hunter, you said ... oh, shit, never mind. Listen."

Hunter exhales, and settles on the flip stool, holding the phone away from his ear, staring at the handset. He takes in a deep breath. Lets it out slowly and interrupts whatever Joe was saying, "You're saying that Sam worked for her? And Dee works for you and MacBeer? Right? A woman, a widow, regardless of how it ... with two kids is involved in all this crap. ARE YOU NUTS? "

"Hawk, I wish it weren't so. Not necessary but we have to keep tabs on her to wrap this up. She is the mystery woman and can damn well take care of herself, and she has. You need to remember that. She can play any role, and has. And incidentally, she's a damn good shot. You need to remember that as well although she doesn't have to be ... would just be a few feet."

"A few feet. I won't do this. Not with her tagging along." He pauses, then continues. "Wasn't there something fishy, more than fishy, with her husband's death? I remember hearing rumors." He pauses for several moments. Then, "You know something. Mystery woman my ass. She's hooked in with ..."

"Not now. We'll talk about this more when you get here. Without her. She'll go ahead." Then he pauses, and his tone of voice takes on a harsh command timbre. "You will do this or you're out. Now. So, is it yes or no? Stay or go? I'm busy and getting tired of your one-liners and bitching. We have a mission to complete and that's all I'm interested in and you better be also."

Hunter stares at the phone. He's sweating. The closet is making him claustrophobic, or he's back in a flak jacket listening to assholes in starched jungle utilities. He remembers something an old sea dog Captain told him when he was a Second Lieutenant. "Decisions made by someone above you in the chain of command will seldom be in your best personal interest." He shakes his head and takes in a deep breath. *Something's sure not right here. But! What would my father have done? Execute the orders? And me? Take Hill 22, or 46, or 229 or 881 or whatever. Does it make a difference? Not if you're in the fight.* His mind running full throttle shifts into the gunfighter's gear. *Always cheat...always win...if you're in the fight. The world remembers Joe Louis. No one remembers Tony Galento.*

Am I in the fight? Yes. Therefore kill everyone in sight. He remembers another gunfighter's rule and mutters it aloud. "The faster you finish the fight, the less shot you will get."

Joe says, "What was that?"

"Nothing. Okay, I'm in, but..."

"No buts. Yes or No? Now."

"Yes. In. Who is Oboe?"

"Never heard of him."

"You sent him. He spoke on your behalf."

"Told you, I never heard of him. Didn't send anyone. Now let's get on with the task at hand."

Hunter snarls, "Okay. Good. Then I have your permission to kill this ghost of Ichabod Crane next time I see him."

"Whatever twitches your trigger finger, teammate."

"Great team, right? It's always *we* until the throwin' of hands start."

"It is a team. The two of us. Just like always."

"Yeah, and you always out-ranked me; you were always in a bunker, and I was always the one laying in the paddy with the leeches and AK47 rounds buzzing around me like pissed-off bees."

"Well, hell, Hawk. I was always the better thinker. You were always better at killing. It is what it is." Joe pauses. "So, get to know Columbo, but be careful. She's a black widow. We'll talk more about it when you get here. Just get squared away. Don't talk to anyone out there in San Diego, including Bradovich. And be here Thursday. And plan to move on to the continent. Preferably into London, then on to Geneva for cash, then on to Rome. From there to Pisa, and wherever the currents and winds take you."

"Joe, c'mom, this is not good. The woman does have a family. Even spiders ..."

"Hawk. Stop. I know what we're doing."

"There's that 'we' again. Joe."

"Right. We. Now listen, please. She knows what she's doing. Has for a long time." He pauses. "See you on Thursday. Call me, or have her call me with your schedule. I mean, after all, she's your secretary. Make like she is one. And stay away from the help." Joe laughs, then adds nothing for several seconds. Nor does Hunter. Then, "Hunter. Don't you do her." Click.

Hunter stares at the phone, holding it in front of him, then deliberately cradles it. Gets up, flips up the seat and table, eases out and locks the closet, returning to the kitchen. Picks up his mug of coffee and takes a sip as he strolls back toward the patio. He gags. *This is bad. It's not just sludge, it's ... it's asphalt.*

He slides open the patio door, drifts out and onto a lounge chair next to the Jacuzzi. He looks out over the same-as-everyplace wood fence and into the fading light. Evening twilight has arrived quickly. The day has swept past, as has the last eleven years, like the old Santé Fe Express. He takes in a deep breath. Takes another sip of the "Black Death." Mumbles, "Whoa!" Then checks his "Hush Puppy" in his rear waist band. Looks at the mug and tosses the sludge onto the grass at the edge of the pool.

"Hell, I don't need paving. I need a drink."

Pisces slinks into his study like a leopard on the prowl. Even his loafers seem to be scratching the tile like angry claws. Rocco pads behind like a trained bear. Robert Camack, aka Roberto Camack Catalano, slides in behind his huge antique mahogany desk as if settling on a tree limb to lay in wait. Only a few items are on top of the desk. An envelope. A phone. A calendar, page turned to today's date. He puts the envelope in top center drawer. Nothing to detract from the beautiful rust colored inset leather desk top. The bear and leopard exchange a glance before the big cat takes in the paneled walls, also in mahogany, shelves on one wall crammed with books never read. Original oils carefully hung on the other walls, as they are throughout the villa. His works of art. Pisces prides himself in his painting.

Bruno, comfortable, casual in deportment comes through the door of the great study and eases toward the desk front. Looks at Rocco and says in Italian, "Good day, yes? Great weather. Better, a great trip for the boss," then looking away from Rocco to Pisces. "Right, Bossa?"

Pisces looks at Bruno, smiles and says warmly in English, "How long have you been working for me? How long have we been friends?"

Bruno, internally warmed, grins broadly, says in English, "Forever, Bossa. Forever. I'm so," then lapses into Italian, "grateful for the chance to work for you. To be with you." Twists his head first one way, then the other searching, for Rocco who has moved. He's behind him but off to one side. Bruno grins and nods at Rocco, seeking agreement, approval or perhaps subconscious understanding. He receives only a granite-like stare. Bruno snaps his head to the front as Pisces speaks.

"Then why are you fucking my wife?" Pisces' eyes are cold and his tone has the feel of dry ice.

Bruno stills, stiffens, eyes shifting in thought but lost for words. He clears his throat, stammers, "B ... Bo ... Bossa. Signore Catalano, I ..."

Pisces raises his hand from his lap like a cobra ready to strike. The "Psssst" of the silencer-equipped pistol, although suppressed, sounds like a cannon in the morgue-like quiet study. Bruno flops backward onto the tiled floor like a thrown sand bag. The collapse of the body is loud, magnified by the silence of the room, sounding like a kettle drum crash. The sandbag quietly pooling blood onto the tile floor. The last fading violins of the concerto.

Pisces looks at Rocco and hisses, "Get him outta' here. Without her," nodding his head towards the bedroom, "seeing you. I will handle everything else."

"Yes, sir."

"And, Rocco. Let it be a warning. Pisces is life and death. Pisces giveth and Pisces taketh away. Pisces is life. To himself, and to those around him. Make sure all our help understand. The crew. Gina ... never mind her." He pauses, turns the calendar page, "Find us another driver. Someone older so as not to make a young man's mistake."

"Yes, sir."

"The man in Pisa. Carmen Messina? He would be good, and he's from here. Get him, but only if you agree and like him. Vet him like a good horse." Pisces laughs. "And make sure he's a gelding." Laughs again. Still with a sly smile on his face, he says, "Rocco, don't make him one. Just find one." He pauses. "Should have thought of that sooner, huh?"

"Yessa, boss."

"Oh, and Rocco. While there, get rid of Antonio. I don't trust him. Make it hurt first, like make him a gelding first if you have time."

"Done."

Dee strolls out onto the patio. Hunter has his back to her, looking out over the backyard fence. The sun is setting. Clear sky, red and orange. A wisp of breeze brings the scent of salt air inland sweeping away what's left of the humidity. It's peaceful yet this is the home where tragedy struck this day. Catastrophe dwelt here but a few hours ago. Dee places her hands on Hunter's shoulders. He leaps out of the chaise lounge, spinning around, dropping his brandy. The snifter shatters on the pool-side cool-crete. He faces her, his MK22 Mod O in his hand, extended at her forehead in less than an eye blink. He stops abruptly, his mind and reflexes registering the moment. He pauses. Relaxes. Drops the weapon to his side. Exhales.

Time seems suspended until he breaks the silence. "Not a good glass day." He drops his chin slightly, and looking through the top of his eyes and shaking his head he rebukes, "You should know better." Raises his head. "At least so I've been told." His tone is icy and sarcastic.

"I know." Her complexion pales, cadaver-like. She stands immobile, tense, like a gunfighter caught without a weapon. She catches her breath. "Hunter, relax. Let's talk."

"Talk? Okay, speak."

"All right. It's late. Been a long day." Color returns to her face. She says lightly, "How about dinner?"

"Dinner? Dinner? Jesus! Are you nuts, Mrs. Columbo?" He dwells a moment, then blurts mockingly, "Partner."

She slaps his face. Hard. Says, "Get your act together, Hunter. It is what it is. Now you know. I know. We know. And now you're no longer clueless, Hawk." She steps back, smiles, turns slowly around as if modeling, tempting some dense sailor. "I am what I am. Angelo is dead. Years now. I'm back working, only in a different capacity since I have children to care for and a family to worry about and an asset to ... to work with, or for."

"Asset. Jesus." Hunter slips the Hush Puppy in the rear waist band of his slacks, and sits on one of those fold-out, aluminum, canvas covered chairs. Every patio has four with an umbrella table. Less tense, more or less peaceful he says, "Well, hell, where do we go from here?"

She says, "How about some dinner?"

"Yeah, great idea. I haven't eaten since ... since this morning, early." He pauses for a second, then says, "How about Lubach's, or there's a new place, Bully's East? I'll treat."

Dee looks at him, shakes her head slowly. "You may be one tough son of a ... gun, but you surely need help. I mean, everyone tells me how lean and mean you are. And today, I mean, wow! But you know what, you just don't seem to think straight all the time. I know. I'm babbling again. That's my weakness. That's my Babylon. But, you. Holy Smokes. I mean, how can we go out to dinner when you can't even lock your front door? The windows only have tarps over them. What's to keep people out? What's to keep the neighbors, or worse, the press, from poking around and coming inside? You're the trained agent. I'm just an out-of-practice assistant handler. A little ol' landlady and clerk-typist."

Hunter sits and stares. Focused but yet not. Studying but wondering. Fidgeting but not. *I've heard about her husband's disappearance. The mystery of it all. The presumption of death. Something's not ... well, shoot.* He nods his head, a smile begins to form, drifts slowly across his face. Eyes lighten with either a plan or mischief, or both. He stands. Looks at his watch, then the darkening sky. The western reds and oranges vanishing fast and turning to ultramarine, and nightfall.

"Okay, you're right. I'll fix something and we'll eat here. Get a fresh start."

"Gee, good thinking, Hawk. But, how about this for an idea? I'll get something for us to eat. You set things up out here. I assume I'm probably a better cook than you and for sure have a better plan. What d'ya think?"

"Okay. You fix dinner. I'll fix us a drink."

"Fine. Let's see. I bet you'll have another apricot brandy. But first, clean up the broken glass so I can go barefoot. Then, get your brandy, and tell you what. Pour me a scotch, neat. We'll sip those, then I'll get busy. And, I'm guessing, you'll want to ask me a lot of questions."

"Yeah, okay, Landlady. I do have a few."

"Get the drinks. And turn on the Jacuzzi. This is going to be an interesting evening to say the least."

Hunter, now on his feet, gazes into Dee's dark eyes. Smiles form on both their faces. Then Hunter laughs softly and says, "You know, you pack a heckuva wallop. A good right hand."

"And that's not all."

Hunter hears a voice reaching from the depths of his brain-housing group. *Hunter, don't you do her.*

Then another from some other depth. *Do her.*

Pisces sits at the table on the veranda. Takes another sip of Chianti. Gina fidgets with the table settings.

Working to make things right, yet glancing often and shyly at Roberto. Then, with a rush of air, seemingly more abrupt than a jet launching from a carrier, Signora Catalano bursts onto the tiled veranda. "Roberto, everything looks so beautiful. The dinner. The fresh catch of the day. Itsa smells so wonderful. I, too, will have a glass of the Chianti." She sits at the table, and waves her hand at Gina to bring some wine.

Anna smiles, leans back, her head sways from side to side with apparent pleasure. "What a gorgeous evening. The mountain, she looks so peaceful. The sea so calm. Life is good. Yes?"

"Yes." Pisces pauses. "It is for most of us. Let's eat." He looks over her head, commands,

"Gina. Signora Catalano and I wish to start. Please serve. And tell Rocco that I wish to see him before he leaves; and you, after supper, in my study. Yes?"

"Yes, sir, Signore Catalano,"

An uncomfortable calm settles upon three diverse horizons. Each with anticipation. Each for a different reason. Each with dissimilar colors. And perhaps, each with a distinctive result. Perchance those enjoying these horizons don't grasp this, or perhaps they do. Don't care, or perhaps they do. The missteps of the ded reckoning process are cumulative so the lapses in the fix feed upon themselves as plotted, growing with time.

Navigators, or in fact predators, will need to check the drift meter or shoot another celestial fix, not forgetting to advance and retard the LOP's so to make a course direction.

Because ... a reckoning, is coming.

CHAPTER 5

"In ten years nobody will remember the details of caliber, stance, or tactics. They will only remember who lived."
A gunfighter's rule

Coilean Muldoon sent a message to the Shanahan lads to meet him at the Metro Pub in town. His anglicized name is Colin, the Irish meaning of which is "whelp." Perhaps as a young boy he was that, however, now he is as ugly as a bulldog, mean as a snake and passes gas more than any three bulldogs.

The two Shanahan lads enter, look around and see the old man, Colin Muldoon, at a far corner table, and he is accompanied by his eldest son, Conor. One would have thought that the father would have wanted a Coilean Junior, however he did breed a whelp and raised him into a Pit Bull...like those originally bred in Ireland and used as "catch dogs" for semi-wild hogs. The dogs can be family companions, as Conor perhaps once was, but now more likely he's renowned for his fighting prowess and nickname, "Pit". A brutish lad with a notable short Irish temper, Popeye-like arms, his stout neck and shoulders melded as one, and a zit-ridden mug of an English Bull, not a Pit.

Both he and his father are hunched over inhaling fine pub grub. The Metro is known for many things, most positive, but its food is of the finest in the city, certainly within the walls of the old city. Danny and Sean Shanahan wind their way through other seated pub customers to the Muldoon table waving both hands to wish away the dense bluish-gray haze of smokers. The lads stand tableside until Colin Muldoon nods. Then they sit. The brutish son, Conor, glances up and sneers at them allowing a string of gravy to dribble on his chin. The elder Muldoon grumbles, "Have a pint?"

Danny Shanahan answers for himself and his younger brother, Sean. "That would be good. The task is over and done with. Not a soul spotted us." He pauses, waiting for a reaction.

Colin grunts, "Tis on me then."

That settled, Danny continues making eye contact with only the elder one of the two. "What is it you wish this night, Master Muldoon, sire?"

Colin raises his ham-like hand with his finger extended and with the other hand shovels another load of fine Irish stew into his mouth. Puts his soup spoon down and swipes his mouth with his sleeve. Watches the waitress, a perky, auburn-haired young lass, leap away with the pint order as his son, Conor, pats her soccer ball shaped butt. She yelps and with a playful grin screeches, "Keep your paws to yourself you overgrown ape and tell your father he's smellin' up this space with his rear-ended belches." The Pit Bull ignores the remark and shovels in another spoonful of gravy-dripping stew into his grinning mouth.

The elder Muldoon, beet red from the remarks but ignores it nonetheless, says to the Shanahan lads, "When she brings your pints, and is gone, we'll talk. That be the way of it. And it will be in the Irish. I'm told you understand."

"Aye. Do you have word of Paddy?"

"We'll talk when the lass returns and is gone."

"So it'll be." They remove their caps and lay them on the table still with a grip on them with twisting hands. They wait, eyes flicking about for the perky barmaid to return. A dryness comes to their mouths at the same time, much like identical twins might experience. Heads twist and turn together, syncopated eyes dart about as one. They look at one another, then for the auburn-haired barmaid again. To Muldoon's eyes. And back. They sense. It is not a good word they'll be hearing. All this while listening to Conor, the zit, slurp his meal, gravy still on his chin and more on the table. The checkered tablecloth beneath the Pit Bull's bowl looks as though he has strained the stew up through the cloth. Mrs. Shanahan, the boys' feisty mother, would slap them silly if they were to eat like that at home. Or have 'em eat out of a bowl on the floor to teach them table manners, which she had done once or thrice when they were young.

The wait is excruciating for the Shanahan lads. Their breaths grow short and their jaws tighten with glum anticipation.

When Pisces and Anna finish dinner, Gina hastens to clear away the dishes nearly dropping one, and does let a fork clatter to the tile. Anna inhales sharply, shaking her head and hisses in Italian, "Inept peasant."

Gina drops another. Utters, *"Scusa!"*

Anna flicks her hand toward Gina as if brushing unwanted crumbs from the table.

The supposed-to-be house mouse retrieves the forks and backs away muttering, *"Mi dispiase."* Then repeats herself in English to please Pisces. "I'm sorry."

Pisces nods not wholly imperceptibly, smiles and says, "No mess. Not to worry. Bruno made worse," and he chuckles.

Rocco makes an unintentional topic changing entrance with a tray holding a snifter and a short fine crystal drink glass. The snifter filled with an apricot brandy from a small family winery in Tuscany. It is their Chianti that Pisces also drinks. The glass has but a splash of *Macallan* fine oak 12 year scotch whiskey on the rocks for the Signora. Pisces more often than not complains about her drinking the fine whiskey on ice, but not tonight. This is whiskey imported by *Rinaldi* and sent to Anna. Rocco serves both and then places a new, unopened box of cigars on the table. As is customary, Pisces opens the fresh box of his *Joya De Nicaragua* cigars, wrapped in their stunningly beautiful Rosado-colored *Nicaraguan Habana Criollo* wrappers. Pisces removes one, and the wrapper. Fingers and feels it carefully. As should be it feels substantial, no bumps, no soft spots.

Anna sits, legs crossed, foot twitching and finger quietly tapping on the table watching him. And by his way of things, not yet sipped her *Macallan*. Her thoughts are as always. This is his ritual. First the cigar and its lighting. Then the inhalation and taste followed by the intense, squinting gaze at the smoke. Then a sip of brandy. A nod that signals the tranquil leopard is satisfied and finished with his ritual, and the feline Anna may have a sip of scotch. Then wait to see what Pisces, her Roberto, wants to chat about, if anything. On occasion he says nothing, finishes his cigar and brandy and takes her here, on the table. Then another brandy and have her again or perhaps just have her perform her specialty. Anna awakens from her thoughts by blinking her eyes voluntarily several times and audibly exhaling.

Roberto Catalano draws on the cigar as Rocco holds a lighted wood match. As expected the draw is easy, spot-on flawless. The first taste, in fact the first one-third palette, will be sweet with flavors of cherries and raisins. The smoke is a beautiful, consistent gray and twirls upward into the night air, and then appears to float from the veranda and drift down the mountain under the sea breeze. Catalano smiles in satisfaction. Rests his cigar-holding hand on the table, and takes a generous taste of his brandy with the other. Nods his head in fulfillment. Smiles. Pauses. He motions to Rocco, dismissing him. Then says as the man is leaving, "Rocco, have one of my cigars, old friend ... one mind you." He jokingly admonishes, "And a glass of brandy if you wish. The last of this. Then open another and set it out here."

Rocco breaks into a broad grin, says, "Grazie mille."

Catalano smiles then lets it turn sour quicker than warm milk. "Don't forget. Later, in the study." Pauses, growls, "Is it tidy?"

Rocco says, "Yes, sir," and is gone, disappearing into the darkness of the villa. The only lights spreading warmth are in the kitchen, in the study, and on the veranda. From the veranda other villa lights stretch down the mountain blending with those of shops in town, and boats and yachts in the harbor below. One of the latter is Pisces' own 98 foot Benetti. It is a Fratelli Benetti design, built by this old prestigious firm and Italian registered. It has two engines with twin screws and a 600 nautical mile range cruising at 12K's. Carries 12,000 L's of fuel and about 8,400 water. It can sleep ten. All teakwood decking and the salons, lounges and bridges are furnished in mostly white leather. It has a crew of five, all hand selected by

Rocco from the DeStefano crime clan in Calabria. Its name is the *Sorridenta*.

Catalano turns to Anna and says, "Bruno is gone. Today was his last day."

She frowns in feigned disbelief. Rattles the ice cubes in her *Macallan*, then rests the glass on the table casually, yet deliberately. "Why? I thought he was doing a fine job. And he was with us ... you for such a long time."

"He broke my trust. When that happens, the person must go. Be dealt with, no matter the time, the relation or whom." He stares at Anna for seconds, watching for some reaction. She grimaces ever so slightly, more a twitch of her mouth, fingers her etched crystal glass then pulls her hand back in her lap. He continues, "You broke my trust. But, you're my wife so you get to stay." His eyes narrow and the leopard snarls, "For now."

Anna stands, flushed, hisses, "Bruno did nothing. I did nothing. You insinuate everything with your eyes and tone of voice, your mannerisms." She stomps her foot hard on the tile. Seeing no reaction and with evidently no immediate response coming, she angrily shouts, "We did nothing you didn't bring on yourself. That you and that slut didn't do. I will not ..."

"Shut up. He did, and you did. And have done for some time now. It will be the last time, or you will feel more pain than Bruno." He takes a sip of brandy and rises slowly from the chair as a leopard might when sensing danger or prey. "And don't think about leaving. You will leave only when I say. You have nowhere to go anyway. You are an orphaned peasant girl, remember. A peasant," reminding her she is no more nor less than the house mouse. "I took you in and made a life for you. A good one. Now, leave. Go to your room. I will be along later, if I choose. And do as I choose."

She jams her arms tight to her hips and thighs, fists clinched, and comes to his end of the table. He methodically places his cigar in an ashtray. She moves to slap him, but Pisces is much too quick, catching her arm midway in motion. With his other hand, he slaps her across the face hard dropping her to the tile floor of the veranda. He reaches down, grabs her by the hair and snatches her to her feet. Growls, "Do as I say, now. Be thankful for what you have." He pauses stepping closer. "Your life."

She snaps, "But you can have your slut, Gina. I can't ..." she screams as he slaps her hard again knocking her backwards, her feet slipping on the tile. She twists as she falls first to her knees, then her head crashes onto the ceramic hardness of the floor. This time she pushes and claws away from him on hands and skinned knees. Tears running from beneath her lids, nose dripping blood. She gathers herself, staggering to her feet. Her face shows a harsh redness from the two slaps, blood oozing from her nose, and a trickle from the right side of her mouth mingles with a tear winding down her cheek.

He says, "Now go. You pushed your luck much too far tonight."

She turns, wobbly on her feet, but her Italian temper and pride force her to stalk away, an angered strut, into the darkness of the villa. Pisces eyes trace her until he sees a bedroom lamp flicker on upstairs. Turns, sees Rocco watching from a study window. Roberto Catalano nods towards the bedroom, flicks his index finger across his throat. Then he points to the room with a demonstrative nod. The head movement is returned in kind by Rocco, and he disappears from the window.

Pisces prowls back to his seat changing his leopard spots as easily as shifting from low gear to drive. Catalano picks his cigar from the ashtray, not dropping an ash. The first one third has burned away. He takes a slow, easy draw and again watches the wisp of smoke circle and drift aimlessly in the night air. The second third of the cigar has the taste of mild Scotch Bonnet, pepper spice with a note of apricots and fresh almonds. Again he takes a generous sip of his apricot brandy which blends so well with his cigar. That or rum. Nothing else. He leans back allowing his body to relax, head resting on the back of the chair. Another draw. Another treat.

With the latter thought processing through Catalano's mind, Gina, as silent as a bird walking on velvet, comes to his side. "Signore, is there something else for the Signore this evening?" She pauses a long moment, looks about again, whispers, "Is everything alright, Roberto?" The velvety words are followed with a coy grin.

Catalano gently grasps her hand, sighs, "Yes, everything is fine. Fine. I will be out here for a time, with my cigar, my brandy and my thoughts." Then he follows with, *"Non ti preoccupare."*

The coy smile is replaced with one of concern. She murmurs, "I won't worry." Then, purrs, "Roberto, ti amo," as she places her other hand on his neck where it joins the shoulder. Squeezes.

He presses her hand, then lets it slide from his, grins and nods, gently pushing her away and says, "I know you do. Later you can show me how much." He brings the Joya De Nicaragua to his mouth once again. As she departs for the kitchen entrance, Pisces watches the young woman swing tantalizingly away. Long dark hair swishing and bouncing on her slender shoulders, she seems to float on her long thinnish legs yet distinctive calves and thighs. She has beautiful hands with long fingers. Like those of a pianist. Gina turns her head, peering back over her shoulder, a wide smile on her flawless face, a look of innocence, like a clear summer day. This affair has been going on for some time. Many times right here on this same table in the sun of early afternoon when Anna has left for town to shop, or to the beach or perceivably to Bruno somewhere cozy in town.

Pisces leans back in his chair, relaxing, drawing and sipping. He glances up and sees the bedroom lamp still on. Sees a shadow pass from the study through the villa. It's Rocco with a tray with bottle, glass and ice bucket. And probably his personal ice pick. Pisces pours himself another brandy. Takes a sip.

Murmurs, "Life is good. Maybe I'll paint tomorrow. The Mountain. Yes, the mountain."

Hunter realizing that she is correct and going out to eat is not an option, asks, "So, what are we having for dinner? Do you want me to grill something out here?"

"No, we're having leftover lasagna."

"Leftover? From what?"

"Always better the second night. Especially mine. A long-standing family recipe. None like it anywhere. Best restaurants can't touch it."

"From what?"

Dee smiles, shakes her head slowly. "Last night."

"Oh."

"I was going to have it last night. But, I lost a bet to ... never mind." She takes a deep breath, exhales, shakes her head. "Anyway, like I said, it's always better the second night." Pauses.

Hunter frowns, "What?"

"Damn, that didn't come out right either." Shakes her head, "Never mind. Get the drinks and I'll run over to my house and get the lasagna, bring it over and heat it here. We can eat out on the patio. How's that? Do you like lasagna?"

"Yeah, sounds okay. I mean, you know, lasagna is lasagna. I've had it. All tastes the same."

"Well, not mine, Marine. I make it with De Cecco lasagna, use both Jack and Mozzarella cheese, and cottage cheese. Sliced hard boiled eggs and great meat balls." She kisses her five finger tips. "Make them myself with ground steak, an egg, parsley and Parmesan cheese. And has onion, chopped garlic in it. Layered just right." She pauses again, tilts one hip, and with a hand on each, smiles and says, "If you don't eat two helpings, I'll give you the best bl...never mind." Laughs.

"I've ever had. Yeah, right. I'll have seconds for sure. Believe me. Go. Bring it. Drinks on the way. Table will be set. See you back out here."

"*Grazie.*" She half-nods and twists her head. "First, I suggest you go see who that is peeking over your fence gate," pointing to the five-foot wooden fence between their houses.

Hunter tenses, leaps quickly to the wall of the house, and bolts around the corner to the fence. Snaps open the gate and finds a young man standing there with a large box-like camera that newspaper photographers always seem to be carrying. Hunter snaps, "What do you want?"

The startled photographer starts to reply when Hunter snatches the camera away, throws it on the narrow sidewalk pavement, and stomps it into more than its normal assembly groups. Then grabs the young man by the throat and slams him against the stucco wall of his house. Snarls, "I said, what d'ya want?"

"I'm with the..."

"Don't care. You're on my property. Trespassing. For all I know a thief, perhaps a demented peeping tom." Hunter drags the man by his jacket collar along the path between the houses to the front and onto Arcola Avenue with the young man scrambling to keep from falling. Hunter shouts to the still-on-duty patrolman at the cul-de-sac. "I thought Bradovich left you here for a reason. If it's to watch me, go home. If it's to keep people away, do your damn job." He shoves the young photographer further into the street. Hunter looks at the young man, "The camera is goin' in the trash. And you're leavin', now." Turns to the cop who is hustling over, hand on his nightstick. Hunter shouts, "Officer, he's yours. He was either trespassing on my property or he's a pervert peeping tom, or both." The young man stumbles the last few steps toward the officer. Hunter turns and strides back alongside the house and into his patio, stopping to pick up the trashed camera.

Dee says, "My God, you have a violent streak or you're certainly not an especially tolerant soul. I sure hope my lasagna meets your approval."

"Well, if it doesn't, I won't eat a second helping and then it could get interesting."

They stand and stare at one another for a decade of moments. Then she laughs aloud. He follows the cue. Both leave for their tasks shaking their heads.

The drinks are good. The lasagna is superb. Both helpings. The place settings are cleared away. Then both go inside their respective houses, change into swim suits and rejoin on the patio and slip into the Jacuzzi. Dee in a pink bikini. Hunter in swim trunks. Each has another drink. The same. He an apricot brandy; she a Limoncello which when she asked for a refill, Hunter raised his eyebrows and shook his head once. It is mellow but has a kick ... like a sneak right hand.

Dee says, "Let's talk. Relax. It's time we know a little more about each other."

"Why?" He senses Zachary's ghost rustling in his brain-housing group and the whispered, *Hunter don't you do her.*

Dee senses either hesitation or hostility. Smiles, says, "Don't get hot and bothered. If we're going to work and travel together as writer and secretary, we should know one another." She moves from the opposite side toward Hunter, with a few slides of her hips or buns.

Hunter says, "I see." And edges two cheek-lengths away. Now opposite one another again, one hand clasping the drinks along the edge. They settle with a moment of uneasiness. Then Hunter says, "Tell me about your family. Where they live? What they do? About your kids."

"Children. Kids are goats, but that's a good start. However ..." Dee begins with her grandparents, explaining with obvious love and caring in her voice that they immigrated here from Italy. That they, her grandfather, Antonio Antonelli DeLuca and her grandmother, Signora Angelina Maria Celebresee DeLuca, owned and operated a winery in the Tuscany area. Her parents with them. After her mother died, and the political atmosphere in Italy was becoming unpleasant at the least, her father, Benito Antonio DeLuca, came here with the grandparents, her older sister Maria, and her. All now live in Napa Valley, running their family-owned winery, *Per Sempre*. "It means, 'Forever'," she murmurs. "DeLuca Vineyards are forever. After Maria and I, Dino and Anna, and after them, their children. Forever."

"Maria?"

"My sister. Beautiful. Smart. A little taller and slimmer than me but still has ... never mind."

Hunter starts to respond, but Dee immediately continues in her rambling, bubbly style that is made still more enjoyable by her husky, contralto voice, saying, "It features premium wines. In Italy, wine is part of life and we want to make DeLuca wine part of people's lives here. Our premium wines include limited quantities of Sangeovese, Pinot Grigio, Rosato and a superb Estate Red Wine. A blend of Cabernet Sauvignon, Sangeovese and

Merlot. Wines that my grandfather and father are knowledgeable about."

As Hunter listens, because of her style of speech he wonders how she got employed by the Agency. They, *we*, are so muted by the nature of their, *our*, business.

Dee continues about her grandparents and her Dad sharing an old home on the sixty-two acres of vineyards and working winery. The house has a large pool, a guest cottage with a smaller pool. Also a wonderful tasting room. This room is a touch of Tuscany, a link with home, and is casual and warm in the middle of the vineyards with an indoor view of the barrel room. It also has a picnic area for tourists. She adds with a quiet laugh, "And it's dog friendly. Hadda' be." Dee laughs again. "My grandfather rides around the vineyards on his motorcycle with a side car... for his dog, Cab. Magpie's momma."

She goes on saying that Maria, her sister, although stunning, is single and basically operates the business, while her father is in fact the Wine Master. She adds, "And my grandfather, besides his motorcycling, continues to add his wisdom, and most importantly, he persists in making his own apricot brandy. So, if you ever get a chance to meet him, the two of you will have something in common."

"What about Dino and Anna?"

"Eight and six. Good children. Love being up at the winery. Adore their grandparents. Oh, and are scared just a bit of my father. He's a tad gruff at times, particularly with Dino. But they love the pool, or pools, and perhaps that's what causes some of the gruffness from my Dad. He worries about them."

Hunter pauses, then out of harmony asks, "How did you come to work for the Agency?"

Dee's pace is not set off with the sudden change of subject and tone. "I worked at Langley before I met Angie. Angelo. He was in the Navy and stationed at Patuxent River. We married; had children; and came here. He wanted to get in on the action. Nam! Those are his words. He was on his way when the ship stopped in Hong Kong. They had a few days off. He went ashore and...and...never came back." She looks away, over Hunter's head and toward the sky for a few moments. Then back to Hunter with a stare as hard as burnt-black biscuits and says, "Just gone. He's listed as missing. Well, now, presumed dead. The children miss him. Especially at certain times, in the evening, bed time, or like when they visit one of their friends. But, life moves on." Dee has the look of a person that wants to talk about something else.

"And you?" Hunter probes.

"Ahhh, Hunter," she lets her sigh drag out in exasperation. She continues, "It's over. I'll never forget him but he's gone. Dead. I've moved forward. Back at work, and someday I'll fall in love again." She sighs again. Then, "Maybe today," and she grins like the proverbial cat.

Hunter shakes his head uncomfortably, mumbles to himself.

Dee stares at him, head tilting side to side. Then laughs aloud. When her laughter fades, she looks at Hunter and with her contralto voice at its raspiest, says, "I've not dated since he's been gone. Not been with another man. He was my first, and last, maybe." She stares at the perplexed look on Hunter's face. *He knows that's not true.*

The cat smile spreads across her face and she says in a whispered voice, "You need to be careful. I'm vulnerable." Pauses for only a moment, then, "And horny."

"Vulnerable? Not hardly."

She laughs again. Louder, lets it fade and says, "Don't get nervous." Takes in a breath, "Now then, tell me about you. Stuff I haven't been briefed on or don't already know." Titters again and takes a sip of her Limoncello.

He does, and as he does so, Dee inches to a spot against his left shoulder. He fidgets some. She interrupts one of his stories from his Harrow-on-the-Hill days by saying, "Don't fret, I've left your other hand free so you can continue to sip your apricot brandy." She smiles, "It's empty you know. Would you like another?"

Hunter squirms just a tad again, says, "Sure. What about you? I'll get 'em."

"Sit still. You've had a long day and you might well need your rest before tonight's over." She pushes herself up and out of the bubbling Jacuzzi. Stands a second, grabs a towel and dries herself quickly, then purposely drops the towel over Hunter's head. "You were gawking. Vetting me." She squats down like a weight-lifter, stares at Hunter for several seconds then reaches to the edge and picks up her glass.

Hunter swallows the last of his brandy. He can't help himself as his eyes are drawn to it. *Not exactly a bikini cut.*

She smiles, pulls her knees together, lifts the glass from his hand, stands and goes into the house.

Hunter shakes his head, refocuses his eyes and thoughts, snatches the towel off his head. His eyes follow Dee across the patio and through the sliding door, and for as long as he can see her gliding across the living room toward the kitchen. He mutters, "This is how this ... or it ... got started last night with Sam. Cripes, Hunter, get a hold of yourself. This is trouble city. Got to drop her somewhere along the line."

He stops. Frowns. Mentally downshifts, wheels screech, beams flick to high. His head tilts to one side. He squints. *My God. Winery. Tuscany. Grandfather makes apricot brandy. That was part of my dream. This is weird. This is the stuff of premonitions or omens or portents or worse.* He jolts back to the here and now at the sound of her voice.

"I'm back and I'm cold. You need to turn the air conditioning down, or up, in the house. So, I'm gettin' in right next to you, big fella," and does, snuggling close.

She murmurs, "Isn't this becoming an interesting night? Like a dream."

Hunter gags on his first sip of brandy.

CHAPTER 6

"Being ready is not what matters. What matters is winning after you get there."
LtGen Victor H. Krulak, USMC

Hunter relaxes in the soothing waters of the hot tub. It's a clear night. Looking seaward the stars are dimmed by the lights of Mission Bay, however the constellation of Orion, the warrior, is easily defined. Hunter continues his mind-wandering gaze. *Just last night I was in here with Samantha. Then in bed with her. Now she's dead, after one night with me. And I'm told it's not related to me. Or to my mission. Bull shit.*

Blinking away his star gazing he takes a sip of his apricot brandy and stares into the night sky again. *First piece of bullshit is that Dee Columbo is only my Property Manager. Second piece is she's my partner, but she's somebody's partner. And third is "we". There is no we in the hinterland.*

He twirls the brandy in his snifter and takes a full swallow. *And now I'm in the Jacuzzi with her and she's got more moves than a Saigon whore.*

Hunter's thought pattern continues to drift. *Ol' Brute Krulak was right about being ready. Hell, I'm ready, and I'm goin' to win when I get there. Alone.*

Another sip. He shakes his head and mutters aloud, *"Si vis pacem, para bellum."*

Dee asks, "What was that? That sounds like Latin."

"It is."

"And?"

"It means, 'If you want peace, prepare for war'."

There's a pause in this brief exchange. Then Dee asks, "Is the p-i-e-c-e, piece or p-e-a-c-e, peace?" She grins like a cat, then grimaces followed by her burnt-biscuit stare, and "With you, I'm sure it's p-e-a-c-e."

He steps out of the hot tub saying, "It means we need to get out of here. This is not preparing for war. I'm going to bed...alone. If you need an escort home, get your dog," pointing to Magpie wandering around the far side of the pool. "Or take care of yourself? I've been led to believe you can do that."

Dee leaps out of the Jacuzzi like a porpoise surfacing at Sea World and snatches a towel from a chair. "That was unwarranted, Kerrigan." She slaps him for the second time tonight, then throws the towel in his face, turns and walks out of his patio gate and into her yard by way of her back gate. Magpie follows, wagging her stump tail which means she looks like she's doing a K9 rumba.

Hunter murmurs, "Watch the hands. Always watch the hands. Good rule." Then chuckles. "I didn't deserve that. Zachary did. Oh well, now and then I just shouldn't be left alone in a china closet ... whatever that means."

He goes inside.
Been one helluva day.

The Shanahan lads have their pints in hand and as the barmaid leaves the table she gets another pat on the rump by Conor, this one with a squeeze. She squeals and punches the Pit Bull flush on the jaw, knocking him off his chair. He stands, kicks the chair over and bellows like a bull. The pub crowd roars with laughter over their rough-house foreplay and shout offensive words of encouragement to both. The barkeep, a pub old timer, pounds his fist on the bar surface, rattling nearby pints. He shouts the ageless pub command, "Mind your pints and quarts me lads. Settle down." The crowd quiets to the buzzing norm as in watching their "p's" and "q's". The barmaid curtsies and promenades away, head swaying and a broad grin with her tongue on the upper lip. The Pit Bull sits, flushed with feigned anger, but still overheated plans.

Waiting a few moments, the elder Muldoon tilts over and waves all three lads closer. Danny and Sean Shanahan lean over the table, heads as close to the middle as possible. The younger Muldoon, Conor, does as well. It looks like an old-fashioned American football huddle. The quarterback, Colin Muldoon whispers, "We haven't heard from your brother, Paddy, for days now. We should have, but we've heard nothing. I am going to have one of our trusted mates in Boston go seek him out and make inquiries. We do know there was a bombing, and in a city where one was supposed to have taken place. But no names have been released. And we have no word of, or from, me lad, Paddy."

Danny Shanahan says, "Maybe he's just on his way home. Hasn't had time to ..."

"I think not. A call was to be made first. That was an order. A must."

"Well then, let me go there to find me brother. He may need help. He may need us."

"No, as I say, I'll have one of our mates go check. You, and Sean here," nodding to the younger lad, "must stay. You are needed here, not there. This is the way of things. The way it must be."

Danny stretches back breaking the huddle and takes a sip from his pint and puts it back down hard on the tabletop. "I should go. Paddy may need me."

Sean blurts out, "And me as well."

Muldoon's face reddens, his whisper is a tad louder and more harsh. "I should have told you nothing. You will not go. You will stay put. You have other duties to do here for the cause. Going there was a one-time assignment for Paddy. The ending of a matter long overdue but not forgotten. Now strap it up, lads, and wait further word from me. Do you understand?"

Danny again answers for both. "We understand what you say. We will wait for the present. But, not too long." He snarls, "Do you understand, Master Muldoon?"

Conor starts to stand. The elder Muldoon pushes him back in his chair. Glares into Danny's eyes and with an equally nasty tone says, "I hear ye, lad. Don't ya press me. Now go and I will tell you what I know, when I know, and if I consider it is necessary. Now, git." He waves the back of his hand as if swatting them away. Conor starts to stand again, only to be shoved back in his seat by his father, causing him to rock over backwards to the floor once again. Conor leaps to his feet, rights the chair, and stands, fists clenched, glaring at his father.

The elder stands. Snarls, "Give it a go, you whelp."

His son sits, flustered. The old man sits, stares at Danny and Sean.

The Shanahans get up, snatch their caps and slap them on their heads and stalk out of the pub, leaving the unfinished pints. The two Muldoons watch them intently. When the two are gone, Colin says to his son, "You keep an eye on those two. If they do something other than what I ordered, you stop 'em. Give them a lesson in following orders. We are in a war, not a family feud or some struggle between clans."

In the Irish, Gaelic, Conor responds. "It'll be my pleasure. I've never liked or trusted any of the three of them."

The elder Muldoon, also in the Irish, orders, "That may be, but not a thump unless they try to leave town or something akin to that. Understand? "

"Aye. Aye, I do." He nods as he speaks. Pauses. Then grins and says, "But now I be having me self another pint or two. Then have me self that barmaid."

The elder Muldoon shakes his head. "Good Lord, Conor. You and every lad under sixty have had her. You be catchin' somethin' that will burn worse than the fires of Hades."

"Naw, not me, father dear." The barmaid returns to the table heeding Conor's wave for service. He hugs her around her waist and says, "I'll have me another pint."

She wiggles just a bit appearing to try to free herself but without serious intent, and says, "And would you be wanting another again, or something else as well?"

"Both."

She wrenches free, smiles, and says giggling, "Then it will be so, laddie."

The elder Muldoon downs the remainder of his pint, says, "Since you won't heed my warning, then you can pay the tab. This one and the one that will surely follow. 'Night, and don't forget your task."

"Aye."

At home, outside the kitchen door in the back of their cottage, Danny whispers to Sean. "We will do as we've been asked. For now. But if Paddy is not home soon ... in a day or two, we will do what we must."

Sean nods. "That we will."

"Until then, stay close. And beware, because we will be watched I assure you. It is the way of The Army." Danny opens the door and he and Sean quietly enter to see a plate of mince-meat tarts on the table and a tea kettle about to whistle on the stove. And two cups for the pouring.

Pisces quietly enters his study and finds Rocco standing, waiting patiently, just inside the door. "Evening again, Rocco." He looks around carefully. "The room looks fine. Tidy. Not a trace. Is everything else done?"

"Yes, except the disposal. I will do that early tomorrow morning. I will take the boat out and dump them. We can trust them, one and all. They're part of the DeStefano clan and have much to lose if found by the authorities. Here or at home." He pauses for a moment, then in a more quiet and cautious tone says, "Boss, you should have used less a caliber in here." He pauses, a worried look creeps across his face. Seeing no reaction, and getting no comment, he continues. "It would have done the job and not been so messy. Bruno's brains were all over the books and shelves, and the bullet fortunately was lodged in your large Atlas and not the woodwork."

Pisces stares at Rocco for several moments, then smiles, "Yeah, you're right. Poor planning. But then I truly don't give a shit. The Walther was all I had in the desk. So, more mess, who cares but you. You are only chewin' on my butt because you probably used an ice pick upstairs. Right?" Catalano pats Rocco on the back. "Talking about planning, have you ensured ..."

"Yes, sir. They are tied, taped and bagged. Canvas. I will weight them down once on the boat. They will stay down. We'll leave about four in the morning. Before the fishing boats go. And we'll stay out and do some fishing. The crew likes to fish. We'll give them a little vacation this way."

"I should have given them Anna first, then dump her. They would have enjoyed the fishing much more."

"Perhaps." Rocco pauses, then allows a slow grin to cross his face. "Perhaps it's not too late." And after the slightest of moments bursts into laughter.

Pisces follows, roaring and chokes out, "You are worse than me, Rocco."

"Yes, perhaps. But seriously, Bossa, you stay here and be seen all day, by someone other than Gina. Maybe go into town. Take a walk."

"Good. Done. I'll do that. Anything else?"

"Yes. I've called Carmen Messina. He will work for us. He's overjoyed. I suggest bringing his sister and her son as well. She can cook and keep house. The boy can work here as a yard man. And, he is a fine auto mechanic already. Can work on the cars and also drive on occasion. Also the boat engines, and perhaps spell a crew member from time to time. I will put them up over the garage and I will move into the main house."

"Good. Good plan, but, you move into Gina's room when you return. She can move to the room next to mine ... For the time being. Until I decide what is best for her."

Rocco says, "Done." Starts to leave and declares, "I will take care of things tomorrow, then I will leave for Pisa late in the day to get Carmen and the others, and will deal with Antonio while I'm there. *Buona notte, Signore Catalano.*"

Pisces nods and to make Rocco feel more at ease for the moment speaks in Italian, saying, "Tell Gina to come in and bring my brandy with her. *Per favore.*"

Rocco nods agreement as Pisces closes the door quietly. Roberto Catalano walks to the huge, soft, rust-colored leather couch on the far side of the study. Sits, leans back with his hands clasped behind his head.

What is best now for Gina is me. Later, we'll see.

There is a soft tapping on the study door, then it opens quietly and slowly. Gina slides through, brandy bottle and snifters in her hands, bumping the door closed with her butt. Her sheer gown is open in front and swishes off to the side from each of her long legs as she prowls across the tile flooring to Pisces. This is not new, but now she moves more confidently, not as a cat stalking a predator but one that has already captured her prey and is going to feast.

"Roberto, love."

Sunday started early for some, like Rocco. It ended early for others, such as Bruno Costa and Anna Catalano. For Gina it also starts early, and for her it continues longer than she anticipated, however this is the first time she has had Roberto purely to herself so that shouldn't be unexpected. Pisces is not a young man, but still a hunter and in superb condition, perhaps starving. Droughts can cause hunger of all kinds.

For the Shanahan lads and their worried mother, Sunday is simply too long as it is. For the elder Muldoon it's an early mass. For the son Conor, it will be one that he will remember for its burning aftermath.
For Paddy Shanahan, it never came.

Samantha McGee never saw Sunday's morn.
For Hunter Kerrigan it is a late morning and a surprise. As he ambles down the hallway from his bedroom toward the kitchen he smells fresh coffee brewing. Then hears sizzling and trailing behind the sound, the aroma of bacon. The sounds and the smells are enhanced by a freshened and a dazzling Antonelli Teresa DeLuca Columbo standing in white slacks, a green silk sleeveless blouse and white-strapped sandals. Black hair glistening in a bit of light coming through the kitchen window that faces East. Hunter stops short of the kitchen.
Before he can speak, Dee says, "Good morning, Hunter. I'm sorry for last night. For yesterday. For everything. It was a horrible day, and night. Let's start fresh today; fresh for the days or weeks ahead." She pauses, tilts her head, holds each leg of her slacks between her thumb and forefinger, curtsies and says, "What say ye, laddie?" Smiles coyly. "Is that in the Irish enough?"
"Close enough for an English version. However, in the interest of not wasting any more time, sorry, let me help get set up."

"Okay. Let's just eat in here. In the booth in the kitchen. It's nice and cozy. Quiet. And we can talk and figure out our next step, or two, or more. So, set the table, please."

"Done. Let me just check for messages first. Okay?"

"Hunter. Come here, first." He does. Dee puts her arms around his neck and shoulders; hugs him; and pats him gently on the back. Whispers, "Pals?"

He pulls away, shakes his head, "Pals," and turns and strides toward his office and the closet.

Dee murmurs, "Maybe more than pals."

"I heard that, Pal. I heard that. Nothing gets by the Hawk," and he closes the door to his office.

Dee murmurs, "Think so, huh?"

And this Sunday has time left on the clock.

CHAPTER 7

*"If you can choose what to bring to a gunfight,
bring a long gun and a friend
with a long gun."*
A gunfighter's rule

Hunter's chat on the phone reveals little new. Zachary tells him they know for sure that Herman Mueller, aka Aries the CIA turnaround agent, was stabbed with a pick-stick, the type workmen use to pick up litter. Then Joe followed with, "However, what killed him were two shots to the head, close in, assassination style." He continues by telling Hunter that there were no witnesses, except if you consider Alberto, the owner of the restaurant. Pauses, then says in virtually a hiss, "He must have known something because he and his entire family were found slaughtered. The local police have no evidence but suspect a local artist named Roberto Muscarella only because Interpol says that is an aka for a known assassin. To us, he's Pisces."

Hunter interrupts the monologue. "Joe, this is weird. Did I tell you about the dream I had? Actually it was..."

"No, some other time, pal. This is important stuff I'm giving you." Joe Zachary goes on to notify Hunter of the villa outside of Pisa that Muscarella leased that is now empty. And of a leased flat in London and likewise empty. Joe suggests that Hunter plan a trip, as an author doing research. Before Hunter can comment, he says, "Since your ID hasn't been compromised, nor you, let's go with it. Be easier and cover your travel."

Hunter frowns, pauses, then asks, "Not compromised? What about yesterday?"

Zachary tells him again that the incident was related only to Samantha, her father, and he being there was coincidence to the PIRA. Joe emphasizes, "That's who's responsible." Then, "Pisces, and anyone that works for him doesn't know you from Adam."

Hunter asks, "What about my father?"

"Well, of course he knew your father. Certainly knows the name Kerrigan but you're not using that name and he doesn't know you. Never saw you. Doesn't know anything about you. Shouldn't be an issue."

"Shouldn't. Would of, should of, great. Personally, I believe the man is a lot smarter than you think. I'll give you the IRA crap. The PIRA on the other hand is a hard-ass group of nasty-minded, irate and unforgiving Micks. They or someone will remember Patrick Shanahan, if that was his real name and I suspect it is, or was. Hell, he's a KIA in a war. Kin doesn't forget nor forgive in that part of the world. They are at least in the top five of assholes per square foot." He pauses, laughs, then chuckles, "Hells bells, my grandfather still hasn't forgotten Pearl Harbor. He won't serve a Japanese person in his bar. Calls 'em 'damn Japs.' It's embarrassing. Anyway, I'd bet Pisces is always tuned to these frequencies and may even have done a job or two for them. And to think that no one knows my real name here is just not true."

"Who besides our people?"

"The people who were with that Oboe clown. My friend Bradovich. Sam. Dee. Probably all the police that were here. That's for starters."

Zachary replies, "According to our Intel, Pisces is not hooked up with the PIRA. Never has been. Don't worry about the rest. We've got your back."

"Really? Got my back? Who had Sam's back?" Hunter pauses, then, "And where does the agency stand on APSF?"

"What? APSF?"

"Never mind, go on."

Zachary's voice changes from business-friendly to a cold-listen-to-me tone. "Hunter, knock this stuff off. We need to get this job done."

"Joe, listen to me. This is important and it's strange. Did I mention to you this dream I had Friday night? The night before..."

"Was it wet or dry? How's that for an APSF line?"

Hunter pauses more than a moment. Then, "So you get it. Dammit, Joe, this is not a joke. It was more a nightmare than a dream; a once in a lifetime nightmare. In it I was in Pisa and I was..."

"Hunter. Okay. Good. Then you should know Pisa well. Now let's move along and get this job done. No more wet dreams; no more dipping pigtails in inkwells; no more dipping ... screwing your handlers; no more IRA. Go find and terminate this Pisces asshole or I'll get someone else and you can get out of the business. Am I clear?"

"You're clear. I'll have a plan and will see you Wednesday night. I'll call first. Have a nice Sunday, Joe. Take Ruth to church or something and read a book on nightmares." He hangs up before Joe Zachary can respond, then heads to the kitchen.

There he slides into the booth, and Dee puts a cup of coffee in front of him and says, "Give me a few minutes and I'll have your 'chow' off the griddle and on the table. How do you want your eggs?"

"Do you get nervous when people don't listen to you?"

"Yes, speaking of which, how do you want your eggs?"

"This is a conspiracy," shakes his head. "Over easy will be fine and plenty of bacon. Thanks." Sips the coffee, "Hmmm, good. Thanks, pal."

"Be nice. I heard you. We'll talk later."

"I will be nice. I am nice. At least I was once upon a...oh geez...there it is again. I'm goin' nuts. I need some time to unwind, clear my mind, and think. How about we go to the beach today, and then I'll take you to dinner at the Hotel Del tonight?"

"Are you serious?"

"I'm serious."

"Wow! Hu ... Hun ... Hunt ...," Dee takes in a deep breath and states matter-of-factly, "What I was about to say was, Hunter, you bet. And, how about this? I know a friend of Angelo's that will give, give mind you, me a room at the Del. We can go over, change, go to the beach, then back to the room, clean up and have dinner. They have a great beach there, you know."

"Yeah, I know. Been on it and all up and down the Strand. That's Navy Seal territory."

"That's all great. I mean, whoopee, or Ooh Rah, or something. I get nervous when people don't answer the question. Don't you? Is that a yes?"

"It's a yes. Great plan, pal."

"Be nice." She walks to the table, says, "Here's chow." Puts the plate with three eggs, over easy, yokes unbroken and the whites looking like rink ice without the logos. No signs of grease. Seven stripes of bacon and two pieces of toast, buttered. She leaves, is back in seconds with hers and slips in the booth across from Hunter.

Hunter says, "Looks great. Smells better. Why seven strips of bacon?"

"It's Sunday."

Hunter shrugs, says nothing and begins to eat the first strip of bacon by hand. His face shows there is a thought inside somewhere, but it just hasn't snapped on yet. Dee takes a bite of her bacon, chews and swallows hurriedly, then says, "The seventh day. Time to rest. Seven strips."

"Yeah, I got that. Makes sense."

"Not really. Hunter, I love the Del. Love it. Can't wait. Particularly the patio restaurant overlooking the tennis courts, and the beach, and the ocean. I love it all." Stops for a moment letting her cat-like smile begin to spread, then coos, "It is so romantic. I hope the moon is out. I'm goin' to wear something that will knock your eyes out." The smile reappears, "It's been a long, long time." She pauses, then quickly adds, "I'm doin' it again, huh?"

Hunter stares at her. *I doubt that.* Then sensing the void says, "Well, we're just goin' to have dinner. Swim and dinner. Remember. And we'll be back before any moon rising stuff."

"Okay. Forget it. What did Mr. Zachary say?"

"To go as an author. Writing a story and doing research. Will be my cover," laughs, "Until it's opened and someone reads the Prologue. I'm letting the idea float around in my mind for a day or two. Not sure about it."

"Sounds like a plan. Seems good." She pauses, looks up and catches his eye. "Not as good as the Del." Grins. He does as well. Then she says, "Are you bringing a weapon?"

He gazes at her for a moment. "Yes, of course. Why?"

"Well, I was thinking it will be interesting. You didn't have one yesterday in your jockey shorts so I was wondering how..."

"I think you said it earlier. Be nice."

"Should I bring mine?"

"You have a weapon?"

"Of course. And after yesterday, I'll be totin'." She takes another bite of bacon, her third strip. Then says, "You know the two rules of *unarmed* combat?"

"Yep."

"Well, in case you forgot, they are," she pauses, dangles a strip of bacon from her fingertips. "First, always bring a gun." She points the bacon at him. A lurid smile creeps across her face, then she adds, "And always bring an Italian girl."

"It's a Jewish girl."

She smiles, "Yeah, I know, but do you know one?" Tilts her head to one side. "Didn't think so. Besides, I'm better." She tilts her head down, brows raised with eyes at the top, and forms her lips in an oval and slides the bacon strip in her mouth, and out again. Then in again, this time biting and swallowing the strip. Wipes her lips with her index finger and thumb, adds, "At a lot of things." Pauses, then with the grin finishes, "And, big guy, you're stuck with me."

"Yes, I am. Just remember. Stuck with, not on or in." Shakes his head, "You make it darned hard to be nice."

"Hard is nice."

Hunter shakes his head, jaws locked.

She slides out of the booth and heads for the kitchen sink taking her plate and empty coffee cup with her. Says, "Let's get a move on. Clean up your dishes. I've got a call to make." Pauses, snaps, "I know, on the house phone, but I'll do it at home."

As the Shanahans leave Mass, Danny spies the Muldoons departing also. He catches the elder Muldoon's eye. The man shakes his head indicating no word. The Shanahan's mother sees this and whispers to her son, "It'll be soon I'll be wantin' to know. They'll not be lettin' me wonder for too much of a time like they did with your father. I'll see to that."

Danny leans over close to his mother's ear, "I know, Mum. I know. We'll be waiting a few more days then I'll be gettin' me own answers."

"And me as well," pipes Sean.

Danny says to both of them, "We'll see. For now we'll wait. It is the son that'll be watchin' us. I'm sure of that."

All three trod toward the house. It'll require a good foot under them, and the Shanahan woman likes her brisk walks. She's still a hearty soul, perhaps more so than her sons know and certainly more than the elder Muldoon, whom she despises, suspects.

Rocco has returned from his fishing trip. To make everything look plausible should he be seen by anyone that matters, he has a good catch of Alletterato and Palamita under tow. Already cleaned and filleted by the crew. Both fish are prevalent in these waters and most catchable during the summer months. He has one large Palamita; near 4kg, about 8 lbs. And he has a few Alletteratos or Bonitos of about the same size, and one slightly over 6kg, about 15lbs. He and Signore Catalano typically fish for swordfish when they both go out. On those occasions they rent a boat and skipper to ensure a catch or two. The area is well known for this great sport fish. Nonetheless he gives all but one of the Alletteratos to an old woman walking on the road. She's overwhelmed and appreciative and probably impossible to locate.

Neither Pisces nor Gina are up and about. So as to not embarrass his boss, Rocco leaves a brisk note in the kitchen for each. For Gina, that a Bonita is on ice. For Signore Catalano, it simply says. "Done. On my way to Pisa."

They take Hunter's Vette. Nine years old is not yet vintage, but getting close. It's white with red leather upholstery. Nary a scratch and glimmers from the wax job. They cross on the Coronado Ferry and head directly for the Hotel Del Coronado. Dee's friend has arranged a room so they are dressed casually for dinner. The swim suits, beach towels and flip-flops are in small bags. The Vette is not built for extended travel and lengthy stays for one, much less two.

The Del is an old and famous hotel. Built in 1888. At the time it was the largest wooden structure in California, possibly the States. Is famous for the movie stars and Presidents that have stayed there. And the movies made there, such as *Some Like It Hot*. The Presidents have included a few old-timers and more recent ones such as FDR, Ike and JFK. When you approach this wonderful old landmark from the boulevard, it can't be missed. A no brainer. Always carrying a fresh coat of white paint and red roofs. The spires can be seen from virtually anywhere on the island, particularly the main one as it stands as a beacon to lovers, romantics, weekend tourists and one-day wannabe's. The Dragon Tree out front is the final web for the spider Del.

Hunter valet parks with perhaps unnecessary words for the young man at work in his clean, crisp uniform. "No spins. No burning any rubber. And put the top up please." He gets a grin and a "yes, sir" in response. Then a tiny squeal of tires as Hunter and Dee walk up into the grand old hotel. Hunter looks back over his shoulder. Dee nudges him in the ribs with her elbow. "You encouraged him. Shouldn't have said a word."

"I know."

"The room's in my name. Let me sign in so it looks more natural since there is no charge. Just a lonely woman treating herself to...never mind. I'll change in the bathroom, you can use the bedroom. I'll do it in a closet if you don't trust me." She giggles. Does what she has to at the desk, turns her head toward Hunter and says, "Then we'll head for the beach. Do you think we can have a small bite on the patio a little later? Not enough to spoil dinner. I love eating out there. It's so...so, I'm doing it again, aren't I?"

"Yes."

"Is that, yes, for a bite?"

"Both."

"Good. Who gets to take it?" Laughs and grabs the keys from the young man behind the registration counter while saying, "Thank you."

The man smiles, fumbles with a file. Then smiles, "Yes, ma'am. On the house. Or on the hotel, or something." He watches Dee's hips as she strides toward the elevators. "Whew!"

After more than a few steps, Hunter looks back. The clerk smiles, lowers his eyes, then his head. The young man takes a deep breath through his nose, murmurs, "If it looks like, smells like, it is ..." and takes another sniff of the trailing edge of the aroma drifting back from Dee. While doing so he notices a man watching the couple from behind a copy of the *San Diego Tribune*. The clerk watches both. When the couple disappears into the elevator, the man folds the paper and lets it drop to the chair beside him. Checks his watch.

The day goes well. Dee and Hunter swim, body surf and have some playful shoving and wrestling in the surf. They have a light lunch and it is on the patio. The only discomfort for Hunter is all the eyes focused on Dee in her tiny, canary yellow bikini with its sheer covering blouse that she has put on for the meal. The yellow sets off her skin tone which is heightened by her tan. Her dark hair frames her flawless complexion and dark eyes. Pink lips, nails and toes. And a better job of shaving.

The staring by the gentlemen guests is a little more focused than on the actual buffet table. The bikini may be bright yellow, but the woman is not a canary, still with her sheer white cover-up tunic, her bravura breasts are like magnets to small pins in the gentleman's eyes. Their eyes move slightly, then back again a tad quicker, then in a flash, rivet on her. Spires in their own right. As Hunter and she eat and chat, Dee, aware of her surroundings says, "Hey, pal, don't worry about it. I'm getting used to it again. Been awhile and frankly, I kind of like it."

"Well, a glance is okay, but ogling is rude. Ticking me off. Oh, and by the way, where is your weapon?"

Ded Reckoning

"Which ones?" She nearly chokes laughing at her own remark. Then says, "In my purse at my feet. And yours?" She pauses a split-second, adds, "And don't you dare ask which one."

"In the back of my waistband. Under my shirt."

"Gee, that must be comfortable. If you had it in the front, possibly the ladies would stare at you."

Hunter looks around the veranda. Then up at the sky checking the angle of the sun and says, "Let's eat and get some more time on the beach. And water. I want to take a swim down the Strand and back before we come in for the evening."

She nods. Takes a drink of iced tea and leans back in her chair. That makes more than a few gentlemen guests more uncomfortable as her sheer white, three-quartered sleeve tunic's draw strings slide unfastened, exposing her full to overflowing yellow-topped bikini bra to two rows of tables facing her. There are a few slight coughs. A shake of the head by Hunter. And hushed, whispered admonishments in the background from the gentlemen's ladies.

Hunter catches himself staring. *They are huge. All that from one rib.*

Sundays begin and end. Some begin in mass looking for help. Some end in the sea where there will be no help. Some end at an airport looking for an Antonio. Some end eating fish looking for respite and restoration. Some end in a funeral home not able to look for anything. Some end in the morgue looking but not seeing a white ceiling. And one ends for two, sitting on a patio with a refreshing breeze looking at one another for an explanation.

Like LOP's, lines of positioning of a navigational fix, they are waiting to be drawn. To be plotted. Not celestial from the stars although many of these are seen tonight by some, but not by others. And not from radio or radar. But more exactly from deduced or ded reckoning.

The maps are out and instruments sharpened.

CHAPTER 8

*"Do or Do Not;
There is no Try."*
Anon

The day has gone well. Hunter and Dee sit on the towels beneath them after an initial dip and body surfing. Dee smiles, looks into Hunter's eyes and says, "*'A sunbeam to warm you; a moonbeam to charm you; a sheltering angel, so nothing can harm you.'* That's an Irish Blessing. Don't know who wrote it, or if it just evolved as so many do, but it's nice."

"It is, and nor do I. But, there's more. However, the sunbeam sounds and feels good, but I'm my own sheltering angel."

Dee cants her head to one side, "And the rest?"

He glances skyward for a moment, then into her eyes. "*'Laughter to cheer you. Faithful friends near you; And whenever you pray, Heaven to hear you'* ... or somebody."

"You're like an encyclopedia. Let's just talk."

"Just a thought to start a conversation, not an end."

They do begin a conversation. Most blather. As a rule typically about each other, answering one another's questions. Some personal. Some innocent-enough sounding probes. In time the chatter wanes and they go back in the water. Hunter for his open ocean swim. Out two hundred meters. Surprisingly, Dee is at his side. Then north five hundred meters, turn about and back south. Dee is still alongside, stroke for stroke. Nary a word. Since they were taken out to sea somewhat, the trip back in is a difficult three hundred meters. A rip current has developed. No more a struggle for Dee than he even with the increasing height of the surf.

On the return to the beach, in the tumbling white-water after the last line of spilling surf Hunter says, "Dee, you're a heckuva woman. I meant to take the swim alone. Needed the exercise ... or exorcism. Didn't mean to drag you along. Heckuva gal."

In the knee-high ebb and flow of the foam, Dee tackles Hunter, driving him into the surging waters and lies on top of him. He manages to raise his head above the receding surf, sputters, "Damn, Dee, I meant that as a compliment."
"Well, guess it was. I over-reacted. Try this as a better response." She kisses him full on the mouth while another wave tumbles and extends itself toward the beach. The foam, salt, and sand of the undertow doesn't interfere with her passion, only complements the taste. She pulls away, says while laughing, "You taste like sea water ... and feel like steel cables wired to an anvil." Dee, water streaming off her body, glistering in the setting sun fosters a picture of a nymph rising from the deep as she extends her arm to Hunter, offering her hand to assist. He accepts and she pulls him to his feet. Nose to nose. They stare at one another for a moment, then amble quietly out of the water. Beached, tired, yet refreshed. One giggling. One stunned. At the towels they pick up their belongings and stroll all the way to the room without saying another word.

Eugene Bradovich enters the downtown office of the FBI San Diego SAC and asks the receptionist, a young, attractive gal, to see "the man", James Ryder. *Strange she's here on a Sunday, especially for a woman of her looks. She oughta' be on the beach or on a surf board. Guess when it hits the fan, everyone picks up some of the debris.* She nods and disappears into Ryder's office. After a few moments, she comes out, holds the door open for Bradovich and politely says, "He'll see you." She smiles and eyes him from top to butt as Bradovich ambles past, and into the neat, clean but usual austere government office here in the hinterlands. *The high and mighty in Washington spend our tax dollars on lavish trappings, all others seem to have pale pea green and white walls, with battleship grey steel desks, chairs and file cabinets. Ryder's does have an imitation black leather couch and wooden coffee table, surrounded by three equally ugly wooden straight-backed chairs.*
A standing Jim Ryder greets Bradovich and points at one of the three chairs and says, "Have a seat. What can I

do for you?" He sits in the chair at the other end of the coffee table. Its four foot expanse creates sufficient chilly distance. Ryder is in his customary blue suit, white starched shirt and a yellow power tie. Is close shaven, eyes steely and well-manicured hands. The walls to either side are adorned with black and white photos of him with local and national dignitaries and there are various degrees and certificates completing the smattering of individual history.

Bradovich is a sharp contrast in his rumpled sports jacket, open collared sports shirt, a tired frown capped with a slight growth of a beard. He growls, "Just thought I'd pay a professional courtesy call and see if I can help. Have anything yet?" He sits, crosses his legs and tries to find a comfortable position for his Popeye-like arms on the chair. He can't and crosses his arms across his chest in a psychological display that would interest a psychiatrist but not Ryder.

Ryder stares for several seconds, says, "Nope. Not much. And we have nothing for the press either and damn sure want to keep it that way for the moment."

"Gee whiz, Special Agent Ryder, that implies I would let the cat, or the IRA bomber, out of the bag. I wouldn't do that. Especially in this case."

"I'm sure."

"Well, San Diego isn't a swarming, sweltering crime-ridden metropolis, but we have our moments. I like to stay on top of things and keep our seaside town clean and tourists happy. A terrorist in town with enough plastic explosives to sink the Coronado Ferry or make Mr. A's rooftop restaurant a sidewalk cafe causes me more than mild concern. So a little heads up and cooperation would be appreciated."

Ryder sits and stares at Bradovich for several seconds. The silence in the room is like a street in old Dodge and the stares like two gunmen waiting to draw. Surprisingly, but rightfully, Ryder breaks first and gets up, steps to his window, his back to the detective. Then turns, shoves his hands into his trouser pockets and says in a civil tone, "We have nothing yet that you don't know. Nothing final back from Interpol or the Brits from the prints or dental. But, from the photo, we do know he landed in New York two weeks ago, the eighteenth. Went from there directly to Boston we assume because he flew from Boston to Washington, D.C. two days later. And left there the next day for here. He must have met someone there because he had ample time to make a same-day connection. Been here about ten days. We believe the target was the girl. So it looks like a contact, or two, put him on the woman here. And by my reckoning, that contact was in Washington. The Boston trip was most likely for check-in, equipment, final words, and perhaps a reunion of sorts. A lot of IRA sympathizers there. Possibly family." He pauses, "And that's it. When we get more I'll let you know. If I can."

"I see. Okay. You know I have some other interests in this ..."

"Yeah, I know. Kerrigan. You two are foxhole buddies, right?"

"Fighting hole Buds. Foxholes are for the Army. Marines don't like the connotation of a foxhole. Prefer fighting hole." Bradovich laughs quietly to see if he gets some reaction from Ryder. Just a smirk. "And, yeah, we were and we are." He pauses again. Then, "And it's my city." Then shaking his head, "You tapped his phone, right? You heard our conversation. You did get an okay?" He raises his eyebrows and tilts his head.

Ryder continues his Dodge City stare. Takes his hands from his trouser pockets. Enough in the old days to cause the gunfight to erupt. But, no weapons, at least in sight, he only steps away from the window and sits at his desk.

Bradovich, out of his chair now, steps in front of the desk and says, "Look, that other agent, Oboe or whatever his name was, is, he isn't FBI. But he's a Fed. CIA I bet. For all one knows perhaps I should be talkin' to him."

Jim Ryder laughs, "Yeah, go ahead. Talk to ole' Oboe or Dobie, or whatever he's using today or tomorrow." He pauses, looks down at his hands that he has now clasped together, resting on the desk top. He lets out a breath. "Ah, Dean, I imagine ..."

"It's Gene, but Detective Bradovich will do fine."

"Yes, Detective. Well, anyway, you talk to Oboe if you can. I suspect you'll never find him, or anyone with that name working for that agency or any agency. Anyway, if you do and he doesn't want to be found, he won't be. Hell, I could be him and you wouldn't know it." He lets out a sigh. "But, you might run across him somewhere ... it'll most likely be dark, dank, and English the fifth language spoken. So go ahead. Look him up."

Smiling, Bradovich asks, "Are you him?"

Ryder laughs, "I told you what I know. Anything else will have to come from someone else, somewhere else," pointing up and east. He pauses again, lets out a long sigh, "I shouldn't tell you this, but the perp didn't die from any fall down a hill. He couldn't have had that much damage if he had leaped from the top of your buddy's favorite restaurant, Mr. A's." Ryder's tone becomes gruff again. "Your boy's feet have shit all over them and no one in the government, the Marine Corps, or any outfit will say anything other than Kerrigan's not involved. His records are already sealed or they were months or years ago in preparation for something. Right now, all I have is two bodies; well, one and parts of another, and they'll be gone tomorrow. So, do me and yourself a favor, go solve something else. This one is over except for finding out about the good Mister Smith." Ryder stands, adds, "And then possibly we, the Bureau, can joust a few Irishmen around, but we won't dislodge them. They're stubborn by nature and don't scare easily. And if there is someone important involved in Washington, well, who knows how deep that may be buried."

"Thanks, Agent Ryder. I appreciate the information. I didn't like your tone at times. Nor you mine. If I come up with something, I'll call." He smiles, "My phone's not tapped, is it?"

Ryder, not amused by the last remark, ignores it. "Yeah, okay. Appreciate a call. I'll do what I can. Just keep the lid tight. But, tell me. Is this guy Kerrigan a knight or a nightmare?"

"In shining armor with more holes, more guts, more smarts, more toughness and more leadership than anyone I've ever met. Smart! Do you know he can remember everything he reads or hears? Everything. He never writes anything down. Guts! He just believes in attack, attack, attack. Shoot, if he has to retreat, he'll retreat to the back of his fighting hole, and no further." He pauses to take a breath. Then continues, "He's an ace with weapons. Rifles, hand guns, knives and his hands. He can see an ant in a cornfield at a thousand yards, and hit it, first shot. Hell, in another one hundred years, in another two hundred years, they'll still be Marines talkin' about him." He pauses again to catch his breath, then adds, his eyes a tad misty, "Hell, he's the reason I'm alive. Agent Ryder, The Hawk could make one phone call and there would be a hundred, more like a thousand, guys standing beside him, like quicker than you can insert a full magazine. He's ... ahhh, never mind. Good day, Agent Ryder. And thanks. Semper Fi." Pauses again, smiles and says, "Oh, Mister A's is not his favorite restaurant. It was just the first place here in town he found that served apricot brandy. He loves the stuff. It makes him believe he's actually civil, urbane, perhaps human." Bradovich turns and strides out of Ryder's office, closing the door behind him and nodding to the receptionist, "Ma'am, should be in church or on the beach with me."

She half smiles, "Or elsewhere. That would be better."

Bradovich stops, turns, and grins. "Okay, I'll remember that."

"Do. Soon."

Rocco takes a taxi from Pisa's Galileo Galilei Airport into the old part of town. It's easier. More comfortable than the buses and trains that are so convenient at the airport. The cab might be easier to track him but who would be doing that. No one should care about his movements. He'd sooner stay closer to the Mediterranean. He loves the sea, but for his purposes on this trip the old Grand Hotel Duomo Pisa on Via Santa Maria will do fine. It has a fine old restaurant serving excellent Tuscany cuisine and has a quiet, comfortable lounge and bar. The hotel is about fifty meters from Duomo Square and The Tower. And, not that far from the *Borgo Stretto* with its elegant cafes and shops. These latter places have interest for Adrianna.

More importantly, the hotel is close to Alberto's Restauranti, and hence Antonio Rizzo. No matter the situation, Antonio will be at or around Alberto's at some point in time. If he feels he's in danger, most likely at the back door, in the alley. There is no other place he can eat free when his money runs out. And then only if they expect him back at work. And it is his only job, consequently how hard will it be to find Rizzo. Besides, one or more of the help will know where he lives. That information can come easy or hard. It makes no difference to Rocco. Everyone knows of the slaughter of Alberto and his entire family. And everyone suspects Antonio knows something about it, even though he has said nothing. Nothing to the local police. Nothing to Interpol. Nothing to anyone. When questioned, or the subject is mentioned, he just weeps, trembles, but says nothing other than he knows nothing. However, Rocco's mode of conversation and gestures are harshly different.

In the late afternoon tomorrow, Rocco will meet with Carmen Messina, Carmen's sister, Rosa and the boy Lorenzo. He will make the offer, which they will not refuse, and make the arrangements for their travel. He will treat them to a fine dinner giving them a flavor of life ahead. But now it is late in the day, and he must call Adrianna. Have her come here for dinner and whatever the evening holds. She is much more than an acquaintance and lovingly accepts her place in Rocco's world. That place pays well, shops well, vacations well and plays well.

In his room, Rocco rings up Adrianna. She answers after only a few rings. In his native language he says, "Adrianna, ciao. It's Rocco. I'm here. Come to the Duomo and we'll have dinner. Yes?"

"And more I hope. I have missed you. You left quickly, and the hole in my heart has not mended yet. If ever."

"Ahhhh, Adrianna, your soothing voice already has me hungry for you. Come."

"I will be there shortly. Should I plan on staying long?"

"At least several days, and then, shortly thereafter a vacation. For that you can shop in the Borgo Stretto."

"Wonderful. And Rocco, I thought I saw your friend Antonio Rizzo yesterday. He was slinking around the alley by Alberto's. He looked exceedingly bad, like a man without a home, and here it is August in beautiful Pisa. Probably wasn't him. Come to think of it, Antonio would never let himself go like that. He is too much a lady's man."

Rocco pauses for a moment. His mind wandering. Then hears her say, "Rocco?"

"Yes, I am still here. He is not my friend. Just a waiter I know that took extra care at my table. I have no idea what's wrong with him, nor do I have any interest in him. He is of no concern to me. My only interest here is in you, and some minor business I have to attend to tomorrow." He pauses, "Adrianna, hurry. I'm hungry."

"For what?"

"You."

"Me as well...for you."

The bathing, showering, and the changing of clothes goes as well as Hunter can manage. It is restrained, and fairly well-mannered, but not non-sexual as he hoped. At least in Hunter's mind. Except, there was the moment Dee entered the bathroom while Hunter was in the shower, opened the shower door and whistled. And later when she came from the bathroom into the bedroom to pick-up her slacks and blouse, wearing only her panties and bra, giggling and jesting, "I heard a saying once. If love is blind, why is lingerie so popular?" The first incident got a shout from Hunter. The latter a groan and a turning of his back pleading with her to be less brazen, and even lesser of a pal.

Regardless, the dinner on the patio at the Del goes well. It is more cultured than the clothing-changing environment and incidents. The conversation is about both their families, and reluctantly for her about a few mutual Navy friends, and for a moment or two, however strange, of Angelo. They each order their own meals, however Dee insists on ordering the wines. These are DeLuca wines for sure and wonderfully subtle. There is no apricot brandy, thus Dee suggests, "This has been a great day, and I thank you ever so much." She leans over and gives him a peck on his cheek. Then continues, "As I see it we can take a walk on the beach, or we can go back and sit in your Jacuzzi. What'll it be?"

"It's late; going home sounds good. Besides I would like my apricot brandy before I call it a night. We've got a lot of planning and work to do tomorrow ... and Tuesday."

"And how about the Jacuzzi?"

"Daggone, Dee. Haven't you seen enough of me in a bathing suit today?"

Dee laughs. "Yes, I have. That's my point, big fella."

Shaking his head in hopelessness, Hunter gets up from the table, moves over to Dee, slides her chair away from the table and with his hand in the small of her back guides her, more a push, toward the exit and valet stand. Once there and when the Vette arrives, the top is down and the attendant is smiling. "Great wheels, sir."

"Thanks." Hunter hands the lad a twenty.

The young man says, "Both sets. And thanks a million."

Dee smiles and says, "Thank you," before Hunter can reply. Slides down and into the sports car and winks at the valet. Turns to Hunter and whispers, "And I have slacks on."

"Yeah, well, he must have been at the beach today, or one of the old geezers at lunch might have said something. Either way, he's right or they're right. Good wheels." He audibly lets out a breath and says, "Not sure how to handle you."

As they round the drive heading out, Dee exclaims, "Oh God, I hope that's a question. Is it a question, Hunter? Because if it is, I can ..."

"I need to rephrase that. I don't know how to take you at times."

"You can take me anytime. Anyway. Any place. Just take me."

"God dammit. That's not goin' to happen, Dee. Something is out of whack here. We're working together 'cause I have to. Ordered. Just partners. Remember that." He pauses, "Ya see, your plan is to 'Do', and mine is 'Do Not', so there's not going to be any trying."

Dee smiles and raises both her arms into the relative breeze above the windshield and in her low contralto voice murmurs into the deflected stream of air, "There will. Is only a matter of time." Sighs. "Tonight would be good."

"What was that?"

"I said, when something is out of whack? What's a whack?"

Hunter removes one hand from the wheel as they near the Ferry landing. He rubs his cheek. Looks at Dee, "You gave me two of them."

She says, "There's a car following us."

"I know. I see it. If it gets on the ferry with us, I'll handle it."

CHAPTER 9

"Be polite. Be professional.
Be prepared to kill everyone you meet."
A gunfighter's rule

Hunter says, "Stay here. Watch the mirror. And remember the three B's."

"I will." Dee reaches into her purse and pulls out her S&W .38 snub nose which is not a stopper nor that accurate unless breath-smelling close.

Hunter snarls, "Cute," as he slides out of the car, stands looking five cars back while tucking his shirttails in so it's easy to get to his M39. He sees the shadow of the driver move and the man eases out of his car. As Hunter approaches the shadowy person, he sees that the man has his hands out in front where Hunter can see them. The man understands the rules. In another step as he closes, Hunter sees the man's face and the teeth of a wide smile. It's Gene Bradovich.

Hunter releases his grip on the M39 in his back belt line and shakes hands with Bradovich. The detective looks and points with his head towards Hunter's Vette and says, "Ol' buddy, why is bra singular and panties plural?" Both start laughing.

"Brad, I haven't heard that pathetic question since you asked that Navy nurse at the Hong Kong Hilton when we were on R&R. Remember what she said?"

"Yeah. She called me a supercilious, snide asshole. I told her I wasn't silly but was super."

"Yeah, you did but she didn't mean what she said. She was just upset that you wouldn't give her a tumble."

"No. That you didn't."

"Yeah, well, something like that. What's up? Why the tail?"

"Just watchin' your six for a time." He shrugs, then, "Talked to the SAC man today. He says they don't have a make on this guy. Don't have anything back yet and that Oboe is a ghost."

"Well, Brad, my friend. I appreciate your concern, but I've got a handle on things. The bomber wasn't after me. It's of no concern to me other than he killed a friend. And ..."

"And a good lookin' one, too." Bradovich lowers and shakes his head, mumbles, "I've seen her before. Knew of her. Nice gal. Married to a Marine Lieutenant once upon a time. He was killed in Nam." Then Bradovich's head comes up, and he says, "As always you seem to be surrounded by 'em," nodding toward the Vette.

"Well, this one is my Property Manager and my assistant. She will be helping me become an author. Good editor and solid researcher. Besides, I never mess with the help."

"Her husband was a good guy. Knew him strangely enough. Just upped and disappeared on liberty one night in Hong Kong of all places. Funny matter is that the Navy CID guy was on to something. Thought possibly it wasn't just a disappearance. But, suddenly it all got scraped. Strange. And now, here she is ... on you like a flea on a dog. Anyway, he would have liked you."

"He did. I met him once. What is this other shit you were goin' on about?"

"Just what I said, Skipper. Just what I said. Remember, if it smells like shit, it probably is. The whole business with her husband smelled bad. Her too."

"Brad, I believe I got the message. And he was a good guy, and possibly a little too tough just to vanish. I'll remember that. And ol' buddy, you remember. This isn't my first patrol nor ambush."

Gene shoves his hands in his pockets, drops his head momentarily, then it comes back up and he says, "Okay, Lima Six Actual. I read you loud and clear. But I've got your back and if you need something, call." He pats Hunter on the shoulder. "Oh, by the way, your home phone is tapped. Feds. Better check both. You guys always have another. And hers, too. And I see you cut the crime scene tape. Put it back if you leave so folks will know you're a law abiding citizen and not a revengeful, obstinate old lion on the prowl."

"Well, I am, but not old. And both what?"

"Phone lines, Skipper. This is ole' Lima One Actual. Remember? Your ever lovin', loyal platoon commander. Followed you into the Vill's more than once. Been to the dance before. Just watch yourself, and if you need something, anything, call me and we'll get somewhere we can talk without echoes. Semper Fi." Bradovich feigns a punch to Hunter's gut and slides back into his own car.

Hunter doesn't flinch. He doesn't take feints. As a rule hammers first. He slaps the roof of Bradovich's car. Bends down to the rolled down window and says smiling, "Roger. Out." And strides away to the Vette as the ferry is about to dock on the San Diego side. Gets in the car and says to Dee, "Old friend. Good to have."

"Yeah, so am I."

Hunter shakes his head, "You never give up, do you?"

"Nope. You might as well though." She leans over and pecks him on the cheek. "That's just to make your ole' buddy back there groan and be in a little pain for the remainder of the evening if he thinks what I'm thinking." She settles back in her seat with a giggle as they bump and clump off the ferry onto the landing. She adds, "You owe me at least two."

"Two what?"

"I've made two moves, so I deserve two in return."

"Okay, a brandy and the Jacuzzi makes two."

"It's one, but it's a start. It's a start."

The Vette leaps forward, screeching and skidding sideways just a bit as Hunter turns and accelerates onto Harbor Drive.

Rocco and Adrianna spend the early evening in the Grand Hotel Duomo's restaurant. The seafood here is splendid and Rocco's only complaint is that perhaps it is not as good as what he can wrestle up at home, more accurately Pisces' home. Adrianna is not diminutive, but in comparison to the hulk of Rocco DeStefano she appears so. She has frosted her hair, highlighting its natural dark brunette flavor. And she is shapely, with slender legs appearing more contoured in her spiked heels; sleepy eyed and moves smoothly and easily like a leopard on a nightly stroll. Rocco is simply huge and thick, neck to ankles with powerful looking hands, but he too moves with the grace of one of the great cats.

After dinner the two adjourn to the bar. He for his *Amaro Fernet Branca*. Good for the digestion and some say medicinal. It got its fame in Milan more than a hundred years ago by its producer, Bernardino Branca. Pisces, although a brandy drinker, introduced Rocco to this treat. Adrianna on the other hand has more simple tastes. Although she enjoys her Sambuco in late afternoon, she prefers *Amaretto di Saronno* in the evenings after dinner. To her it is like Sambuco but with less alcohol. This is important because she will be expected to be active and attentive this evening. To be not so is not good with Rocco. His behavior can be his behavior; hers is to be as expected or better. Between sips and fresh drinks they dance. The tiger and the leopard. Moving smoothly and easily but the striped cat looking dangerous as his eyes continue to prowl, to search.

At no time during the meal, or now, does Rocco bring up Antonio's name. He cares, is interested, but he will discover what he needs to know about locating Antonio Rizzo tomorrow or the next day, or the next. Then he will visit with the man. No need to hurry this task. Patience is a pleasure of the hunt, as the kill is the pleasure of persistence. Tonight is for himself, and Adrianna. Tomorrow for Carmen and his family, and Pisces. Then perhaps a few more days with Adrianna, then Rizzo and his loose tongue. Besides, Rocco's apparent leisurely visit will cause Antonio to worry more, then when nothing happens, become curious. Then careless.

Adrianna stares at Rocco after this last dance set. She finally gets his attention after enduring the minutes of his wandering mind. It was his mind, not his prowling eyes. She had glanced around, and there is no competition in this old hotel bar tonight. When their eyes connect she says in her native language, "Rocco, the hole in my heart needs mending. Let's tend to it before the band leader and surgeon Branca tires of their favorite patient, yes?"

"Ah, yes, because Rocco DeStefano may tire of Branca and the music, but never of Adrianna. And I remind you, my love, it is always you that begs for breathing space."

She leans forward, nibbles his ear. "Not this night." Then whispers, *"Ti amo."*

He smiles, shakes his head slowly and in a whisper in his native language and accent, "I believe I too love you. And now may be the time in our lives to enjoy that, and life."

She replies, "Good. Wonderful."

As they stroll out of the bar, into the reception area and towards his room, they do not see the straining eyes watching from the darkness in the far corner of the lobby, away from all activity.

To the delight of Gina, Roberto Catalano has decided to spend the evening, and the next several days on his 98' Fratelli Benetti inanimate toy, the *Sorridenta*. With an aft sun deck. Its sun deck will keep Gina occupied for at least some of the time. In addition it has deck space for fishing or diving. It's the fishing that attracts Pisces, at least during the times he is recuperating from time with his animated toys, such as Gina now. She is insatiable. And like her, the fresh caught fish make wonderfully tasty and fulfilling meals.

They leave after dark to minimize observation. Not that it would draw much attention, but little is good, none, better. He takes the *Sorridenta* out himself, then once in deep water allows his crew chief to take the helm and the crew member chef to prepare and serve dinner. They cruise for a time after dinner, then anchor up for the night. There is always one armed crew member awake at all times on watch. And all the crew know better than to ogle Gina for the consequences are grave. And that is not a play on words as one crewman discovered when Anna was aboard some time ago.

After dinner Roberto and Gina sit on the aft sundeck. Catalano has one of his specially ordered *Joya De Nicaragua* cigars and his brandy. Gina sits at his side. Quiet. Staring at her man now, running her finger up his arm, across his cheek. Nibbling at his ear and neck on occasion as he takes in those effortless draws. She samples his cigar at his prompting, and she does it in an evocative manner. Her life has changed. For how long is always a question when around Pisces, perhaps not around Roberto Catalano. But then, when is Pisces present and when Roberto Catalano. To live is to know.

Gina squirms in her chaise lounge and nibbles on his ear again, breathing a whisper, "I am wet. I need you now," and nips his neck and suckles his ear lobe with her lips.

Roberto tosses his about spent cigar overboard and growls at his tigress in heat, "Then here and now it will be," as he tumbles onto her, tipping over the chaise lounge. It is here on the decking as he pulls a white leather seat cushion from a bench with one hand, lifts her skirt with the other and with both plunks her panty-less butt onto the cushion.

Once near home, Hunter turns onto Jutland, by-passes Atwell Street, his usual turn that runs into Arcola at the cul-de-sac. Instead he goes a long block further and turns into the top end of Arcola, lights off, and stops. He looks down towards his and Dee's homes, and the cul-de-sac at the bottom of the hill. They sit for several minutes. A police patrol car is still parked against the dead-end railing on the cul-de-sac. Hunter says, "Brad's word is his bond. As long as I'm here, someone is going to be out front, or somewhere close. I guess that's good. Let's go." He turns the lights back on and drives down the slight hill and into his garage. They get out and go directly into the house through the inside garage door. Hunter heads to his room saying, "I'm going to change, okay? Be back in a jiffy. I'll meet you in the tub with the drinks."

"Okay. And I'll just have some of that pancake syrup you call brandy."

"Heard ya. Be nice."

Dee murmurs, "I'm goin' to be more than nice." *Utterly clueless.*

Hunter returns, pours two snifters of apricot brandy and goes out onto the patio. He hands one snifter to Dee who is already in the sunken Jacuzzi at the end of the pool. Sets his down and slides in next to her. Turns slightly, then lurches back from her like a hooked yellow tail. "Dammit, Dee. You're not wearing a damn thing. Where the devil is your ..."

"I know. I know. But I hate to put on a cold damp suit. Sorry. Just don't look. Besides, the bubbles hide everything."

"The bubbles don't hide a damn thing. Nothing does."

"So?"

He picks up his snifter, takes a gulp and growls, "You ... Are ... Dangerous." Takes just a sip this time slides a good two feet away. Then inches another foot from her, sliding his brandy snifter along the ledge. She laughs at his defensive choreography.

The mood changes as quick as a toad's tongue when Hunter begins talking in a business tone of voice about his plan. The tone and the substance get her undivided attention. For the first time today, and yesterday late, she seems to have her mind on something other than seducing him. She asks questions here and there, but most of the time she is intent on listening. Nodding in agreement or comprehension. At the end he pauses, takes a last sip of brandy and says, "Well, generally, what do you think of it?"

"I think it'll work. I don't think Zachary will like it. Probably won't go along with it, but then, who knows. You're the boss."

"Yeah, it would seem. But if not, in the end, I am my own sheltering angel. Besides I'm not going to tell them everything. They just want me to get it done and quickly." He pauses for a moment. Grins. "Hey, I'm ready for one more before we call it quits for the night. We'll go over this in detail tomorrow and get done what needs to be completed." He feigns a coy smile and asks, "What say ye, lassie?" He starts to get up.

Dee says, "Sit down, laddie. Ready me is and I'll be gettin' some pints." She laughs, then, "And that's as close as an Italian girl can get to sounding like an Irish lass."

"Did great, however let me get the drinks. I don't want you to ..."

"Sit." She slides over to his quarter of the Jacuzzi with her snifter in her hand. Snatches his glass, then stands on the seat, facing him, straddling Hunter while he remains seated in the tub. She shuffles forward several inches, leans over ever so slightly, hesitates one moment as he is face to...well, certainly not to face. Dee whispers, "While I'm gone, rethink your definition of partner." She giggles and steps up and over his head, taking the snifters into the house, water dripping onto his face from her thighs and ...

Hunter sits staring. A blink or two. Mutters, "Hmmmm. Gives a bit of a tang to the water." Turns, stares after her. "Good Lord, all that from one rib."

When Dee returns with the half-filled snifters, Hunter looks away as she reenters the Jacuzzi. When she settles, and this time it is beside him, she says, "Well?"

"Well, what?"

"I can tell by your tone of voice that you're miffed. Not muffed." She lets out one of her throaty, evil giggles. "I just thought that if you got a glimpse of all of me, you would truly appreciate what you're missing and consequently I would see and get what I'm missing. I realize what you've been saying all day. I understand your reasoning. You just don't seem to ... I just thought ... that eventually nature would ..."

"Shut up and listen to me. Not hear me, listen."

Dee starts to render another lilting remark but is silenced by Hunter hurling his half-full brandy snifter against the fence between their two yards. He stares at the fence for a moment, then glares at Dee. "We are not going to do it. We are not going to have a relationship. This is a partnership, and not by my choosing. It's all business or it's not going to be any of your business. I made a mistake today by taking you to the Del. If we get personally involved, one or both of us will die. It is to be hoped only one more person is going to die and that's going to be Pisces. If others die it will be collateral damage and nobody I know. I'm going to hunt the bastard, Pisces, down and kill him, and I can't do that with images of your pussy in my face or us screwing our brains out. Do you understand that?"

Dee's eyes narrow to slits. "Yes."

"Good. Because if you don't, one or both of us will die. Now I'm goin' to bed, and I'll see you over here in the morning. After breakfast. Do you understand that as well?"

"Yes, sir."

"Good." Hunter stands and says, "Night. I'd offer you a hand ..." He turns and heads into his house, disappearing in the darkness of the living room. Within a minute his bedroom light comes on, it's reflection bouncing from ripple to ripple in the pool as a cooling breeze creeps across the yard.

Dee sits virtually motionless in the Jacuzzi sipping her brandy staring up into the misty night sky. It resembles June gloom. She remains inert until she sees Hunter's bedroom light blink off. She turns her head and stares at the bedroom window for several moments, then murmurs, "You're right." Takes a sip of brandy. *And thus it will be, and you'll be surprised just how efficient and tough I am. But when it's all over, Hunter Kerrigan, you will wish you had taken the moment ... or moments.* Another sip while her mind continues. *"Mister. I've known of you for some time. I've seen your Bio and I've been briefed. And Mister, I've heard the sea stories."* Her next sip of brandy drains the snifter. She says loud enough for it to carry to at least the bedroom window. "So, Mister BAE ... that's big ass ego so beware because this Hawk's tail feathers are ruffled." With that last comment, Dee pushes herself up and out of the Jacuzzi. Places her snifter on a nearby table, and departs through the back gate leaving behind her towel, the still cold and damp yellow bikini and a large lump of pride or hate. Neither attracts flies, but always attention.

In his bedroom, Hunter stares at the ceiling. Mutters, "Pisces, I'm coming." Then rolls over on his side, slides his hand under the second pillow resting it on the M39 and closes his eyes.

From one rib, damn.

CHAPTER 10

*"Have a plan.
Have a back-up plan because the
first one won't work."*
A gunfighter's rule

Rocco's Monday is productive and satisfying, however not nearly as pleasurable nor exhausting as last evening with Adrianna. He meets with Carmen Messina and Carmen's sister, Rosa. And the boy, Lorenzo, as well. All three are excited about working for Mr. Roberto Catalano and enjoy the luxury of dinner at *Vecchio Dado's* on *Lungarno Pacinotti*. It's an old, warm family-owned Restauranti, and Rocco's treat includes a table outside with a view of the Arno River. The vista is made even more exquisite by the presence of the striking Adrianna joining the group. Certainly for the young man, Lorenzo, who turns the color of tomato paste when she catches him gawking at her. Nonetheless the dinner goes well, and Rocco gives them instructions for their travel to the villa and for settling into the living quarters over the garage. It is a two-bedroom apartment with bath and a kitchen with an adjacent eating area. The boy can sleep in a small room in the garage below with its own facilities. Rocco explains that the master of the villa, Mr. Roberto Catalano, will be gone, and that he, Rocco, will be returning in a few days to make the necessary introductions when Master Catalano returns. Meanwhile his instructions are to settle, give the villa a good cleaning, keep the grounds trimmed and orderly, cars tuned and running, and pantry stocked. He tells them where to shop and to keep the inventory up to the level listed. And liquor cabinet always up to the desired level. And he emphasized, no substitutes here. Carmen and Rosa depart happy; Lorenzo departs infatuated. Rocco will instruct the boy later on the dangers of ogling the women of the villa.

After the three leave, Rocco leans over and in a low, animated tone says, "Adrianna, how about the *Salza?*"

She squeals in delight, "Oh, yes! Yes. I passed there today while shopping and was tempted."

The *Salza* is the *Bar Pasticcerice Salza*. It is known for tempting people off *Borgo Stretto* for sugar-induced wickedness. It's been here for over fifty years. The desserts are delicious unlike the English dessert trays that look wonderful but lack taste.

As they get up to leave, Rocco clasps his hands together in a rubbing motion and says, "Wonderful. And we can walk from there to the hotel to work off our over-indulgence. Come, that taxi is ours," and he leads Adrianna from the Restauranti. Inside the cab, on the way, Rocco adds, "We'll go to Rapallo later tomorrow for a few days or more. Yes?"

"Yes. Oh, yes, yes, yes. Wonderful. I will have to shop in the morning."

"If you can walk."

"Ohhhhh, well now." Then mischievously, "We'll see who says 'Oh pleasa stoppa' first."

Rocco laughs, roaring like a tiger in his haunt.

The taxi driver continues along, saying nothing but glancing into the rear view mirror from moment to moment to watch the gestures while listening to the verbal foreplay that continues. He has no reason to notice the car that has been lagging a full three-car lengths behind since leaving *Vecchio Dado's*.

Muldoon sits at a far corner table of the pub. His customary spot, always unofficially reserved for him although it is not necessary this rainy Monday night. There is a meager crowd on hand. His son, the Pit Bull, is his shadow as always. The two of them watch as the Shanahan lads wind their way toward them through and between the tables and past the bar. When they arrive, the elder Muldoon nods at the two empty chairs across from him. Danny and Sean sit and say nothing. Not a greeting, just a stare from both. In seconds, Danny thrusts his arms and hands outward shrugging his shoulders, as if saying, "We're here, what say you?"

Colin Muldoon's face begins to color. "Not even a 'Hello' or a 'Good Evening' is it?"

Danny replies, "Where is Paddy?"

Conor Muldoon stirs in his chair. His father Colin's face ripens to the color and look of a tomato. He too stirs uneasily in his hard-back wooden chair. He clasps his hands in front of his body, resting them on the tabletop. Grimaces, and says in a hushed voice, "My contact's report is that the girl is dead. Paddy did his job. Saints bless the lad. And that ..."

"What about Paddy? Where the devil is he?"

"I'm about to say, lad. 'Tis not easy. It appears that Paddy fell down a steep canyon and died from the fall. The U.S. Federals are involved. That is all we have. My contact is staying there to dig up more. He will ..."

"Paddy is dead, snarls Danny. "My brother is dead. And you say ..." The lad stops in mid sentence slamming his fist on the table. Then gripping the edges of the table with both hands he barks, "Paddy Shanahan did not die by falling down. Shanahans don't die by tripping or stumbling or falling down. Perhaps Muldoons do, but not a Shanahan. Someone pushed him and killed him." He pauses, breathing heavier. "Who?" Then louder and red-faced, "Who, damn you, who?"

The Pit Bull starts to stand but is pushed back in his seat by the elder Muldoon's arm. Colin Muldoon's face is still red, not as deep as before, but the mixed expression of anger and frustration is still waxed over his jowls. "You listen to me, Danny, me lad. This is all I know for now. I will have more in a few days. Until then, remain calm." He pauses, leans over close to the Shanahan brothers and in a whisper says, "You have a duty tonight, lads."

"We'll be havin' no duty tonight, nor any other night, until you tell us all there is to know, or Paddy is back here, in his home. And speakin' of that, if he is gone, what of his body? What then?"

Muldoon drops his head to his chest. Raises it as slowly as a curious turtle coming to the surface. His beet colored face has faded to his natural ancestral potato farming Irish hue. He unclasps his hands. They remain on the table but in closed fists as huge and craggy as rocks on an Irish meadow's stone wall. "All right now, lads. I'll be givin' ya a night or two off. But you will stay in touch and be where I can reach you when I have more word. And if Paddy is truly dead, I and the Army will arrange to have him returned home to rest whenever they release his blessed heroic Irish body. Are you clear on this?"

"We are clear. And when you get all your information." Danny's distinct pause between his comments emphasizes his anger. "All your ducks in order. We'll be wantin' to know what the Army will be doin' about his death? His killer? 'Cause Shanahans don't die by falling down. And Shanahans don't take lightly the killin' of one of our own." Danny pauses, glowering at the elder Muldoon. "Am I clear?"

Conor Muldoon does stand now, pushing his father's hand aside. "You two be doin' what me father says or I'll be breakin' the both of you in two like the rotten little twigs ya be ... like I've been wantin' to do for years."

The father puts his arm across his son's body. With the other points a finger at the two Shanahan lads and says, "Nary a word. No more talk. Go and wait. Now. Be good, lads."

Danny and Sean stand for a moment staring at the younger Muldoon, fists clenched and veins bulging in their arms. "You're right, Master Muldoon. There will be no more talk." Danny turns, shoving Sean before him, and both stride towards the exit not caring about who they bump on the way out and in fact do shove some noisy pint drinkers aside.

The elder Muldoon yanks his son down into his chair by his belt. The old man stares after the two Shanahans. Then says, "There's goin' to be trouble from those two. If it comes to that, we'll have to make the good little Mrs. Shanahan a true childless widow." He stops to get his breath and allow his blood pressure to drop. His color goes from that of a beet to that of a peeled potato. He raps his knuckles on the table top, and says to his son, "Now get that full breasted barmaid that gave you the clap over here so we can have a pint or two."

"Pa?"

"Shut up and get me a pint. I'm stressed out enough."

"Yes, sir."

Hunter finishes his morning run. The first in several days and it shows. He went up Arcola to Jutland, down the hill to Moreno, then south to the intersection of Balboa Boulevard. Turnaround and back north on Moreno to the end and circle back to the bottom of Jutland. Up Jutland to Atwell, and down the one block of Atwell, finishing in front of his house. The patrol car is still there. Earlier one other had "picked him up" on Moreno and trailed along, about a hundred yards back. With his M39 tucked in the waistband of his shorts, the contingent of him and the squad car are well prepared. For what, no one knows, certainly not the patrolman.

Hunter waves goodbye to the patrol car behind him on Atwell and to the parked cop on Arcola. He enters his house to the sound of clattering dishes, the aroma of fresh coffee and the scent of a woman smelling like a field of wild flowers.

He sees Dee and says, "I thought I told you to ..."

"I know. I know. You did. But we're not enemies. We're partners, and I just thought you would like some cereal with fresh cold milk, juice, coffee, and have your partner join you for the start of the day. If you would have invited me, I'd run with you. Now go get cleaned up and come back and sit down. And no fussing. I'm just going to have some coffee and toast myself. I've fixed you a healthy breakfast. Good, Lord." She exhales, "It won't ..."

"You're doin' it again."

"I am. You're right. Go, get cleaned up."

"Gone." Hunter turns and heads down the hall towards his bedroom and a quick shower.

Dee's eyes follow him, not watching his stride instead consuming his body. She murmurs, "What a waste." Shakes her head. *Clueless.*

Hunter and Dee finish breakfast with little conversation. Idle chatter at best. As they wrap up putting things away, Bobby and Richard, the two handymen arrive. They immediately go to work installing new windows. They have a truckload of windows since they cleverly contracted to do the house across the street and a few others in the neighborhood also damaged by the blast. They also brought along split rails to mend the fence in front.

Hunter and Dee adjourn to the patio for a discussion in privacy. Once there, she says, "I promise to be good."

He starts the conversation with, "Good. Now then, let's get down to business."

Hunter explains the plan. She will be going with him. An author and his secretary slash editor. First to her parents' home in Napa Valley where she can visit her kids and family."

Dee injects, "Children."

Hunter frowns and goes on announcing it will look good, natural and will set things up to cover her absence. Then back to Frisco and fly to D.C. They will leave here this afternoon. Leave Napa Tuesday morning, he'll meet with Joe in D.C., and leave there that night for London. She'll precede him to England, not being with him when he meets with Zachary. They'll be in London only to check a lead. Then on to Geneva for cash, ID changes if necessary, and on to Pisa via Rome. In Pisa he, and only he, will find and meet with this Antonio Rizzo, and then both he and Dee will visit the recently deserted villa of Roberto Muscarella, aka, Pisces. From there, it will be dead reckoning navigation to wherever Pisces has alit.

At the end, Dee starts to ask a question but stops as Hunter raises his hand. "Just a minute. I've already talked to Joe early this morning. The D.C. briefing won't take long. I told him I didn't want the colossal mass of information that he, his analysts, and all the other alphabet agencies will have. Don't want the hoards of briefers and side-kicks. I just want the hard facts from him for the chase. Leads. A picture of Pisces and an agency sketch of him as he might look today. Who he has around him and who else is looking for him. Anyway it will be short. All I need is one good sniff and I'll track him, tree him, and waste him. If possible, make him hurt first ... for my parents." This vengeful statement in view of the fact that Pisces murdered his father and mother in London years ago when Hunter's father was about to expose Pisces as a turncoat, double agent. Both were with the agency in those years. He ends with, "Now, any questions?"

Dee registers an astonished look reacting to the merciless statement at the end of his monologue. She collects herself and says, "Mister Zachary isn't going to like, nor let me go along to Europe. The facade here is fine, but not there."

"I'm not telling him you're going. As far as he knows, you'll be staying with your kids in Napa on vacation and ..."

"Children."

"Dammit. Now where was ... ahhh, yes. We'll just have to get Maria and your father to cover for you. You'll always be out. They can take calls, messages. Just BS and miscommunication. In a few days we'll send Maria to Italy, the Isle of Capri, and tell anyone that asks that you and Maria are on vacation. She being there will be proof enough. By the time anyone knows different, it'll be too late, and if I'm as good as I believe I am, Pisces will be history and I'll be back here writing my novel."

"Okay, hence I won't be at the meeting in D.C."

"Nope. On an earlier flight to London. We'll meet there."

"Where?"

"At The Ritz in London. On Piccadilly. Hop a taxi from Heathrow. I'll take care of the arrangements."

"Look, since I'm supposed to be the secretary, I'll do that. And all other arrangements. It will look better. Look real."

"You're right. Do it. I'll give you the info, you look 'em up and tell me the arrangements. As we travel, I can always look clueless."

She smiles, tempted to respond but only affirms. "Wilco."

He returns the burnt biscuit stare, "Wilco? Will copy. I'll be damned. You need to use 'Roger' also, and often."

"I know your military jargon."

He grunts. Two burnt biscuits staring.

There are other questions by both. And, Hunter gives her the necessary travel and lodging information she needs. At the end he asks, "Do you know your other neighbor well?"

"Roger."

"Good, smart ass. Go there to make the calls. My phone is tapped. Possibly yours as well. The whole place might be bugged. Bottom line, I don't want to screw with it now." He shrugs, says, "I'll give you some cash. Pay her more than it costs. Just tell her your phone is out of order and you need to hurry."

"I know what to do, besides, she's not home but I know where she leaves a key."

"Better."

When Dee returns to Hunter's house she's toting a clothing bag and a small box-like matching case. The windows are finished, and Frick and Frack are working across the street. Hunter is sitting in his office, a clothing bag hanging over a chair. He looks at Dee's baggage, says, "Too much gear. Take only one. We can get anything else we need as we go."

"The clothing bag is a small, simple bag with bare necessities in it, and the other is my make-up bag. Every woman carries one."

"Put the make-up in a brief case. Anything that won't fit, stuff it in the clothing bag. We'll buy what you need. May have to leave in a hurry and leave stuff behind. Possibly running, therefore face cream, perfume, sprays and powder puffs won't help."

"Okay. Got the point. We're travelin' light. Should I go braless and only wear pantyhose?"

"You're a real smart ass." He hesitates, then, "I'm surprised the airlines don't charge you for excess baggage with those ..."

"You won't think they're excess if you ...come to think of it we have a few hours before we leave." Her grins turns to a frown, "Ahhh, never mind. What's next? "

"My slip of the lip. My fault. Let's go out to the patio. I have something else to tell you. You need to know."

"Oh yes. The scene of the crime, the Jacuzzi."

Hunter shakes his head. Dee laughs. They head for the patio. Hunter grabs two glasses and brings along the pitcher of iced tea Dee made earlier. They sit at the "everybody-has-one" round patio table with an umbrella in the middle. Matching chairs of course. He pours the tea.

Dee says, "Thanks. That was nice. You actually have manners. Now, what else?"

Hunter leans forward in the chair. "Please don't interrupt until I'm finished. I had a dream Friday night, or to be more precise, early Saturday morning. I mean, after I, we, I mean Sam...whatever. After I fell asleep."

"Look, Hunter, let's not ..."

"No, listen. Please. It's important. Important to this mission. Possibly to our lives." His tone, and the simple words "mission" and "lives" change her disposition. Hunter tells Dee of his nightmare. Mueller being killed in Pisa by Pisces. His meeting and killing of Antonio. The meeting and working with Devorah, the Israeli Mossad agent. And later her brutal assassination. He leaves out the matter of the relationship the two had. The assault at Pisces' villa first in Pisa, then later in Amalfi. The East German agents' attacks on him in Pisa and London. His and her involvement and stay in Tuscany at Dee's grandparents' winery, and before that right here, pointing at the spa and the house.

Here she does interrupt, gasping, "Tuscany? But how? They haven't been there in years. This is weird. Hunter, I ..."

"Yeah, I know. Hush. Listen." He continues on with the clues, the killings of three of his former girlfriends here in California, and the collusion between Samantha, Joe and MacBeer. The killings of Samantha and Joe. The killings in Johannesburg that coughed up clues of MacBeer's deceit and collusion. And his finding of Pisces on the Isle of Capri, and the strange death of Pisces arranged by him but completed by the Israeli's. Finishing with, "An entire mission, only it was a dream." Shakes his head then continues, "A one-time nightmare. Can you imagine? All that in one dream ... nightmare. Dreams take seconds. This went on and on, forever, or seemed like it, I guess." He pauses again, continually shaking his head.

After a moment, says, "Now, Sam is dead. By the PIRA. They shouldn't be involved, but the bastards will become more so. The Mueller killing, in Pisa, turns out to be real. And, there is an Antonio Rizzo. Oddly, I am supposed to track him down and question him because the agency believes he knows where or how to find Pisces. There is a villa in Pisa where Pisces lived. Empty now, but he did live there. Like in my dream. And your grandparents. They don't live there now, but they did. And they are in the winery business. And your father does live in Napa Valley like he did in my nightmare. And you have a sister named Maria that ..." He doesn't finish his thought. "God, I don't even want to go into that part." He puts his hand up stopping Dee from reacting. Then goes on, "And the part about you and me. Our relationship. I mean we were doin' it here, in Italy, and in your grandfather's guest house, for Pete's sake. And the stuff about your grandfather and his apricot brandy. I mean, this is way off the page. Is it a dream, a nightmare, or is it a premonition? What?"

Dee sits staring at Hunter. Starts to take a sip of iced tea but puts the glass back down. Looks into Hunter's eyes, searching for a moment, then says, "Hunter, it's a premonition if you want it to be. To me, it's a dream. Nothing more. A little weird but a dream and we, you, should treat it as such."

"Dee, it doesn't make any ..."

"Okay, it's a premonition, and we'll treat it as that. And if it isn't. No harm done. The only people that will know will be the two of us. We just go execute your plan. An author and his secretary, writing a book. We follow any leads we have or get. We follow your nose and mind what the dream is telling us as we go. It or something that's connected will lead us to this man, Pisces, or whatever his name is today, or tomorrow."

They both sit back in their chairs, legs stretched out and touching under the table, staring out over the fence. Lost in their thoughts for the moment. He thinking of the one-time nightmare. Her, what else. She nudges his leg with hers, grins and says, "I'm better in real life, even with excess baggage. Wanta' make a dream come true?"

Before Hunter can respond, a voice from behind them with a distinct Boston accent says, "Pardon me, but a reporter from the local paper told me..."

Hunter is up, spins around, leaps at the man before the sentence is complete. His deliberate left arm swing has shoved Dee off the chair, arse over teakettle and into the Jacuzzi. His right hand clamps on the man's neck while his left foot sweeps the man's feet from beneath him. The intruder lands hard on the concrete patio. Hunter is on top of him like a hawk on a plump rabbit, pinning him down. His right hand digging into the man's neck grasping the Adam's apple.

The back gate to the patio bursts open like the starting gate at Del Mar.

CHAPTER 11

"An appeaser is one who feeds a crocodile--hoping it will eat him last."
Winston Churchill

"Hold it right there, Mr. Kerrigan. I got him covered." The patrolman stationed at the cul-de-sac now stands on the patio after bursting through the back yard gate.

Hunter releases his grip on the intruder's throat and starts to stand. The man props himself on his elbows, looking to get to his feet. Hunter smashes the man in the forehead. A jack-hammer-like blow with the heel of his right hand. The intruder's head bounces off the concrete of the patio with a stomach-turning thud. His body goes limp and his head slumps to one side. He's unconscious. A trickle of blood appears on the Cool-Crete of the patio.

Hunter mutters, "Damn, that'll stain Columbo's patio." Takes a quick glance. "Where the hell is she?"

With his S&W .38 revolver in hand, the patrolman shouts, "Cripes." Hunched over, head craning forward he takes a step toward the limp body pointing the weapon with both hands at center mass. "Hey, I said I had him covered. Didn't need to do that. Now he's out cold." The officer bends over, checks the man's pulse. "Yep, alive. Out cold."

"Yeah, well, he started to move so I put him down. Will be easier to cuff. And knock-off the shouting. Remember he's the bad guy here. He broke in."

The officer spins around, startled and unable to answer Hunter as Dee bolts up from the Jacuzzi's still water like a spinning dolphin at Sea World. She pulls herself out sputtering and spitting water. Her skirt sagging from the water's weight yet adhering to her thighs as if pantyhose. Her blouse soaked and clinging to her breasts, and her hair hanging straight covering her face. She is in heels and thrashing about attempting to gain her balance while pulling her hair away from her eyes.

Hunter laughs. Dee glares at him, then swings and misses him, losing her balance and stumbles into the Jacuzzi. The patrolman has gathered himself, and when Dee resurfaces he asks, "You okay, Miss?" He quickly glances at the intruder and sees he's still unconscious, turns his attention back to Dee who is climbing out of the Jacuzzi, heels in hand and showing a lot of leg.

"It's Ms. Columbo, and yes, I'm fine. Just wet and pissed."

Hunter adds, "And safe."

The officer checks the man on the concrete. He's beginning to regain consciousness. The cop rolls the man over, cuffs him, then rolls him back over and drags him to the stucco wall of the house. Using both hands on the shoulders, he props the man up and asks harshly, "Who the hell are you?"

With an obvious Irish brogue, tainted with a distinct Boston accent, the man grumbles, "The back of me head feels like a smashed potato and me forehead feels like it was hit with a hammer. All I was trying to do was ask this lad here …"

"Mister. Before you say another word, I need to warn you of your rights." The patrolman reads him his Miranda rights, then asks, "Do you understand?"

"Yes, but by all the saints …"

"What's your name and what'dya doing here?"

Hunter says, "You are at the least trespassing, and more likely something worse. Now start talking fast." Then to Dee, "Ms. Columbo, why don't you go inside and dry off. Change clothes. I believe you said you were about to leave?"

Dee nods an understanding and having already stepped out of the Jacuzzi, sprints on the balls of her feet around Hunter and the officer to the gate while snatching a towel to cover her breasts.

As she leaves, the man says, "My name is Mickey O'Rourke. I'm from Boston, here visiting and trying to find out what happened to my friend, Patrick Shanahan. I was told by a reporter at the local paper …"

"Your friend, who?"

"Patrick Shanahan. I was told he died here Saturday morning."

The patrolman shouts, "Your friend was involved in a bombing and killed a woman."

"Listen Mister," Hunter hisses. "A friend of mine was killed here Saturday. This friend of yours did it. The police are investigating and ... and you listen carefully. That's the extent of my knowledge. Now, you broke into my house. Anything else you have to say, tell the patrolman at the station or on the way. My understanding is that your friggin' friend took a header off the cliff down there." He pauses, then says to the patrol officer, "How about getting this guy out of here and downtown? And call Bradovich from the car right away."

"Mister Kerrigan," Hunter cringes at the use of his name by the patrolman, "I will do that. Will you be pressing charges?"

"Only if Bradovich thinks I should."

"Well sir, I will have to notify the Agent Ryder of all this. Mister Kerrigan, sir, our instructions are ..." his words trail off relative to the intensifying stare from Hunter.

Hunter snarls, "Do what you must, but I would call Bradovich right away if I were in your shoes. I don't know this jerk or the guy he's talkin' about. Get him outta' here," and shoves the man's shoulder with his foot, toppling him over onto his side, his head scraping down the stucco wall on the way to bouncing off the Cool-Crete again.

O'Rourke snaps, "You not be doin' that, lad, if I were not all tangled up with these ..."

Hunter leaps at the man, and with his right hand jerks him to his feet, shoving him against the stucco of the house. "If it weren't for this officer here, you'd be dead. I might do it anyway," and draws back his left hand.

The patrolman grabs Hunter's left arm and shouts, "Enough. Hold it. This man is under arrest. Now, let him go."

Hunter yanks his arm free releasing his grip on the man's shirt and tie. Hunter growls, "Get him outta here. Pronto."

"I will, sir. I understand." The officer grabs O'Rourke by the shoulder, yanks him to his feet and says, "Let's go. And shut up, you're goin' in for breaking and entering."

The man begins to speak. The officer yells, "Shut up and get movin'," as he pushes the groggy intruder through the open back gate that's hanging from one hinge.

Hunter enters his house and goes directly to the closet in his office. He dials a number. Waits.

Then says, "Joe. I'm about to shove-off. Just got paid a visit from a guy from Boston, name of Mickey O'Rourke. Broke in my house."

"You mean today? What the hell?"

"Yeah. Just now. In town poking around. Snuck in and surprised Dee and me. The police have him. The guy out front who is supposed to be preventing all this has him in custody. O'Rourke was asking about his friend Patrick Shanahan."

Joe Zachary moans, "Jesus. What is going on?"

"You tell me. Remember, you're the one that said this doesn't involve me. You and Oboe. I will see you shortly, as planned. And, Joe, get this joker off my back. Out of my life. And away from my job. Quickly, or he's gonna be collateral damage."

Hunter answers a few questions from Joe. They talk for another several seconds. Hunter hangs up, closes and locks the closet. As he walks into the hallway, he sees Dee coming in the house through the sliding glass door that leads from the patio.

Hunter picks up his clothing bag. Says, "C'mon. We're leaving for the airport. Get your things," pointing to her luggage on the couch in the living room. They have been reduced to a cloth clothing bag and a briefcase. The bag is Navy blue with a gold "USN" and aviator wings stenciled on it. The briefcase is brown leather and a flap top with straps. Hunter adds, "We're goin' in your car. Nice bags. Wear a neon sign why don't ya?" He snarls, "Change the Navy one before we leave the country."

Dee stammers, "Bag?" Then spits, "Sign? I'll give you a ... My car?"

"Yes, no one is watching you. We'll go in through your back door. Load up in the garage. I'll lie on the back seat. You drive out like any normal day."

"Got it. Let me get my things and I'll be over in a sec. I'll lock up behind me."

"That's your job. You're the friggin' property manager."

Hunter hears Dee sputtering or muttering as he leaves through the gate and into her backyard. He uses the gate latch to hold it in place and up. Dee closes and locks the sliding glass door behind him. Picks up her clothing bag and briefcase, leaves by the side door locking it as well, goes down the path to her back gate, and into her house.

Minutes later, with the patrolman gone and no replacement in sight, Dee backs out of her garage. Stops and gets out of her car. Pulls the garage door closed. Lowers her sunglasses from atop her head and slides into her car behind the wheel. Closes the door, backs out of the driveway and goes up the hill on Arcola. She takes a route other than the one she would ordinarily take when leaving their houses.

After a few minutes, Hunter says from his cramped position on the floorboard in back, "See anyone following us?"

"Nope. No patrol cars. Only a new Caddy and an older car, convertible loaded with children."

"Good. Keep watchin'. I'm staying down until we park at Lindbergh."

"Roger! Oh, and next time you save my butt, don't smack me so hard." She hears Hunter laughing and muttering. She says, "What?"

"That was the best part of my day."

"Well, if that's the case, all I can say is that you're easy to please. Bubba."

"Sticks and stones will ..."

"Shut up."

"Roger."

Danny Shanahan lets the lace curtain slip from his fingers at his mom's front window. He continues to peep out from the corner of the pane of glass. Glares over to his younger brother, Sean, sitting in his father's old chair by the stone fireplace. "Muldoon has some bloke posted outside, watching."

"Just one?"

"No, two. One is in back as well." He pauses for several moments. Then speaks deliberately, "Do you remember that meeting about two months ago in the back of Michael O'Rourke's cobbler shop?"

Danny comes away from the window and sits in his mum's chair in front of the fireplace and across from where Sean is sitting, in his father's.

Sean watches him settle, says, "Aye, I do."

Danny pauses, eyes squinting a tad, then asks, "Didn't he mention his brother in Boston? Said something like, 'Mickey is becomin' a Southie' or something like that? Do ya remember?"

Sean nods his head slowly, and says, "Aye. Aye, I do, come to think of it. What a lucky guy gettin' to live and work in Boston. A lot of good fortune for that Mick, I'd say. Not havin' ta stay here bein' bossed around by Muldoon and that clod of a son he bred out of that sow he calls his 'Woman'. Besides, the Brits were lookin' for him, hard. Still are. He'll play hell getting back in the country."

"Yeah, but me point is, he was, like Muldoon, part of the old IRA. He and Muldoon made the split together, and he and that arsehole bein' tighter than ticks, I'd bet a quid or two they still are."

"Meanin'?"

"Meanin' that's Muldoon's contact. In the U.S."

Sean thinks for a spell, then says, "Yeah, I believe you're right. He must be the one." Sean sits staring at his brother for several moments, watching Danny gaze into space. The light bulbs are nearly visible. After more than a few moments, Sean mutters, "Don't see where that will help us. Mickey won't be talkin' to the likes of us. Only Muldoon or possibly his brother, Mike, from time to time."

"And perchance another."

Sean shakes his head. "Certainly not the clod."

"Ah, Sean, me lad. You be right, but a little slow on the up-take."

"How's that? I wasn't last night at chess. Fourteen moves and you were done."

"True, but me mind was elsewhere. Now then, brother dear, doesn't Mr. Mickey O'Rourke have a daughter livin' with his brother, Mike, over that shop. Helpin' 'bout the house since old Mrs. O'Rourke passed away and their father long before her?"

"Yes, and a pretty lass she is, and not that fond of her uncle and the way he treats her. Often talks about goin' to America to stay with her dad. But he won't have it, least ways any day soon." He pauses, grins. "Ahhh, she's a looker, she is. Lean, lanky, and with more than two handfuls of boobs, but with a religious streak from her chin to 'er knees."

Danny leans forward in the chair, "You be knowing her well, lad?"

"Oh, she's always been sweet on me. I've been with her a time or two, or three, more actually but the parish priest has her ear and she's keepin' her knickers on, her knees tight and rubbing themselves raw." Sean sighs. "I be comin' close the last time but ... ahhh, well, better to be free and a bit horny than tied down and punching leather with an awl for her uncle."

Danny leans back in the chair, his arms close to his chest and his chin resting on his thumb and index finger. A grin spreads across his face and he nods his head like a puppet on a string. He stands, pounds his right fist into the palm of his left hand.

"Sean, me lad. Let's go up to our room. I have a plan I be wantin' to discuss with you."

Danny starts for the stairway with a crooked finger motioning Sean to follow.

After the PSA flight lands in San Francisco, Hunter and Dee hurry from the plane, and with only carry-on luggage, they uselessly beat most of the flight to the rental car agency. The agent moves at a pace of a drunken snail although smiling and customer satisfaction pleasant. The rental is a Ford Custom 500. Hunter and Dee lay their clothing bags flat in the trunk on top of her briefcase and head north for Napa Valley and her family's vineyard.

The traffic at the airport and in the city slows them. It should be only about an hour and fifty minute drive, but it will be longer today. Nonetheless, the delay isn't noticeable because of the conversation the two are having. For the first time, no digs, no jabs, and no innuendos. Dee, as Hunter did on their Hotel Del ride, fills him in on some Napa Valley history. First regarding the Yount family and vineyard, and of other famous families. Then about the Napa Valley Vintners and onto her family's winery, *Per Semper*. And finally one piece of useless trivia: that being the original settlers here, the Wappo Indians, named this valley, Napa. Meaning the land of plenty.

Hunter laughs and says, "The Wappo Indians? C'mon. That sounds like one of the names of the Marx brothers. Groucho, Harpo and Wappo." He roars in laughter at his own joke. Dee gives him a playful punch on his arm.

After a few minutes, she says, "Turn right at that next road." He does, then in less than a mile she motions, "Turn in here. We're home."

Hunter turns as directed, goes under a brick and stone archway. A kept fresh painted sign reads, "DeLuca Vineyards and Winery" and under it the words, *"Per Semper"*. Hunter says, "Forever." Smiles, "That's nice."

"That's right, you speak and read Italian. And several others."

"Yeah, and one for sure you don't. Gaelic."

"Got me there. Take a right up there," pointing, "and we'll head for the house."

Hunter smiles, "Head for the house." Then sees it. "Wow! Little Teresa DeLuca did well for herself."

"Little Teresa DeLuca does a lot of things well. Oops, broke my word. Oh well, we're here."

Hunter pulls onto a circular driveway and stops in front of a smallish but gorgeous two-story stone and masonry house that whispers Tuscany from every curtained window and from every ledge and crevice. The gardens in front, and in the circle, are in full bloom and have the look of a woman's touch. Dee says, "Oh-oh, here comes, Cab. Should have brought, Magpie." Hunter gets out on the driver's side; Dee doesn't wait for him to come around the car. She's out in a quick slide and greets the leaping Cab, the family Lab. Still sprite for an old timer.

Hunter stretches, strolls around the car, looks about and says, "Man, what a place. Wappo was right."

"The Wappos were right, and you ain't seen nothin' yet, Marine. Wait 'til my granddad gives you the tour on his cycle. You'll love the sidecar, and love more the leather helmet with goggles that go with it." She laughs. Then says, "Here they come. Cab was first. Now the clan follows. And you watch out for Maria, she'll eat you alive."

"Really?"

"Yes, literally."

Hunter stands dumbfounded as he is introduced to the DeLuca family. Dee's grandmother is picturesque. Tall, slender, shapely and regal looking. Hair silvery gray but she's still agile, graceful and light in her movements. Her husband, Signore DeLuca, is also tall, distinguished looking with a grey mustache and a mischievous smile. Cunning might be more accurate. Dee's father is taller and also thicker than his father, and has a tanned, leathery look from his work and movements about the vineyards. The sister Maria is more like her grandmother than Dee, but only in height. Both she and Dee have robbed the breast pool and long, shapely leg pool of possibly billions of genes. Hunter smiles. *There must be at least twenty short-legged, flat-chested Italian gals walking around angry and lonely in the Tuscany countryside.*

In a maddening tangle of bodies they all shake hands, smile, utter "hello's" and "good to meet you's". For Dee, and hugs and kisses. Maria asks, "And what is it you do, Mister Hunter Kerrigan, that requires my sister to travel clinging to your side?"

"I'm an author, or, would-be author, Ms. DeLuca. Dee is my editor and assistant."

"Are you published?"

"No, ma'am, not yet," says Hunter politely.

Dee admonishes, "Maria, please."

Hunter adds, "Hope to be soon."

Maria runs her hands through her long, black hair. Shakes her head and hair. "Interesting. Interesting indeed."

The grandfather, Signore DeLuca edges forward, and slowly asks, "Mister Kerrigan, if you are not published, how is it that you can travel with a ... what was that?"

Maria says, "Editor and assistant, Grandpapa."

"Yes, yes. That sounds expensive to me for a writer that has not, ahhh, written anything as of yet."

Hunter although uncomfortable, smiles, says, "Yes, well, in light of the fact it's your granddaughter, you have every right to ask. To be concerned."

"I do, and I am, sir."

"Well, to keep it simple, I'm a former Marine officer who has left the service to write. I have an extensive background in language and grammar. Have traveled extensively and lived in Europe. And come from a story-telling family. I happen to have a large retainer from my employer and I have funds that I have saved. I'm unmarried, thereby unattached with no debt. I also have some family wealth. And ..."

"Employer?" Maria interrupts.

Dee's father, Benito Antonio DeLuca, adds, "Good point, Maria. Employer, not publisher. That sounds suspicious to me, but then I'm only a poor old winemaker."

Maria shakes her head. "Poor you are not, Papa. Old, only chronologically; certainly not in spirit. And wise. And a father, and a damn good one."

Hunter injects, "I meant publisher, but it looks as if they treat me like an employee. Just a slip of the tongue."

Maria with a sister, cat-like grin mutters, "I wish."

Dee smiles, "Me three."

The grandfather who has been shifting his weight from foot to foot, looking uncomfortable, cuts off his granddaughters verbal foreplay with a harsh glance, then to Hunter, barks, "And, you have no attachment to my granddaughter, nor intentions? This is all business? An unpublished author, traveling to, wherever, with an assistant, to write a novel with no title and you are an unknown. I don't think so. I have a lot more ..."

Maria interrupts, "Grandpapa. Later, please. Now we should let Mister Kerrigan get settled in the guest house. Then you can take him on your motorbike for a tour and grill him at length. I'm sure he will be most willing to spill the beans once you get him in that sidecar. Or torture him in your cellar."

"No, I want ... Ahhh, yes. Yes." Signore DeLuca pauses. Then, "It's not a motorbike," looking at Maria. Continues, "And, yes, we may go for a tour. But first, I live a long time in the old country. I smelled Mussolini and his Black Shirts long before others. I can smell ... smell, what you say, ah ..."

"Bull shit, Signore DeLuca, bull shit," says Hunter.

"Yes, thatsa right. Bullshitta. I smell the Agency again, Antonelli Teresa DeLuca."

Senora DeLuca gasps, pushes her husband on the arm. "Such language. In front of ladies."

Benito DeLuca, silent for most part, again asserts himself. "Pop, you're right. As usual as a matter of fact, and this I know from experience. I don't like the look of this."

Dee shakes her head, "You're right, Pop. And Grandpapa, you're right as usual."

Hunter shoves his hands in his trouser pockets, drops his head to his chest. Slowly brings it up and says, "You're correct, Signore DeLuca, and Signore Benito DeLuca. Signora. Ms. DeLuca."

"Maria will do."

"Yes. Maria. Anyway. All of you. Yes, I work for the Agency as does Dee once again. We have a simple job to do. Gather some information and make some observations. We'll be traveling together. My disguise is that of an author, traveling with his editor. Writing a story. It will appear to others that we are professionals in our trade, nothing more. For now we need to have an excuse for Dee leaving her home in San Diego. This is it. She is on vacation here, visiting family and her children." He pauses, and looks at Dee with a smile. She nods approval. Then he goes on, "Later, Maria goes to Capri and Dee joins her there. All cover-up." He stops, looks around confused, asks, "By the way, where are the children? Dee, you haven't said a word."

Signora DeLuca says, "They are in town with friends. At the movies. Escorted, of course. They will be home shortly."

Dee smiles. Hugs her grandmama, "That's fine. Go on, Hunter."

"Oh, okay. Backing up, what we need is an alibi for Dee. If anyone should call, someone here, Maria, Dee's father, or grandparents can simply say 'Yes, she's here, but not at the moment.' Then take a message until we return or call."

"More bullshitta," says the grandfather. Then, "Teresa, are you working for that man, DeBeard, again? I no like him. And you know I always believed there was something strange about the way Angelo just ..."

"Grandpapa, it's Mr. MacBeer. And, yes, I am in a way. Actually though I work directly for Mister Kerrigan here. And, you always let your old way imagination go too far."

Hunter is frozen in his place. Stance and face readable. It's gone in a nanosecond.

Signora DeLuca steps forward. Claps her hands, getting everyone's attention. Says, "Papa, quiet for now. You take Mister Kerrigan on a tour. He is our guest. We will have someone put his things in the guest house." She pauses, then, "Teresa, you come inside. Put your things away and visit with your Grandmama, and father, and sister. Anna and Dino will be back inside the hour. Come now, everyone be nicea and I have dinner to prepare." She claps her hands again, only this time in glee saying, "Gooda, I'm again surrounded by my whole family." Hunter says, "Thank you, Signora."

The old man says, "Come, I give you a tour but first we visit my wine cellar. I need a brandy after all this."

Hunter smiles, says, "I hope that's apricot brandy because I love it," pauses a moment and asks, "Is this in the torture chamber?"

The Signore grins as wide as the Grand Canyon, says, "Ohhhhh, yes. Possibly both, but first my own apricot brandy. I've been making it for years. Long before the wine. Come." The two leave, the old man's arm draped over Hunter's shoulder. There is nothing like something in common to put aside a problem. At least for the moment.

Dee's father and his mother, the Signora, walk together toward the house. Maria and Dee follow with arms around each other's waist. Dee carrying the clothing bag, Maria the briefcase. A vineyard worker hustles toward the guest cottage with Hunter's bag.

Maria says, "Your Mister Kerrigan is a hunk, sister dear. You will remember since we will once again be rooming together this evening, that I am a light sleeper. Incredibly light." She giggles.

Dee gives her a squeeze with the arm that is on Maria's waist, "As I am, sister dear. I would not want to find you tip-toeing to the guest cottage in the wee hours."

They both laugh. Then Maria says laughing, "Maybe we both should."

"Perhaps."

Maria bumps her sister with her hip. Shrugs. Smiles.

Dee is not smiling and her jovial mood fades into an all-business mask.

As Hunter sits in Signore DeLuca's dark, dank wine cellar, waiting for his brandy, he's taken with a flashback.
Unbelievable. It is a premonition.

CHAPTER 12

"If you are not shooting, you should be communicating, reloading and running."
A gunfighter's rule

Neither was correct. Neither could go on. With both appetites satisfied they collapsed in each other's arms and slept until mid-morning. Not wanting to lose control, and control and bravado is everything with Rocco, he says, "Adrianna, darling. I look forward to Rapallo. We can swim and walk, and you can shop while I fish."

Adrianna squeals in delight from the tub where she is soaking in lavender scented suds born of perfumed soaps and bath oils. Rocco continues his shaving. She sits upright in the tub, picks up the spray shower head and pulls the bath plug as she stands. Says, "I feel good this morning. This was what I needed to recover from last night," she smiles as the suds wash away from her breasts, and down her long legs still knee deep in tub water.

Rocco is pleased with himself over her coy remark. She knows how to please a man in every way. Now finished shaving and having showered earlier, he leaves the bathroom saying, "Let's hurry. We'll drive. It's a little over a hundred kilometers and will take but a few hours. We'll keep this room. Travel light. Take what make-up you need and what you wear. You can shop there for whatever else you need."

"More new outfits?"

"Yes. And whatever else you want."

This is music to Adrianna's ears. *Shop. The drive will be scenic along the coast. The restaurants in Rapallo and nearby Portofino and Santa Margherita Ligure with their fresh seafood will be a gourmet's delight. Romantic scenery. And Rocco each night.*

Rocco adds to Adrianne's thoughts by shouting from the bedroom, "We'll be staying at the Palace Hotel. Our room will over look the town and the Tyrrhenian Sea."

She gasps, "The Excelsior Palace Hotel?"

"Yes, it's over seventy years old. Warm and comfortable like old slippers, like you and me. He pauses. "I have stayed here before, on business, of course," pausing and catching himself. He laughs, then pretends to clear his throat. "This will be romantic. Who knows where it will lead?"

"How longa we stay?"

"Ahhh, I don't know. A day or two, perhaps more. No real hurry. But I do have to return here. Have a routine task to do for Roberto."

Adrianna comes into the bedroom from the bath. She is not dressed and prowls to the closet mirror. Stops, examines her body in sensual moves and poses, first cupping her breasts with her hands, and turning slightly in each direction. First holding them, then not. Then facing the mirror again she glides her hands down her body. Initially over her abdomen and continuing down each leg, as if smoothing silk, as far as she can reach without bending. She turns slowly, facing Rocco, her head canted to one side.

Rocco groans, "Momma mia, Oh ... ohhhh, if we only had time."

Adrianna crooks her finger motioning to Rocco and murmurs, "Take the time. We have some of that for all this."

Rocco slips out of his loafers. Says, "I called Roberto this morning. He is home. He has met the staff and is pleased. Told me not to hurry but to finish my work before I leave." He is hurrying and fumbling his words that have nothing to do with the moment or his humid feelings. In his haste he clumsily steps out of his slacks. "Oh, Momma mia. Adrianna, you are a goddess."

Adrianna finishes Rocco's struggles by taking off his boxer shorts as he closes with her, ready. He mumbles, "You smella good, likea ahhh ... ahh..."

"I am good, and it's hungry," as she rubs her palms up the inside of her thighs, then her forefinger and middle finger of her right hand continue up to where she pleasures herself more, groaning. She continues the stroking, picking up the temp.

Rocco's eyes have followed her hands. Now, his lips follow the path. Then him.

The tour goes well. Signore DeLuca is pleased that Hunter is an apricot brandy enthusiast. Dee's children, Dino and Anna, arrive back from the movie. The choice turned out to be interesting and perhaps appropriate. It was a Disney movie, *Smoke*, with Ron Howard as a fourteen year old boy mourning the loss of his father and not happy with his mother's selection of a man to marry. The boy finds the dog, a German Shepherd, and later the owner is found. Dino and Anna are not caught up in the story as much as they are interested and excited to meet Hunter.

After the tour and brandies, and before dinner, Hunter takes Dino and Anna swimming. Signora DeLuca shoos her daughters out of the kitchen. They leave more than willingly, change, and join the children and Hunter in the pool. After many dives from the board, most of which are refined common ones the three adults sit on the pool edge watching Dino and Anna swim with an occasional annoying diving board cannon ball from Dino. Hunter is surrounded. Children in front; Dee sitting on one side of him; Maria on the other. Both of the women in one piece white swimsuits, in preference to bikinis, an acquiescence to their father and grandparents. Nonetheless they are hip and thigh to hip and thigh with Hunter.

Dino swims up to the three and asks, "Mister Kerrigan, are you married?"

Anna treading water next to Dino offers, "He's not. Mom told me." She ducks under the water, bobs up and says with a broad grin, "How 'bout my mom and Aunt Maria? They're both beautiful, huh?"

Hunter flushes, struggles to his feet, and says, "Dino, I'm not married. And, as you, I have no plans in the immediate future to do so. None. Out and out none. And, Anna, darling, you're right. Your mother and aunt are beautiful and probably have boyfriends and suitors lined up that are much more attractive."

Maria looks up and coos, "I don't have a one. Nary a one. But I'm close." Tilts her head to the side wearing a coy smile. "Is your name, Close?" She giggles coyly. "And I too love my grandpapa's brandy. And, I've never been married, as a result you could be the first to have my ..." she pauses, emits a low laugh, "My undivided attention in the family wine cellar." She laughs a tad louder, "Gotcha, huh?"

"Could be, but I don't think so. However, do you also make apricot brandy?"

"Sure do, tiger. Better than my grandpapa's."

Hunter smiles, looks down at Dino and Anna. "Anyway, guys, you watched one too many Walt Disney films. And I'm not Earl Holliman, who incidentally is the new guy in the flick, and you don't need the dog, Smoke. You have Magpie. And guys, I'm not Earl. However, I assume your grandmother wants us cleaned up and inside for dinner and that is what's important. Because what I am, is, hungry." Hunter scurries away toward the guest house to change.

Maria looks at Dee, whispers, "There is fire, little sister, fire. Whether it is real or just your usual smoke is the question. But, since you've already had your turn at bat, I believe it should be my turn at the plate. When do you two have to leave?"

"Not a chance, sister dear. Trust me, he won't be available to you. Besides, we're leaving in the morning."

"Well, the night is young."

"You're not."

"Shame on you, Dee darlin'. Experienced is the word I would use."

Dino struggles out of the pool unintentionally breaking up the spitting and hissing. With only a few scrapes of fur on the ground he says, "Mom, did I say somethin' wrong? Mister Hunter looked angry. I didn't mean anything bad."

Anna, now out of the pool and standing alongside of Dino chirps, "He'd make a great dad, Mom."

"Or uncle," adds Maria as she stands.

All head for the house and dinner in single file. Dee trailing with no response.

Rocco, in his own eyes, flushed with conquest and Adrianna, in her own eyes brimming with confidence and success, wait outside the hotel by the valet stand. They will depart in minutes for a reasonably short but scenic drive to Rapallo.

Four other sets of eyes, not flushed nor brimming, but darkened from fatigue watch closely from two separate corners. Two sets of eyes emit signals to the other two. The latter two walk to their car, slide in and wait, watching. One of the sets of eyes, not in the car, strides into the hotel to the front desk. He spends a few minutes at the desk asking questions, then returns to the street and his partner. He signals the two watching in the car. The hand signal is for them to follow; we'll stay here. A nod of understanding by one set of eyes in the car, the unique looking woman in the passenger seat of the black Fiat.

The valet brings Rocco's rental 1970 Alfa Romeo Spider Veloce curbside. He opens the door for Adrianna while Rocco slides in behind the wheel. They depart, leaving a small plume of exhaust smoke at the valet's feet. The two sets of eyes on the street watch. The other two sets of eyes follow at a safe and inconspicuous distance. When both cars are out of sight, Mossad Agent Itzak Levi turns to his partner, Namir Dayan, and says in Hebrew, "The desk clerk says Signore DeStefano hasn't checked out of his room. Will be ..."

Namir, shakes his head and says, "Itzee, speak English. We're supposed to be American tourists or Italian citizens. Not Israeli's. Today, it's English. Besides, it's easier for me. Too much time in American schools, I guess."

Itzak starts over again. Namir tells him he has the gist, continue. Itzak does as he's asked, and in English, "He will be returning by the weekend, possibly Sunday. They are holidaying in the Rapallo area. The desk clerk gave me the name of the hotel."

"Fine. We'll wait for Marnee or Reis to call. After the maid service is finished here, we'll go up and have a look around. Until then, let's eat ... at Alberto's. And check for

Antonio. He should be gaining confidence by now. Becoming careless."

Itzak sighs. "Ahh, more pasta," he holds his stomach. Then asks, "Why don't we just get this over and get back home?"

"Do you know where our man is?"

"No." Itzak feels his stupidity.

"Well then, we'll have to let the good Signore Rocco DeStefano lead us to our assignment. The damn man has disappeared," he laughs, "like virgins in Jerusalem."

Itzak asks, "Where are the Germans and the Americans? I haven't seen anyone else watching DeStefano. I don't know, possibly they have something better?"

"Headquarters thinks not. They believe the East Germans and the Russians don't care as much as we and the Americans. And that the Americans are on the way. Our contacts say a new man but they don't have anything on him yet. We'll do what we've been doing. Follow the scent. And watch for Antonio. His scent or odor shouldn't be difficult to smell and follow. The man has disgusting hygienic habits and lives in a trash heap, or at least he did."

"Fine. Alberto's it is. Let's at least get some exercise and walk there."

They leave, chatting and gesturing, like any other tourists in Pisa.

As Hunter and Dee enter the terminal, Hunter says, "Okay, we'll split up here. You to your gate and flight. Me, to mine. Don't forget, taxi to Grosvenor Square, then another to the hotel. Check to ensure you're not being followed although that should be unlikely. If so, go to a different hotel. Stay the night and get a flight home in the morning. You'll be done. Otherwise, get some rest. I should be there tomorrow morning in time for an early breakfast. Questions?"

"No. Got it. I'm not a dummy you know." She shakes her head, then follows with,   "Everything is arranged.

Have a good meeting with your friends." Dee turns and heads away not looking over her shoulder.

The meal the previous evening went well. The conversation light, the laughter heavy, and the brandy after dinner warming. Hunter took Dino and Anna swimming again after dinner. The dip was short. A four-thirty in the morning departure, or as Hunter stated it, "O Dark Thirty," is early. He thanked her father and grandparents for dinner, the hospitality, and their cooperation. He gave a polite goodnight nod to Dee and Maria and hugged the two children. Then was off to the guest cottage with a full snifter of apricot brandy. The DeLuca family remained up except Dee and the children. It was past Dino and Anna's bedtime, and Dee's also since she was to be up and ready at O Dark Thirty.

However, Hunter had a visitor.

Sean Shanahan and Mary Kate O'Rourke have been sitting in Peador O'Donnell's beautiful and meticulous old pub for the better part of an hour, sipping pints and talking of this and that. Some ad hoc musicians have stepped forward and are setting up to play, a tradition at this historic pub. Sean clasps Mary Kate's hand which is resting on the table. He turns in his chair and faces her, leans closer with a look that turns into a gaze, and if truth be told, sees Mary Kate for the first time.

She is a buxom lass, yet petite. Brown hair that is glistening in the pub lights and has dark brown eyes that brighten when she speaks. Her lightweight beige sweater is not barmaid tight but does show off her figure. Her chocolate brown skirt and matching shined slip-on shoes show her to be a neat, well-groomed and naturally wholesome lass. Pink lipstick and nails, and hair in a pony-tail freshen her look to match her tongue. Fair unblemished complexion, and with all else gives her the perfect look of a touched-up photographic portrait. The lilt in her voice adds sparkle to her words, and her sense of humor lends life, perhaps beyond reality.

Before he can speak, she places her other hand on his and says, "Sean, you're up to something, I can tell. This place is wonderful, and the music is grand. You know I'm more than fond of you, but my aim, and that of the church, is to marry and give me self to that man and me life to him. You've been me love for a good time now and have not taken one step toward my aim except tryin' to get me knickers down around me knees. Tell me then, what is different this night, Sean Shanahan of Derry Town?"

"Mary Kate, you are a brash, beautiful Irish lass. Take a moment to be shy and listen to me, for I am more than fond of you. Always have been. Since long before we knew of such things, let alone talked of them."

"Do you love me, Sean Shanahan?"

"Yes, I do Mary Kate. But let a man have his say."

"I will, Sean, but not until I tell you that I love you as well. And have since the first day I saw you wearing your scruffy short pants with shirt tails out flappin' in the harsh wind, and skipping stones on the River Foyle. In the park. Do you remember that? You turned and stared at me with your hands on your hips and sayin', 'Did you see that, lass? All the way across.' I love you, Sean Shanahan. Now say what you will, or want."

"Ahhh, Mary Kate O'Rourke, you may be impossible to live with, but I'm wanting to do just that. Since you are not only the most gorgeous lass in all Derry, but the most proper, I need to ask your father to allow me to court proper-like. And declare my intentions." He pauses, shrugs his shoulders. "How can I ask? He's not about, and I don't know where he is."

Mary Kate leans close to Sean, pulls her right hand from his grasp, leaving her left still holding him firmly. Cups his face with her right hand and brushes kisses on his forehead, cheek, and ear, then a nip on his neck and finally an open and long kiss on his lips. Several tables around them applaud and cheer. The fiddlers stop and bow from the waist with full smiles. Then start playing *She Wears My Ring*. The crowd cheers again. Mary Kate and Sean sit facing each other, flushed red but smiling and laughing. When the song is over the crowd cheers again, and the quartet of fiddlers bow and go about their music for the night starting with another ballad, *The Rose of Tralee*.

Sean brings Mary Kate's left hand to his lips. Kisses her palm. Whisper's, "I love you, Mary Kate, and want to marry you. How can I talk to your father?"

"First, he's in America. Boston. And I will call him tomorrow at his shop there. Tell him this wonderful news and arrange a time for you to call, or perchance he will come home and allow you to do it all proper-like. How's that?"

"That's wonderful, luv. Now, let's have a fresh pint and listen to the music. Then take a walk after, though it 'tis a harsh wind startin' to rear its teeth."

"A harsh wind is it. You wouldn't be pokin' fun at me, now would you?"

"No, but I will be kissin' you again before I bring us another pint."

"That's good because up to now I've been doin' all the liftin'."

"Mary Kate, you have a quick and sharp tongue. But, I be guessin' it will be worth it all."

She cups her hand on his face as he leans in, whispers in his ear, "You won't be guessin' for long, Sean me love, and you won't be wantin' another." She kisses him full on the lips, long, working her tongue with his. Then eases back. She feigns a bite to his nose and whispers, "Maybe we can change the order of things if me father doesn't march to our beat." She squeezes his hand, adds, "The pints, Sean. Surely you're not that easily distracted?"

"I am by you. But, the pints it will be." Sean gets up and heads for the bar sooner than waiting for a barmaid. All are more than busy now serving tables and pulling away from groping hands of dirty ole' men, and a few young lads as well.

At the bar Sean orders their pints. Waits.

Danny will not believe this, and I bet I'm in her knickers before Saturday night confession.

CHAPTER 13

"Bring a gun. Preferably bring at least two guns. Bring all your friends who have guns."
A gunfighter's rule

    Rocco and Adrianna arrive in Rapallo in the early afternoon, check into their suite overlooking the town and seaside, and immediately enjoy a snack at a street-side cafe before they start Adrianna's shop 'til you drop routine. Rocco's patience runs thin frequently. Thus they incorporate respite stops at quaint sidewalk cafes for a glass of Chianti. In time the setting sun on this western coastline is not only picturesque but a cue to wander back to the Excelsior to freshen up and dine at its Eden Roc Restaurant.
    The Israeli's, Agents Marnee Kaslar and Reis Hazzan, also check in at the same hotel getting one of the smaller rooms. Although not as expensive, in time, the cost will draw severe commentary from Headquarters though they will be reducing expenses by sharing. Twin singles will ease the strain on the budget but not on Reis. Nonetheless they begin the tail quickly, often changing leads to avoid being spotted. The good news is that Rocco is not on a high alert although casual his checking on a tail is habitual. Adrianna is oblivious to such things.

    Adrianna is wearing one of her three new outfits for dinner. The Eden Roc seaside dining room of the hotel has a breath-taking view of the fading glow of the sunset. The patio is covered by a white awning. The tables covered with draped white linen are adorned with fine silverware and a white porcelain pots of freshly cut flowers. Each table is candlelit and the soft white and blue lights surrounding the patio create a warm ambiance Rocco and Adrianna sit at a table for two, on the balcony rail. The restaurant, as one would suspect, specializes in seafood all freshly caught from the Tyrrhenian Sea. Life for these two is good it would seem, certainly for Adrianna.

And as it is it would seem for the pair of eyes watching from a far corner table. A young couple, looking like tourists, or lovers, or conceivably both. They speak in Italian in hushed tones. Part of the selection process for Marnee and Reis was that they speak several languages, Italian and English being two. They have been educated in Jerusalem, the United States and elsewhere abroad. Both have worked assignments in Italy several times. They have the dark hair and complexion of a native of this country. A warm picture of two young lovers, vacationing, however in reality, each missioned to kill, and have before, with their hands or any weapon to include the ones they are carrying tonight.

Marnee whispers, "We should finish and move on. Go hang out in the lobby bar. My guess is that Romeo here is going to sip wine and then head for the boudoir for the evening."

"I agree. I hope she doesn't cause him to have a heart attack or stroke before he leads us to our man."

Marnee laughs, more a snicker. "He wishes ... well, not for an attack."

"Let me sign the check and we'll leave. We're going to have our hands full tomorrow. He's going fishing, or thus it appears. She however ..."

Marnee smiles, finishes, "Primp, shop, primp and get set to get ready to do it over again. And again. What a life."

"You can do all that except the shop portion. I'm willing."

"If you suggest this again. Even think it again, your choices will be the tub or the floor. And if you blink, the hall."

They leave quietly, ignored by the room of still filled tables, and certainly unseen by Rocco sipping his wine, gazing at Adrianna and the seaside view.

Hunter arrives at Dulles International Airport. He is to meet Joe Zachary here, and he will depart from here later on a Pam Am 747 for Heathrow in London. Dulles, with its unique design, was dedicated by President John F. Kennedy on November 17th, 1962 and is still to some extent a white elephant. It's an inconvenient twenty-six miles from downtown Washington and not an easy trip from the suburbs. However, times are changing and the flight options are much greater than at its conception. Particularly if you're a Texan and want to fly the colorful Branniff Airlines.

Hunter finds Joe in a bar in the terminal, sitting in a far corner table. The restaurant portion is not full and those here are all seated at the bar, busy drinking, talking, reading papers or people watching. And those being watched are the few females passing through the terminal, most seem to be "stews". Most young. All beautiful, but none in the same league with PSA stews.

Hunter sits next to Joe, both have their backs to the wall and are facing out toward the terminal. Hunter says, "Does Ruth know you're out here watching the skirts?"

"There's better where I work, and more of them every day."

"Not better than PSA, believe me. Long legs, big on top and hot pants ... and breath, but speaking of work, what'd ya have for me that's new?"

"Glad to see you're focused. However, inside the folded newspaper in front of you are some photos and artist sketches. Pretty good. You can take the paper with you. Everything else we know, you know. The trail stops in Pisa." Joe passes. Takes a sip of coffee. Looks at Hunter, asks, "Did you want some?"

"Naw. Had too much on the plane."

Zachary takes another sip, continues. "He stills owns that London flat. His is empty we think. The other three are still leased; run by a property manager. He's paid from Geneva. The rent goes to Geneva. We have nothing else of a paper trail. Interpol doesn't either. Don't have or can't get anything regarding money transfers. Do know it's a huge account. Millions upon."

Hunter asks, "Any in Italy? Elsewhere?"

Joe says, "We have nothing in that regard. Hell, he could be dead for all we know. Except, one of his henchmen, Rocco DeStefano, was in Pisa, at least as of yesterday. And that guy, Antonio Rizzo, that I suspect everyone is looking for, hasn't been spotted yet. We think he went to ground in Pisa. If not, he's gone. If you find him, you may find out where Pisces is or went. And, if you can get to his other henchman, Bruno Costa, you could for sure find his boss. Of course, either might kill anyone that asks a question. You'll want to be careful. Both pictures are inside also. And Rizzo's as well. He's a good lookin' guy. Probably a lady's man so the gals at Alberto's must know something of him. But he must know that Pisces is looking for him, hard."

"Okay. What about Patrick Shanahan? And O'Rourke? And any other of their cohorts?"

"Was just going to get to that. Patrick Shanahan is, was, a hit man for the PIRA. No doubt. His target was Samantha for the reasons I've already described. Shanahan has two brothers back in Ireland. Both in the Army. Both on the Brit's suspect list, or people to be watched. The Brit's say those two, Danny and Sean, younger than Patrick, are still in town. Derry. The Brit's don't think the PIRA will seek retribution. Shanahan was a casualty of war. No one killed him. He fell off a cliff." He pauses. Then, "I agree with them. He's not a problem, or it shouldn't be for us. For you."

"Well, Joe. I tend to disagree or why would this gent, O'Rourke, been dispatched to find out what went on? And find me? Come to my house? Joe, I know this IRA splinter group is a vindictive bunch. Hard corps. Clannish. Hell, Joe. In weaponry they've advanced but mentally they haven't moved much beyond axes, spears and clubs. My guess is that either they, or if not them, the two brothers will want some blood. Mine."

Joe nods agreement. "You may be right, but MacBeer doesn't think so."

"MacBeer," Hunter snarls.

"Yeah, well, we'll fix that but for now, be careful and I will stay with it. For your sake if not the Agency's. As a friend. And handler. Now, Marine, the bad news."

"Bad news. Where was the good news? I've got a gut feel I'm going to be one pissed-off Marine in a second or two."

"Former Marine, but, yes, probably more than pissed." Joe pauses, stalls some more by looking around the entire bar and concourse area, exhales loudly, says, "O'Rourke is gone."

Hunter stares at Joe. Takes his right hand and rubs his forehead hard, then moves it down, squeezing the bridge of his nose with his thumb and index finger. Looks up, sighs, "Gone? Where? And how the hell did that happen? The police had him?"

Joe exhales again. Eyebrows raised. Grimaces. "There must have been a team with O'Rourke. After he left your house in the squad car, there was an accident. Not an accident per se, they were rammed by another car. The patrolman got out, was knocked unconscious by one of the men. They un-cuffed O'Rourke and fled. The car was found later abandoned at the airport. The descriptions of the two men were vague at best from the patrolman and three eye witnesses, two of which were street people." He pauses, "You know, they even have them in San Diego. Probably wear Bermuda shorts though. Anyway, they weren't interested or didn't want to get involved."

Hunter listens, his head held in both hands, slumped nearly to his chest. "Wonderful."

"SDPD and the FBI put out an APB. Notified Immigration here and in Canada. Bradovich was playing it straight and was having O'Rourke brought directly to the FBI head shed. For his cooperation, he was invited to attend the interrogation. Obviously, there was none. Bottom line, O'Rourke is gone, as are his two buddies. The FBI is watching his home and shop in Boston, and the Boston PD has the APB." Joe gazes at Hunter, "Sorry, pal. We, they, them, us, whomever, fucked-up."

Hunter doesn't say anything for several moments. Joe continues to stare at him, then shifts his gaze to the ceiling, other tables, bar, and finally back to Hunter. Hunter is not glaring at Joe, but the look is focused. The stare of his eyes are like ultra-thin ice picks, punching into the retina of Zachary's eyes. "Joe, this convinces me. They, the PIRA, are wanting revenge for Shanahan's death. And they either suspect or know, or want it to be me, or don't give a damn. To them, it's me. They are going to try to find me and kill me. You need to find this O'Rourke asshole and kill him. And his two friends. And the Brits need to pick up the Shanahan brothers and stow them someplace. I don't need these bungholes chasing me while I'm looking for Pisces. After that, we can take care of the IRA or whatever they call themselves nowadays."

"We'll try, Hawk. I'll put everything I can on this. O'Rourke has a brother in Ireland. I've already sent one of our assets to watch the man and check him out. See where it leads. Perchance to a local leader. The Brit's will be helping."

Hunter shakes his head. "O'Rourke has a brother? In Ireland? Let me guess. He's in the Army too, right?"

"Apparently. Twin brothers as a matter of fact. Mickey and Mike."

Hunter's eyes roll to the top, "And one is married. Right? To Minnie, who works for Looney Tunes, the Irish version of the SAS and CIA."

"No, but Mickey is married and has a daughter, Mary Kate. We're watching her also. She lives with and works for her Uncle Mike."

Hunter breaks out laughing. And does for a good two or three minutes. Then with tears in his eyes, says, "Joe, if this wasn't damn serious, it would be funny. I mean Roadrunner cartoon funny. Is this a script for Disney?" He laughs again.

The Hawk pauses, wipes his eyes with the back of his hands. His face turns to stone. He hisses, "Joe, find 'em. Kill them all. Mickey, Mike, the two buddies, the brothers, and Mary friggin' Kate. Kill them all or they're goin' to kill me, or damn sure try. And if they do try, Joseph Jackson Lee Zachary, there will be collateral damage strewn along my path that will make the fire-bombing of Tokyo look like a family picnic. Understand?"

"Hunter, we can't kill them all. Good, Lord. We'll get O'Rourke back or find him. The others, we'll watch, and if they make a move, we'll move right along with them."

"Kill 'em, Joe." Hunter picks up the folded newspaper. "Or I will. You did say, Derry?" Peeks inside the fold. Tucks it under his arm, says, "Anything else? I've got a plane to catch."

Hunter is standing beside the table now. Joe looks up, mumbles, "MacBeer." Looks down at the table shaking his head. Then back to Hunter.

Hunter sits. "What?"

"I'm smelling old cheese. I'm seeing shadows. I'm smellin' dead bodies. I'm diggin' and gettin' old bones and cadavers. He's so dirty, *Tide* has found a formula yet to help. Watch your six. Be careful. Especially of Columbo, even though I put her in the game with you. I promise you I will do everything I can and will tell you what I find, when I find it."

"This is incredible. Unbelievable. Staggering. Mind-blowing or boggling, or whatever. And in Technicolor. Okay. I'm leaving. Stay in touch. And tell everyone that might come near me that I'm not going to be polite. I'm not going to be professional. I'm going to kill everyone I meet." He turns to leave, takes a step. Stops. Returns. Pats Joe on the shoulder a few times, says, "Thanks, Joe. Semper Fi." Then turns and leaves toward the Pan Am departure area.

Joe remains seated. Stares after Hunter. Whispers, "Semper Fi, ole buddy. Semper Fi. I will try or die." He sighs, "And no further than the back of my fighting hole, Hawk. Not one inch."

Mary Kate calls her father. She is a mixture of tears, giggles, and prayers. The time difference should work. Her dad should still be in the shop. If not, she'll call his number at his flat in a few hours. Like here, he lives above the shop. He might stop at a local pub for a pint and some darts.

She gets no answer and hangs up after ten rings, each counted on her fingers as her one hand rests on the table top beneath the wall phone in her uncle's living room. He is at a pub for sure. She believes in her heart that she must tell her father first, or at least try as best she can to do so. After she puts the phone back on the wall, she looks out the window onto the narrow street below, then to the sky above and whispers, "Mama, I've found me a good man and one that I don't think is involved in all this rubbish. I miss ya, Mama," and blesses herself as she steps back from the window.

Dee arrives at Heathrow Airport in London. With only carry-on luggage, she is off and through customs in short-order. Regardless of traveling First Class on both flights, and in spite of the reasonable comfort of the First Class Lounge at JFK airport, she is tired. The first class seats were spacious. The food good, and the drinks comforting. But, hour upon hour, for all practical purposes a full day of traveling is tiring.

Outside the terminal Dee does as instructed. Takes a cab from Heathrow to Grosvenor's Square. Gets out and walks a short distance and then takes another cab to the hotel. Once there, she carries her own bags into the lobby. Sits at a table in the lounge area and has a cup of tea. After about forty minutes, and finished with the tea, she registers. As far as she can tell, no one followed her and no one here is showing any interest nor is acting suspicious.

Once in the room, she hangs up her few outfits, takes out necessary items from the briefcase and places them in the *loo*, freshens up and comes out into the suite. Opens the drapes and looks down on Piccadilly. *Nice. Never been here. Still alive at this hour.*

She goes to the phone sitting on an antique maple table in the drawing room of the suite. Dials a number from memory and waits. Two rings.

The voice on the other end says, "Hello."

Dee responds, "It's me. I'm here."

"Okay, good. The plan has changed a bit. It's a little more complicated. The good Mister O'Rourke has escaped, been kidnapped, or assisted. He's not been located. But he will be soon. The belief around here is that he was assisted by two of his comrades at arms. That of course is not true. His comrades in arms back home will get a little feisty. As a result, be alert. Nonetheless, your role hasn't changed."

"Understand."

"Has the subject tumbled for any of your wily ways?"

"No. To the contrary. He's rejected everything. Mind is focused."

"Well, after this afternoon he will be depressed and vulnerable. I suggest you be more demur. He might submit, so be careful. Although that might make everything easier, it would not make me feel good at all. I want you to know that."

Dee pauses, says, "Don't worry. Anything else for now?"

"No. It is what it is. Be careful. Call in."

"Are we still on our path?"

"Without a doubt. The time is close. I am about to be free. Days away. Week at the most."

"You know it's been a long time."

There is a pause for just a moment, then a sigh, "I know. As for me. We wasted precious time. But, we'll make it up. We're nearly there."

Dee clutches herself with her one free arm, then sighs, "I just will never understand."

"Understand what?"

"How we got ourselves in this position, and how you managed the Angelo situation."

"It wasn't easy. But, let's not think about all that now. Darling, hang on. One week. Tops. Then we'll not only be together again, but away. Far away." There is a pause. Then, "We need to hang up. Bye." Click.

Dee stares at the phone, hangs it up, then pulls her other arm around her thus she is sitting, clutching herself with both arms, and shivering slightly in August, and the air is not on.

CHAPTER 14

"If you are going to go through hell, keep going."
Winston Churchill

Pisces stands on his veranda gazing out over this quaint old town he's chosen for his final home and the glistening blue of the sea beyond. He sips a *Nero d'Avola* red wine, a Sicilian product. It's popular with the locals but not to his liking. He prefers the Chiantis he orders direct from his favorite winery in Tuscany. Along with the apricot brandy. And of course, the cigars from his long time trusted friend at their source. He looks at Gina at his side. Places his arm around her waist and pulls her close. "Gina, what of your family? Where are they? What do they do? I should know these things, but I don't." He gives her a squeeze, a kiss on the top of her head, nuzzling his face into her thick, dark hair. He takes another sip of wine. Ponders, "Gina Pappalardo? An old Sicilian name. Right?"

Gina looks up, gives him a kiss on the cheek, smiles and responds, "No worry, Roberto. You cannot know everything. It is true I have a Sicilian name. But, my mother died years ago, and my father left. I don't know where. I have no family here other than you, Roberto. I have been working ever since I was a little girl. At times living in the streets. Bruno found me serving tables in that cafe at the bottom of the hill when he brought me here to work as a housemaid."

"No one? No relatives? Friends? No person to miss you?"

"No."

"That's not right. Not good in life."

"I have you, Roberto. And that's good. That's life. And now I just want to keep you happy. Are you pleased with me, Roberto?"

Pisces pulls her close, nuzzles her hair again and whispers, "More than you know." He pauses. "But, I have something to do now," his tone different, detached, coarse.

"Have Rosa fix us some dinner. Some Cannoli with ricotta cheese. And not too sweet. Later we will sneak away for some private time on the boat. Just the two of us. Yes?"

"Yes," and wraps her arms around him, kissing Pisces full on the lips. She pulls back and says, "Tomorrow, can I go shopping in town?"

"Of course. Yes. That's a good idea. Tomorrow."

In his study, Pisces waits for Rocco to call at the prescribed time. His fingers drumming on the desk top. Stopping. Then starts again. Stops. He sips the *Nero d'Avola*. Puts it down and shouts, "Rosa, come here and bring me my Chianti ."

Minutes later Rosa appears. A bottle of Chianti in hand with a fresh glass. He nods and gives a sweeping motion toward the other. She takes the glass away, nods, and scurries from the room. Pisces waits a few seconds and then bellows, "Rosa. Rosa."

Again she bustles into the room, flushed and slightly bent. Pisces stares at her, points to the bottle of Chianti and his glass. Shrugs his shoulders, hands and arms out to the side. Eyebrows raised, his head juts forward.

In a mixture of Italian and English, Rosa, whines, "Sorry, Signore. I forget. Sorry." She pours a glass, leaves the cork out letting the wine breathe. She's not sure of this, but her husband Carmen told her of this. What he didn't tell her was that Roberto Catalano is an impatient man. Also not likable at times. And she, as well as Carmen, were expecting him to be gone when they arrived. That is what Rocco told them.

Pisces nods, and flicks his hand dismissing her. As he does, the phone rings and he snatches it from its cradle. "Yes."

The voice on the other end says, "Signore Catalano, it is Rocco. Checking in as you asked."

"Yes, Rocco. Are you still in Rapallo?"

"Yessa, sir. Planning on ..."

"Well, the new help has arrived already. You didn't school them well. Make sure that gets done before I return next time. Speaking of that, you must leave Rapallo soon and get on with your business in Pisa. But before you do, make some calls. I met a woman of interest in town yesterday. Stunning. Intelligent. And she has the most delectable ... never mind. I want you to find out more about her. I believe she is a widow. If not, she should be or will be. Her name is Russo. Chiarina Romero Russo. Owns some shops. As I say, bright, perhaps wealthy. Dazzling."

Rocco asks where she is from. Pisces tells him along with some additional information of what he knows of the Russo name. Then he says, "Besides being beautiful, she is interested in painting. She saw one of my pieces in town and likes it. And me, I think."

Rocco replies, "What is there not to like of you, boss? I will do this right away and tend to the other matter in a few days. Will that be satisfactory?"

"Yes. And disregard my angry tone. Have a good time with your woman. But get me some information and get rid of Rizzo. I will be gone for several days. Leaving tonight."

"Where to?"

"Taking the *Sorridenta*. Call me tonight before I go. This is important to me."

"Yes, sir, bossa. Will you ..."

Rocco hears the click before he can complete his comment. As always, conversations with Pisces end when Pisces is finished. On the phone, it's a click and dial tone. In person, it's his back as he leaves, or the hand dismissing everyone and everything. The words, and the person. And every so often a pistol shot is the dismissal. Or an ice pick. Whatever, it's a dismissal.

Rocco places the phone in its cradle. Immediately makes a call to the lady's town and makes the request for the information, followed with gruff orders including the time table. This time it is his click. Then he ambles into the bedroom. Adrianna is sprawled on the bed, naked. Laying on her side with her head propped up on her hand, supported by her elbow resting on the bed. Rocco groans, "Adrianna, love. You are gonna kill me."

"I hopea not, Rocco, but one time before we go for a stroll. It will be gooda for your heart and your appetite."

She rolls onto her back, thrusting her arms up and forward toward him. "*Rocco, facciamo l'amore.*"

He drifts toward her, disrobing as quickly as possible. "*Sei bellissema. Incredibile.*"

Hunter grabs a taxi from London's Heathrow Airport. He changes cabs three times before finally stopping at the Cavendish Hotel in the Mayfair district of the city. A hotel over 150 years old and steeped in tradition and legends such as Rosa Lewis, considered the Duchess of Duke Street that ran the hotel in the 1800's. It was rebuilt, modernized in 1966. Hunter waits to register, sitting in the ornate and luxurious lobby of this hotel with over two hundred rooms. However, it is not the hotel where Dee is registered and waiting.

When reasonably satisfied he has not been followed and is not being watched, Hunter registers, goes to his room and hangs up his clothing bag. He's had plenty of time to mull over Maria's late night visit to the DeLuca's guest cottage where he stayed his one evening in Napa Valley. He ran her comments through his mind during both flights. From San Francisco to Washington, and from the Capitol to London.

His thoughts return to that tryst. *She is truly an attractive woman. Like her sister, Dee, Maria has black hair, dark eyes, well proportioned and an inch or two taller. Same dark complexion and same overt sexual aggressiveness, only sincere. However, although she ensured I was fully aware of her interest in me, it was not the purpose of her visit. She sat me down, and sat directly across from me on the edge of a chair she pulled up. Her hands folded in her lap, calmly, yet her fingers were twitching and entwining. Not only nervous, but scared. Spoke for an uncomfortable hour or so, information pouring out. Then when finished with her story and answers to my questions, she got up to leave. Hesitated, and then seeing no other type of interest on my part, shook the hand I offered to her and opened the door to leave. Stopped, and with her eyes welling with tears, said, "Please be careful, exceedingly careful."*

She smiled and lamely pulled the door closed, quietly, only the muted sound of the click. Then she reopened it several inches and whispered, "I am single. I do make apricot brandy. And I'm going to come after you Hunter Kerrigan, before or after this, whatever it is, is over. Night. Bye." And pulled the door closed once more. For the evening.

After mulling over Maria's conversation again, Hunter leaves his room and the hotel. He strides the several blocks to the Pisces flat, or flats, on Cork Street. There he watches the building for fifteen minutes, then satisfied that he is still not being followed or watched, and that the Pisces flat is empty, he enters the building looking back, checking for intent eyes. Then turns to his task, picks the lock to the flat and enters by sliding sideways through the door.

There is another flat in the building, owned by Pisces, and it's leased. The occupant appears not to be home at the moment. Nonetheless Hunter closes the door quietly and walks on the balls of his feet on the carpeting or rugs as much as possible and off the wood floors. He searches the two-bedroom, two-bath flat painstakingly. Every closet, every cabinet, and every drawer in this fully furnished, spit-polished clean flat. Not a bit of dust to be found. A barracks ready for the Inspector General. Not even a scuff mark on the hardwood flooring.

There are two features especially noticeable. One is that there is no security system. The other, oddly enough since all else is meticulously clean, is the odor of cigar smoke. It's in the drapes, curtains, rugs and furniture, and especially strong in the living room which has a dark stained oak Victorian-style settee and four matching chairs. The settee is not antique but for sure of superb quality and expensive looking. There is a matching time and foot-worn cushioned stool that fronts it. Dark stained oak end tables with lamps are at the side of each chair and at each end of the settee. Each table has an ashtray. On one table next to the settee there is a well-used, large ceramic ashtray.

Hunter stands in the room. Shakes his head in disappointment. *Same location as the dream. Thank God, no reception committee and not the same inside.* He audibly exhales. *Nothing. Not a single scrap of paper.* He mumbles softly, "Even the blotter on the desk by the door is new. Nothing here." He gazes around the room in disbelief. He sits on the settee. *Not that comfortable, but classy. There is a TV. Doesn't match anything in here.* He stares at it for several minutes, and the fireplace off to its side. *Sat in here, watching TV and smoking cigars without a care in the world.*

He sits for several more seconds. Puts his hands on his knees and pushes himself up, mumbling, "And leavin' bodies strewn all over the damn town, the world."

Including my mom and dad.

He glances around the room again, then as if his thoughts and eyes mesh at exactly the same moment, his gaze settles on the hearth. Something in the far back darkened corner of the fireplace catches his eye. A glint.

Hunter steps forward carefully, crouches down on his haunches, reaches in and picks the object out of the shadowy crevice. A tiny, infinitesimal gold ball. He warily loosens the tight wad with care, unraveling it deftly. A stunning wrapper. His eyebrows arch. It's a cigar band. Intact. He reads the label aloud. "Joya De Nicaragua."

I've heard of these. Expensive. Big time.

Then mumbles, "Okay, Joe. Goin' to give you a chance to do your stuff." And he leaves the flat as unobtrusively as he hoped he had arrived and entered. At the front door he checks the street. Left and right. Twice. Strolls back towards the hotel.

Two pairs of eyes watch from inside a shop. One whispers to the other as if the man they are watching could hear. "That's him. Has to be. I'd bet on it."

The other acknowledges in the same tone. "We are. Let's go. Be careful. He's good for someone new."

Back in his hotel room, Hunter calls Joe. After several preliminary exchanges about the trip to the flat and cigars, Hunter says, "Find out from this firm if they ship to customers in London or somewhere in Italy. My guess a Roberto something or other. Same name, two or more addresses, and perhaps a recent change. Or a name like that, with a recent change of address or addresses and cancellation of the others ... like this one, and the one outside of Pisa. And Joe, I'd bet he has a personal contact there. Like the owner or general manager."

Joe responds, "Will go one better. I have a man in Nicaragua now. I'll have him make an official call. No, by God, it'll be personal, influential ... and persuasive. And I'll get back to you, pronto."

Hunter acknowledges the response and tells Zachary where he is staying for the moment, reminding him it is different than the plan. .

Hunter then calls Dee. She picks up after one ring. Says, "Hello."

"Dee. Hunter. Listen carefully ..."

"Where the devil are you? I've been worried sick. Have you seen the papers or the TV? My God, even here you've made the news. That guy ..."

"Calm down. Yes, I have. Now listen. Check out of the hotel immediately and go find a clothing shop. Buy a couple of British looking outfits. Keep checking your six. Take a taxi, in fact take two or three, to the Cavendish Hotel. It's in Mayfair, 81 Jermyn Street. Corner of Duke and Jermyn. I'm already checked in using our Bravo ID. Go to the desk and ask them to ring your husband and have him come to the lobby to meet you. Or, if they'll give you a key, come up. But we want the desk folks to know and remember Ian and Sally Hansford. And while at the desk have them make dinner reservations for us at their restaurant. It's the Petrichor or something like that. Okay?"

"Got it. I suppose I understand all this mystery. How long have you been in town?"

"Got here on time. Thought I was being tailed." He fabricates his reactions. "Went through four cabs, two tube rides, one going and one coming back, and a bus and a short walk. Wasn't anything that I could spot. Had a feeling. Keep sensing eyes on me." The latter two comments not part of his fabrication, but an affirmation of real sensory input. "We're probably okay, but we, or I, now have some problems. Get a move on. We'll talk about the changes when you get here."

"Okay. See you shortly. Glad you're okay. God, I was scared to death."

"Not to worry. Now, move it."

"Anything in particular?"

Hunter pauses, then says, "You're still at it. Knock it off." He hangs up, and calls the hotel's Concierge obtaining a list of the best, the most prestigious cigar shops in the Regents Park, Mayfair area of town. Memorizes them as he does everything. Hangs up and waits for Dee to show up and for her to make a show of that.

Mary Kate sobs uncontrollably as she and Sean listen to her Uncle Mike tell them the bad news. Her father is missing. Reported kidnapped although Muldoon thinks something is astir or afoul. And that Patrick Shanahan was killed, no accident. Perhaps by the police but most likely by a man named Hunter Kerrigan who was a friend of the girl targeted. Sean holds Mary Kate firmly, consoling her while gritting his teeth and suppressing his own emotions. Tears, both of sorrow and anger, hate.

The O'Rourke lass can't stop and her uncle is not helping by prancing about the room, red-faced and swearing. Hurling threats aimed at the police, the Kerrigan man and whoever they are that took his brother. And also toward Muldoon for not killing everyone involved. Of course, that's not possible. Not yet. The news is fresh and unclear. Not absolute. A lot of speculation from the American press and that aspect jumped upon by some daily, scandal oriented rags here. But, no pictures of the Kerrigan man.

In due course, Sean is successful in calming Mary Kate and guides her to her room to rest, perhaps sleep. He tells her, "I'll be back later to see you. I need to see my brother and my mum."

Mary Kate sniffles, "Oh, Good Lord, your brother. I was thinking only of me self. I'm sorry, Sean. Oh Jesus, Joseph and Mary." Her sniffles start again and quickly turn into sobs as she mumbles, "Of course, me love, of course. Go."

"Will you be okay?"

"Yes, and no. I will be better when you return to me."

Sean leans over as she lies on the quilted spread on her bed. Brushes his lips upon hers and says, "Rest. Sleep. I'll be back shortly, and before I leave I'm goin' let your Uncle Mike know where we stand. I stand. Is it right by you?"

"Yes, Sean. 'Tis right by me."

He gets up from where he has been sitting next to her on the bed and allows her hand to slip from his as he turns and leaves the room.

In the living room, Sean says to the uncle, "Sir, it is perhaps the wrong time, but as I was going to ask Mary Kate's father, your dear brother, I'd be wantin' to court her, proper like. As a result I be asking you. But understand, first I must be with my brother and my mum. Then to see Muldoon. And then a duty to perform. Do you understand, sir, and do I have your permission?"

"Aye, I understand and ya do. Now get along. I will be seein' you and Muldoon me self at the pub." He nods. Offers his hand. They shake.

Sean nods and leaves. Once down the flight of stairs and onto the street, he begins to jog toward his home. Fists clenched, and his teeth not clinched only because of the need to breathe as he picks up the pace. However, the tears do flow now that he's alone.

Muldoon sits at his usual table in the far corner of the pub. His massive hand wrapped tightly around his pint. His other forged into a fist. His pit-bull son across from him. Silent, brooding and beet-faced. Veins throbbing with every angry heartbeat.

The father hisses, hatred dripping from every word like venom from an asp. "My source called again. The press is saying that this Kerrigan man chased and killed our own Paddy Shanahan. He says the police and Feds are saying nothing of much."

His son, Conor blurts, "Let me go and ..."

William F. Lee

"Shut your face, Conor. I'll be doin' the talkin' and thinkin' here. Like I was sayin' ..."

"Bellowing be more like it."

Muldoon, the Irish father in him, and the PIRA leader as well, backhands his son across the face. Conor rocks back in his chair, tipping over his pint on the table. The empty pewter mug roles off the table and rattles on the floor.

"I said shut your chops, and I mean just that, lad. Now then, as I was sayin', they found Mickey's body floating in the bay. In that filthy bay in that far away city. Damn. DAMN. There will be blood let for this, I swear on all the Saints."

Conor is quiet, having been severely admonished. He recovers his mug but has no ale to cool his overheated radiator.

Both turn and look at the same time towards the commotion at the door of the pub.

The Shanahan brothers have arrived, along with Mike O'Rourke, and are stalking toward the table like hungry lions on the hunt.

CHAPTER 15

*"Flank your adversary when possible
and protect yours.
Don't drop your guard."*
Two gunfighters' rules

Rocco says, "Sweetheart, go soak in the tub and relax. I have another call to make. Then we will go out and splash some paint on this town. Show off another of your new outfits. We will have to leave tomorrow. The boss says."

"Oh, Rocco, my love. I will do as you ask. But, I could live here forever." She raises her eyebrows, and smiles. "But only with you." She pushes herself off the bed and saunters, naked, to the bathroom. She dips her head and rotates it, eyes focused on Rocco's, and says, "Only with you. But, do what you must. I will soak until you call me," then after another two steps, again turns her head, peeks over her shoulder and smiles, "or until you come join me." She gives Rocco an inviting waggle of her hips, closes the bathroom door behind her.

He stares at the closed door. Erotic visions racing across his mind. Then, when he hears the water running, it rinses him back to reality. He moves to the phone and calls an associate in Palermo telling him where this woman, Chiarin Romeo Russo, lives. Rocco informs his friend what he must know and instructs it done by this evening. His confederate on the other end of the line groans, and mumbles, complaining. Rocco interrupts the whining, "This is not a request. This is an order. Do it." Then in a warmer tone, Rocco closes by telling him not to call him, that he will call back this evening. Then adds, "You will be well rewarded, my friend. *Grazie.*"

When he finishes the call the water is no longer running. He can only hear Adrianna singing an aria from Puccini's, *La Boheme.* Her voice is strong and good. But, as in everything, there is a gap between good and professional. However, Rocco believes she is capturing Mimi's plight.

He strolls out onto the balcony. Dwells a moment or two on what his boss, Roberto Catalano, might be up to, then dismisses the thought. *I do what I'm told and what I must. Life is good for me. Not so for Bruno. He didn't listen.*

Then says aloud, "A soak will be good in the bath oils, and Adrianna will make it even better."

Rocco knows the time in the bath will make him forget Pisces, but not for long. But for the moment to be sure.

Dee arrives at The Cavendish and makes more of a splash than the front desk clerks bargain for, and they react by ensuring the dinner reservation and presenting her with a key to her husband's room. Anything to rid themselves of the "lady". They maintain their British reserve for longer than most, but the indignant Sally Hansford has gotten the best of their English steadfastness. When Dee, Sally to them, leaves the desk for the elevator, one clerk whispers to the other, "Poor Mr. Hansford. Seems like such a nice chap. A gentleman he is."

The other replies, "She's a ruddy bitch."

Once at the room, Sally Hansford inserts the key, unlocks the door and pushes it open. She picks up her briefcase in her right hand. Enters the room with her clothing bag slung over her left shoulder, bulky and heavier from her shopping trip. She feigns staggering under the load. Finds Hunter, or her husband for the moment, Ian, slouched in a chair next to the phone offering no help.

He smiles, and carrying a grin says, "Ah, Lady Sally. Cheers. Rest your tush. Put down your bag and briefcase before you wilt. And relax your weary British bones."

"Hunter, you ..."

"Ta, ta. It's Ian, dear. Ian Hansford from Manchester. You need to remember that. Gad, we've been together for years. I take it this Hunter chap is your lover, or some such understanding?"

"You wish, or better, we can start that arrangement here."

"I knew it the moment I said it. My mistake. Again, not a chance. Now then, put things up. Sit. Would you care to have something sent up, or will water do?"

"Water's fine. Give me a minute or two." Sally Hansford goes about emptying the outfits out of the bag and hangs them in the closet. Pushes his one suit, one shirt and slacks to the side, then kicks off her shoes and takes the briefcase into the bathroom. Within minutes she's back, a bit refreshed but still with a crabby look on her face. Her opening remark is a clear indication of her frame of mind.

"Tell me again why we're here, and not where we were supposed to be."

Hunter does. Same story about the tail.

"Bull-pucky. If you're going to stick to that, fine. Okay. Here's one for you." She plants her hands on her hips and steps directly in front of Hunter. "Tell me what the hell my sister was doing visiting you at the guest house." She pauses, staring at him waiting for an answer. When one doesn't come immediately, she snaps, "Well?" Folds her arms beneath her heaving breasts. "This ought to be good."

"Well, I was hoping you weren't aware of that. Embarrassing but innocent. At least on my part."

"I don't care what's embarrassing and what's not. I doubt innocence on either part." She keeps her arms as is but now begins to rock back and forth. "What was she doing there? Better yet what were the two of you doing there?"

Hunter says, "Dee, she came to make a pass at me. I wasn't having any of that and calmed her down and explained it had nothing to do with her. That I was on a job and didn't have time nor the longing to get involved. Same as I told you. It's no different. So, get over whatever is buggin' you. Besides, if you knew she was there, you knew she wasn't in the place long enough for anything to happen anyway."

Dee, now having found a chair, shifts uneasily in the seat. She takes a long, slow drink of the iced water, glaring at Hunter over the top of the glass. Finished, she places the glass down wittingly on an adjacent table. Exhales audibly and says, "Well, okay. I suppose you're right. I mean about the length of time." She pauses, "But you give me twenty minutes alone with you in any room, much less a bedroom, something will happen." She looks intently at Hunter. "You're not that ... what was the word, innocent." She stands, then immediately plops back down in the chair. Tilts her head to one side. "Do you have an interest in her?"

"No. Nor you. How many times do I have to tell you? This is business. A damn nasty business. You should know. If I hear this subject from you again, or anything close to it, I'm sendin' your butt back. And remember that, because we will be in this room alone, together, and perhaps others before this is over." He stands, then says, "Now let's talk about what we need to do. In London."

"Fair enough. What?"

He tells her that they will check out Pisces' former flat, and also talk to the other tenants if possible. And to the leasing manager if he's about. He tells her the next step will depend on what, if anything they find. If nothing, he explains they will eat dinner here, or leave and go elsewhere but will make enough of a scene to be noticed and remembered. Lady Hansford and her timid English husband. Then says, "Later you make arrangements for us to depart for Pisa, via Geneva and Rome."

Dee nods. "Is that it?"

"Yep."

They finish their water and leave together after each makes a quick wardrobe change. One in the bedroom, one in the loo. A couple, visiting London. The English gentleman and the proper bitch, accents included.

Agent Ryder, sits on the edge of his desk, glances at Detective Bradovich, then stands and walks behind his desk. Takes his habitual warm and friendly stance by thrusting his hands into both pockets, back to the window that overlooks downtown San Diego with the bay in the background. "I've been ordered to conduct this press conference and level with these folks. More or less level. Facts as we know them. Your people okay with that, Gene?"

"Yep. I'm not going to add anything. Stickin' to the same story, if asked, that you guys are running the show. We're helping where we can." Bradovich scoffs, "It appears that we didn't do such a bang-up job of that." He gives a short kick in space, "Cripes, a perp being kidnapped from a patrol car." He sighs. "Sorry."

"Okay. Let me throw on my coat and we'll face the vultures. Let them pick at our bones."

"Your bones." Bradovich laughs.

Ryder grins, "Yeah, my bones. But after my bosses finished with me earlier there isn't much left."

The press conference doesn't go well. Agent Ryder makes an announcement and answers only two questions, one reluctantly, and then he simply leaves. Before going he told the gathering that a woman was murdered, identity known but being withheld until next of kin can be notified. The assailant was a Patrick Shanahan, a visitor from Ireland. He placed a bomb in the woman's car and detonated it in front of the lady's boyfriend's home. Shanahan was chased by the lady's boyfriend but not caught. Running from the scene and from the boyfriend, Patrick Shanahan jumped or fell over the edge of the ravine and tumbled to his death. His body is being retained at the city morgue until an autopsy is completed and all forensic evidence collected. Later that same day, the lady's boyfriend was paid a visit by a Mr. Mickey O'Rourke, an Irishman, now a U.S. citizen, living in Boston and ostensibly a friend of Shanahan. O'Rourke was arrested for breaking and entering, and while en route to this office was kidnapped by two armed men. The car involved has been found and impounded. O'Rourke's body was found in the bay hours later, close to the ferry landing. The kidnappers have not been identified, and consequently not found. The investigation is ongoing.

At the end, Agent Ryder is asked if the Irish authorities have been notified. He answers, "They have." Then he is

William F. Lee

asked for the boyfriend's name. He replies, "A Mr. Hunter Kerrigan. A former Marine and now an unpublished author, or more accurately, a writer." He holds up both hands, announces, "That's all for today. Thank you." And he turns and gets on the waiting elevator that will take him to his office and a scheduled meeting with his staff.

The abrupt departure after only two questions causes a rash of shouting and other commotion. The local media and press begin shouting questions, then complaints. No one sees Detective Bradovich slip away. Not to his office. There would be no sanctity there. Knowing that and with thoughts of his Marine buddy on his mind, the detective slips behind the wheel of his car and drives. Nowhere in particular at first. Then after a few blocks he swerves onto Pacific Coast Highway and heads for the Marine Recruit Depot. And the Officers Club to have a drink in solitude, or better yet with a few fighting hole buddies.

Back in his office, SAC Ryder while conducting a meeting with his agent force, says to the group, "You know, those kidnappers were way too good. Knew too much. Experts at the craft as well as leaving not a trace of evidence. Anywhere. Car. Body. The clothes are missing. We got zip. Nothing."

The group nods in agreement. A few mumbled comments are uttered. Then Ryder says, "Except, however vague the descriptions are, something is nagging at me. One of the artist's sketches. The nose?" He pauses. "Can't get a handle on it."

He slaps his hands together, says, "Okay, let's get to work and go through this again. Piece by piece. Second by second ..."

"Nose by nose," interrupts one of his agents.

"Yeah, and go to all those dank, dark," he pauses, "that's it!"

"What?"

"Later. You gents go. I have a call to make."

Rocco telephones his source. The information on the woman, Chiarin Romero Russo, is straight forward. His man tells him that the lady is a widow. A wealthy one at that. Her husband died two years ago. She still runs the remaining two shops, both of which are up for sale. One near closing and the other has an offer. She is off-the-page gorgeous, mid-forties, and an art enthusiast. She loves this region but prefers a different location. A cleaner city. She is looking to move and in fact visited a town of interest lately. Her home is also for sale. She has no lovers but does have one suitor, a prominent politician in the city. Except he is married and the rumors are that is a problem with the lady. Rocco asks, "How wealthy?"

The voice on the phone replies, "Net worth, several million. These last sales will be more than supplemental aide."

"Is she truly beautiful, or just so for her age?"

"Stunning, for any age. Tall, slender, nicea body. Dark hair and eyes. Looksa like a model. Momma mia, if my wife looka like her I would not waste my time on the phone with you in the evenings. I woulda be home."

Rocco laughs, then says, "*Grazie. Buono sera.*"

After hanging up, Rocco pauses for a few seconds with his hand on the receiver as it rests in the cradle. Takes in a breath, then dials his boss, Signore Roberto Catalano. When Pisces answers on the first ring with an impatient tone of voice, Rocco feels a pinch in the pit of his stomach. Nonetheless, he passes on all the information about the Russo lady. Answers a few questions. The conversation has the tone of a business transaction. But then, it is. Near the end, Pisces asks, "When can I expect Rizzo out of my life?"

"As soon as I find him. Tomorrow or the next day. I've been informed that no one has seen him but his apartment is still rented. He's not in it. Hasn't been there since ... since the accident, and the landlord has three months advance in his hand. So, I guess he intends to return when he thinks things have cooled down."

"Don't get informed. Get him. I want him cooled down. Cold. I don't want him running loose. Now go fuck your lady and go kill Rizzo. Quickly. Do you understand?"

"Yes, sir, bossa. Yes."

"Well, good. We're on the same track as usual. That's why we're so good together. Now then, you have a nice evening. I'll be leaving on the *Sorridenta* for several days." Click.

Rocco stares at the phone. Mutters, "Nothing changes ... except the women, and the villas." Slams the phone back in the cradle and returns to the bedroom to finish dressing for the evening, muttering along the way, "but it is to be hoped for the last time."

Adrianna is dressed, in an all white slacks and jacket outfit. With one button too many undone in the front of the jacket, it displays her bountiful cleavage. The snow white of her pants suit shows off her complexion, now darkened by the sun here in Rapallo. She says to Rocco, "Pleasea hurry. You have given me an insatiable appetite."

His frown is replaced with a wide grin, "For what? Dinner or me?"

"Both. Dinner first to satisfy one. Dessert to tease the other. And a hastened walk back here to warm me for my playtime. I will have all there is to have this evening." She pauses, then, "The sound of the telephone slamming tells me we are leaving in the morning. So I must make the most of this evening. Yes?"

"Yes. I have work to do."

"And?"

"We will see. Possibly I will have to leave Pisa."

"Well, then, let us make the most of this evening. It may be the last."

Rocco, who has finished dressing, puts his arms around Adrianna and says, "Don't say that." And they leave their suite for another evening of dining on the hotel's patio overlooking this tranquil town and sea.

Marnee and Reis will be overlooking as well. At least the on dining. They will not be watching the seascape.

Roberto Catalano and Gina Pappalardo stand snuggled together at the helm as he guides the *Sorridenta* clear of the harbor and out to sea under the watchful eye of the craft's crew chief. Gina is breathtaking on the flying bridge with her hair blowing and twisting in the incoming sea breeze. She asks, "Roberto, darling. Will we be safe going out so far this evening? "

Pisces squeezes her strongly around the waist. "Of course, love. I'm an expert seaman, but the crew chief has his eye on things and he and the crew will be taking over momentarily. Then I can spend all my time on you."

She giggles, "On me?"

"Well, most of the time. We will cruise. Visit ports. Eat wonderful fresh fish that I will catch. And we will make love whenever and wherever the urge overpowers us, and we'll do it to the rise and fall of the swells. To the rhythm of the sea. And your energetic hips."

"You make it sound so wonderful, Roberto. I am a lucky woman. But what of the crew? Won't they ..."

"No. They will be out of sight and minding their business. It is wonderful, or will be."

She sighs, "And how long is ... will it be?"

"Forever."

Gina laughs, tilts her head, "And when is forever?"

"When it ends."

Gina stands motionless, except for the gentle rise and fall of the *Sorridenta*. After a few moments she mutters, "When it ends. That doesn't sound so romantic."

Roberto stiffens slightly, but not enough to be noticed by Gina. He responds in a warm, loving tone, "It is both romantic and poetic." Pulls her close and whispers, "At least I mean it to be." Kisses her on the neck, then nuzzles his face in her blowing hair. Then in full voice, "How 'bout we go below and have an apricot brandy or and two." He pauses, "We will sip as we slip out to sea. How's that for romantic if not poetic?"

"Bravo, Roberto. Bravo," and she grasps his arm nudging him on the way.

He gently pulls free, moves close to Gina. Kisses her tenderly and whispers, "You go ahead. I'll be down in a few minutes. I need to have a few words with our helmsman here. Go. Pour the brandy and get comfortable."

She returns his gentle kiss, smiles and slithers away toward the ladder way and salon below.

Pisces' eyes follow her, or more readily her hips. Then he motions his crew chief to him. Says, "We're past the point but take a little more northward, then come hard a port and parallel the coast."

The man answers, "Yessa, sir. We got it, sir."

Pisces nods, then checks the barometer. All is fine. Tunes the radio to a weather channel. Listens. Is fine as expected. He claps his hands together, rubbing them and sternly orders, "I want to be alone. Keep the crew out of sight and taking care of business. Tell the chef I will let him know when I want dinner." He strides away, not waiting for an affirmation for there is no otherwise response to a Pisces' wish, order.

At the ladder way he pauses.

All is well and will be better soon. I'll have another artist in the family.

He strolls down to the salon.

CHAPTER 16
"Only hits count. The only thing worse than a miss is a slow miss."

A special gunfighter's rule

Hunter and Dee, as Ian and Sally Hansford, hike to Pisces lease property on Cork Street. As Hunter had done before, both now observe the flats for a good thirty minutes. Hunter enters the vestibule of the flat as he did earlier in the day. This time he waits before picking the lock to the inside door as Dee continues the vigil from across the street. She sees nothing stirring as a result of Hunter's movement and entry. After a final glimpse about, she follows him.

Hunter whispers, "See anything?"
"No."
"What about the windows in the other flats? Anything odd?"
"Nope. People doing what people do, move about."
"Okay, let's go inside. No security system out here and nothing out of the norm with the door." Again he picks the lock and they both enter the flat. Hunter acts as if it is the first time here and checks for security measures inside and is careful of his footfalls. He warns Dee to stay on the carpets and throw-rugs. Dee nods and does as instructed.

After both search the flat and find nothing except a well-furnished apartment for lease, Dee whispers, "Zilch, except the smell of cigarette smoke. Is strong, especially here in the living room."

"Yeah, the guy must have been a chain smoker." Hunter shakes his head and whispers, "I hate the smell of nicotine. We'll have to take a shower when we get back to get rid of it."

"Together?"
"Dammit, Dee," he hisses.
She smiles, shrugs her shoulders. They leave as quietly as they came in.

As it appeared from the outside, the other three flats are occupied. Hunter and Dee ring each flat. They talk to the occupants, one is the property manager. He is having tea when they arrive. The others are preparing to do the same when Dee and Hunter ring. Afternoon tea is truly more than a ritual here, conceivably a sacrament. At the least a tradition and as steeped as the Dover Cliffs. Dee and Hunter get no information of value from this group, to include no invitation to tea. None have ever seen the man in Flat One. The Property Manager is more talkative than the others, but still curt. He informs them early on, "I'm only the PM. Didn't know the chap. Receive my check for my labor every month and happy for it. He pays me handsomely to mind the flats and to mind me own business. I do that."

Hunter asks, "From whom?"

"Meaning what."

"Who pays you?"

"The bank."

"Can I see a stub, or a deposit slip? Something?"

The PM hesitates, then says, "Are you and the lady with Scotland Yard?"

"No."

"Then who?"

"Private investigators."

The PM pauses again, then says, "My. I say. Well, sir, and madam, you will have to bring the gentlemen from The Yard with a warrant or something. I only manage the property and do not have a ghost of an idea about the person of whom you ask. Anything else, sir? Madam?"

"No. Guess not," Hunter moans, then adds, "Anything more you can tell us?"

"It is for lease. Interested?"

"Not really."

The gentleman smiles, nods his head toward the door, and extends his hand in that direction as well. "Pleasure. Have an agreeable day. What's left of it. I'll be back to me tea. Cheers."

Hunter and Dee half-smile and leave. She murmurs, "Madam, my ass." Glances over her shoulder, hisses, "Ta,

Ta, arsehole." Hunter grasps her elbow and hurries Dee along.

Once outside they look about, see nothing suspicious and move down the block to Brewster, then quickly to Old Bond Street. Hunter hails a passing taxi. Asks to be taken to St. Martin's Theatre. There they stride energetically several blocks to the tube station at Covent Gardens. Take the underground back to Green Street and stroll separately the four or five blocks to Jermyn and The Cavendish Hotel where they join forces again having not spotted anyone tailing them. As they amble through the hotel's lobby, Hunter whispers, "My paddy instincts tell me eyes are on us."

Inside their room Hunter immediately takes what he needs to the loo, showers and dresses. When finished he tells Dee that while she's getting ready, he's heading to the lobby for a drink and will wait for her in the bar. She agrees, adding, "Have mine ready, please."

Hunter nods and leaves, each have unwittingly satisfied a need of the other. Such is deceit. It is what it is.

He takes the fire stairs to the bottom floor, and leaves through a back entrance into the mew and hurries to the nearest of two cigar shops in the Regents Park area. The first yields nothing. At the second he finds that a Robert Camack of Cork Street has been ordering special cigars for years. The brand name, *Joya De Nicaragua,* in particular the *Antano.* The wrapper is identical to the one Hunter found in the hearth at the flat. Several questions provide little else of value except being shown a receipt signed by Camack from the last order in June of this year. The owner has no other addresses nor forwarding information. Hunter rushes back to the hotel. Selects a seat at the open-end of the bar, orders two scotches, neat, and sits surveying the lobby.

He spots a set of eyes and is relieved to some extent knowing his paddy instincts are alive and well. The man is reading a newspaper, legs crossed, ankle over knee, and occasionally turning a page with a glance around the lobby along with a fleeting peek at Hunter.

Another sip of the scotch and Hunter detects a second set of eyes. These entering the hotel. The woman glances quickly at the first set of eyes then moves to the far corner of this ornate lobby. She sits. Orders. Minutes later a pot of tea, cup with saucer, and a small plate of powdered sugared sweets are served by a proper looking uniformed gent.

Hunter sips his scotch, catches the eye of the woman and nods with a contemptuous smile. Turns his head quickly and holds the eye of the young man reading the paper. Nods. Then glances back to the woman.

Black hair, dark eyes, tan complexion. Fine-looking honey. Mid-thirties. He notes her long legs, crossed ladylike with a foot bouncing nervously.

Their eyes meet again over Hunter's glass as he takes another sip of scotch. He tips his glass. *Israeli's. The Stassi don't have any woman that sexy. If they did it would be a Warm War.*

As soon as Hunter leaves, Dee streaks to the room door, steals a look out the door peep hole, then presses her ear to the door. Opens the door and peeks out into the hallway. Confident he's gone, she scurries to the telephone, dials a number, and drums her fingers on the small desk top, waiting. Hears the ring. And a second time. A third, then.

"Hello."

After a momentary pause she says, "It's me. We've changed hotels. We're at The Cavendish St. James, I believe it's called. "

"Why? Is he suspicious of something?"

"Don't know. Although he believes he's being followed."

The voice on the other end says, "He is."

Dee pauses. Then, "That means me as well."

"Yes, but they will stick to him. Or if they lose him for some reason, follow you back to him. Either way, we win."

Dee hesitates, "Why am I here?" Then, "Never mind. We went to the flat. Nothing. We're leaving tomorrow for Geneva, then Pisa via Rome. At least that's the plan."

"Good, okay. Listen, this is a quick update. O'Rourke is dead. Shanahan is dead. No one knows who. Well, I

know, of course. And people who need to know, will know. The Irish will be looking for Kerrigan 'jolly' soon."
"He's not using that name."
"What name now?"
"Hansford."
"Okay. Sure, that figures. Anyway, I'm pretty sure I know all the ID's he'll use and I'll get them known. He won't use any twice that's for sure. But, keep me informed each time he changes nonetheless. Let me know ahead of time if you can. And be careful."
"I will. Are you okay?"
"Fine." A pause, then in a hushed tone, "Cover your pretty ass."
She too pauses, then also whispers as if someone is listening, "I wish you would."
There is no sound for several seconds, then, "I will, soon." Click

Dee stands holding the receiver. After a few seconds she places it back in its cradle. Saunters to the closet. Disrobes deliberately. Naked as she steps out of her panties, she gazes at herself in the full length closet door mirror and mutters, "How could anyone not want this?" Turns, takes another look over her shoulder at her butt, whispers, "Nice. Still tight," and wiggles to the loo to prepare the bitch, Lady Sally Hansford, for the staff of the restaurant.

After an obligatory amount of time for a proper Lady to prime, Sally Hansford arrives at the lobby bar to collect her drink and husband, Ian, exactly in that order. After finishing the drinks Ian and Sally Hansford drift to the hotel's restaurant under the watchful yet obviously uncomfortable eyes of the Israeli couple, now together, sipping tea. Dee and Hunter wait to be seated, and order two more scotches after another short delay. When the drinks arrive after a bit of a time lag, Lady Hansford complains of the service. Too long to be seated; too long to take the order; and too long to wait. She makes a scene, her voice becoming more shrill with each complaint. For her finale she takes the napkin from her lap and slings it at the frustrated and defenseless waiter. She stands, hands on hips, toe tapping, glaring at Ian. He shrugs, fumbles with his pocket and places the exact amount between the untouched drinks under the lady's watchful eye. Sally Hansford, in a huff, prances out, pleased with herself. Ian glances at her, and as he steps away he drops two one-hundred pound notes on the table. He looks about and trails meekly behind his wife.

The waiter mumbles, "Ruddy bitch." and after a darting glance around, furtively pockets the bills.

Outside, Hunter turns to the doorman; however, Dee is already off the curb and on the street. He hastens to the curb and hails a taxi for the two of them. Inside, he gives the cabbie the only direction he needs, "Annabel's." It's a fashionable and popular restaurant, bar and hangout in Berkeley Square. After several minutes, Hunter is not astounded to see they have a tail. In fact, two. Working in singles and no doubt the two from the lobby. *Israelis can be good but these two might get momentarily enamored with Annabel's and get careless again.*

Hunter laughs softly at his thoughts.

Dee says, "What?"

"We're being followed. Don't look back now or when we get there. Just hang on my arm and drool."

"I'm not allowed to drool."

"Figuratively you do around me all the time."

She hisses softly thus the cabbie can't hear. "You're an egotistical bastard."

"Play nice."

They arrive at Annabel's on Berkeley Square. As soon as they enter, Hunter whispers to the hostess and presses a wad of cash into her hand. He whispers in her ear again. She smiles. Gives Hunter's hand a playful squeeze and leads them through the crowded room, past the loos and to a side entrance. Hunter whispers to her again, kisses her on the cheek. Her smile is warmer and returns the peck on the cheek and says, "Anytime, killer."

Dee scowls at the woman but says nothing.

Hunter and Dee hasten along Hill Street. He whistles down a passing taxi. Hunter directs this one to Cecconis, a restaurant in the Mayfair District. It's a place to see, and be seen, by those in the rarefied social atmosphere of the city. Those not stratospheric go unnoticed although in this venue it's possible to be thought as somebody. One would think it's not a place to hide, but then again, it is. People on the run would more likely adorn a pub stool.

At a table inside sipping what he prefers, an apricot brandy, Hunter is sure the tail has been waggled free. He is also positive they'll encounter them again. Most likely at The Cavendish which prompts Hunter to devise an alternate plan.

Dee is nursing another scotch, neat, having taken to the Lady's taste, when Hunter asks, "Sally, my darling. Do you have all your ID's in your purse?"

"Yes, why?"

"Good. We'll finish these and leave."

Rocco and Adrianna enjoy a serene evening before ordering. They sip more than one glass of wine on the hotel's restaurant patio that overlooks Rapallo and the sea beyond. They finally order and take pleasure in a Caesar Salad made at tableside, then both have freshly caught Alletterato, Bonita for dinner, with a mixture of fresh sautéed vegetables and buttered pasta. When the meal is over he sips brandy and she Limoncello until darkness intimidates this seaside resort town. Rocco decides to forego the walk to and from the Bar Pasticerrcia Salza for their dessert. Adrianna doesn't resist. She is anxious for more love-making. An art form for her, and besides she is aware of Rocco's growing restlessness.

Rocco is anxious to return to the room. For the first time he has become aware of a particular young couple in the restaurant, pretending to dote on one another but not able to act as if watching Rocco and his lady without pretext.

He and Adrianna nonchalantly leave the restaurant but stride urgently to their room. At the door, he tells her to go inside, pack everything. His and hers. Adds, "Don't ask me any questions. Do it, now. And, wait here. Make no calls. I will be back."

Adrianna nods. She is a woman in love, but not a fool. She has known Rocco a long time and is aware of his menacing circle of friends. Neither he nor his associates are keen on questions.

Rocco takes the elevator to the lobby. Sits at the bar, orders a brandy, lights and smokes a cigar which the barkeep offers only to special guests of the hotel. He has another drink, pays the tab leaving the man a generous tip, and strolls outside. He stands beneath the broad awning over the entrance. More a canopy. He inhales the fresh sea air feigning to relax and benefit from the joy of a typical Rapallo evening in August. He draws on his cigar, watches the smoke twirl and dissipate quickly while he's rocking back and forth on his heels. Drops the half-smoked butt, crushes it with his foot. He takes a step to the side and speaks to the valet who listens intently, nodding his head. It is an intense conversation. Rocco presses money into the valet's palm, then strides to the side of the hotel. At the corner of the building he darts into the now pitch-black, cobblestone alleyway. Ducks into a shadowed architectural crevice and waits for his prey as still and quiet as a leopard in tall grass.

The Israeli, Reis, opts to follow Rocco. He tells Marnee to remain behind but move to a corner of the lobby where she can see both the entrance and the elevators.

Marnee complains, "We should stay together. Act as a team. Not separate. Remember our rule."

"Something is up. You watch for her. I will follow him." Reis adds, "And I'm not unarmed".

She stares at Reis. *And I am a Jewish girl.* She says instead, "And?"

"He is not leaving but is up to something. Either way, he won't leave her behind but she is involved in some manner."

"I still think I should go with you. Work in tandem."

"No."

"It will be as you say. You are the leader."

Marnee retreats further into the lobby, finds a corner and attempts to blend with a tall billowing potted plant.

Reis watches the front entrance but able only to see the left shoulder and arm of Rocco. When he sees Rocco move off, Reis waits for several moments and strolls outside, feigning wanting a breath of fresh air. He stops under the canopy. Not seeing Rocco, he inches forward in the only direction Rocco could have gone. Toward the alley. Looks, sees nothing. Glances around at other options. There are none. The Israeli steps into the alley, unfastens his jacket button. Reaches back and checks his weapon in the back waist of his trousers. He carefully jiggles the Walther. It's awkward with its silencer on, but finds no tangles. Ensures the safety is off.

After several steps, still not seeing anything other than tar-like blackness and yet darker shadows, he continues to creep deeper into the alley. He eases his weapon from his waist. Not wanting to frighten anyone should a worker suddenly appear in the alley, he holds the weapon in one hand, tightly alongside of this leg.

He continues to inch along. *Should have brought a Jewish girl.*

Rocco reaches out from the shadowed crevice in the wall, hand over Reis' mouth, snatches and spins Reis into the building's side. Reis' nose splatters as it hits the coarse surface of the stone wall. The Walther drops from his hand. Rocco slams the Israeli's face into the wall again and again. The third time Reis crumbles to the alleyway cobblestones. Rocco stoops down and grabs the Walther and fires. *Pfsssst. Pfsssst.* Reis' face explodes as the rounds exit. Bone, blood and flesh splatters mix with the grit and grime of the unattended passage.

Rocco has a quick look up and down the alley. He tucks the pistol in his waist. Drags the Israeli by the ankles to a large trash bin thirty feet deeper into the alley. Picks him up and shoves him over the edge of the bin. Climbs up and in himself, scoops hands and armfuls of trash over the body. He climbs out, wiping his jacket and suit trousers as tidy as he can and then wipes the weapon clean with his handkerchief. Looks about again, then takes several paces and drops the Walther down a drainage grating and dashes to the back end of the alley and around the corner of the building. Strips off his suit coat. Removes everything from the pockets and rips off the two labels. Jams the labels, a pen and the dinner receipt in his trouser pocket. He stuffs the jacket in a trash can, again digging and piling the contents on top of his deposit.

Returns the lid and hastens to the hotel through a back entrance and up the fire stairwell to his room.

He slips inside. Asks, "Ready?"

Adrianna responds with a nervous, "Yes."

"Good. Wait." He rushes to the phone and calls the front desk and has his bill quietly readied and brought to his suite.

A few minutes after the clerk has taken full payment and a sizable tip, Rocco and Adrianna go downstairs using the fire exit and rear entrance. They step outside and into their waiting car. They leave hurriedly but with less enthusiasm than when arriving, passing the trash can with Rocco's coat as they depart. Lumbering behind them is the huge sanitation truck, here to empty the trash can and the dumpster.

Inside, Marnee, nervous beyond what her patience can bear and better sense dictates, checks her weapon in her waistline and steps toward the lobby entrance.

Where the hell is Reis?

CHAPTER 17

*"Train like you plan to fight.
Hard and dirty."*
A gunfighter's rule

Marnee had seen Reis go outside and disappear into the shadows beyond the entrance. Laid-back in manner yet wary, she steps outside. Surveys her surroundings. Sees no one other than the valet coming back to his curbside stand. Using Italian, Marnee asks if he's seen the two gentlemen that were outside several moments ago. The valet answers saying that he has been on a break and didn't see anyone. Adding, as if an excuse for his being away, "No business this timea night. Makea no difference. People come and go. I don'ta remember no one."

Vexed and disgruntled, Marnee comes back inside to the front desk and asks the night clerk if the DeStefano couple has checked out. The clerk shrugs and says no without checking.

Marnee steps away and out of sight of the desk clerk. Reaches inside her pant suit jacket and fingers her weapon in the waistband of her slacks. She stalks outside, gazes around and sees nothing but the silent and dimly lit streets surrounding the hotel. She arbitrarily chooses to go to her left. Eases a half-block up the street. Stands, hand inside her jacket at the back. Compressed against a wall.

Sees nothing.
Hears nothing.

She grimaces edgily. Drops to a crouch and calls out to Reis in a loud whisper. Nothing. Moves sideward several steps. Tries again slightly louder. Same result.

Stands, slides her hand from inside the jacket and returns to the front of the hotel staying close to the buildings. She sees a different young man at the valet stand. Approaches him and asks him the same question with little conviction. The answer is an abrupt no but with a quiver in his voice and on-edge eyes. She moves closer to the young man and asks again. Marnee is a unique beauty. Midnight dark eyes, like bottomless inkwells and expressionless at times as this, like a shark. Her nose is a prominent feature along with thick lips and wide mouth. Uncommonly big for her face, but in a mysterious way, ravenously attractive. Sexy, alluring, but not model-like. A look and personality that suck a man in and make all other women look common. The valet sees only the shark in her. He remits a shaky, frightened, "No."

"Another, 'no'?" Marnee takes two lightning-quick steps and gets into the boy's face. Snarls, "Listen you little shit, there were two men out here. Where did they go?"

The valet responds defiantly, "I told you. I saw no one." His misjudged bravado gaining strength, he shouts, "I don't know what you're talking about, bitch."

"Bitch?" Marnee slaps him in the face. Twice. Quick. Palm, then backhand.

The young man staggers a step back, hands belatedly raise in self-defense. Then he draws back his fist. Marnee snatches his wrist, twists his arm behind his back, spins him around, and sweep kicks his feet from beneath him. The valet lands face down, half on the cement of the entrance and half on the antiquated cobblestone surface of the street. Nose bleeding and stunned.

With her hand still on his wrist now bent behind his back at a forty-five degree angle, and a knee in the small of his back, Marnee growls, "Where did they go?"

The valet grunts and points with his free arm towards the alley. She lifts her knee from his back, releases his wrist and stands. He begins to push himself up aggressively, spewing internationally understood obscenities. Marnee stomps her foot in the back of his head, smashing his face to the concrete again. Snarls, "Remember, you tripped and fell." She rolls him over onto his back and at the same time snatches her switch blade from her jacket pocket. "Anything else and I will come back and slice you up like a salami." She grabs his tie and with a flick of her wrist slices it off beneath the knot. Drops the loose end on his chest and steps away. The young man, bleeding from his nose and mouth, eyes looking like glass implants, remains as still as a toppled statue as Marnee departs toward the alley.

Inside the alley she inches along, her Walther in both hands. Arms stretched-out in front forming a narrow triangle. She scans with her body, eyes and weapon as one. The alley is as black as a witches heart, and Marnee's vibes are all in F Sharp. She inches past the dumpster.

Stops. Surveys her immediate sphere of vision. *Messy like most trash areas.*

Listens. *Talk to me, Reis.*

She calls out his name in a coarse whisper. "Reis." Again, nothing.

Suddenly something whooshes past, brushing her shoulder. She turns and jumps backward, staggering into a building wall opposite the dumpster. Her Walther swings to the target.

Damn cat.

The dumpster cat scats down the alley. Marnee sees and hears nothing else. *Scared the pee out of me.* She inches to the far wall of the alley, inching along, staring to the end. Nothing.

Stands motionless for a few moments, calls out in the hoarse whisper again. "Reis." Pauses. "Reis." Nothing, just the cat turning the corner at the end of the alley, tail in the air.

She returns to the front of the hotel. The valet jumps aside, one hand raised in self-defense, the other fumbling with a handkerchief trying to curtail the dribbles of blood from his nose. Since he is not being attended by anyone, Marnee assumes he got her message. Nonetheless she takes a quick step in his direction, then slides her weapon back under her jacket and into her waistline. Marnee feigns a move toward him. The young man leaps behind the valet stand. She stares at him menacingly, then turns and leaves.

Inside the hotel, Marnee hastily checks the lounge area and the bar. Not a soul other than the barkeep sitting on a stool at the far end reading a book. She goes to a house phone near the front desk and calls her room. No answer.

Knowing the DeStefano's room number, she dials that number. It rings to pointlessness.

Marnee stalks along the front desk, drumming her fingers on the counter as she slides to the end where there is a flip-top entrance. She glances around the lobby. It's empty. She ducks under the counter and hisses at the young night clerk, motioning him to come to the end.

The young man approaches not cautiously, but busily, motioning with his hands for Marnee to leave. To get out from behind his counter, his space. When he arrives, he points and waggles his finger at Marnee as a prelude to his scolding. She snatches his wrist, jerks and spins him around and into an alcove inside "his space" and out of sight of the lobby. His body slams into the wall, his intended words still in his throat. Marnee spins him around facing her and grasps his personals in her hand and squeezes, clamp-like, and pins him into a corner in this closed niche. Her grip is like a robotic claw.

The young man manages an out-of-breath soprano squeak.

She hisses, "Where are they?"

Only a half octave lower he groans, "Gone. Out the back."

"Have you seen my friend?"

The youngster leans over even more as she tightens the vise. "No. No. Please. They paid and left."

"The car?"

"Brought to the back."

"By who?"

He yelps again as she re-snatches his privates and squeezes harder. "Alfredo." The robotic claw tightens. "The valet."

"And you?"

"Brought the bill to his suite. He payed the bill and tipped me."

"Not enough." She releases the young man to his exhaling of breath and whimpers. Then knees him in the groin. Hisses, "Not enough." Marnee rumbles out of the alcove and turns to see the valet entering the lobby. He looks wide-eyed at her, turns and darts back outside probably frantically wondering how a woman so sexy can deliver such punishment.

The dark-eyed, tanned-skin Marnee turns back. Her short, thick black hair still in place. Her beige pantsuit jacket strained to retain her breasts and the slacks, though flowing as she moves, can't hide the round firmness of her butt. The clerk is bent over in a semi-crouch, shuffling tenderly out of the alcove and to his position near the register. He looks back, still in disbelief that so much nastiness is ingrained in such a fine-looking woman. She glares at him, growls, "Say one word and I'll come back and cut them off. Everything."

She strides outside once again. Grabs the valet, Alfredo, by his throat. Snarls, "You lied," and knees him in the groin. She releases him and lets him drop to his knees, bent over at the waist and head resting on the concrete next to his valet station. Marnee looks down, shrugs. *Give him credit. Didn't leave his post.* She smirks, says, "Remember what I said."

She steps toward and turns into the alley. *Must find him. He's hurt, I know it.* Leaps and staggers backward as a huge trash truck roars and rattles out of the alley, rumbles around the corner snorting carbon-monoxide from its twin exhaust pipes jutting upward alongside the cab into the darkness.

Marnee stares after the truck momentarily, then steps into the alley again for another look-see.

Where the devil can he be?

Has to be dead.

The meeting at the pub, although potentially volatile, is as calm as Irishmen can be with pints in hand. No one is shouting, but all are red-faced and ranting. The elder Muldoon reaches a decision amidst the clamor. Slams his fist on the table for silence. The din stops and all eyes turn to him. For whatever reason after the disrupting slam of his fist, he then waves heads to huddle up and he hisses only slightly above a whisper, "This man Kerrigan must die, and he will die knowing it's in payback for our Paddy." He goes on, but now in a low growl, "And the killer of me good and dear friend, Mickey O'Rourke, will meet the same fate. As God is me judge." Muldoon takes another whalelike swallow from the pint, then adds, "Whoever they or he be."

Venom dripping from every word, Danny Shanahan asks, "Where is this Kerrigan bastard?"

Colin Muldoon takes a gulp of his pint and responds, "I don't know, lad. But I give me word I will find out, and he will be yours and Sean's to handle." Another gulp from the pint, then, "As you wish. And the Saints be with ya ... as they are with our cause."

Danny and Sean nod, drain their mugs of ale and bang the heavy pewter mugs on the wooden table. Here, each regular has his own pewter mug, stored hanging on the mirrorless portion of the wall behind the bar. A cheer goes up from this fiercely independent yet clannish group. Their ancestral nature is hardworking, accustomed to hard times but would fight as soon as spit. Muldoon orders another pint for the group from the barmaid. She is no longer adored and fondled at the tableside by Muldoon's son. Conan Muldoon is still recovering from the urinal gripping sensations of his one-night love affair with the free-living lass.

Sean Shanahan shakes off the Muldoon offer with his head, wipes his mouth with his sleeve and says in a low tone, "I believe I will pass on another pint and visit Mary Kate. She is in need of a friend in her grievin'." He looks to Mary Kate's uncle and asks, "Is that fine with you, Mr. O'Rourke?"

"Aye it 'tis, my lad. It 'tis. I will be along in due time to see if my brother's grievin' daughter is near recoverin' from this tragedy. If one ever can." He shakes his head, "Have 'er make you a nice cup of tea, Sean me boy."

At the table a few in the group snigger and mumble but are careful that nothing is heard by O'Rourke and the Shanahans. It would be considered sacrilegious or worse, fightin' words. Mike O'Rourke needs only a flint's spark to ignite his temper, and less for the Shanahan brothers. However, restraint is difficult for the pit bull, Conan Muldoon. He's been admonished and whacked already this day by his heavy-fisted father and wants no further schooling thus he remains silent but sneering.

Danny Shanahan pats his brother on the shoulder, nods and winks. "Go, little brother, and give Mary Kate a hug, and tell her I'll be sayin' some Our Father's for her and her dear departed dad."

Sean's face reddens barely enough to be seen by Danny much less the others, and he pushes away from the table. He shuffles toward the pub's door, pretending he's not anxious. In his heart he is sure he wants to comfort Mary Kate, but in the dark recesses of his mind he has other plans. One, is to bed her, of course. And two, is to see if she has any more information of her dad than her Uncle Mike and the elder Muldoon have let on. Both endeavors would be good, but the first would be great and the latter will do on the way out.

When the younger of the Shanahan brothers arrives at the O'Rourke door and rings, it is opened a crack by Mary Kate. The lass peers out, smiles, clad only in a light flannel robe with its untied cloth belt dangling. She opens the door wide for Sean and with the suction of the door, her robe as well. She makes no effort to grasp the robe closed as she gently pulls Sean inside by his belt buckle.

As they climb the steps to the flat above the cobbler shop, she murmurs, "Wonderful of you to come, Sean, love. I was prayin' you might would, 'though a Hail Mary or two I was sayin' for my father." They stop and face one another at the top.

Sean hesitates as his eyes scan the gap in her robe. "I only stayed for the one pint." He shilly-shally's for a moment, then adds, "Your Uncle Mike says he will be along in due time and for you to make me a cup of tea." He receives no immediate reply only a gentle tug on his arm.

Now, the robe more than slightly agape, Mary Kate inches closer to Sean. She hooks her finger over his belt buckle and pulls him close, nestles soul-deep, rubbing her body wantonly on his. She whispers, "Tea it will be, but in due time." Brushes her lips across his and takes him by the hand. "Come with me," and leads him down a narrow hallway to her room at the rear of the flat.

Sean murmurs, "Do ya think it's a good idea what with your uncle comin' along be ..."

"I do," as she pulls him along with one hand and sheds her robe with the other.

The sea is like an enormous pool of ink. There are gentle swells but no whitecaps. The sky is bright with stars but moonless. The *Sorridenta* slips along at less than cruising speed, rocking gently with its running lights and mast lights hinting at its presence. Below in the master lounge, propped up by pillows with their backs against the headboard, Roberto Catalano and Gina sip brandy. Clothes strewn from the door to the bed. One chair toppled over after its use as a prop. A venturesome night of love-making, ended.

Gina sips the last of her brandy. Slides down from the pillows and slithers fully onto the large bunk-style bed. Sighs, "You are too much for me, Roberto. I dreamed of it being so ... I am worn out and sleepy ... and drunk." She feigns a kiss, "I am sorry. I can't ..." her voice trailing off in drowsiness.

"You have only whetted my appetite, and we have barely begun, sweetheart. Let me pour another brandy for us. A booster shot." He sits more upright and turns to the bed table, reaching for the crystal brandy decanter.

She sighs, voice more or less inaudible, "No more, please. I cannot stay awake. I've had much too much already."

Pisces turns while still seated and stares at Gina. Her eyes are closed. He leans over and whispers, "Sleep tight. I'm going to have one more topside. Then I'll be back to join you." He leans over and kisses her forehead.

She murmurs an unintelligible response as she pulls the bed sheet to her neck.

Pisces watches another few moments, then stands and slips into his cotton khaki shorts that are part of the foreplay debris on the carpet. Steps into his slippers, more of the same, checks Gina again, and saunters out.

He sits on the after-deck, leaning back, absent-mindedly naming constellations. "Orion. Chair of Cassiopeia. The Big Dipper." He leisurely sips his brandy between mutterings and allows the night to slip by.

Several miles ashore there are lights flickering from a small rural and nameless coastal town. At sea, not a boat in sight save a cruise liner on the dark, indistinguishable horizon. His crew in their quarters except the helmsman on the bridge, out of sight.

After another brandy, Pisces takes in a deep breath and exhales warily. Stands, opens the top of a bench seat and takes out a roll of gaffer tape. Much like duct tape, only it doesn't leave a sticky residue when it's removed. He quietly moves inside and to the master lounge where Gina is not only sound asleep but has rolled onto her back with the sheet having fallen away slightly. He stares at her half-naked body. Shrugs his shoulders. Exhales thoughtlessly.

Pisces tears off several pieces of the gaffers tape. Leans over and pulls the sheet the remainder of the way down so Gina is entirely uncovered. Then scrutinizes her for a moment as he sits. She hasn't moved, nor does she now. He softly grips her ankles, pauses, then pulls her legs together.

He mutters, "A first for her," and grins. She is unconscious. Too much brandy late tonight, and too many vodka martinis before and after dinner. Pisces grasps her two wrists and folds them over her abdomen. No hint of a reaction from her.

He quickly tapes her ankles together, then her wrists. Then carefully the same with her knees. Pisces dwells a moment, watching. Next he manages to work another piece of tape under her waist and up and over both arms slightly below her elbows. He does the same across her chest. She takes on the appearance of a mummified Cleopatra. Gina stirs, but only with a slight movement of her head to the side. He takes another piece of the tape, quickly and tightly places it over her mouth and nose, and pinches it tight at her nostrils. Then quickly presses the tape securely in place with both hands. Hurriedly pulls the sheet up, clamps it down across her breasts, and pins her shoulders to the bed. He leaps on top, straddling her at the thighs.

Her eyes snap open as she turns her head from its side. Tries to raise it, and does an inch or two, neck straining. She can move nothing else. Eyes bulge in terror. She thrashes like a hooked carp on a dock. Knees violently attempt to move but can't. Her head snaps from side to side. She gasps for air that won't come. The struggle devours her oxygen and drains her allowable time to remain breathless. Then abruptly the struggle stops. Eyes go blank. Her body no longer straining. It's limp. A patched and taped rag doll.

Pisces holds her in this position. Sitting, insensitive as a giant boa squeezing the life from its prey. After several minutes he slides off Gina, pulls the sheet down, stares at her, then checks for a pulse. There is none. He stands, wipes his brow with his forearm. Takes a few steps backward and sits in the now righted chair, to collect his thoughts. *That was easy enough.*

Miles later, Gina lays lifeless. Skin tone and texture changed to resemble a porcelain figurine. Pisces stands, moves to the bed, and carefully pulls off the tape. Picks-up his once gorgeous maid and foolhardy lover, carries her to the after-deck and unceremoniously drops her into the deep.

He mutters, "Sleep well. Nothing personal." Expressionless he watches her body slip ghost-like beneath the surface, drifting with the unseen current. If found, a nameless, intoxicated, careless yacht traveling beauty.

Pisces rushes below and gathers up all Gina's belongings from every boat space where she might have left some personal article or a piece of clothing. He carries them from each closet, drawer, cabinet and shelf to her suitcase laid open on his bunk. When done he takes it to the after-deck, makes several gashes in the leather with a galley knife and drops it over the side.

Roberto Catalano saunters into the master salon. Has another brandy, lights a cigar and thinks of the woman of his dreams. *Chiarina.*

CHAPTER 18

*"The faster you finish the fight,
the less shot you will get."*
A gunfighter's rule

After another tour of the alley and the back of the hotel, Marnee doesn't find Reis or a clue of his whereabouts much less existence. During her search she checked the dumpster knowing it would be empty, but longing for some shred of evidence. Only in its emptiness was there hope, but in reality it was dark. Marnee returns to her room and calls Itzak Levi and Namir Dayan, her two Mossad compatriots in Pisa. After explaining the entire course of events, including the dumpster facts, she is told by Itzak, the Team Leader of the group, that Reis is most likely dead. Further that before his body turns up, she needs to be gone.

She is instructed to check out of the hotel. Take everything belonging to Reis out of the room and return to Pisa immediately. Itzak tells her that he will take care of notifying headquarters, and they will deal with the consulate in Rome. Further, if per chance Reis is alive, he will find his way back here or home. Itzak adds, "Unfortunately, I don't believe that to be the case. Mossad Headquarters will get some people out to the dump and throughout Rapallo."

Marnee listens, and after a few more questions of her by Itzak she moans, "I cannot make myself believe I should leave without Reis. Either alive or with his body."

Itzak sighs, "Marnee, Reis is dead. And Rocco DeStefano also made you. Reis' body has been dumped, probably in the dumpster, and it has been emptied. This is not a first for us. DeStefano killed him, then got rid of his body. If he had the time he would have killed you as well, or tried. He didn't for whatever reason. He fled. You need to get back here. We need to find Rizzo, get what we need and put him to death if necessary."

"Yes, yes. I agree."

"Good." Then in his native language, *"Savlanut."* Continuing he says, "As the proverb tells us. 'The only truly dead are those who have been forgotten.' Reis is not forgotten." Then back in Italian, "He will lead us to Rizzo, and then to Pisces. We will find Pisces and kill him for what he did in Jerusalem, and we will kill Rocco for what he did to Reis. Understand?"

After a pause, she responds. "I do. Yes, *savlanut*, patience. You are right. I will be out of here shortly. In Pisa in a few hours. *Shalom.*"

She places the phone in the cradle and goes about packing. Everything. Hers, his, and all in her bag to include his knapsack. Looks around the room, checking. Itzak's quote reminds her of another. *When you have no choice, mobilize the spirit of courage.* Her thought fades and she retreats to the lobby and checks out. The clerk is different, but it looks as if the chatter about her has at least made the rounds of the help, if not management. It makes no difference.

The valet brings the car. He is an older man but it is obvious the lady is known curbside as well. The man is all polite smiles, knowing or otherwise.

Marnee climbs into the rental car, screeches and bumps away on the cobblestone street, her mind on Pisa. *Will do it myself.*

It's early morning, much before dawn when Rocco and Adrianna return to Pisa and the hotel. They go immediately to their suite seen only by the night clerk and a half-asleep bellhop. The latter is summoned to carry Adrianna's bags, crammed full from her shopping in Rapallo.

In the suite she does not unpack. Simply has the half-awake bellhop drop the newly purchased suitcases on both bag racks at the foot of the bed. Rocco tips the bellboy as Adrianna dashes to the bathroom. As the young man leaves, Rocco hangs the "Do Not Disturb" sign on the outside handle, closes and latches the door. Then, pulling off his shirt he saunters to the bathroom as well. Both freshen up and when finished, come out together, stripping off clothes and dropping them on top of the bulging luggage on the racks. They clamor into bed, Adrianna's insatiable appetite needing nourishment. For her, everything is like it's a finale, or the first time after an enforced prolonged absence.

Adrianna knows nothing for sure, but suspects something. For her, life simply goes on and she must have Rocco. And hold on to him. To her, he is whatever he is. For her, he is life, a good one at that and she's aware her sands are ebbing.

Finally, with both appetites feverishly nourished, they turn onto their backs content and exhausted. Both pull up the sheet. One knows what is ahead; the other does not, but is buoyant.

For Rocco, everything is clear. He's on familiar terms with his job and goes about it without emotion. He always has ever since he's been with Pisces, or Robert Camack, or Roberto whomever, to include, now, Catalano. It's his only life. Before his home was in the streets and alleys of Rome and Calabria. Now his home is in villas and on verandas, however the nature of his work is in and about the social cesspools of the world. Today he will find Antonio Rizzo, deal with him, and go home to Pisces. Adrianna will be left behind with promises of his return and money to spend. He will have her dealt with in time if necessary, and who knows, back at the villa perhaps Pisces will be occupied with this new woman and leave his scraps, Gina, to him. Willed so to speak. Certainly nothing akin to what Bruno discovered. Only if Pisces makes her his gift. If not, there are always others. Something new from Taormina.

Hunter pays the tab at the *Cecconis*, leads Lady Sally outside and hails a taxi. Says to the cabbie, "Heathrow. Air France terminal."

Dee responds, "Heathrow. Where the ... what the hell?"

"We're going to Geneva," in softer tones so the driver can't hear, "and we'll travel separately but on the same flight." He turns his head quickly to check behind the taxi. Nothing. "We'll stop long enough there for me to get some more ID's and money. Also I will take you to the Rue du

Rive. Great shops, best in Europe. Hell, window shopping there is practically an international sport."

"Shop for what?"

"Clothes. Surely you've guessed? We're not going back to the hotel. For both of us, but particularly you."

"Then what?"

Hunter, keeping his voice low, says, "Take the next step. We'll talk about it later. First things, first. Get out of London without our two friends having a clue. Nor anyone else. The Israelis lost us and are probably back at The Cavendish. And there was someone else. Looked like one of our assets. They'll realize in a few hours that something is awry, but it'll be too late. We'll be gone."

"Well, that's good."

"Yeah, but there will be others. Waiting for us wherever we go. The trick is to go where we are expected and still not be seen, or go where they don't expect and not be found."

Dee says nothing for several moments, then asks, "Who are we this time?"

"I'll tell you when we get inside." He looks around outside, then says, "We're just about there." Pauses, then adds, "And still without our friends."

"Wonderful. The problem is that all this sounds a lot like your damn dream. London. His flat. Now, Geneva, for money and ID's. Rome. Then, Pisa. You're not following your premonition, are you?"

"Nope. It's coincidental maybe, but things will be changing rapidly." He laughs softly. "Used to be called deduced reckoning, D E D, ded reckoning." Chuckles again. Then to the tune of a famous song he softly sings, "On patrol again ..." his voice trailing off.

Dee asks, "What's this 'On the go again' routine' and the Deduced reckoning? Are you going to let me in on all this mumbo-jumbo you're spewing or are you going to continue to chortle?"

Hunter smiles, "Chortle? Hmmmm. Remember what the Irish say. 'A handful of skill is better than a bagful of gold.'" He leans forward to pay the cabbie, says to Dee, "We're here. Let's get a move on it. We only have thirty minutes to catch the flight if my premonition is accurate."

"That's not funny, wise guy."

Hunter signals the cabbie to keep the change which is more than modest, less than to be remembered. He slides out behind Dee as the driver says, "Thanks, mate." Hunter takes Dee's arm and leads her briskly to the Air France counter. There he purchases two tickets for Geneva only. Both he and Dee use new ID's.

Walking away from the counter, she utters, "Aimee Badeau. Mr. and Mrs. Laurent Badeau. Refreshing." She laughs at her own humor.

"I got that. Well, all for a purpose. We're on Air France. I speak French fluently. French is the predominant language in Geneva. We can pass for French, and if you'll either hold on to my arm, or rant and pick at me, we'll even appear married."

"Given a choice, I'll nag."

"You'll wish you were nice when you see the shops on the Rue du Rive." They jog to the departure gate to find the flight is in the final stages of boarding. The couple, Badeau, board without incident. The stewardess inside the aircraft hatch exchanges pleasantries with Laurent in her native language. To Hunter's surprise, Dee, or more accurately Aimee, asks her a question in French regarding the seat numbers. Then whines to Laurent, again in French, to let her sit by the window since he's changed his mind about being separated on the flight.

The flight to Geneva is about two hours and forty minutes. Laurent spends this time napping. Aimee spends hers staring out the window at the channel, French coastline and later the Alps. She sips coffee while Laurent rests. At Geneva's Contrin International Airport they quickly clear through customs and stop at a restaurant in the airport to eat. Both use the restroom facilities to freshen up. For Hunter it's the face and hands. Dee, the same although she does have back-up in her purse to put on a decent new face, and perfume which will at least disguise what Hunter can't.

Upon returning to the table, they order breakfast, coffee first. Strong and black. As they muddle through the meal with nothing more than idle chit-chat, Hunter constantly surveys the goings-on in the airport, particularly this concourse. Sees nothing suspicious.

After the third cup of coffee, Laurent says, "Aimee, I've got to make a call. There's a bank of phones across the concourse. You wait here, okay?"

"Why don't you pay the bill and we'll both go. I'd like to call home."

"Call home? What the hell for?"

"To let my folks, or Maria, know that I'm okay. And check on my children."

They both stand to leave. Laurent hesitates for several moments. Aimee signals a question with her head jutting forward, eyebrows raised. He says, "All right. But don't tell 'em where we are, or were, or going. Okay?"

"Yes, that's fine, except I'll have to make a collect call, so they'll know."

Hunter grimaces, "Yeah, right. But nothing else."

"Got it. Who are you calling?"

Laurent drops more than enough cash on the table to cover the breakfast check. As they take a few steps toward the bank of phones he says, "I'm going to call ahead. Make some arrangements and to chortle with Joe." He steps into a booth and closes the door.

Aimee mutters, "I'm too tired to give ..." her voice trailing off as Hunter slams the booth door closed. *And I need a shower and clean clothes.* She goes down a few booths, puts in a few coins, and makes a collect call to the number she's memorized. Again it rings, several times. The hello on the other end is a tired one.

She says, "Hi, it's me. We're in Geneva. We left in the middle of the night without checking out and we're now traveling as Aimee and Laurent Badeau."

First comes a grumble. Then, "Okay. Excuse me," followed by a clearing of the throat. "I was asleep. Let's see, why did you call?" Another hesitation, this one void of sound effects. Then, "You're on plan, right? Geneva, to Pisa through Rome?"

"I guess. He's only purchased tickets to here and he's making a call now to make arrangements. At least that's what he said."

"He's right there?"

"Yes and no. He's in another booth." She hesitates, follows quickly with. "Don't worry. He can't hear. He's two or three booths away and thinks I'm calling my children."

"Well, okay, but we probably need to hurry this along. Avoid any suspicion." A pause, then, "All right, everything seems on track. By the time you get to Pisa, everyone, meaning the Israelis, East Germans and probably some angry Irishmen will be looking for Leanardo Frati, and his wife, Caterina. The name he will be using."

"What about me? When do I finally drop out of sight?"

"When he's dead, then pick the best time. I don't care who kills him. Them, Rizzo, the police. Push him into confrontations. Even you if no one else does. I need Kerrigan dead. In Pisa."

"I thought ..."

"Just see that it gets done, darling. Put him in or get him in a confrontation by making it easy for him to be found. In Pisa is best. That will give the Italian government a lot to think about. Two American government employees killed in their country, in Pisa, within weeks of one another. With the Israelis and Germans there, and the Italians will know that, the finger of blame will point in at least two, possibly more, directions. But not ours. Okay, anything else?"

"No, I guess not, but ... but what about Pisces?"

"Pisces? Pisces is my guy. Our guy."

"I thought Rocco was our guy?"

"No, no. He just works for my man. And he'll be gone soon as well."

"WHAT?"

"Calm down. We're a team. A threesome. And I paid him off so we do Kerrigan and he does his guy. Then he goes his way and we go ours. All square."

"That's ... this is ..."

"Brilliant, huh? More than brilliant. Now, you take good care of yourself. Be vigilant and cautious. We have a wonderful life ahead of us." He emits a soft chuckle. "Better than the President and First Lady." He chuckles. "Yep. Better. Now remember, Kerrigan must die. That's a must." Then a whispered, "I love you." Click.

Dee stands in the booth, gathering herself. *I do love him. God forgive me, but I do. Always have.* Exhales, and digs into her purse. Opens a compartment at the bottom. She confirms the name of Caterina Frati by checking the passport and accompanying credit cards. *This is my last one.*

Dee takes in a deep breath, pulls a tissue out of her purse and zips the bag closed. Inhales deeply again and steps out of the booth. Glances around, moves a few steps and sees that Hunter is still on the telephone. He signals her with his index finger. She nods, tugs at her purse looking about at the maze of people moving to and fro. Sees no one watching her. Wipes the perspiration from her brow. *I can do it. I can.*

In the other booth, Hunter continues his brief conversation. He's had two. The first with Joe Zachary who gave him a name, Roberto Catalano, and an address in Taormina. The new shipping address for the cigars, with a new surname but still Roberto. Still, Pisces. The die is cast.

This last call nears its end. Hunter says, "Listen, Maria, I'm sorry she hasn't called. For the kids' sake, and for your parents. More than sorry. But we knew it would be coming to this or worse someday. We know what she, they, are capable of doing. I want you to know I've got everything under control."

"I hope so. But, what about us? Am I weird for thinking there's an us?"

"Listen, there isn't. Just isn't. I thought I made that clear. I have a job to do. You do as well. You're either with us as planned or you're an accomplice. I realize this is perhaps your worst nightmare. Mine as ... never mind. It's a nightmare. Trust me, there is not an us except as a team. Now, I've gotta run. You'll have to leave for that vacation and go where I told you. Wait there until you hear from me. If you don't hear in a week, get Dee and go home. She'll be in Pisa."

"I ..."

"Go, I will be there within a week. I've got to go. Bye." Click.

"I will." She hesitates then whispers, "Hunter, I know in my heart we're goin' to do it someday." All this to the buzzing and clicking of a long distant line shutting down.

He steps out of the booth, takes out a handkerchief and wipes his brow. Says to Dee, "Hot as a sauna in there. You get through okay?"

"Yep. Everything's fine. Folks, Maria, children. Want me home."

"Well, to be expected." Hunter smiles, "Let's go to the bank and get some monopoly money and spend it on Boardwalk or Park Place."

"What bank?"

"Rothchild's. Big bank. Is located in over thirty countries, and best, one is in D.C. Makes things easy for us. This one is on Rue du Rhone, not far from where we go after that. We'll take public transportation. Taxis are hard to find in this city and ..." abruptly whistles down a cab. Pumps his fist, "Our luck is changing. Now, don't forget. We'll speak French. If you're not comfortable, go to Italian. Some of that here too, and a little English. Prefer not to speak any English here. You can handle all this, right?"

"*Oui*, and the Italian like a native. A onea, twoa ..." accompanied with a coy smile.

Hunter only shrugs. Mr. and Mrs. Badeau, Aimee and Laurent, a happy, in-love French couple slide into the taxi. Hunter, using French, says to the driver, "Take us to the Rue du Rive. The best lady's clothing shop you know."

The driver smiles into the rear mirror, *"Oui, Monsieur."*

Laurent leans back, smiles at Aimee and says, "When we get there, you use the

Badeau credit card to shop. While you shop I'll take care of things at the bank and meet you back at a shop we choose. Say, two, two and a half hours?"

"I thought you said we were going to get some money?"

"You're right, I did say that. But on second thought, I don't want the bank officials to see both of us. And they will. I have to get into the safety deposit box set up there for me."

"What if something happens?"

"Like what?"

"Like anything."

"Well, use the credit card and go home ... to Maria, the kids, your family, whatever. They miss you, right?"

She stares at him. "Children. And, yes." She cocks her head to one side holding the stare.

Hunter reciprocates and when she looks away, he turns his gaze out the window, feigning taking in the sights.

Aimee sits quietly. Stares straight ahead over the front seat and out the windshield. *I hope I can do this. I need to; I'm in too deep.*

Laurent, both tired and refreshed. Continues to look intently out the window. *Didn't even call. She's in on it. Again. And she's gonna' try to do me ... do me in. Been tryin' the other every other hour.*

Maria DeLuca sits alone, staring at the cradled phone. Her pink cotton robe half open, but covering some of her sleep ware, a thigh-length tee shirt she purchased years ago at Yosemite with "A National Treasure" stenciled across the front. She remembers their first meeting. Arranged clandestinely and hidden from all except Hunter's old Marine buddy, Findlay, who was stuck at Headquarters Marine Corps tour for fast track Lieutenant Colonels. His place was a safe house, an apartment in Bailey's Cross Roads in Virginia. It was a terrifying meeting but she thought she struck a chord with Hunter. Wasn't any music but in her heart she heard notes. Discernibly not Hunter. Maybe it was Findlay. He kept vetting her.

Then her thoughts drift back to another time, a few months ago when on a routine business trip for the winery, she was picked up by agents and brought to another clandestine location for yet another secret meeting. Findlay met them and he escorted her to the same place. His. Hunter was there with Joe Zachary. At this meeting it was apparent they knew everything about Dee, her lover, about Angelo, and about her knowing and not disclosing everything. Hiding the truth, the facts from the family, from the law, and even from herself. Under the surface she was a head case. And Zachary had a plan, and she didn't have any options any longer, at least not affable ones. And, of course, they took her deposition. And what amounted to a plea bargain. Each distressful and yet a relief.

Maria's reflections persist as she continues to stare into nothingness. She visualizes and lives sensations of the day and especially the evening afterward with Hunter. An incongruity to the interrogatory meeting earlier. The seemingly connection at a non-business dinner. The contact, although only a handshake again, it was warm and seemed to linger. perhaps only to her. Then her yearning and craving held moderately in check by improbability but more so by Hunter's words and lack of action. Her life and comfort zone had changed, transcending into a region of petition and longing.

Maria gazes at the phone a moment longer. Tears trickle down her cheeks. Then the soberness and horror of reality strike once again.

My Lord, what has my sister done? What is she about to do?

She dials the first number, then bangs the phone back on the cradle.

I love him. I think.

She dials the number Hunter gave her. Exhales, relaxing as best she can.

What am I thinking? That's a dream. This is a nightmare.

The first ring startles her back to the moment.

CHAPTER 19

*"Move away from your attacker.
Distance is your friend."*
A gunfighter's rule

"Mr. Zachary, it's Maria DeLuca. Hunter asked me to call."

"Yes, he told me. Are you going where he suggested?"

"Yes. Tomorrow."

"Okay, go and come via D.C. A ticket will be waiting for you at American. If you're concerned about your safety or your family's I'll arrange for security. In addition, I'll have you met at the airport and brought to a safe house in Arlington." He pauses. "The city, not the cemetery."

"Understand. Let me think about your security offer. I haven't even talked with my parents yet. It's all so ..."

Joe lowers his voice to a more soothing, fatherly tone saying, "You have to do that. There is no good time, but not doing it or not doing it in time could be irreparable. Call me back when you've had that conversation and thought about the security issues. Then when you get here we'll go over things one last time. You can go over the deposition and add to it if you need. Okay?"

"I guess, Mister Zachary. I'm frightened."

"I understand. I do. And, it's Joe, if it'll help."

"Okay, Joe. I ... I'm deeply saddened and embarrassed about all this. Scared. Actually, terrified. For my father, my grandparents, the poor children. I'm ..." her voice cracks, "scared skinny. Literally. I look like a scarecrow in the mirror. It must be noticeable to others. I want to do the right thing, but?"

"I know. You are doing the right thing. Hunter will be in touch and help if and when he can. If not, I'll put a person on it like I mentioned. Somebody that you can trust and that knows Hunter. Travel with you if necessary. To be close." He hesitates, then says, "Maria, this has to be done. If not, people are going to jail for a long time at the least. You are either with us on this now, or you're going to be with them. In jail or dead. This is not a game, it has to be done, and now."

"I suppose."

"Maria!"

"Yes, I know. I understand," Maria sighs, then, "You know I'm attracted to him. More than attracted. Those meetings, the dinner. I sense he knows, but he doesn't seem to be interested. It's like it's nothing but a job to him."

"Maria, he cares. Just not the way you want. This is a dirty business. You keep your mind on our business here. I can assure you, Hunter's is, and remember, he's an operative. He's not a nice person when he's working. Probably isn't when he's not, either. Now, hang tough and get on the way. In effect you don't have an option." Joe pauses once again searching for a clincher. "Maria, and keep in mind, Dee's children are going to need you. Perhaps as a mom."

She pauses, then, "You're right. I'll see you tomorrow, probably late. I'll call and confirm everything. And, Mr. Zachary, get me some support, and thanks for your wonderful reminders and tips."

"It's part of my job, and I'll get someone there, Maria."

Maria hangs up. The tears gone. The face thinner. The lines harder. Her eyes darker. She stands, starts for her living room where her dad and grandparents are relaxing. She knows that today will be a long day for her and the DeLuca family, and longer ones to follow.

Tragic, painful days ... And longer months ... Years, possibly.

As she nears the room and hears her grandfather speaking, she mutters to herself, "Better send someone good. I'm coming apart."

The driver lets Aimee off at the shop, *Pivoine Su*, on *Cours de Rive*. Laurent asks the driver to wait and he slips out with Aimee. Says, "I'll take care of my own clothes. Going to the bank first, then I'll get some duds, and after that, back here to meet you. Two hours. Enough time?"

"Oui." She smiles.

In French as well, Laurent says, "Yes, I remember. After here we will go back to the airport and leave for Rome and Pisa. I'll make the arrangements while I'm at the bank. We'll be leaving here as Leonardo and Caterina Frati. You've got 'em, right?"

"*Oui.*" Another smile, this one feigned.

"Okay. Go crazy, but remember, only one bag and that has to be a carry-on."

Aimee, more exactly Dee, nods. No grin. Not even a smirk. No sarcastic remark. Only a hard stare.

He shrugs without caring, yet noticing, and slides back into the taxi he's been holding with the door closed. Says to the driver, "Sorry for the delay. Rothschild's. *Near Rue du Rhone, 18 Rue de Hesse* I think."

"*Oui, Monsieur,*" and the taxi pulls away.

Aimee turns and looks up and down the *Cours de Rive* with feigned interest. Stares at her trembling hands. Mumbles, "I'm going to come apart. Talking and planning is one thing. This another."

Roberto Catalano has directed his crew chief to take his pride and joy, the *Sorridenta,* westward past the main port of Palermo, and further west past the point of *Reserva Naturale Capo Gallo.* Then southwest around the jut of land near *Silno Orea* and into the *Gulf of Castellamumarl.* This stretch of coast is a combination of sand and the vibrant blue of the *Tyrrhenian Sea* that contrasts the stark colors of Sicily's scorched earth. Here they anchor at the *Marina di Mondello* in *Terrasini,* and he will find a place in town to rest and freshen up before contacting the woman, Chiarina Romeo Russo. The crew will stay aboard. No shore leave.

After making the necessary anchorage arrangements with the Marina's old salt-like owner, Roberto follows the old man's advice and hikes the short distance to the *Le Oasi B&B* in the center of *Terrasini.* The B&B is an old family-owned and operated house, restored and remodeled recently.

The town is beautiful to anyone's eyes, but to the painter in Catalano, he focuses on the old sea-worn pastel colored buildings and the streets near sea level with their flowering trees, orange and palms. He takes in the edges of town where the *Aloe Cactus* and *Fico di India*, prickly pear cactus, hug the rocky coast. And from his study of this town before leaving his villa in *Taormina,* Pisces knows that *Terrasini's* name comes from the Latin, "*Terraesinus*", meaning coast filled with caverns.

He mutters, "Might stay awhile. Perhaps paint some of this." Then louder, as he stops in front of his destination. "But, first things first. Chiarina Russo." He claps his hands in anticipation. Then struts into his "peacocks roost" to be, at least for the moment, the *Le Oasi.*

Once in his room and settled with his face and hands freshened literally and his mind figuratively or at least painlessly readjusted, Roberto sits at the small desk with the telephone. He reaches for his wallet and removes the folded note page he transcribed when talking with Rocco. Dials the number, listens to the four rings, then hears, "Good afternoon, Signora Russo's residence." Roberto hesitates a moment, having a little difficulty with the greeting since it is in Sicilian. The Italian Meridionale-estremo language group is customary here, but Pisces has not lived here long enough to become comfortable with its use. In addition, all regions have their own dialects as well. Fortunately for Roberto, this woman's dialect is Messinese. From the Messina area, near his villa in *Taormina.* He's already become accustomed to its use. She must have moved here, which is not common. Most Sicilians remain in their regions.

Regaining his wits, Roberto replies in Italian, "Good afternoon. Can I speak with Signora Chiarina Russo? This is a friend, Roberto Catalano. The Signora and I have met."

The woman replies, "One moment, please," now in pure Italian.

After several instants, a voice on the line murmurs, "Signore Catalano, hello. What a pleasant surprise. So good to hear from you, and although you warned me that I had not seen nor heard the last of you, I thought perhaps I had."

Roberto keeps the conversation in Italian. "Well, hello. Yes, I always keep my word, especially to such an intelligent, beautiful woman and a patron of the arts as you. May I call you, Chiarina, as I did when we met?"

"Yes, certainly." She pauses. "Would you prefer we speak in English, although your Italian is exceptionally good? Incredibly natural, and no hint of Sicilian yet." She laughs softly.

Roberto switches to English. "Yes, that would make it easier for me, and I recall you speak English as well as any American, and several other languages as I recollect."

"Yes, well, English it will be apparently. Are you here, in *Terrasini*? If you are we must visit. See one another. Yes?"

This is too easy. Roberto responds, "As a matter of fact I am. Came here on my boat. She's moored at the marina and I am staying at a B&B in town that was recommended to me. The *Le Oasi*. I would be ..."

"Yes, that is a fine, old family-owned business. My husband, Giordano, God rest his soul, helped the owner finance the remodeling a few years ago. But, so much for that, we must get together. But you must be tired. It is a long trip in a boat."

"Well, it's more like a small ship. It has a crew of five although I often handle her myself. It's enormously comfortable. Anyway, I want to see you very much but I thought I might rest and clean up here, then perhaps we could have dinner in town at a ristorante you suggest."

"Yes, and no. You rest and freshen up. But we will have cocktails and dinner here, at my villa. I will have my cook prepare something special from the area, a fresh tuna dish. And some Cannoli with ricotta cheese." She lowers her voice to a husky whisper. "I recall that being a favorite of yours."

Roberto is taken back. *This woman is more than I imagined.* "Yes. Yes. It is. Sounds great. But, are you sure? It seems like a lot of trouble."

"No trouble. And bring your swim trunks. We will swim in my pool, and at sunset we'll gaze out at the sea which is always a beautiful oil in the making. However, instead of painting we'll sip some of our local wine. As an artist and seaman you will like its flavor. It has wisps of the arid Sirocco winds and salt of the sea. And potent, I caution you." She emits a soft laugh. "The wine and a few sips of Limoncello can make one wobbly kneed and weak-willed."

"Hmmm, well then, I will be cautious. But are you sure, this seems so much?"

"Absolutely. You charmed me once. I want to see if that is a fact or just my lonely, untamed imagination galloping emancipated."

"Emancipated. Well, wow." He pauses, reflecting on his jubilant sounding response. Then quickly, "Listen to me. Like a wild, young man." He continues but with a smoother, more mature tone. "What time is best for you?"

"Five-ish. And bring both."

"Both?"

"Yes, Roberto. Bring wild, and the young man. I realize this sounds assertive but I have been hoping you would call, and this is better. You've come."

"I'm looking forward to it. I will rent a car and be ..."

"Nonsense. My driver will pick you up. Close to five. I am anxious to see you once again. My goodness, you came all this way in your boat. How romantic. Bye."

Roberto puts the phone back in its cradle and stares at this particular stylish and antiquated device, then through the window over a few roof tops and out to the *Sorridenta* resting peacefully at anchor less like the slave ship it's been. He gets up, takes the few steps to the bed and flops onto his back.

I think I'm going to need my rest.

As his master begins his respite, Rocco awakens from his. Adrianna is already up and dressed. She says, "Good afternoon, Rocco darling. You slept soundly. That must mean you were at least as satisfied as I."

"Ahhh, that I was. That I was. Why are you dressed?"

"I thought I would go look about, perhaps participate in my second favorite past time, shopping."

"Shopping? Do you ever tire of it? I will soon run out of money."

"Ahhh, but that never seems to happen, Rocco darling. But, if you prefer I not."

"No. No, go. I am going out for a short time anyway. I will meet you at Alberto's for dinner."

Adrianna hesitates for a moment, grimacing. "Must we? Alberto's brings back such horrid thoughts. Besides the wonderful handsome young man, Antonio, is no longer there."

"We can go elsewhere. You choose. I'll meet you back here. In the lounge. The bar, at sunset. Yes?"

"Yes, thank you, darling." She comes to the bedside and kisses Rocco on the cheek as he sits up and swings his legs over the side. As she turns to leave, he gives her a lover's swat on the butt. Adrianna squeals in delight, feigns strutting, hips swaying like a street-walker on the prowl as she makes her way to the door. Waves goodbye over her shoulder and is gone.

Rocco gets up, steps to the telephone, dials while sliding into the seat.

After a few moments, Rocco says, "Have you found him yet?"

A pause of several seconds, then Rocco blurts, "Where?" Listens again and asks, "Is he there now?" Again moments pass, then Rocco stands, says, "Keep an eye on him. I'm coming right now. If necessary, keep him there," slamming the phone to rest.

Rocco shoots to his feet. Growls, "The little prick is ruining my vacation." Nonetheless he claps and rubs his hands together vigorously on the way to the closet.

Always good to stay in practice.

In a closed tool shed behind the Muldoon row house, he and the Shanahan brothers meet. Of course the pit bull, his son, Conor, is in attendance. The elder Muldoon sits upon a work bench, hand resting on a vise. Conor stands to his left, leaning against the bench, busy picking strands of corned-beef from between his teeth. Danny and Sean Shanahan sit against the weather-worn wooden walls, each on a rickety, three-legged old wood bar stool. They are across from Muldoon. Eyes fixed on the large, gruff old Irishman.

Danny asks, "Why are we meeting here? Why not our usual so we can have a pint or two?"

"'Cause, lad, no one must hear what I am about tellin' ya. No one." The statement captures the Shanahan's attention immediately.

"And that is?"

"My source in the 'Colonies'," and he laughs with use of the word, "informs me that the murderer of your brother, Paddy, that Kerrigan gent, is in Europe. Not only that, but he passed through London and is now on the continent as we speak."

The brothers slide off their stools. Eyes flashing anger.

Muldoon continues. "He is on his way to Pisa, in Italy. He is searching for a man named Antonio Rizzo. And, he has company. A woman is traveling with him pretendin' to be his spouse. They will be using the name of Frati. Leonardo and Catarina."

Danny steps forward, virtually hissing. "We need to go there. Now. I want revenge. We want revenge for Paddy ... and the Army."

"I know, lads. And it will be so. The cause will support this mission with the cash and the weapons you be needing. You will be leavin' this very night. Driving to London and flying from there. We will cause a scare to draw attention so it will be easier for the two of ya to slip out of the city here. Now go get what you need to travel and meet me in the alley behind Paddy Collins' garage. One hour. I will have everything you need."

Danny clasps the elder Muldoon's hand and says, "We won't be lettin' you or the cause down. Nor Paddy, for sure." Sean comes forward, does as his brother did, and they leave, bursting through the door. Each giving the cool Irish air a fist pump and the loose gravel in the alley a kick.

Conor Muldoon clears his throat and asks, "This is good news. How can you know so much?"

"Me source is good. The best. The conductor of the orchestra so to speak." He laughs and claps his son on the shoulder, continuing, "And we'll be gettin' paid handsomely for it. Can you imagine that? C'mon now, we've work to do."

"We. I never see any of the 'we'."

"If ya did, you'd waste it on that trollup."

At Langley, John MacBeer, the DCI, glances at his watch. Calls his secretary on the intercom and asks, "What time is my next appointment?"

The scratchy reply drones the device. "A meeting in one hour. Upstairs. On the Pisces project."

"Get Zachary on the phone."

"Yes, sir." The click ends the low rushing sound on the intercom, much like the squelch knob on a field radio did in his younger days.

MacBeer has little patience, but it isn't tested. In moments his buzzer signals his secretary's efficiency like an angry bee. He glances at the light, punches the button, and picks up the phone. "Joe?"

"Yes, sir."

"Get up here and brief me on the Pisces' mission. I haven't heard a word from you in days." Click.

He gets up from behind his desk, ambles to his conference table bringing his coffee. Sits, and leans back in the chair, both hands clasped behind his head, looking out his office window for several minutes. Huge cumulus storm clouds have built up late in the day and are preparing to vent their anger on Virginia, hence the sky isn't forecasting a sailor's delight.

Finally, John MacBeer half sighs and half mutters, "Must be an omen."

"What's that, Chief?" Joe Zachary says as he enters.

"Nothing. Sit. Start talking and no bullshit. I want hard facts. An update. I've got a meeting upstairs in less than an hour. Only on this project of yours. Seems strange."

"My project?" He looks with raised eyebrows at MacBeer. "My project? Really? I didn't think anyone was that interested. Bigger things going on in the world. Did you know, hear, that the Israelis lost a man in Italy? At a seaside resort of all places. And ..."

"Get started."
"Yes, sir."

CHAPTER 20

*"Be careful not to make
a woman weep."*
A proverb

After a few ticks and tocks over one minute, Joe Zachary stops and says, "That's it. We haven't heard from him since London. If he's left, I assume it's to Geneva, and then on to Pisa."

"I understand his schedule. His plan. I want to know what he did or found in London. Where he is right now? What am I supposed to tell the boss, and then the President? We don't know? Are you nuts?"

"Sir, this isn't a high priority Op. You said. 'no rush, just get it done.' And you said it was a good opening assignment for Kerrigan, particularly since what Pisces did to his family." Joe pauses, looks at his notes. "The killing of Ms. McGee is a much higher priority than this. And so is what happened to the Irishman, O'Rourke. We're running into nothing but an universe-size black hole on that front. Along with these we still have Black Ops boiling in Southeast Asia, let alone I've got five operatives in Germany that are up to their a ... their butts getting those sources out. The ones you demanded we must have. This Pisces issue is just a routine, back burner job as far as the Agency goes. Your own words ... Sir."

John MacBeer settles in his seat, slumping almost. His complexion pales back to his normal office pallor after his unrestrained explosion. "You're right." He inhales deeply. Rubs his hands together, relaxes, then clasps them together under his nose. "I'm getting upset about nothing. Continue your brief."

"Yes, sir. Sure you're okay, Chief? Seem a bit out of sorts."

MacBeer shakes his head quickly several times, motions with his index finger to continue and not dally while saying, "No, no, no. Get on with it."

Joe Zachary looks at his folder and in a steady drone ticks off the status of each Op or project. It takes a solid thirty minutes of rapid fire, staccato-like comments, along with Joe pushing several photos forward for MacBeer to view. Then snatching them back and going on to the finish, ending with, "Questions, sir?"

"No. Good job." Then after a brief hesitation he asks, "Will Agent Kerrigan get this done? I mean, he's shiny-penny-new, and possibly I should have had you put someone deeper in experience on this Pisces Op."

"He'll be fine, sir. Pisces is going down ... as is everything and everyone involved. Soon. And, sir, rest assured when I hear anything, I'll keep you on top of it. Won't leave you in the dark."

They both fix their eyes on each other. Unspoken words being exchanged. The moment seems longer than it is since each knows more than what has been said and each is assessing the other. They both want this introspecting staring to end. Two stags with full racks of antlers. Charge or walk away. MacBeer clears his throat and stands. Joe closes his folder and stands as well. Thinking the meeting is over, he takes a step toward leaving when MacBeer asks, "Joe. What kind of man is this Hunter Kerrigan? I should have studied his file more closely. Perhaps I should have gotten to know him better. You know, I knew his father well. Extremely well. Fine man. Loyal to the bone."

Joe Zachary stops and turns as if on a bungee line, before the question is finished. Asks, "What?"

"You heard me. What kind of man is Kerrigan?"

"No, I mean about his father?"

MacBeer frowns. "I said I knew him well. Fine man and loy ..."

"Yeah, you did, and the consensus was he was set-up. Somehow. Well, anyway, about Hunter Kerrigan." Joe pauses, gazes directly into his boss's eyes, a slow grin spreading across his face like a young boy being granted permission to play doctor by the neighbor's daughter. He brings his file folder to chest level, tapping it on his tie.

"Well, John, a Sergeant of his, Skip Raye, I believe that was his name, probably said it the best I've ever heard when he was asked that same question by their Battalion Commander. He quoted an anonymous saying. It went something like this: 'Well, sir. He's the type of man that when he arises in the morning and his feet hit the deck, the Devil says, Oh shit, he's up'. That's the best description I ever heard of Hunter A. W. Kerrigan, the Hawk."

MacBeer, frustrated, stands and with his palms pressed hard down against his meticulously polished mahogany conference table, uncharacteristically stammers, "Wh ... What?"

"Yes, sir. And, sir, he is The Hawk, and The Hawk is out ... sir." Joe smiles, his burnt toast dark eyes sparkling as he nods a departing, "Yes, sir. The Hawk is out and I'd hate to be a rabbit running." And strides out of MacBeer's conference room as his boss stands mute, stunned, perplexed and flushing scarlet as he sits once again.

His secretary eases into the room, says, "Mr. MacBeer, your meeting is in ... Sir, are you all right?"

"Yes. Yes." He feigns a polite smile and returns to his desk, picks up a folder and adds, "On my way. Thank you."

His secretary titters as he brushes past, "Mr. Zachary sure seems up today. Like the proverbial cat."

"He did, did he?" He buttons his suit coat and marches out of the office. As the executive elevator doors slide open like a slow yawn, John MacBeer steps in and turns about, staring out through the still yawning doors. Then, finished and alert again, the doors hiss close.

John mutters, "This needs to end. They all need to die ... Pisces, Kerrigan, Dee, Zachary and DeStefano when he finishes it for me."

After gathering more than sufficient cash, additional passports, ID's, credit cards and such from the bank, Hunter calls Joe again and passes on to him his rough plan and schedule. Then he catches a taxi and picks up Dee where they agreed, the shop *Pivoine Su*, on *Cours de Rive*. She's ready and bounds into the taxi and they ride to Geneva's Cointrin International Airport amidst traffic and Dee's shop-til-you-drop babble. There, as Aimee and Laurent Badeau, they stop for a bite to eat of airport restaurant food. At least in Geneva, and other European airports, it's better than the US of A airport saturated fast-food garbage. After ordering and sipping iced-tea while listening to Aimee describe her new outfits, one of which she's wearing, Laurent interrupts, "Good. Sounds great. Beautiful on you." He pauses, puts his hand up, palm outward, and continues. "Now then, we have a slight change of plans."

"What? What's happened? Is there a problem?"

"Nothing. No. A precaution only. We're going to split up so as to not arrive together. You'll take a flight to Pisa ahead of me. I'm goin' to hang back and watch. Then follow, and watch. Then hook up with you."

"Watch for what? Anything in particular?"

Their food order arrives. Bratwurst sandwiches on pretzel rolls and a pile of sauerkraut. Hunter puts a finger to his lips, waits until served and the waitress departs leaving the check on the table. Then he continues. "Ah, let's see. Oh, yes. The Israelis. Others. Anything out of the norm." He takes a forkful of the kraut. "Mmmm. Good. When you get to Pisa, get a taxi and go to the Grand Hotel Duomo on Via Santa Maria. It's in Duomo Square, a few minutes from the Tower. We'll travel as we are, but separately and check in as Leonardo and Caterina Frati. The room is reserved." He takes a gigantic, famished bite of the mustard-loaded brat sandwich. Chews frantically and while still not done, says, "Tell them your husband will be along soon. Stay in your room until I get there. If I'm delayed, order room service if you need it. Got it?" Takes another bite. Slurps, "Try the Dusseldorf Mustard. It's great."

Aimee hurries to finish her mouthful. "Yes, I've got it. How far behind will you be? Try the what?"

"A few hours. Perhaps slightly more. Not long. The mustard. German, great taste."

"Okay. Now then, how do you like this outfit? Be truthful." Takes a healthy bite, chews a few times and points at the mustard, adds while chewing and swallowing, "That is good."

"The outfit looks great. Especially on you." He stuffs in the last of a bratwurst sandwich. "Let's go." He stands.

"I'm not fin ..."

"Yeah you are. We've got to hurry. Your plane leaves in thirty minutes. C'mon." He motions to the waitress, leaving cash on the table. Waits a moment while Aimee stuffs in a mouthful of the brat sandwich and then clamors to her feet. She wipes her hands on a napkin and snatches her bags half choking on the brat. He leads her by the arm toward the ticket counter. As they rush along, Hunter says, "You'll be going through Rome. An hour lay-over, then change planes to Pisa. Keep everything with you. Be watching for any tails, suspicious looking people. Singles or in pairs. Anyone. You know the drill. If you see something out of the norm, sit at the nearest cafe to your departure gate and watch for me. I'll check before I leave when I come through. Okay?"

"Yep."

"Good. Here we are. I'll get the tickets."

Hunter, as Laurent, does just that including his later flight. Then he hands Aimee a envelope with the tickets, some cash, gives her a husbandly peck on the cheek, smiles and waves her along the concourse to her gate. Aimee, glancing back every few seconds, scurries along since they've called the flight for boarding more than several minutes ago. Hunter sits across the concourse, deep inside a dimly lit bar and grill. From the darkened corner table he watches Aimee and everyone else coming, going, sitting, and standing. Then one late and hurrying boarding duo, then at the last possible moment a second. From their dour clothing and general looks Hunter is certain they are eastern bloc. Cheap suits, a few of the ties showing the creases from not being untied, only tightened and slid down to remove. Heavy, scuffed shoes. One duo he doesn't recognize but his bet would be they're Russian. This is based on his "ded reckoning" since one of the men in the other duo he recognizes. His walk is with a nearly indistinguishable limp. He's a Stassi agent. A known assassin, Helmut Faust. His last name means fist, and Helmut has hams for hands.

Someone is drawing a crowd.

Hunter continues sitting, watching until the plane departs. Stands, strolls to a newsstand and purchases a local paper while still watching the departure gate and surrounding area. Then sits again for a time reading his *Tribune de Geneva* and watching the ebb and flow of activity in the terminal. He sees no other Russian and German duos. Finally, when satisfied all is to his liking, he goes to another terminal and arranges a charter flight to Calabria as Alfonse Battaglia.

Alfonse's plans are different than Leonardo's, Laurent's, and Ian's. But never from Hunter's.

Roberto Catalano steps out of the front door of the *Le Oasi B&B* to find Chiarina Russo's 1971 white Mercedes-Benz 280 SL Roadster and chauffeur waiting. The driver eyes Roberto who is wearing beige linen slacks, pale blue short- sleeve shirt worn loosely and white slip-on loafers, no socks. At first a polite smile of acknowledgment, then a nod of approval of the person. Roberto knows the man is more than a chauffeur. His age hints of a left-over from when Giordano, Chiarina's husband, was alive. Nonetheless Roberto is politely welcomed, the door held open, and as he slides in, the driver asks in reasonable English, "Do you minda the top down?"

Roberto smiles, looking up at the cloudless sky, "No. Is fine. Wonderful in fact," and takes in a deep breath.

The driver closes the door and scurries to the driver's side, slips in, starts the engine which hums to life sounding like a piano's bass keys with the soft pedal applied. They leap away from the *Le Oasi* as the driver says, "Not longa. Only three or four kilometers unless you would likea to see the city centre. Signora Russo wanta you to seea some of our town."

"Sounds good to me. Drive on, ahhh ... " Roberto shrugs and raises his eyebrows.

"Benito."

"Good. Yes, Benito, the tour sounds like just the ticket before ... whatever."

Benito frowns, not unnoticeably. Nonetheless, the tour goes well and adds only a kilometer or two for the trip to Chiarina's villa. Roberto Catalano realizes they are close when they leave the main roadway and slow for the travel down *Strada Vicinale Frammina Morte*, which Roberto recognizes from a map he viewed. Then turn again onto another paved but more narrow roadway, *Viale Mediterraneo,* which parallels the Tyrrhenian Sea. Benito slows, turns and eases onto a gravel road that leads to the Russo home, which is truly a villa by the sea. Roberto sits back for a few seconds taking in the view of the white stucco walls and red tiled roof of the villa while Benito hustles around the hood of the 280 to Catalano's side of the Mercedes.

Why would she want to leave all this? We should keep both.

Roberto's thought is interrupted by Benito opening the door of the car, and Chiarina opening the front door of the villa. She and Roberto meet halfway between the car and the villa. She opens and stretches out her arms, palms gracefully up in a warm polite manner saying, "*Buona serva, Roberto.*" They hug gently, she brushing each of his cheeks with hers, then floats back, leaving her right hand extended. Says, "*Ciao.*"

Roberto clasps her hand, smiles, responds, "*Ciao.*" Then quickly in English, "Hello again."

She nods, whispers, "Hello, again, it is." Her smile is as brilliant and soothing as the sun which is moments from resting its edge on the sea, directly beyond the villa. The tone and mood is set. It will be warm, two recent friends meeting again as if the acquaintance was lengthy as opposed to new, and both comfortable speaking English for the moment, Italian when necessary or perhaps in passion. The path is clear. Where it ends, one is perhaps unaware; the other, certain.

They enter the villa with Chiarina leading followed by Roberto, and of course Benito lagging but a few paces behind, still watchful. The entry spills immediately into a moderately- sized living room with all white walls, dark wood trim everywhere showcased by the similarly trimmed huge panoramic windows overlooking the veranda and the sea. The vaulted ceiling with dark rafters gives the room both a vision of size and a feeling of comfort. It has a large, stone fireplace which sets on the tiled floor. The furniture, with the fireplace as the focal point, is all large, pastel-colored soft stuffed chairs and sofa. Chairs with foot stools, tables alongside with magazines that cry "read in comfort" and the couch whispers, "snuggle fireside". She inadvertently interrupts the room's ambiance by asking, "Would you like to see the rest of my home now or later?"

Roberto, lost in the moment, fumbles with, "Why not now so you can show me where to leave my swim trunks. You did say to bring them?"

"Yes. We'll see if you need them. But come, let me show you about."

The dining room is also in white with dark wood trim and a table that seats five. The veranda can also be seen from here. This room leads to an enormous kitchen, galley really. Further, down a hallway beyond, in the back of the villa are three bedrooms, all with views of the coastline. The master also has a white motif with dark wood trim around the windows and rafters. A wrought iron king-size bed, matching tables. A dark wood dresser setting under a huge mirror. A large wood burning fire place and with the flowers, paintings, and pillowing, the room has a softness about it regardless of the white. It has a colossal master bath to include a large Jacuzzi circular tub with a view of the sea beyond.

She shrugs, smiles, says, "I like to relax. Here, by the fire, and the sea view." She turns and says over her shoulder, "Leave your trunks in here. On the bed. Come," her hand trailing behind leading him and searching for a warm touch.

One of the other two bedrooms is for guests. The other is obviously in use. The two share a bath, but the bath is definitely feminine. She and Roberto only peek in the doors of these rooms, and then she hurriedly leads him to the veranda, poolside to a small table in the corner, directly over the cliffs. The view of the coastline is colossal. She sits at the table, pointing to a chair for him. As he sits, a maid appears on cue. Chiarina says, "This is Estella; Estella Riebello, my aide, chef, helper but mostly a friend and confidant ... and frequently my dinner partner along with Benito. Stell, this is Signor Roberto Catalano."

Pisces swallows hard. Grins, eyebrows raised. Estella is lovely. A petite but well-endowed natural redhead with greenish mischievous eyes. Pisces gawks, then quickly Roberto smiles, utters, "*Ciao*". The moment is instantaneous, and lost, except for the Pisces mind. Stell graciously nods with a hesitant impish smile, perhaps having noticed the momentary ogle.

Chiarina says, "I hope wine will be fine. As I said, I do want you to at least taste our local wine."

Roberto answers quickly, "That will be wonderful. Let's see now, it has a wisp of the arid Sirocco wind and a taste of the sea."

"You listen well, especially to the romance of the grapes. An artist's trait and outlook I would think." She looks to Estella, "Two, and bring the bottle in the event we decide to relax for a spell." She tilts her head away from Roberto, toward Estella, says, "Stell my dear, what are you planning for dinner, and when?"

"A tuna casserole. Fresh caught today, and Cannoli with ricotta cheese as you suggested. Served when you wish, Chiar. Signora." An ever so slight grin creases her face.

Chiarina looks at Roberto, head now tilted toward him, and with a playful look on her face says, "Late, after dark and a swim?"

Roberto nods approval. "Both, or more readily all. My favorites." Smiles and reaches over and gently squeezes Chiarina's hand. Estella floats away as soft as a wisp of the arid wind, leaving Pisces mind to wander. Wonder.

I bet she's part of the package, the team. And at bat, a lot.

Then Roberto grasps the moment and senses and sees only Chiarina.

She says, "It is wonderful of you to come. To visit. And the timing is perfect."

"Thank you. I have thought of it often since we met in *Taormina*." He pauses, asks, "How so? The timing?"

"I'm leaving for *Taormina* the day after tomorrow. Going to look for a villa there. I am moving from here. In truth from Palermo, and my past I suppose."

Roberto smiles. "This is such a scenic location. A warm home. It would be a shame to leave it. Not sure I would do that. But, perhaps I can be of service. You're welcome to stay as a guest in my villa while you search. My staff would be at your disposal. You could come and go as you please." The spider pauses, then, "It would be my pleasure to help."

Chiarina sits pensively, gazing toward the setting sun on the sea.

Weaving his web, Roberto adds, "Perhaps you should keep this as well. It's charming."

After a few additional moments of pensiveness, the stunning widow smiles, nodding slowly. "Perhaps. It does sounds inviting. Let me dwell on the thought. Here comes Stell. I hope you enjoy this wine."

"I'm sure I will." He watches, but not too closely, as Estella places the tray on the table, sets the two glasses, opens the wine, then pours a sip for Signora Russo's taste. Chiarina instead offers the glass to Roberto. He sniffs the wine, gives it unrushed swirls in the glass and takes a sip. Eyebrows up, and with a nod, says, "Wonderful. Sicilian. And it is of this region."

Chiarina exhales excitedly, motioning for Estella to complete the pouring. When she does, she leaves as Chiarina and Roberto gently clink their glasses and both say at the same time, "To a warm friendship."

Chiarina tilts her head in astonishment, laughs. "My word, what a coincidence, or perhaps an omen."

"An omen. If so, a warm one too, or three perhaps."

CHAPTER 21

"To be sure of hitting the target, shoot first and call whomever you hit the target."
Anon

The Shanahan brothers sit in the car behind Paddy Collins' garage. Windows down as the elder Muldoon goes over the instructions once again telling them to drive to London's Heathrow airport and park in the long term area. Wipe the car down carefully as a precaution. Do not speed on the way; there is ample time for the 617 km trip. Inside Heathrow, go directly to the BEA counter and check-in. Sean interrupts, "What does BEA stand for?"

Muldoon angrily replies, "Jesus, Joseph and Mary. May the saints ... where have you been, laddie? The British European Airways." Colin Muldoon wipes the drool from his mouth with his sleeve. "Where the blazes have ya been for the last ... ahhh, never mind. It will be a direct flight to the city with the ... ahhh ..."

"Leaning tower. Pisa. And where I've been is here, fightin' the war. Here where it 'tis and well ought to be. Not where you got my brother, Patrick, killed you blundering, babbling, drooling baboon."

Muldoon's son, Conor, leaps for the car window and is met with Sean's fist, knocking him back but not over. His nose red and bleeding and lip split, both a result of his usual eyes-closed, pit bullish charge.

Sean starts to clamor out of the car as he shouts, "C'mon you over-stuffed cocker spaniel. I'll ..."

His venting and fury is cut off by his brother Danny's hand clasped over his mouth and jerking him back into the passenger seat. Danny pins Sean's to his side. At the same time the elder Muldoon grasps his son in a bear hug with Paddy Collins stepping between the struggling and staggering Muldoons and the car. The raging Conor screams, "I get me hands on you, I be killin' ya as quick as lookin' at ya ... ya skinny pig-shit runt of an Irishman."

The elder Muldoon has Paddy Collins, a monster of a man, pull and wrestle Conor away into the open garage. Colon goes on and finishes his instructions with, "Danny, after you get to Pisa, go to the hotel I wrote down on the slip of paper. Kerrigan should be there already or on his way. Others too, perhaps. They be all government people like we're useta dealing with and   Jews, Krauts maybe. And a big Italian loot named Rocco. He's some kind of enforcer. Be careful of 'im. But if necessary, kill 'em all, but Kerrigan for sure. If 'tis messy, get out of the city and country anyway ya can. Hike it if ya must. If not too messy, take a train to Venice, and from there a train to the channel. Ferry across and get to the car. Be careful there that the car is not being watched. If that be the case, leave it. Then get home best ye can."

Danny nods, says, "I've got it. We'll be off now."

"And be bringing some of our money back if ya can."

"I'll not be worryin' about money. You have a pint or two ready when we get back."

The elder Muldoon is forced to grin. "Aye, then. And lads, be as courageous as lions and tough as whet leather." Muldoon winks and waves to the brothers. Then he turns to Paddy Collins and his son who is still mildly struggling in the garage, says, "Enough, Conor me lad, or it will be the back of me hand."

The Shanahan brothers drive off. Sean says, "I'm goin' to kill that ape's son one day soon. When we get there we should kill Kerrigan and let the others be. They're not our business. Nor the business of the Army. They're Muldoon's personal business. He wants only to let it be known the Army has no boundaries, or better, he personally has none."

Danny nods, "You may be right, little brother. We'll see. Ya know, it may be that this Kerrigan lad is not the one. He's Irish clean through I'd bet. It might not be him. It might all be Muldoon's doin' somehow and the tale is his nasty blarney. I don't trust 'em. He's up to more than Army business here."

"Aye. We are of one mind then. Yes?"

"Aye." Danny takes his eyes from the road for a second, glancing at Sean. "We are."

Rocco unfolds a reason why he must leave to Adrianna. Tells her to pack everything. His and hers, and leave nothing here. Then drive home to Roma. He softens his tone and adds, "I'll call. I promise. Soona. Tell you where I'll be, and if you want to come, good. This time we will be together forever."

In her eyes the welling tears overflow, streaming down her cheeks. She says nothing, only nods. She understands the nature of this man, and enough of his business. Adrianna whimpers, "I love you. I will come to you."

They kiss and embrace. She holds tight, trying to make it last. Feeling it to be final. It lasts only seconds longer. Rocco pulls away, utters, "Yours." Points and motions with his head to a cash stuffed large brown envelope on the small phone desk. He turns and dashes out of the room slamming the door behind him.

Rocco takes the exit stairs down to the basement level, then another separate stairwell up to the kitchen thereby avoiding the lobby area. He pushes through busy apron-clad chefs and uniformed servers to the rear entrance and out into the alley behind the hotel.

The apartments where Antonio is holed up are less than a kilometer from the Hotel Duomo. Nice, upscale which leads Rocco to believe Antonio is there with someone, probably a girlfriend, and he has several. The young man is good at capturing hearts but not with keeping his lips sealed. He likes lira too much and would sell Rocco or his boss, Pisces, to the highest bidder, or any bidder. Antonio's problem is there are not many bidders in this city, and those few there are know of Rocco which makes Antonio's market place as empty as a beggars pocket.

Rocco arrives and sees his informant casually smoking a cigarette in the doorway to the apartment building. The man drops his cigarette, grinding it with his foot as Rocco approaches. The man leans toward Rocco's ear, whispers, "305." Rocco shakes the man's hand and says, "Wait here. Be my eyes and I will pay you well," then squeezes the man on the shoulder in a gesture of loyalty and assurance and disappears through the apartment's outer door and into an entranceway with mail slots.

All but a few have names. More important they all have apartment numbers. Across from them is a closed door with a sign "Manager" engraved on its tarnished brass plate. Rocco checks the mailbox again, sees the numerals 305 and a meaningless name. He mutters, "305. At the back." He strides quietly down the hall and uses the fire stairwell going up. He doesn't need the sound of the elevator to alert anyone, especially Antonio. Also not the likely snoopy manager. On the way up he takes his Ruger .357 out of his beltline and affixes the suppressor, the silencer. He slides the weapon in his front trouser waistband.

At apartment 305 Rocco presses his ear to the door, a few inches below the imitation brass numerals. He hears nothing. Carefully tries the knob. It's locked of course. Presses his ear to the door again, and again hears nothing. He presses harder. After a few more moments he picks-up a muffled gasp or scream. Feels a slight bump but not from the door. A muffled thumping sound. He smiles. Takes a few steps down the hallway, runs his hand along the wall. The thumping is stronger, the noise is obvious, and the gasps are a mixture of groans, grunts and muffled screams. He smiles again.

Bedroom to the left. Having a go. His mind slips away for a second thinking of Adrianna. *A screamer.* Smiles, then dead-pan instantly.

Rocco returns to the door in three giant soft steps. Easily picks the flimsy apartment door lock. Pulls out his Ruger .357, and in silence opens the door. Steps in swiftly, eyes and weapon functioning as one searching the interior. Nothing but the diminishing sounds of spent ecstasy and ended satisfaction from the bedroom to his left. He opens the door and steps in, says, "*Caio, Antonio.*"

The young brunette sitting astride Antonio with her head drooping forward, hands braced against the headboard, emits a startled yelp and spins off her lover. She lands in a sitting position, mouth gaping open, eyes saucer wide and legs still spread open. Rocco adeptly moves the muzzle to the right. Pfsssst. Pfssst. A double tap. A professional, tight pattern like quotation marks without the swirl. She is thrown back on the bed. What's left of the back of her head clunks on the headboard just beneath the splattering of her blood, brains and bone on the wall, headboard and pillows. A collateral spray splashes the side of Antonio's head at his ear.

Terror stricken, Antonio attempts to turn and get up. Rocco fires again, hitting the young man in his left shoulder joint. More blood and bone splatters. Antonio screams and spins back to his left. Before he can move again, Rocco has pushed the door closed and is sitting at Antonio's side with the muzzle of the weapon pressed hard directly under the chin. Rocco grasps the young man by the hair. He says, "Antonio, my man, we need to talk."

He struggles to get up. Rocco puts a second round into Antonio's other shoulder. As powerful as the .357 is, the hollow point may go beyond the headboard, but not through the wall. Besides, Rocco knows this is the last room on the floor therefore on the other side of the wall is stone. Antonio lies in anguish, writhing in pain near shock but trying to grasp his shoulders with his hands. He can't. Rocco presses his hand on the boy's forehead, says, "Antonio, who have you told what you saw by the university? And at *Alberto's*?"

Antonio, tears flowing free now. Eyes of a terror-stricken deer. He shakes his head vigorously. Gags while trying to speak.

Rocco asks, "No one?"

The boy trembles in dread, the blood oozing from both his shoulders pooling makes squishing sounds as he rigorously shakes his head, "no".

"Antonio?"

More of the same, sobbing, shaking of the head regardless of Rocco's grip.

"And of me? Antonio?"

The young man continues his energetic yet terrified denials. Whimpering. Trying to scream but Rocco has retightened his grip over Antonio's mouth after his severely animated "No's". The coppery smell of blood soaking the sheets and pillows saturates the room. On Antonio's left, it mixes with the girl's.

Rocco says, "No one, huh? You know what? I believe you, Antonio. I do. If you had, you would be gone. Taken the money and ran."

Antonio's face contorted with fear begins to become less tense registering a glimmer of hope. He is still trying to grasp his shoulders as the huge Italian stands.

Rocco smiles, says, "But, I don't trust you." Pfstttt.

The fifth of the six rounds in the cylinder hits Antonio in the center of his forehead. His side of the headboard now matches the girl's. It's less than hers, smaller in circumference. Not a matter of intellectual capacity but of the number of shots. Still it manages to spray off the headboard and onto the girl's face.

Rocco takes out his handkerchief. Moves to the bedroom door and swipes around the spot where he remembers pushing it closed. Uses it to open the door, wiping as he closes it. Wipes the knob on the outside. Strides into the kitchen, rummages through cabinet drawers until he finds what he needs. Then with handkerchief still in hand moves quickly to the apartment door. Does the same with the apartment door after glancing up and down the hallway before exiting into the open. Then he dashes to the fire exit and heads down to the first level two and three steps at a time and not touching the iron safety railing. At the bottom he carefully and quietly opens the door a crack. Looks out. Sees nothing, enters the hallway and tiptoes to the front door, opens it and slides out joining his associate. Rocco nods a thanks and thrusts his lira stuffed hand out. The man clasps the money as Rocco hugs him, and buries an ice pick in the back of the man's head at the neck, ramming it up into the skull.

The man slumps into Rocco's arms, and the big Italian lowers him to the white and black tiled floor. He leans over and fits his .357 in the man's hand. Wipes the handle of the ice pick clean. Then looks out the door, first one way, then the other. Sees nothing. Smiles, lights a cigarette and walks briskly away from the apartment toward the hotel.

In the hotel lobby, the Israeli agents, Itzak Levi and Namir Dayan, have been joined by Marnee who has not had the opportunity to check back in to the Hotel Duomo. Only time to be briefed on the current situation here, and that no one has found Reis, or wishfully so, his body. Itzak and Namir are solemn-faced when they see Marnee's face register astonishment by degrees with each word. Then she freezes, staring. They realize something is amiss and turn their heads to follow her gaze.

Adrianna is checking out, bags being toted to the door by the bellman. He will need to make a second trip. Alarmed, they stand from their lobby chairs tucked away in a far corner. Itzak whispers, "Marnee, watch her. Check the desk. Namir, check the back and alley. I will look upstairs. Five minutes, or less, back here. If not, the other two go to the one not here. Move."

They do. Namir at a brisk walk. Marnee at a casual stroll to the front door, only to see the Alfa Romeo waiting at curbside. Valet at its door. Itzak striding to the elevator. Regardless of their pace, it all is unnoticed in the busy lobby and lounge.

Within the five minutes all return. Marnee says, "The valet says she's headed for the airport. She's taken the big man's bag along with hers."

Namir blurts out, "Saw or found nothing in the back or on the way. Kitchen help are saying nothing, but they have that look."

Itzak remains calm. Says, "He's gone. The room is empty and being cleaned by the maid. Let's get to the airport. I'll drive."

Marnee says, "Okay, we can take my car. It's still at the curb."

All three stride briskly out the entrance and into Marnee's rental car. She lurches into the backseat. Itzak and Namir up front. Itzak extends his arm and hand backward, says, "Key."

Within less than a half of a kilometer, they pick up the Alfa Romeo with Adrianna at the wheel. Rocco's car.

Within another half a kilometer Itzak shouts in Hebrew, "Harah!"

Marnee leans forward. Also in Hebrew, asks, "What?"

Namir answers for Itzak, again using their native language. "She's not headed for the airport. Looks like she is headed out of town."

"Maybe home," as Marnee now leans her elbows on the back of the front seat.

Itzak says, "Well, wherever, I hope she has less petrol than we have.

All three are silent for several moments, concentrating on Adrianna who they have allowed to be a few cars ahead. Finally, Marnee says, "Oh boy. You know she is from Rome. I believe she is going home and he is either going to meet her there, or he is gone. And I assume the latter."

Less than a few moments pass when Itzak orders, "I think you are correct. But we cannot follow her. We must go back. Call in. They can have someone in Rome track her down. We have to find Rocco. Somehow." And then again, his anger is vented, "Harah!"

Itzak slows, pulls over to the right, and makes a U-turn, heading back into Pisa and the hotel. After going about a kilometer toward town, he mutters loud enough for the other two to hear, "It is easier to guard a sack full of fleas than a woman in love."

Marnee laughs and says, "Sorry, it is not funny."

Namir shakes his head. "Nothing will be funny when the Chief is told."

"And that is my good fortune," Itzak sighs.

Maria DeLuca sits in her seat as the American Airlines flight climbs out over the Bay Bridge and continues its slow ascending turn to the east and New York. She decided she didn't need a chaperone. She's in the last row of First Class, As a result when she pushes her seat back, she'll have no one's knees to worry about, but plenty else. Her troublesome discourse with her family did not go well. In time, for her or for her dad or grandparents, the talk with Dee's children will be difficult at best and more likely, tragic.

The trip will be long, tiring. First, Washington and another meeting with Joe Zachary. Then for whatever their reasons, to New York's JFK. Then Rome, onto Naples, and the helicopter to the Isle of Capri. A long time to dwell on her sister's escapades, deceptions, and deceit. Spells of going over her conversations with Hunter and Joe Zachary. The painful expressions, sobs and denials of her family. And spells of thinking of this man she believed she loved yet only knew for a few scattered days and without an ounce of return, only the yield in her heart and mind's eye.

Dee as an adulteress? An accomplice? My God, what has she done?
What have I done?
What am I about to do?
"Do you care for a cocktail, ma'am?"
"Oh. Oh, my God. Yes, please."

CHAPTER 22

"The best way to forget all your troubles is to wear tight shoes."
Anon

While on board her flight, Dee, aka Aimee Badeau getting on and aka Caterina Frati upon debarking, noted the late boarders and watched as they sat in the rear of the plane. Caterina could feel their prickly presence and burning stares while she sipped a glass of wine and watched the Alps below slip beneath her window. The shabby foursome did become uncomfortable when she glared at them as she slipped off her shoes after she returned from the rest room.

Here in Rome it is apparent she is now the target or they expect her to lead them to one. Either way, something is amiss, and as a result Caterina Frati does exactly as Hunter ordered. She does not board her connecting flight to Pisa; instead she sits in a conspicuous spot at the ristorante nearest to her would-be departure gate. Waiting for Hunter to arrive and do his thing.

The two Germans mill about, gazing into shop windows full of items that only tourists would purchase, then move to a newsstand. They finally come to rest at an adjacent gate's waiting area, each paging through a local magazine. Catarina's observations cause her to wonder. *Businessmen, tourists and workers. Everyone looks the part except this pair in cheap suits. They look like something out of an old, black and white Humphrey Bogart or Edward G. Robinson movie.* She mutters softly, "They need a better wardrobe department."

The Russian duo, much the same except less obvious in that they are yards down the concourse at a shoe shine stand nonchalantly getting their scuffy brown shoes polished by a babbling old Italian man with gnarled and stained fingers lonely for conversation and eager for business.

The earlier call for her flight, and its subsequent boarding call reminders, caught the attention of the two duos producing anxious glances toward Dee and one another. The scene has diminished from Bogart and Robinson to an Abbott and Costello standard. The duos watching each other while pretending not to watch Dee, or Catarina, or whoever she is at this moment. An airport "who's on first" routine. A thin line of perspiration forms on Dee's forehead. Hands tremble. Even her thoughts seem to quiver.

When the time comes and passes for Hunter's flight from Geneva to have arrived, and the boarding for the next flight, his, to Pisa is called, Dee shifts uneasily. No Hunter. She would like to feel or sense his presence, but doesn't. She mumbles, "Hunter, you...." her eyes trolling the concourse, other shops and waiting areas as her mumbling turns to thought. *He'll appear, his soothing, confident voice will tell me to be calm, and then he'll crumble the duos like plastic mannequins.*

A body tremor brings reality and she murmurs, "I'm losing my mind. He's not here. He's not coming. He's gone."

She blinks. Regains focus. The Pisa flight has departed. She inhales deeply.

Everyone appears to be getting edgy, including the waitress who has poured yet another cup of espresso for the lonely and chic lady sitting in her stylish blouse, slacks and shoes, with the not-so-elegant clothes bag draped over one of the other chairs at the table. As another hour passes, Dee's attractiveness and panache fades into distraught expressions and glances. The German duo splits, one window shopping nearby and the other to the food bar in Dee's ristorante. If he were home or in NYC he'd order bratwurst sandwiches, piled high with sauerkraut, on a pretzel roll. However, he's in Roma and fumbles with two meat ball sandwiches and plastic glasses of red wine. When he hands it to his partner, he spills a splash of wine on his associate's suit.

Dee sourly laughs to herself. *Can't hurt that suit.*

The two Russians, shoes shined at least twice, move closer. One sits in a waiting area. The other makes a purchase at a newsstand then returns to sit with his partner. He takes out a pen and dabbles in his magazine. Dee stares. *Do they have crosswords in Russia? Difficult to imagine.* However, no one in this cast is convincing or committed to the play. Only to waiting. And watching.

Forehead dry, hands steady now, Dee as Catarina, hails the bored waitress. Then stands, nods and slaps cash on the table. Smiles for all to see, snatches her clothing bag and strides with a pronounced hooker's gait to the bank of public telephones. Steps into the booth, sorts through some coins, and enters what she is sure to be sufficient. Dials, making her collect call.

During a few exchanges with an operator, and the persistent clicking and pauses, Dee notices one of the Russians has moved close to the phone. She snaps open the door, glares at him, extends her leg out of the booth and stomps her spike heel into the toe of his newly polished shoe. He yelps in anguish, and hops away toward his teammate, scarlet-faced and sputtering, while drawing the quizzical attention of a passersby. Dee slams the door and hears, as if on cue, the operator asking the person on the line to accept the call or not. It is accepted and the voice says, "Dee, I know where you are from the operator, but why? What's happening?"

Dee whispers, "Hunter is not ..."

"Speak louder. I can't hear you very well. Hunter is what?"

Louder, and accelerating her rate as she often does, Dee snaps, "Hunter is not here. He didn't show. And I'm being followed by two different teams of two men. Both are poorly dressed. Cheap suits and if you can believe this, white or light gray socks. With dark suits. My God they look like European Archie Bunkers. I don't ..."

"Dee, you're off and roaring. Calm down."

"Yes. Thank you. I'm a little edgy right now." She takes in a deep breath, and peers through the glass of the booth. "Okay." Another breath. "Now, where was I? Oh, yes ..."

"Dee."

"Yes. I'm fine now. Well," accentuated with a sigh, "based on his yelp, I'd say one is Russian. The other crudely dressed duo could be from anywhere in eastern Europe. What am I supposed to do?"

"One second, darling. How do you know this guy is Russian?"

"Because I understand the F-word in Russian." A pause. "In any language actually."

"What?"

"That's what he screamed when I stomped on his foot while he was trying to listen to me on the phone." A snarly tone has crept into her responses. She continues and explains Hunter's plan, and why she has remained in Rome. Then goes on, "He's not here. He's not coming here, is he? I know that I didn't miss him or something like that. That bastard is on to me. On to us. So, now what?"

There is an uncomfortable pause, accompanied with the intolerable noise of fingers drumming on what might be a wood table. Added to that is the accentuated rustling sounds coming from her shifting and twisting in the booth trying to get comfortable. The tight shoe allegory is not working. She hisses, "You there? Now what, dammit?"

"Okay. Calm down. Wherever he is now, he will be in Pisa. May be there already and it's apparent he's trying to dump you. So, get on the next flight to Pisa. Go to your hotel as expected. I'll have one of my men who has been tagging along go there as well. I'll arrange a flight for him." His tone of voice changes. "And don't shake those four idiots. Let them come along thinking they've got you covered. They'll be cared for there in Pisa. You ..."

"How?"

"How what, Dee?"

"You said they would be cared for. How?"

"I'll handle that. They won't be checking in. They'll be checking out. You stay out of the way and in your room. Order in until my man tracks you down. Possibly Hunter will show up. If he doesn't that'll mean he has information we don't. So if he doesn't show, stay closed-up until my man contacts you."

"Wonderful. What is his name?"

"Oh hell, Dee, I don't know what name he's using at the moment. He hasn't checked in yet. Probably trying as we speak. But he will use my name and speak fluent Italian so you can speak with him as a native. Will draw less attention in public. Questions?"

"Yes, how much longer is this going to go on? I'm getting nervous. I didn't bargain for any of this. I'm beginning to feel I'm going to have to do ... do this myself. I want this to be over and us gone. I want you. You and me. You prom ..."

"Dee. You're doing it again. Calm down, darling."

"I know. I know. But this has gone way beyond ... I just want you and I want us to be gone."

"Dammit, Dee. We knew all this when you pleaded for me to get rid of Angelo. I did that. It was part of the deal, and now this is as well. Now get that hot Italian blood to simmer down and regain that vineyard toughness that allows you to conduct business. Business as normal. You had it once, now get it back for just a few more hours, days. This will be over soon, I promise. And we'll be long away and far wealthier than you or I or anyone can imagine." There is a pause on the line. He can hear deep breaths being taken. Finally.

"Okay, I'm fine," then in a more resolute tone. "Let me get on with it."

John MacBeer softens his voice, says, "It'll be soon. Now, be careful and next time call me only at the number I gave you. Bye."

Click. A rushing noise. Then nothing. Except four sets of eyes staring at the booth although it feels as if all in the concourse have stopped and all eyes are focused on Dee, more accurately Caterina Frati. Of course, they aren't. Only Frick and Frack, and Bogart and Robinson.

Dee takes in a deep, calming and yet sinister breath. Steps out of the booth, unbuttons two top buttons on her blouse and heads to the ticket counter. *If they're goin' to stare, give them some cleavage. And hips.* She wiggles, jiggles and bounces on her way.

Lookin' good, huh guys?

Alfonse Battaglia, or Hunter in a wig, mustache, and the thickening of his dark beard steps from his charter flight, a private early model of a French Cravelle. Before debarking, he scans the area from the tarmac, outward. Everything registering. It's a small commercial airport at *Reggio di Calabrea,* and now there are no other aircraft incoming or departing. Two commercial jobs parked in a hangar. That's it. Possibly it's because the city has a major crime war going on at present. Except for the car and driver he arranged waiting to take him to the boat to cross the *Stretto di Messina* and into Sicily. There he'll travel by the hotel's pick-up bus, the Hotel Lido Mediterranean on *Via Nagionale* in Taormina, Pisces' new home town. The hotel is close to *Spisone Beach*; close to town, has its own private beach, bar and lounge and a new and helpful concierge. He calls a yacht dealer, gets a line on a 78' Stephan's launch that just came on the market. Alfonse will take a walk-about, just a wealthy tourist enjoying the warmth of August and the smell of sea air. The concierge will have a car waiting to take him to the yacht dealer in the harbor.

Roberto Catalano and Chiarina Russo enjoy their wine poolside, watching this August sun settle on the Tyrrhenian Sea. The red glaze on the sea's edge makes ancient seafarers' fears of a flat earth seem true. The chat between the two is of each of their villas, his boat, real estate on his seaboard and advantages of his village of Taormina, as opposed to this western coast of Sicily and the thickening of the smog over Palermo. The port city is busy and growing fast, perhaps too fast. No conversation about Taormina could be void of the recent eruptions on Etna. It is the largest active strato-volcano in Europe and just a few months ago, April and May it had vigorous activities ruining wonderful farmland, ski slopes, forests and fruit orchards. The May activity brought huge crowds and assumed something of a fiesta atmosphere, and enterprising locals brought in pizza stalls, Coca-Cola and beer stands while others fished large lumps of molten rock out of streams near the boccas and beat them into ashtrays to sell to crowds of tourists. Still in all, Chiarina is adamant about leaving the Palermo area.

As dusk rapidly swallows her villa and pool, Chiarina takes a last sip of wine from her glass. Roberto reaches for the bottle which is empty. She puts her hand over her glass, smiles. Estella has arrived out of the shadows with a fresh serving of wine and snacks still wearing the seen-everywhere black and white maid outfit obviously minus undergarments. Chiarina stands, stretches. Her long, sea-side tanned, slender legs accentuated by her heels and white shorts. She undoes her full, thick pony tail letting her hair cascade around and below her shoulders like a velvet curtain dropping on an off-Broadway stage. Her smile turns from one of pure happiness to one of suggestion as she says, "Roberto, I believe we should swim, and perhaps play before dinner."

Catalano nods as he stands. "Sounds wonderful. I assume I can cha ..."

His words hang in a white puff as printed words in a cartoon strip as Chiarina slips out of her emerald green, sleeveless blouse dropping it in her chair before stepping out of her shorts. Regardless of the wide swath he has cut through life, Roberto is motionless and momentarily speechless.

Chiarina cants her head to the side, eyebrows raised and hands on hips after simply allowing her shorts to lie at her feet. She coos, "You like?"

Regaining some form of composure he utters, "I like." Cocks his head, inhales deeply, "Oh yeah. God-damn! I sure as hell do."

"Then hurry for I feel like a young girl again." Trailing her fingers across his pale blue shirt she steps to the edge of the pool. Dips her left toe in the pool, utters, "Good. Warm." She turns at the waist, chin tucked in and down, then adds. "Cold would be refreshing but not good." Giggles softly. She looks to Estella who is standing at the table's edge watching Roberto finally begin to strip off his shirt. Chiarina engages Estella's eyes, says, "Stell, come join us. Three is always more fascinating and pleasurable." Then all in one motion, turns back, sits and wiggles from the edge into the pale aqua water as smooth as a water moccasin and looking as menacing.

Roberto slips off his loafers and hurriedly tries to get out of his beige linen slacks. Staggering and tripping in haste. Estella is out of her simple maid outfit which did not include panties and a bra, and teasingly strolls past the struggling Pisces. She is a pure redhead and alluringly pink. Estella is in the pool alongside Chiarina faster than an aircraft carrier cat shot.

As his trousers tangle around his ankles, Roberto mutters aloud as he finally steps out of the heap, "Oh man, how good can it get," already becoming aroused to the delight of Stell and Chiar.

Chiarina, with Estella swimming on her back doing lazy circles around her, chirps, "Better and I hope you're up for it."

Roberto launches into the pool's warm water and soft lights like a hungry croc.

The inky night sky has swept dusk under the Sicilian carpet. The soft pool lights remain on and the veranda lights help spread a warm glow to the table in the corner, overlooking the cliffs and sea. Chiarina and Roberto relax in terrycloth robes at the candle lit table. His hair slick and combed; she with freshened make-up and her hair blown dry and cascading over her shoulders. Estella has already poured two glasses of wine and is serving a freshly baked tuna casserole and Cannoli with ricotta cheese. She is now in a fresh, relaxed outfit of slacks, halter and a full apron. It's as if the previous splash party was not spontaneous. Possibly planned and habitual, perhaps common place. Whatever the rhyme or reason, it was both a dream and not. Roberto thinks, if ole' Bobby Camack from the streets of Philadelphia could see me now. This is Eden, and the serpent has been satisfied. Well, hell, he can. A comment by Chiarina brings him back to the table, and life as it is.

Once dinner is over, Roberto slides a little deeper in his chair. Takes a sip of Limoncello that Estella has brought Chiarina and him. Fingers the glass, turning it slowly on the white linen tablecloth. Estella nods to her lady, teasingly trails a finger across the back of Roberto's neck as she leaves, saying to him but for all to hear. "Etna is teenage boy compared to you, Signore Roberto."

Pisces turns his head slightly but only catches a whiff of Stell's perfumed scent, however sees Chiarina brush the robe from her thigh, uncross her legs, re-cross them and push the robe from the other thigh. She whispers, "Now you choose for tonight, Mount Roberto. Me, her, or both?"

Roberto sighs. *Life is good.*

As it is to the rabbit that no longer looks for the hawk overhead.

CHAPTER 23

*"Once you're in a fight, it's
way too late to wonder
if it's a good idea."*
A gunfighter's rule

    Sean and Danny are already seated in the coach section of this Alitalia flight from Roma to Pisa. They see the woman they know from descriptions Muldoon gave them. She enters the aircraft long after other first class passengers are on-board and seated. She hangs a clothes bag in the cabin closet and sits in her vacant seat, on the aisle. The two lads see four other late-comers scurry aboard trying to look casual while hurried, anxious to get seated somewhere. They bump and squirm to the rear of the aircraft but not excusing themselves for their hasty rudeness. The Shanahans don't know Franz Bauer and Helmut Faust. Nor do they know Ivan Zharkov and Jaska Maklakov. And based on those same descriptions the Kerrigan man is not on the plane, and it appears that he won't be as the forward hatch is closed by the attendant. However the lady is on board and that has to help them find the American in Pisa. A bonus is she doesn't know them since she saw them in the terminal waiting area and again here on board without a flicker of alarm or recognition.
    Sean, squirming in his seat as the plane backs away from the terminal, whispers, "Danny, I'm havin' me a lot of second thoughts about this."
    "Aye. Me as well. But we're in it now, but I do wonder about it all."
    "Do ya think Muldoon is lying?"
    Danny cocks his head toward his younger brother and replies, "Muldoon would lie to the Almighty to earn a better spot, so it would be nothing to lie to us except to gain something for himself, and perhaps the cause, but by and large for himself."

Minutes pass then Sean sighs long and wistfully. "Ahhh, well then, did I tell you I love Mary Kate?"
"Aye, ya did."
"And you and Mum?"
"Aye, but don't be givin' me a kiss."
They laugh at the remark. Their first since the beginning of the trip so perhaps it is a nervous one as well.

The three Israeli's sit in a far corner of the lounge at the Grand Hotel Duomo in Pisa. They listen to a Mossad compatriot sent from Rome tell them what all Pisa and Italy already know and the world will as well by evening. It is that Reis, their teammate and Marnee's partner, has been found dead in a trash dump outside Rapallo. Reis will be returned home after the authorities are finished. However, the three are reminded to get on with their mission, which now also includes terminating Rocco DeStefano since all are positive that only he could have done this. Unfortunately, the Mossad has no new information as to the whereabouts of Rocco, nor Pisces. The messenger agent does tell Itzak, Namir and Marnee that the woman traveling with the American agent, Kerrigan, is on the way here. She was spotted boarding a plane in Roma. Unfortunately, they have no information on the whereabouts of the American. The agents first lost him in London. Then they lost him in Geneva and he wasn't in Rome. The Mossad compatriot sighs and says, "This is perhaps the largest collection of embarrassed Mossad agents ever." All hang their heads a moment at the statement.
The briefing continues and as it wanes, Marnee, lost in her thoughts, stares out the windows of the lounge which overlooks the street. Suddenly, in a harsh whisper directed at her teammates, "Look. At the curb. Coming in and in a hurry."
All turn and look curbside. Then their eyes follow Dee through the front door and up the marble stairway opposite them, to the registration desk. They watch as she hurriedly checks in, constantly looking around and behind her. The woman leaves abruptly, fingers hooked to a

clothes bag over her shoulder, heading for the elevators. When the elevator door closes, Marnee gets up to see where the indicator stops. She signals her partners, then descends the steps to the polished marble of the ground floor. She eases out the front door and lingers on the street as a tourist might, contemplating which direction to stroll. She instantly absorbs the madness of this game as the Russians arrive by taxi, and yet another odd looking duo, closing at roughly a trot, toward the hotel from the direction of the Pisa Centrale Train Station. Marnee turns in the opposite direction, and crosses Via Santa Maria, as if heading for the shops.

Itzak and Namir will see what I am up to. The key is Rocco and I have a nose for smoke and that always leads to fire.

Two sets of gentlemen sit at opposite ends of the beautiful dark-stained but modern looking bar at the Hotel Duomo on Via Santa Maria. Bottles of every liquor known to man line the glass shelves in front of the mirrored wall behind the bar. To one side is a square support pillar, also stained dark, filled with black and white photos of celebrities and wanna be's. Neither duo know of the other. Sean and Danny Shanahan drinking ale, Itzak and Namir sipping soda water with a twist of lime. Their common bond now is the TV in the corner blasting the news of a murder of a young man and woman here in Pisa, and the finding of the Israeli tourist murdered and left in a trash dump in Rapallo. The Israeli's know of one and make the connection of the other. And they know Marnee has now gone off on her own. A trait not admired by her teammates nor Mossad headquarters, but it is Marnee and it works. The Shanahans know only that the woman, Dee, registered as Caterina Frati, is here and with any luck will lead them to the American, Kerrigan, or whoever he pretends to be this day. The news makes them think of home and of the aftermaths on the morns following all PIRA missions.

Sean takes a sip of his ale, mutters, "Vibes. Bad vibes. The news is tellin' us something, Danny."

"Aye. We'll keep a sharp eye about us."

"Ahhh, Danny, me brother. My mind keeps slippin' to home. And the beauty of our land. The visions of the Cliffs of Moher, River Blackwater, Killarney Lakes, Gap of Dunloe and such. And Mary Kate ... and Mum ... and Paddy. Then comes the ugliness of The Army, and Muldoon, and his idiot son. All of it. There is a better way and a better life I think."

"Aye."

"We should follow that path perhaps."

"Aye ... and find meself a Mary Kate."

"And soon."

"Very soon. Yes indeed. You're not thinking about kissin' me again, are ye?"

Another nervous chuckle is shared.

Hunter, as Alfonse Battaglia, is settled in at the Hotel Lido Mediterranee on Via Nazionale in Taormina. Only Joe Zachary knows Hunter is here, and that is because Joe obtained Pisces current address from the cigar manufacturer. It's in Taormina. A luxurious Pisces habit that has become a ded reckoning LOP for Hunter. He needs only two, perhaps three LOP's, clues, for the fix. Tomorrow will bring a well-disguised reconnaissance, followed by a nighttime one as well. For the moment, Hunter sits on the terrace overlooking the beach on the aqua blue Mediterranean. It is covered with the yellow and white beach umbrellas, beach chairs, and the beautiful people who can afford this resort. A few yachts, to include the 78' Stephan's, are anchored a hundred or so meters offshore and several smaller, quicker boats are pulling water skiers up and down the shoreline, between the anchored yachts and swimmers. One can't miss the large number of shapely young women in tiny bikinis and more than a few are topless. *I could love Europe. And not shaving, in truth, is sexy on most, at least these here.*

Alfonse takes a sip of the Chianti Reserva from Tuscany. Then another as he recaptures his thoughts of the last several hours and in particular his update from Joe Zachary.

Antonio, the possible lead is dead. An Israeli agent is dead, murdered. A MacBeer man is headed to Pisa, and Dee. However, the target lives here. And the big guy, DeStefano, has most likely gone to ground and if not caught or killed will show up here sooner or later. Either way he will be handled, but he's vital to finish this mess ... a sophisticated thug with more ties than an eyelet field boot. Complex as a spider's web but yet as simple. Then Hunter mutters another rule by some gunfighter somewhere, "Squeeze, don't pull. Watch, don't blink. Move, don't wait." Then a tad louder, "Missions change; warriors don't."

"Sir, would the Signore care for another, or perhaps a menu?"

"Oh, excuse me. Ahhh, well, just talking to myself and admiring the scenery. Yes, another will do just fine. No menu, I will eat inside later. Thank you."

"No problem, Signore." The waiter leaves smiling since they both have not only spoken in the native language, but Hunter's, Alfonse's, is marinated with the dialect of this Messina area.

When the waiter returns with Alfonse's wine, he takes a moment to suggest that the Signore take time to tour the Etna eruption sites. The waiter adds that he had, as well as most Taormina citizens and visitors had, especially the dry waterfall in the Cava Grande where the lava had flowed like a great river of glittering red and orange streams. He adds wistfully, "Not so now, but still ..." he shrugs and smiles.

Alfonse nods, smiles and thanks the man. Follows with, "I will. Perhaps the day after tomorrow. First I want to walk about the town. Take it in. Locate a friend if I can. A painter. Perhaps you have heard of him, Roberto Catalano?"

"Ah, yes, Signore. Signore Catalano. He stayed here for a few days some time ago. A notably generous gentleman. He is an artist. A painter of oils and lives her now," pointing up over the hotel toward the bay and the cliffs beyond. "Big, big villa. Keeps to himself except when he paints."

The waiter prattles on for several moments, then hurriedly excuses himself to attend another table where a beautiful woman is waving frantically for service.

Hunter glances at the woman. *Can't blame him.*

Then he sets off to the concierge's desk and his limo. He's made his decision and will purchase a practically new 78 foot Stephan's. The previous owner brought it to Taormina, then passed away less than a week after his purchase. His wife is not a seafarer so the launch is available at an easily negotiable price. It has a cruising speed of 11K, max of 13. The launch has five cabins, sleeps nine and has three heads. Has an open salon, large formal lounge and an aft sundeck. It is done in beige leather and mahogany furniture and trimmings. The decks are all teakwood. Hunter has it registered and named *The Marnies* after an old Marine joke about an Air Wing snuffy who painted Marnies on the tail of all the planes in his squadron. A slight spelling error. Anyway, Hunter laughs softly as the paperwork is being completed. *I'll understand it.*

Rocco moves quickly on foot to a public phone and makes a call to an old friend that has done him many business favors in the past. This old friend can only take calls from a few people, and Rocco is one, perhaps the most important. He is as good as Rocco at his trade, but a recluse by historical necessity, which is good. Drago Brafa is a friend, and also a Sicilian by birth. Drago comes to Rocco, picks him up and they drive to Drago's home near the river in Pisa. It is small, old, and attracts no attention. Nor does Drago these days.

Over a much needed glass of wine with Drago's animated grunts, homemade sign language and Rocco's nodding replies, Rocco finally arrives at his topic. "Drago, how would you like to come to work for me? Home in Sicily? Even near your Messina?"

Drago smiles. Pauses, then sighs. His response is his normal guttural sounds, grunts and sign language but his demeanor is excited and one that exudes appreciation. This is Drago's means of communication since his tongue was cut out by the Nazi's and left him for dead twenty-seven years ago. He survived, was found and resurrected by Rocco who understands the language of Drago. The interpretation is, "Home. Ah, that sounds wonderful," but the notes also carry a mysterious melody. "For you old friend, or for your employer?"

"Well, yes, for my employer, of course. But, day to day, for me. You will have little if any contact with him, and for that you will be thankful, yet well rewarded."

"Will I live in this place? And what is it I will be asked to do?"

"Yes, Drago, you will live on the premises. At the villa. You will help provide security. And help me with some tasks from time to time. And with some at hand now. Tasks you are familiar with and have done many times for your country, and after, for me. Have I ever wronged you? Have you not always been handsomely rewarded?"

"By you, yes. That part is true, but I am not as strong and quick as I once was, so now I must use more of my mind in completing tasks. Perhaps plan better. Not too much charging as a bull might."

"Drago, I know all that. Let me get to the point. I need help now, here in Pisa, to get rid of some people. Then we will go to Sicily and get lost forever. With our women. Do you have a woman?" Rocco pauses, getting no response to the women remark, he continues. "The pay is good. The villa is spacious, and the work will be quiet and uneventful. More like retirement, only with better benefits than most."

Drago sighs. Stares at his friend and many-time confederate, and labors through his questions. "Do I understand you correctly? You want me to kill, or help you kill some people here? Then we leave quickly and quietly for Sicily. There it will only be security? Bodyguard? Working for your employer? And I have your word, that once home, the killing is over?"

"Yes. That is it. You have my word. And you will be richer than you can imagine."

"Imagine?"

"Well, perhaps not imagine. But richer than you are, or can expect in your lifetime."

Drago pauses for several moments. Looks around his small house. Smiles. "I will do this for you, Rocco. Done. Tell me who, where and when." He smiles, "Soon I would imagine."

"Yes, soon and, ahhh ... more than a few. Good, Drago. Downright good. First, another glass of Chianti to wash the taste and smell of Antonio from me. Then my plan."

The man rises, grunts, "Yes, Bossa."

After her arduous and nerve racking trip, Maria DeLuca arrives at the La Palma Hotel on Via Vittorio Elmanuele III on Capri. The one that Hunter told her about in his dream. "Nightmare," she mutters. "But real now, and gorgeous." The flights were long. The meeting with Zachary seemed longer but was brief, succinct and cool. The flight from Rome to Naples, was a puddle-jumper or more apropos, a vineyard-jumper. The forty-minute ferry ride across the Bay of Naples was beautiful and refreshing. Mind clearing in a fashion. The hotel she has learned was first established in 1822, modernized and added to several times over, but its distinctive trademark symbol, the palm tree, remains in front.

The view from her room is breath-taking. The old town and the sea. The room like the hotel is grand, and she has been told by an eager Desk Manager of its clientele over the years. Royals, such as King Constantine of Greece, if one has an interest in such things. She thinks, *the stars that visited here such as Sophia Loren and Gina Lollobrigida would be of more interest to Hunter than the good King.* She laughs softly at the thought, then sighs at the reason she is here, Dee, her family. The man, Hunter, will destroy all that, and yet maybe, possibly provide salvation and restoration in some strange unforeseen way.

Unpacked, showered, and dressed she again reads the message given to her when she registered. "Maria. Don't try to reach me. I will call late tonight. Have a nice dinner. Try Mamma Gemma's. Ask for directions. H."

She places the message on the small desk holding the telephone and leaves for da Gemma Ristorante on Via L'Abate. When she asked of the ristorante Maria was informed by the gentleman at the desk that Mamma Gemma and her husband, Raffaele, started this now famous eatery in the early 1950's. It's in the historical center of Capri. Its walls are adorned by dozens upon dozens of photographs of famous people, and many not so famous, but all have visited and eaten at this ristorante. And all have for sure seen the most famous of the photos, that of Mamma Gemma in her famous red apron.

Maria is ushered to a small table in the corner with a wonderful view of the town and the entire room. When the waiter arrives, Maria asks in her best Italian, "Would you have by chance an American Wine from the DeLuca Reserva?"

The waiter's eyes brighten, pleased with the native language from this new stranger, but more so by the request. "Oh, yes, of course. The only one we have. The family was originally from the Tuscany area and had a wonderful winery there. We like to think of them as one of our own, or at least Momma Gemma did." He pauses, then, "You know of this wine? This family?"

"Yes. I am the granddaughter of Signore and Signora DeLuca. Maria DeLuca."

The waiter bows graciously, rises, looks around, arms spread palms up and smiles, "Then your first night will be as our guest." He smiles, shrugs, "I am family. May I suggest a bottle of the Chianti Reserva?"

Maria nods her head, smiles demurely, and murmurs, "Thank you, Signore. It will be my pleasure, and the Chianti will be an excellent start to this evening."

The waiter takes Maria's hand, brushes her fingers with his lips, and scurries away to get the wine and notify others of their special guest this evening, and of course bring the Ristoranti's photographer back for a picture of him and Maria DeLuca, for the wall of course.

Maria relaxes, smiles and nods to a few tables of guests who have overheard the waiter's remarks and certainly observed his flamboyant gestures. Her turmoil hidden in a tourist moment.

I'm here. Should have brought the escort.

CHAPTER 24

"Anyone worth shooting is worth shooting more than once. Ammo is cheap."

A gunfighter's rule

The ring of the telephone is a shrill interruption to the peacefulness of the Russo villa.

"*Salve,*" the woman continues in her native language and dialect. "Signora Russo's residence. This is Estella."

Rocco replies in same. "Estella, is Signore Catalano present, please?"

There is a pause, then the soft voice says, *"Questo dipenda?"*

"*Il mio name a' Rocco DeStefano. Io sono suo amico. E molto importante.*"

Another pause accompanied with a sigh. Then in a husky whisper, *"Attendere un momento."*

Standing at the wall phone, Rocco drums his fingers on Drago's kitchen counter as moments that seem like hours drag by. The hurried tedium is broken by Roberto Catalano's harsh voice. "Rocco, speak to me and be quick." Then in a bit warmer tone, "I am pleasantly occupied."

"*Si. Ciao.*" Rocco continues in his native language. Easier for him; about the same for Pisces although irritable. "Antonio and his unfortunate girlfriend are no longer here. And better, they spoke to no one."

His tone of voice back to harsh and brisk, Catalano replies, "Yes, I know. Although I have little time to myself here, I have heard the good news on TV."

"What isn't on the news is that the clans have gathered here. All looking for Antonio, or perhaps me, to lead them home."

"You will not let that happen. Understood?"

"Yes, it will be so. To assist I have hired an old friend, the 'Silent One'. You remember him? He will help me dissuade the clans and he can be trusted."

"Ahhh, yes. Awfully good, but he's a bit soft in the jowls and more grey in the temples these days. Yes?"

"*Si*. But still excellent and most important, trustworthy."

Roberto Catalano pauses. One can all but hear his mind shifting through the gears, Low-Low, Low, and finally, Drive. He asks in a whisper but maintains his coarseness, "And who are these interested clans?"

"The same. From the north and both dressed poorly. And of course the constant companions from the Middle East. They have never forgotten your trip to Jerusalem."

"*Si*. They never forget. Shit, from the beginning of time they remember." He pauses, then, "But I heard something on the news about them."

"Yes, they are one less. Now three, at least here. Probably more coming."

"You have a plan?"

"*Si*. We will dispense of our friends this evening. All of them. And the extraordinarily beautiful lady who is also here. The mistress of your close friend."

Another pause from the villa on the west coast of Sicily. Longer than before. Long enough to cause Rocco to utter, "Bossa?"

"Yes. I'm here. The lady. Ahhh, yes. Okay. Do it. Put an end to all this. For all time. Everything to bed, finally. Then, come home. Bring the silent one with you, and we'll let him settle in peace and comfort. With the two, or three, or four of us." Pisces laughs, then, "And, I have something special for you."

"I will do. Our friend will be pleased." A short pause, then, "What is special? Did it answer the telephone?"

"You will see." Click

Rocco has learned from experience that Pisces' surprises can be either colossal or fatal. Most have found the latter to be the case. Bruno certainly did. As did Anna. And before her, many. He mutters to himself, "And now Gina, I'ma guessin'. Well, I too have surprises."

Drago comes into the kitchen and grunts, "All finished? When do we get started?"

"Now."

"Tonight?"

"Of course. The night is always kind to the silent and the deadly."
"And the swift?" grunts Drago. He pats his belly.
"Swift enough, and remember, ammo is cheap."
"Yes, a common law in the trade."

Hunter walks the town. A reconnaissance patrol in tourist mode and dress. A tourist sees what they want and expect. The beauty and the historic. However, the scout sees all that and more. The hidden; the darkness; the shadows; and the unexpected. And he sees it as he will at night.

Taormina is old; is quaint; and many sections are crowded with tourists. The distance from the Lido Mediterrainee to Pisces' villa is further than Hunter anticipated as it relates in time to traverse on foot. At patrol's end he spends the remainder of the afternoon observing the villa. It's beautiful. Spacious. A veranda with pool which has a covered sun deck and two uncovered. Also a four-person Jacuzzi-Spa. Two floors with an attached building with garages. And only a low stone wall. A five minute walk to town and no more than a five-minute drive to the beaches. Can see Etna although it must be 50km's, and from the pool area can see Naxos's beach and the Ionian coast. Even has what appears to be a wood-burning oven, perhaps for pizzas. More important there are three servants occupying the quarters above the garage, and no security, at least for now. Hunter mulls this last observation. *He wouldn't have needed any if he hadn't made the mistake with the cigar wrapper, and the ordering. The first, tiny. The second, fatal.*

A few deliveries come and go with ease. But, seemingly no Pisces. Through his travels today, Hunter knows that Roberto Catalano's boat, the 98 foot Benitti, *The Sorrento*, is gone and has been for several days. Gazing at the villa from the late afternoon shadows at the end of the street, Hunter thinks, *The help will be a problem. They have no place in this. Only Pisces and his man, Rocco. Possibly his woman if he has one. Hell, he always has one.* He pauses again. Another look, then starts strolling away from this beautiful area of Taormina knowing he will have to change hotels tonight. As he continues to amble down the hill towards town he thinks of what he has seen. *The servants. Two older people and a young lad. Probably a woman somewhere. And of course Pisces and Rocco when they return. And they will. And they will die.*

At the bottom Hunter stops, looks back for a moment. Turns and strides away at a hurried pace. *I can't avoid this fight, and I may just have to go into a survival mode and clean up the collateral damage, bodies, later.*

Having returned from his walk-about patrol, Alfonse Battaglia hurriedly checks out of the Lido Mediterrainee hotel claiming he must return home because of an illness in the family. The valet loads the taxi, Alfonse tips him generously enough to satisfy the young man but not so much as to attract attention. Then he has the driver leave, appearing to head to Messina and its airport. Shortly after a few turns, a trip through town, a stop and park to stroll along a street looking for any possible tails, Hunter arrives at his new destination. The Atahotel Capotaormina on Via Nazioale. The hotel was founded four years ago and built on top of a cliff. A short hike to Pisces' villa. Hunter takes a classic room in lieu of their offerings of an Executive, Superior or a Suite. He'll draw less attention although all who come here attract some form of notice because of its exquisite nature. The hotel, established on the top, has lounges and pools down below. One being a salt water pool located at the tip of the property. Everything overlooks the exquisite blues of the ancient Bay of Naxos and Mediterranean Sea.

After a shower and change of clothes, Hunter as Signore Alfonse Battaglia, goes to the hotel's La Scoglura Restaurant for a drink or two and dinner. He is seated at a table on the terrace highlighted by its stained wood decking and frame, with its bar and other tables on the other side of the glassed wall and sliding door. The restaurant of course specializes in Sicilian cuisine with the seafood all fresh caught that day.

Having been served, Signore Battaglia relaxes at his table with a glass of Carricante, a white from the Etna area. It is mild, not as strong as many other local wines, and will blend nicely with the seafood feast he is entertaining. And perhaps just one glass of Malvosia with its golden amber color from the island of Li Pari near Messina after dinner. Then a stroll of the hotel grounds enjoying the view and return to his room, dress for his evening patrol to Pisces' villa, and perhaps inside if the opportunity presents itself.

"Is the Signore ready to order, sir? We have some excellent choices this evening."

Signore Battaglia feigns surprise of the waiter's arrival and responds in Italian. "No, not yet, and I know of the choices. It is a difficult decision. As is the entire menu, but I may go with one of the choices and let you decide which for me."

"That would be an honor, Signore. I will think on it long and hard. In the meantime, just one more glass of the Carricante?"

"*Si.*"

The waiter returns shortly with the wine and leaves Hunter with his thoughts as he sips his Etna wine.

Gotta get inside tonight while it's empty.

And call Joe later.

And Maria ... gotta keep her cool. She's shaky. Need to get her some help.

MacBeer's man has arrived and sits with Dee in the cocktail lounge. They talk in whispers as the two Irishmen and the two Israelis at opposite ends of the bar separately pretend to be in deep conversation as they watch Dee. Also with occasional eyeball sweeps of the lounge and lobby area. The Israelis of course see the Russians. Sean and Danny Shanahan don't know who they are but saw them and another clumsy pair board the plane late. And they can't clearly see the man's face who is sitting with the American woman, but they think he may be the man, Kerrigan. What they do know is that there is more going on than they bargained for, or perhaps want.

The two Russians sit in separate chairs in the lobby, table between the two, one smoking a cigarette and feigning relaxation after dinner while the other leafs through a magazine pretending interest.

The two Germans, believing the lobby is already too crowded, stand outside, across the street in a closed shop doorway hidden in the shadows of the night. Drago, smoking, nonchalantly is leaning against his recently inherited off-duty taxi. The driver in the back seat, neck broken, is forever off duty. The Silent One simply waits for the plan to unfold.

Rocco has slipped inside the hotel from the rear alley and has found what he wants. Two unlocked cleaning and storage closets. One on the ground floor in the rear, and one on the fourth floor, just at the end of the hallway near the Queen Bee, Teresa Dee DeLuca's room. Returning below he stacks rags, towels, face cloths, rolls of toilet paper and boxes of tissue in the closet, then douses them with lighter fluid. Then empties a plastic bottle of tile cleaner and fills it with more fluid. Using a cleaning rag, he fashions a long enough fuse for the bottle so it'll burn for a few minutes. Rocco lights the cloth fuse, leaves the door ajar and dashes to the fire exit, then up three steps at a time to the fourth floor.

He repeats the process on the fourth floor using less materials, and with a shorter fuse. He leaves that door ajar as well and walks to the other end of the hall. When he hears and sees the explosion at the other end, he breaks and pulls the fire alarm. Starts down the hallway screaming "fire" and shouting for people to get outside. He senses the explosion below hearing another alarm going off and people shouting. Next are the announcements over speakers in the lobby and internal PA system ordering people to evacuate the building and not to use elevators. The latter is emphasized again and again. The hallway on the fourth floor comes alive with people rushing out of rooms, some screaming, some shouting instructions, all running for the fire exit after excitedly finding the direction to run. Rocco struggles with the crowd's surge, but he shouts and creates as much panic as he can until he reaches Dee's room. No one notices him stopping, picking the lock, and entering as opposed to following the herd. He's just another panicked body at a room door.

All of the room floors are being evacuated as are the lounges, bars, and lobby. Men and women in all forms of garb, pour onto the street in front. Bartenders and hotel employees hurry people outside. The fire engines, lights flashing, have begun to arrive. Police cars screech to a halt, sirens screaming and their blue lights flashing adding to the eeriness of the night. The guests, employees, and other people gather outside, backing away, to watch the building, inside and out. Police cordon the street forcing the crowd backwards towards the shadows of the other side. It looks and sounds like London, Tokyo or Berlin in the '40's, except there are no flames. Merely a little smoke is visible which in itself creates more babble and hence a louder crowd din.

Drago backs away from his inherited taxi and eases over behind the two Germans who have inched away from the doorway, drawn by the events. No longer in the shadows. The two pops, each silenced revolver shots, are not even remotely heard over the sirens of the last few fire engines arriving or over the pandemonium of the crowd's shouting, talking and gasps. No one notices anything happening behind them. The Germans slump to the ground like flour sacks dropped from a truck bed. Drago has shot each twice, double taps, so quickly that the second of the two barely reacted. One shot, up, in the back of the head, and the second at the base of the neck, angled downward. With the about simultaneous thuds of their bodies, Drago glances around, seeing that no one has seen or heard anything other than the commotion, jerks the bodies back into the doorway and darkness. He leaves, walking close to the backs of the crowd to where the two Russians are standing, at the back of the mob scene at one end of the crowd, watching the people in front of them but more the entrance of the hotel.

Drago takes the same two quick shots each, same angles. They too drop. The pops of the two double taps not heard. However, the spray of blood and bone seems to float in the air above the back edge of the crowd. Most dissipates unnoticed except for some of it that a few people seemingly wipe the dampness from their necks or shoulders as if it were a mist or spray of water. They will determine otherwise in minutes.

Drago is gone like a ghost in a nightmare. He melts away behind vehicles and crowd, moves unnoticed up to the corner, then around it as if a fleeting shadow. Unnoticed except for one person, who follows at a careful distance.

Marnee, hugging building walls, thinks. *This is the Italian's work and this man will lead me to him. And to Pisces.*

Rocco, confidant that Drago has dispensed of the Germans and Russians watches from the window of Dee's room. A table lamp lit as it was when he entered, as well as the door being relocked so it too will be as she left it. He sees that the circus is ending outside. Nothing damaged he's sure except inside of the hallway janitorial closets, and a little smoke on two floors. He hears the stomping of firemen's feet and their shouting as they ensure all is well on this floor. The alarms have ceased. The hotel night manager is on the PA system encouraging people to come back inside, and return to their rooms or take advantage of free drinks for all in any of the bars or lounges. Rocco goes over his plan in his mind. He will wait in Dee's clothes closet and when she returns, kill her quickly and quietly thus getting rid of the last of those that can hold a hammer over his head. The last that can ruin his and Pisces' retirement ... and Drago's, maybe. He would like to take his time and make it hurt, but he still has the Jews to terminate.

The two Irishmen, Sean and Danny, are quick to return to the bar and claim their reward for the inconvenience. The hotel's offer is being taken advantage of by a staggering number of guests. Fire officials are still roaming the building. Some police. Staff has returned and all are busy cleaning up, serving, with a few foolishly running about with little direction, jabbering about the events.

The Israelis, Itzak and Namir have returned to the lobby. They stand in a far corner, not interested in the mollifying beverages. Itzak whispers, "The Irishmen are back inside. Not the Russians. And I don't see ..." He stops as both spot Dee reentering. She and the well dressed American gentleman that was with her earlier enter the elevator. Itzak continues, "Well, I do now. As I said earlier, that escort has CIA written across his back like American footballers."

Namir replies, "Yes, and watch. It'll stop on four. This is getting interesting, and also for our two Irish friends. We and they are the only ones in here who seem to be watching that duo."

"You're correct, friend. It's stopped on four and I sense..." For the second time within minutes, Itzak's comment is interrupted. This time from screams and shouting from outside the hotel. Guests are now surging to get inside, while other curiosity seekers fight their way out. The few policemen inside race toward the entrance. The circus has erupted again and the clamor inside is momentarily silenced when a guest races in shouting, "There are dead men all over the street. A murderer is loose."

The surge both ways continues along with dozens of screaming women, and the shouts of police warning, "STAY INSIDE. PLEASE. STAY INSIDE, " over again and again.

Itzak and Namir calmly fight their way through the crowding, shoving and pushing flow. They arrive outside, ignore the police shouts and work their way to the edges of now both frightened and excited guests, passersby, and lingering curiosity seekers. They nod to one another, splitting up. Each goes to the crowd gathering around each site despite police warnings and cordoning. Moments after each has seen the Russians and Germans, they find one another. Itzak shakes his head, "It's the two Russians. Assassinated. Professional."

Namir replies, "Same for the Germans, and I suspect more than a routine problem with the taxi. The police found what is probably the driver in the back seat. His neck, snapped like a chicken."

Itzak orders, "We've got to get back inside and check the woman. The Italian has to be responsible for this. Everything. The fire, and all this."

Namir adds to this assessment. "He's got help. Possibly one, or more."

The two Israelis fight and claw their way through guests, the curious onlookers, the police and firemen into the lobby. Itzak says, "They're gone. Where are the damn Irishmen?"

"The hell with them. Where is that big fucking Italian? We better check on the lady. And watch our own ass." Namir tugs at Itzak's arm, "And where the hell is Marnee?"

He replies, "I would suspect outside. And on to the person responsible out there."

CHAPTER 25

"Use cover and concealment as much as possible."
A gunfighter's rule

Rocco hears the room door open as he squats, waiting, in the room's clothes closet. He has his M951R Beretta with suppressor in hand, elbows resting on his knees, weapon pointing up and out. His head is slightly canted so his ear is nearer the closet door. He hears a man's voice say, "I better go in and just check around."

Then the reply from the lady. "Really? I like the sound of the first part but why the latter? We left with all the others and it was locked."

"Yeah, I know. But Mister MacBeer would kill me if I made a mistake and let something happen to you."

"Oh, that's warm and enticing. What can happen? Kerrigan has vanished. I don't know where he is and could care less at this stage. Besides your boss is a long way off."

The agent shakes his head side to side, eyebrows raised and mutters, "Right." Takes in a breath, drones, "Nonetheless, checking is in order. In here first."

A pause, the sound of a shower curtain rustling, then, "The bathroom is clear. Hey, stay away from the window."

Rocco feels the vibration of footsteps on the floor coming toward the closet. The man's voice, closer now, agitated and more pronounced, issues another warning. "GET AWAY FROM THE WINDOW. NOW. Please."

The agent grasps both knobs of the double-door closet and swings them open as if using a chest exercise cable. Rocco stands and fires. "Pfssst." The first round hits the agent in the chest as Rocco rises. Then with the pistol's suppressor one inch from the agent's forehead, "Pfsssst." The back of the man's head explodes spraying blood, brains and bone toward the inside of the room. Part of the spray splatters on Dee as she nears the foot of the bed from the window. The sagging agent is blown backward from the two 9mm hollow point rounds and drops like a felled buffalo. Rocco steps over the body quickly and fires a shot into Dee's chest. She staggers to the foot of the bed, falls backward on the bed. Her face is splattered on her right side with a portion of the agents head. Blood surges through the center of her sheer blouse. She tries to speak. Rocco quickly looks around to check the room door. It's closed, but not locked. Several quick steps there, snaps the lock and fastens the security chain, and back again at the foot of the bed. Dee lays, face up, gasping for air. The sound of the sucking chest wound is distinctive. She struggles to raise herself on her elbows. Mouth trying to form words. Eyes bulging with terror and senselessness.

Rocco leans over, inches from her nose and says, "Angelo was a good man. A good Italian man. Too fucking good for you, but orders were orders. Just business."

Dee's face exhibits shock and confusion. Her vocal gasps and the wound's sucking sounds are interwoven into the murkiness of death. She drops from her elbows to laying flat on her back, legs dangling over the end of the bed. Blood pulsing from her chest, running through the sheer white blouse, and seeping down her side to the plush decorative green and beige bedspread. More blood oozing underneath from the exit wound.

The huge Italian leans over even closer. Kisses her forehead. Hisses, "I wish I could make it hurt more but I don't have time. So, this is for Angelo. For loving and trusting a whore." Rocco lifts Dee's skirt, shoves the Beretta up between her legs and fires a round. Her body shudders, flopping up and down like a fish's final effort on the wooden planks of a dock. Rocco smiles, snarls, "And this is for mea and my bossa, and his *amico* in Washington." Another silenced pop. A single 9mm round between her eyes. Her body completely limp now, eyes cold and lifeless, staring at the ceiling, seeing nothing. The bed spread now a soaked and splattered coppery-smelling canvas of blood like a contemporary artist's rendering of death at sunset.

Rocco stands and scans the room. Moves to the closet, takes out his handkerchief and wipes the door knobs clean. *That's all I've touched. Except the room door.*

He quietly steps over the agent's body and moves to the room door and his exit. *Got one more job to do tonight.*

He is stopped by a tapping at the door, followed by a voice speaking Italian, "Ma'am, this is room service checking to ensure guests are safe and secure? Are satisfactory?"

Rocco stands motionless. *The Italian is good, but not native. Shit.*

The tap is repeated, but louder. The question is also repetitive and louder. However, there is another voice whispering, indistinguishably. Then the original voice again, "Ma'am," not in Italian, "we know you are in the room. Are you safe?"

The door handle rattles as it's tried from the outside. The other voice speaks, not in a whisper, but louder, in a grimly, hushed tone. "I know she's in there. This is her room. They came back up."

"Yes, but possibly to his room."

"He's not registered. He hasn't checked in. Perhaps this guy is Kerrigan?"

Itzak says, "We need to go in. Ready?"

Namir looks both ways, sees no one in the long hallway. Steps back and peers up the hall to the elevator. Whispers, "The elevator is still here on this floor. This isn't smart nor the ..."

His comment stopped by the sound of the door's chain being removed and the lock snapping open. Both Itzak and Namir have their weapons in hand, at arm's length and the side of their legs. The door swings inward as if sucked open by a tornado. Rocco fires four shots, two each before either can raise his weapon. One each to the heart, and one each to the face. Both lurch backward into the hallway wall which is splattered with blood and skull remnants. Itzak and Namir thump to the carpet smearing separate streaks of blood on the wall on the way down. Rocco fires another suppressed round into Namir. The slide of his Beretta locks to the rear. He changes his magazine with another ten round mag and fires a final shot into Itzak's face.

He wipes the door handle both inside and out and steps all the way out the door, walks hurriedly to the exit stairwell door being careful not to be heavy footed. He takes the steps two and three at a time until reaching the lobby floor. There are still excited guests milling about. People surging in and out. The police have not yet been able to get the full control needed. There is no aftershock calm, and although certainly to come, no lockdown yet.

Once outside, Rocco melts into the crowd and confusion, and drifts across the street and around the corner. As he walks in the shadows of the buildings intent on meeting Drago at their prearranged location near the park, he thinks of the Irishmen. *They can be spared. They are no threat to me.*

At the bar Danny and Sean continue to sit, sipping their third ale. Watching the crowd, taking in the din of the commotion inside and out. Danny, the elder brother leans over, chin not wholly resting on the younger's shoulder. "Laddie, I be thinking we need to leave this place. It's beginning to look like the riots of '69."

Sean turns toward Danny, "It tis. You're probably right, brother. Probably right. But, a good night's rest before we put a foot under us won't hurt. And give us time what we're goin' to tell Muldoon."

Danny takes a gulp and snorts, spraying some ale and bits of chewed peanuts. "Fuck Muldoon." Then he takes another, the last, and in a hushed, sing-song manner says, "Rather, brother dear, think of this. At some time real soon, real fucking soon, the police are going to lock this place down and question every guest. Every person in here."

"So, we've done nothing wrong. The barkeep can attest to that."

"Yes, well, that is so, but I be thinking if I were the police, 'What are two young Irish lads from Londonderry doing here in Pisa with all this going on? Might be wise to run their names with the Brits.'" He pauses for another gulp. "I would. It's not as if we're a couple on vacation nor will the Brits say, 'Oh, it's just those delightful Shanahan lads.' What say ye, laddie?"

"Aaah, yes. Well now, the morn dawns and it's not a pretty one regardless what the Lord says about painting another. Let's finish and get a foot under ..."

Sean's words have trail to a whisper, then drag to a stop. Both brothers, startled, stare at the commotion happening at the front desk. The desk clerk is losing all composure, yelling for the Manager and the police. The rush away from the desk is frantic, exceeded only by the police and firemen's dash toward the clerk.

An elevator door hisses open, a woman bursts from within, screaming, "They're killing everyone. All of us are doing to die. My God, help us! Help us!"

More shrieking women and shouting men stream out of the fire exit stairwell, racing for the outside doors.

What was ebbing is now a tsunami again.

Chiarina pulls herself up the chrome ladder from the pool. Her naked body glistens from both the water's lights and the moon. She snatches the annoyingly ringing patio telephone from its cradle on a nearby table, snaps, "Russo residence. Now is notta a good time." She listens for a few moments then turns to Roberto Catalano who is now side stroking to the edge of the pool. "It's for you. Your man says it's important."

"I'll take it," and Pisces clambers out of the pool, also naked and not fully settled. Takes the phone from Chiarina and says into the instrument, "This better be damn important."

Rocco whispers, "It is. They are all gone except the two Irishmen who can be the blustering one's problem."

"Wait a second." Pisces muffles the phone against his thigh, looks to Chiarina and says, "I must take this. We can con ..."

"We will continue but inside. It will be warmer, but then perhaps not if you don't hurry." She turns but grins over her shoulder and snatches a towel from a chair back. "Don't be long." She strolls, hips swaying, towel dangling from her hand trailing along as she moves toward her room off the villa patio.

Pisces mutters, "Damn. She's going to kill me before I get her home." He puts the phone to his ear in time to hear Rocco say, "What was that. I didn't ..."

"Nothing. Not important. Now tell me quickly where we are on this final matter."

Rocco explains quickly about the Russians and Germans. Goes into detail about Dee and her traveling companion, and also the easier than expected collateral damage to the Israelis. Explains why not the two Irishmen when Pisces questions him. Then finally says, "It is time to come home. Yes?"

"Yes, and I will be there in two days with guests. By boat. You get there as soon as possible and ensure all is well. And Rocco, are you sure no one saw you?"

"No one that is alive."

"What about, Drago?"

"Well, of course, but he will not ..."

"Do not bring, Drago."

"But ..."

"You will only need Estella, and me of course, for friends. And Chiarina as my wife. Drago is a witness and is useless to us. He can only be a problem. Let him be known as the tormented one. The butcher of Pisa."

"Yes, that is better. It will be done. What about Muldoon?"

"He knows nothing of us. Besides, our American friend in Washington will take care of him and he will be pleased to do so, and know that I will leave him be to retire, albeit alone. It is over for us. No one knows our whereabouts except our friend and former partner, and he will never say a word nor go this route again." He pauses, then, "And oh yeah, Rocco, call our friend and make sure he understands what has happened and that it is over. Our relationship. Or the package will be mailed."

"Done. Okay. Okay. Now, Bossa, is this Estella ..."

"She is everything you can dream of and puts your Roma friend to shame. Trust me."

"Oh, I do. I do. On my way."

"Good." Click. As usual the conversation is over when Pisces says it's over. He walks into the villa, finds Chiarina sprawled on her bed. Nude. Dry. Refurbished. And ensuring she is moist.

"Roberto, come. Take me again."

Rocco hears the click, stares at the phone. Then steps from the booth and looks about. He walks the several yards where Drago has been standing in the shadows, watching for intruders, followers.

Rocco whispers, "Drago, my friend. It is done. We go home," and grasps the huge man, hugging him. Then removes his right arm while still clasping the man with his other and slapping him on the back in joyful pretense. Rocco quickly removes his Berretta from his coat pocket, shoves it under Drago's chin and fires, releasing his left hand at the same time. Drago sprawls backward into the building wall, the back of his head gone. Then slumps to the walkway, both legs resting on the cement, limp, toes pointing to the sides. Rocco wipes his weapon clean of prints and carefully places Drago's hand around the butt, finger on the trigger guard, then the trigger. Also a print next to the safety. Then allows it to drop alongside the man's hand. Rocco takes his extra magazines and places them in Drago's pockets. Ensures his friend still has his weapon, and steps back. *Life is better for you now ole' friend. No more people pointing and laughing.*

Rocco looks around, seeing no one, strolls up to the street's park, turns left and heads away on its dimly lit walkways.

My God, I should take that butcher now, but I need his boss. It's the mission, and getting more personal by the moment. Marnee slips along the wall, around the phone booth. Needlessly checks the body, and continues ahead following her prey. *I'll call Itzak and Namir first chance I get.*

Hunter watches the villa. He checks his watch. *Three hours since lights out. Quiet night. Let's go inside. See what I can find and take a look at the killing zone.*

CHAPTER 26

"Someday someone may kill you with your own gun, but they should have to beat you to death because it's empty."
A gunfighter's rule

After his late night reconnaissance of the Pisces villa, Hunter knows he will have to complete his mission only at night, and only inside. Otherwise there will be too much collateral damage. While inside Pisces' study he found the package. Photocopied its contents and replaced all as it was. To take it now would be an advertisement. When he completes his tasks he will recover the original. The security is lax. The old man or the young boy walks the inside perimeter once after dark, and there is no alarm system. Pisces' bedroom is obvious; and one of the guest bedrooms, also obvious, belongs to the bodyguard, his henchman, and they are a good distance apart. Out of wall thumping and screaming range. So, the villa will be the venue and silent and deadly the menu, and if time permits pain will be added to the entree. The problem will be if Pisces and Rocco bring guests who will be staying when they come home. If that is the case Hunter knows he will have but two choices. One, get them out of the villa somehow without raising any suspicions, or it will look like D-Day.

Now, safely back in his room he strips off his all-black garments, takes a shower, dons his skivvies and snaps on the television with the volume low for covering noise. He has calls to make. However, the picture captures his attention immediately. It is the Italian version of breaking news. The massacre in Pisa. He listens to the talking heads for several moments, then dials overseas and Zachary's number. It automatically transfers after four rings to where he is, or going. He's in the site room and answers on the first ring after the transfer.

"Joe. Hunter."

Without any acknowledgment, Zachary embarks on his discourse like a fusillade of 4.5 rockets from a multiple-launcher. "The shit has hit the fan, everywhere. It's all over the World and the US media is in a feeding frenzy. Here's what I know are facts from where I sit." Zachary races on at speed-reading rates telling him that Dee is dead along with a traveling companion and that the Italian press and authorities are still reporting her as Caterina Frati and the male gentleman unknown for sure although the hotel register shows a reservation for a Frati couple. "We know her companion is our boss's man. Once she's identified, some of our friends might think it's you. That might help us." Zachary continues, telling Hunter that the two Russians and two Germans have been murdered and that they were following him and Dee. "Obviously you lost them." Then he continues with reports that two Israelis were apparent victims outside of the Frati woman's room. Dee's room. These were not the London people. This is a team that lost a partner in Rappel earlier. Zachary gasps for air, says further, "I mean, Hunter. This is like a herd of Zebras were let loose in a lion's cage. And the guy that worked at the restaurant, our friend Antonio Rizzo, he's dead. Assassinated in bed along with his girl friend. And now ..."

"Joe, take it easy, man."

"Right. Right. As I was saying, and now, a deranged, handicapped man, assumed to be the killer of everybody, has been found in a nearby park, dead by a self-inflicted gunshot. Are you shitting me? Who are they kidding?" There is a pause before Joe adds, as a feint stab of humor, that Pisa is resembling the United Nations headquarters with the arrival of foreign government suits and a murder rate like Gotham City. Joe finishes with, "Contact Maria and let her know what happened and have her tell her family. Everything. I will get someone out there to stay on top of things and assist them. However we can. Mainly keeping people away for at least a few days."

"Joe, we need to get them out of there. A safe house, or better, bring them to Maria. To Capri. And I'll get Bradovich to do all this."

"Who?"

"Eugene Bradovich. My buddy in San Diego. I can ... we can trust him. For sure."

"I'd sooner use an agency asset."

"That could be a MacBeer asset."

"Yeah, that's possible. Well, okay. Bradovich it is. You set it up. Just move some of your money to him and tell him to use cash only.

"Done. It'll keep the DeLucas away from people, the media, and especially our friends. Also, we can close ranks and they'll be close to Dee. Well, I mean her remains. You have the embassy collect and hold the remains until we, I, get it untangled and into some form of calmness." Hunter pauses, half chuckles and adds, "Actually I'll be diverting their attention adding Taormina to Pisa's woes."

"Okay, sounds good. You get in touch with Maria and get the ball rolling. ASAP."

"Roger, and I'll confirm."

"And listen, Kemo Sabe, the shit is hitting the fan so fast here that the city will be completely fertilized before the morning papers are out. Get your job done, and bring back the package."

"Joe, I already have a photocopy of the package."

"What? Oh. Great. Send it. But to Ruth, gift wrapped or something."

"Wilco. My plan is to bring back the original after Tonto's buddy rides. Unfortunately, right now I don't know where 'our' friend is. Only where I hope he'll be coming, and soon. I'm guessing his man will be here soon. I need both here to make it easy. And, Joe, I've got the place juiced, so if push comes to shove, there may not be much left. It could look like Hiroshima."

"Oh shit." He lifts his butt from the seat letting some gas wander away. "Well, get it done. I've got to get to the President. First with MacBeer and then, somehow without him. Gotta run. And remember, the faster you finish the fight, the less shot you'll get."

"Geez, Joe. Cut the crap. I haven't touched the trigger yet and we've got more bodies than at Anzio."

"It's just a rule. And I'm worried about you."

"Joe, go see the President, and while there by yourself, tell him I said hello. And that I'm okay and have his back."

"You know him?"

"Yeah. Extremely well. We're buds of a sort. He owes me, and Ruth in a way."

"You never ... Ruth? Not one of those ... one of those bimbo set-ups. Damn. I would have never ...none of this is in your file."

"Joe, just tell him what I said. And tell him when I get back we'll have a pop together. Bye."

Hunter looks at the phone resting in the cradle. Glances at the TV again and the talking heads. Then sits at the small desk staring out the window overlooking the pool below, and the bay beyond. The pool gleams an aqua green hue and the bay abounds with flickering lights of moored yachts. He sucks in some air, then dials Maria in Capri.

Pisces heads directly west out of the harbor, before turning northeast. He will pass Trapani, and shortly turn due east and pass Carini and Palermo, hug the coast until he coves up for the night in the Milazzo area. Then in the morning, up anchor and haul ass, round the northeastern tip of Sicily, past Messina, and south through the *Stretto di Messina* to Taormina.

On board the *Sorridenta* with him are Chiarina and Estella. The weather is clear, breeze light, the mood is spirited although dampened in Chiarina's eyes by the horrifying news early this morning from Pisa. Estella is getting herself and Chiarina settled on board by dutifully stowing baggage in their respective compartments. She in her own, her mistress's in with Roberto. The bulk of their luggage is being taken to Roberto's home by Benito, Signora Russo's driver. He will drive straight through and will be waiting. While Estella busies herself, Chiarina lounges on the sun deck with the master of the *Sorridenta*.

"Roberto, this is wonderful. Wonderful! Yet wrong somehow. It is hard to enjoy all this knowing about that horrible massacre in Pisa."

"It is sad. Tragic. But not of our concern. Put it out of your mind."

"Yes, I should. But why did this ... thisa unspeakable, appalling act happen? What could cause such dreadfulness? Who would do such a thing? And, why?"

"I don't know, sweetheart. It's beyond my comprehension. The world is incredibly ugly at times. Too ugly. But we can't do anything about that except live our lives the right way. Pleasantly. We can hope for a miracle, but unfortunately not rely on it. In life there are just more ups and downs than a fiddler's elbow. Let's not talk of the downs. Leave us enjoy this trip, ourselves, and what's before us. Follow our hearts. You know, the heart sees better than the eye."

Chiarina moves from her seat, snuggles close to Roberto and coos, "Yes, you are so righta. Perhaps a poet besides an artist."

"May be, but to be fair some of those words are the thoughts of others, not mine. Just heard them somewhere and like the tone. They're good medicine."

"Ahhh, Roberto. You are my medicine. And in all the righta doses ... and places."

Pisces stares at her, asks, "And Estella?"

"For shame. Shame. She is a diversion. For both of us if we choose. If you do not like this from time to time, I will shed this wicked behavior. After all, I needa only you now."

"And I only you. We will steer her towards Rocco. It will be a match made in ... made in Taormina." He chuckles and hugs Chiarina.

"So it will be."

Estella interrupts, "So what will be?" and pleads for help onto the sun deck with a bottle of wine and three glasses. Having her plea answered, adds, "I heard some of that. About good medicine. But, whatever. For now, wine tops the list of all medicines." She smiles, steadies herself on deck, and with Chiarina and Roberto holding the glasses, says, "Allow me," and pours the velvety carpet from the bottle into each crystal glass. "A fine Chianti."

Roberto raises his glass, says, "I heard this toast from a fine Jewish gentleman I encountered a few years back. It's a Jewish proverb I think. It goes something like this,

'When life is at stake, don't follow the majority.' We won't." He smiles, "Trust me."

In unison the ladies clink his glass and say, "To hell with the majority. And we do." Both laugh, then Estella adds, "Remember, a man without a woman cannot defend himself against seductions ... whatever that means." She giggles, adds. "That too is a Jewish proverb."

"It means, life is good." Roberto slides in his lounge chair. Stretching out and holding his glass of Chianti on high. "Yes, life is good. Two exquisite, pleasing women. Mellow wine. Clear weather. What could possibly be better?"

"Rocco," hesitantly questions Estella as she looks from one to the other. The air becomes still. The water calms. It is apparent the Mediterranean Sea has withdrawn from the conversation.

Chiarina drops her chin, "You heard?"

"Yes. I love diversity and what happened the last few evenings. Nevertheless perhaps I will love Rocco."

Roberto sits up, swings his legs over the side of his chair, struggles to his feet and gives Estella a firm hug. "I'm sure Rocco will topple within seconds at the sight of you. And you for him. But, if not," and he puts his other arm around Chiarina, "we will do what you two wish. Whatever pleases the two of you."

"You please me, Roberto. As does, Chiarina."

Chiarina blows a kiss to Estella and chirps, "Okay. We will do as "we" wish. Now let's enjoy this wine, and if it will return, the breeze from the sea, and the view." She kisses both on the lips. A peck, yet with a flick of her tongue for teasing and a taste.

Pisces tightens his hug on both, then releases them and returns to his chair. Stretches out once again and gazes out to sea. Feels the breeze return from its moment of calm. Smiles. *Good. A new life, and perhaps a new way of life.*

"Maria, Hunter. Please listen for ..."

"Oh, Hunter. Thank God. Have you seen the TV? Heard the news? My God, that's where Dee is." Her voice rising with each thought. "That's the same hotel and where you were supposed to be. Oh, Lord, I ..."

"Maria, listen to me. If you aren't sitting down, sit down. Now." He pauses. Getting no response or reaction, adds, "Are you sitting?"

"Yes. Good God, Hunter, I have this ..."

"Calm down."

"I can't until I know ..."

"Maria, please. I'm sorry, your sister ... your ... Maria, Dee is dead. She is the one in the news ..."

Hunter's words are drowned out by her scream. Not one. Rather, one after another. Her shrill voice breaks into sobs and a gasping for air. The clatter of the phone hitting a table rattles in his ear. The thumping sounds of fists hitting a hard surface is transmitted so clearly he can more or less feel the vibration at his own desk here in Taormina. More screams, interlaced with profanities and a string of "Oh, God, no's." Then some, "I did this to her, my God." Several times. Moments seem like hours. Time, however vital, always seems like eternity in these instances. And valuable time is passing in Hunter's mind.

Hunter shouts again for Maria to pick up the phone. To calm down. Finally a calm ensues in the form of a quietly weeping Maria saying, "Oh, Hunter what are we going to do? What can we do? Does my family know? Oh, Good Lord, what are the children going ..." and the sobs return, gaining in volume. The inhalations are throaty, the gasps for air deeper. Quiet comes. But, like a hurricane passing a landfall, the eye follows offering only temporary relief.

"MARIA. Maria. Get on the phone. Get a grip. We have to take control of this. Now."

Still weepy, she responds, having gained some control in the eye of the storm. "Okay. Okay. Tell me how. Was it like they are reporting?"

"Yes. She was assassinated. We believe Dee was shot by Pisces' body guard. Probably the same man that killed Angelo." The weeping begins again, quickly going to sobs.

Hunter waits for several moments even though time is prized. His system always runs icy under stress. It always did. Does now. He orders, "Maria, get a grip. However

horrible this is, remember, you know all this. You know what Dee did and was up to. Jesus, she was having an affair with her old boss. Again. They had Angelo killed. It has backfired in the worse possible manner. I'll help you. The family. The children. If I can. And I will take care of the man, the men, that did this. But you and I have to take care of business. Now. Are you up to this?" He pauses, again allowing precious moments to pass.
"Maria, get up for this. We have to act now. Suck it up, Maria. NOW, dammit."
"Okay, you bastard. I'm ready."
"Good. Now then ..."
"I didn't mean that, Hunter." She inhales deeply. "Do you care for me at all, Hunter?"
"Of course. You're a helluva gutsy lady. Great American. A patriot. I mean ..."
"That's it?"
"Well, yes. Pretty much. Well, a friend of course. Listen, this is business. A war in a way. And, you're in it with me, us. So, I guess buddies too."
"Buddies? Okay. Let's get on with it."
"Right. Now then, this is what we must do."
Hunter tells Maria the plan and of Bradovich. All will come to Capri and wait for him, Hunter. When he arrives, all will be finished and they can take Dee home. She acknowledges. He says, "See ya. Bye." Gone.
Maria hears the click, a buzzing, and the pounding of her heart.
And no more tears. There are none left tonight.

Danny Shanahan looks away from the window of the laboring train as it climbs. However hard it is to turn away from the beauty of the Alps, his younger brother's pensiveness is stronger medicine. "Where is your mind, Sean? Tis not here."
"You're right. Not here. Not in Pisa. It is at home. With Mum and Mary Kate. Where I should be and will be. I hope."
"That's a good place for it to be. Me as well ... well, not with Mary Kate, but home and with Mum. All of us. We

will be there, perhaps not soon enough, but soon as possible."

"And what of Muldoon? And his idiot son? And the others?"

"I don't know, but the Shanahan family will go its own way. I will see to that."

"I was thinking Danny, I can ..."

"Think of Mum. And Mary Kate. And making me an uncle. And get some sleep, it's a way to go yet."

"Aye, it tis. And we'll make it. Won't we?"

"Aye, we will, as long as you don't kiss me."

A chuckle. Nervous and not.

John MacBeer paces his office. Then sits at his desk. Then up again, and paces. *I need Pisces dead. Now. God dammit! Dee, you fucked this up.* He kicks his desk. *No, I should have never ...*

He hears the static of his intercom come to life. "Sir, Mister Zachary is on the way in. You and he have a meeting with the President in less than an hour."

MacBeer reaches to the desk to respond as Joe Zachary enters. He looks up but pushes the button regardless and says, "Thanks. On the way." Stands from his stooped position, nods at Joe Zachary and asks, "Are we ready? Anything new?"

"No, sir, nothing new except Kerrigan wasn't there. He's alive."

MacBeer jolts to a halt. "I know ... Kerrigan? Why wasn't he ... wasn't he ... well, where the hell is he?"

"Don't know. Only know the guy found with Dee was your man. By the way, what the hell was he doing there?"

"My man. You mean an agency operative? Right?"

"Well, I guess. Thought he worked only for you. Anyway, that's all that's new. I'm ready. You know, boss, you're not looking so well. Are you okay? Look pale, and perspiring like you have a touch of the flu or something."

"I'm fine. Fine. Let's go."

Zachary pats MacBeer on the back and says, "Well, sir. Good. And oh, when we finish I'll need a minute alone with the President."

MacBeer stiffens and stops. "Why? What for? This is most irregular."

"Well, it's personal. Ruth and the First Lady are old friends. She has a message she wants me to deliver for her. He'll understand, probably better than I." Zachary prods MacBeer along with a gentle push and a couple of pats on the back.

"Oh, okay. I didn't know that. I mean that Ruth knew the first family."

"Yeah. Crazy, huh?"

"Well then, let's take two vehicles. I don't want to wait."

"Already arranged."

"Huh! Oh, fine. Yes."

CHAPTER 27

"Do not attend a gunfight with a handgun, the caliber of which does not start with a '.4' "
A gunfighter's rule

    Marnee's tailing of Rocco DeStefano is thorny from the "git-go", especially through the dimly lit park, and then by taxi through Pisa to the airport. The streets in town are clogged since many are blocked by the police, and they are bursting with sirens and flashing lights of the emergency vehicles. Once at the airport and determining Rocco's destination, Marnee gambles and gets on the aircraft first, sits in the rear, busies herself with an out-of-date magazine as they fly to Reggio Calabria. Next a trip to the docks and a ferry to Messina in Sicily. As a Mossad agent, Marnee knows her history; consequently her time in and getting through Reggio Calabria is fraught with trepidation.
    The city is unique in itself, and is menacing as it relates to Rocco's family name. Reggio Calabria is beautiful although being ruined by a crime war, bordering on revolution, which if one thinks of its history is not necessarily surprising. Sixty-six years ago the city, and a huge percentage of its population, were destroyed by an earthquake at 5:21AM in the morning which incidentally is about the time of day Marnee and Rocco arrived from Pisa today. However, the earth is tranquil at this moment in history, ostensibly not hungry although across the strait Etna belched and regurgitated its innards just a few months ago. However, in 1905 some 25,000 souls perished from the quake here. Most of them as they rushed to the sea for safety and were met by a ten foot tsunami. Three other tsunamis hit finishing Mother Nature's reminder. Also, the same quake killed more than twice as many in the town of Messina, across the strait. Reggio Calabria was rebuilt of course, but again destroyed not by nature, instead by a British air raid in 1943. Raised from rubble once again and certainly more modern it

flourished for years, however now it's being ravaged by a political war and crime wave. The 'Ndrangheta, a mafia-type crime organization is the cause. The city is home to 'ndrine, such as Condello-Imerti and the DeStefano-Tegano clans, warring against one another. Marnee is aware of the DeStefano name in the latter clan and is keen to leave, although to remain hidden on the ferry ride to Messina will be difficult. However, she does it well, mingling with the tourists, visiting mainlanders and the home-bound Sicilians.

In Messina, Rocco is met by a young man driving a black, '71 Mercedes-Benz 280 SEL 3.5 sedan. Marnee is hard pressed to lease a rental car and get on the road hoping to catch-up to the southbound black, 4-door 280 within 50 miles. There are dozens upon dozens of possible destinations. She has no time to call Mossad headquarters but has caught glimpses of the TV news in terminals and overhears worried conversations on the ferry. She knows firsthand, of course, of the killings outside the hotel, and now knows something of the carnage inside. She knows of Itzak and Namir's murders. She is enraged, so the problem is not just staying with Rocco hoping it'll lead to Pisces, but to reclaim her calm and business-like attitude and approach. This is more than difficult since it was Pisces that assassinated her uncle, a highly respected member of the Knesset, a few years ago in Jerusalem.

The mind games are intense for Marnee. Now in a strange location. Destination unknown. No back-up. No plan other than to terminate two men and any that interfere.

She drives south and catches up to Rocco's Mercedes as they travel through Santa Teresa di Riva. She supposes the young man driving, with Rocco lounging in the rear seat, is making it a leisurely and relaxing trip for the "gentleman" returning home. She passes the sedan so as not to create any suspicion for coming-up on them so rapidly. Marnee keeps tabs in the rear view mirror from less than a half kilometer ahead for several minutes, then slows and allows the Mercedes to pass her. As it does she holds a road map between her head and the side window pretending to check and navigate as she drives. Only the youngster driving gives her a glance. After this she follows, hanging back a quarter of a kilometer or more when possible.

Her thoughts are all over the spectrum of recent events. She knows others were onto Rocco. Probably for the same reason: Pisces. She wonders where are the Irishmen and what do they know and if they, and others, particularly the Americans, are far behind. And where is the American that was last seen in London and did not arrive with the lady? Or were the Russians and Germans only following the woman, and if so, why? Her thoughts return to the present as, up ahead, the Mercedes slows and eases off onto a side road with signs announcing Taormina.

Marnee mutters, "Now, big man, lead me to your master and payback time."

Alfonse Battaglia, Hunter, joins the tourists on another warm, sunny afternoon, taking a walkabout in Taormina which for him includes watching and strolling by Pisces' villa. His timing is opportunistically lucky as Rocco arrives. The sedan parks in the villa's drive adjacent to the garage and servants quarters. Tour map in hand, baseball cap and sunglasses masking his face, Hunter sees Rocco emerge from the car. *Big man. But a dead man walking.*

The old man caretaker and his wife the cook, housekeeper and maid, huge smiles spread across their faces, rush to greet him. The young man is holding the car door open. There are hugs, more smiles, and chatter. Greetings over, Rocco strides away toward the villa's patio stretching his arms outward and upward, twisting his neck to relax, the old woman at his side, chattering and gesturing. Rocco nods. Stops, says something to the cook and maid. She turns and heads toward the kitchen. He continues to a veranda table and sits. Legs stretched out in front and hands and arms reaching skyward. Then recoils into a shoulder hunching sitting position of home at last. Worry free.

Okay, one down. Bet the other is not far behind. Hunter folds the map and responds to one of the couples wandering about. He takes their camera, along with a few animated instructions, then positions them so the villa is in the background. He takes their picture, and another facing out toward the Mediterranean, as requested. Politely refuses one with them at their request. As they thank him profusely, a faded black Fiat, woman driving, rounds the corner, approaches, slows to a crawl at the villa. Nearly stops, then speeds up and goes on its way. Hunter takes in the action in his slow-motion like mind. *Beat-up car in a posh neighborhood and the face of the woman driving I've seen before.*

He pauses, watches the car until it turns at the end of the street, then smiles and nods to the picture-taking couple again and strolls away from the villa like a wandering tourist.

Know that woman. He takes two strides down the hill toward the corner and stops quick as a jackass hit by a two by four. He mutters, "Devorah. Can't be. Can't be."

He shakes his head. *Why not. It's another friggin' omen. I gotta get this over with.*

Hunter hurries on his way back to the hotel.

Done. And out.

Marnee pulls up to the first and closest hotel she finds after passing the villa. It's the *Ataholtel Capotaormina*. Turns the car over to the valet who at least feigns surprise when he asks to take her bags and she tells him she has none. He shakes his head and takes the rental heap away. Marnee stands for several moments looking at the pools below, and beyond them to the Bay of Naxos and the Mediterranean. *Beautiful, but it's going to get sullied.*

She strides into the hotel and up to the registration desk. While registering for a classic room, expensive but least so, she asks the clerk in her best Italian, "Where are the closest lady's shops? In the hotel? Elsewhere if necessary. But close."

The response is that there are two in the hotel shopping concourse. He points the direction. And adds, "There is another shop but a few blocks away. The remainder are below, in town."

Marnee smiles, nods, takes her key and strides, hips swaying, toward the hotel's shops. She, like Rocco, is traveling light, although she does have exceptional personal baggage. The clerk is fascinated by the walk and the baggage, as is the valet who has returned and entered to tell the idle bellhops of the dark haired, busty and leggy lady with the cheap Fiat and no bags.

Hunter trails the valet through the front door and catches the end of the matinee performance. He too stares until the lady is out of sight, however for different reasons. He questions the clerk and jokes with the young lads. *It's her or a twin.*

He nods to all and whisks through the lobby and returns to his room to take mental stock, call Zachary, clean up and eat later. *Need to make another recon of the villa and somehow check out the lady.*

He gets an overseas line and dials Joe "Z". Waits through the clicks, static and buzzes for the ring.

"Zachary."

"Joe, it's me. Give me an update on the Israelis in Pisa."

"Interesting you ask. Outwardly they are enraged, but dreadfully quiet inside. Three dead and one, a female, is missing and presumed KIA. They are angrier than a swarm of hornets. A lot of cries of outrage to the Italian government, but deep inside not saying much, and that ought to be worrisome to some folks. Why the question?"

"She's not missing and is sure enough, simon-pure, bona fide alive. She's here. Saw her today."

"Enough with your vast dialect, Champ. How do you know it's her?"

"You remember my nightmare? Well, ..."

"Don't start that again."

"Well then, trust me, she's here. I know. And you can bet her pals are finding out just about now. How long do you figure before they'll have help here?"

"If what you say is true, Hawk, possibly a day, maybe a two." A slight pause, then, "No. They always work in teams. Experienced together. They'll send a team. A good one. So that may well take three days."

"Well, Joe. She knows where the villa is. Tailed the big guy there from wherever. Probably, Pisa."

"So, what's your plan?"

Hunter sighs. "To end this, now ... as soon as the target arrives. Those two only I hope, but I'm geared to take the house and staff down around their ears."

"What about her?"

"Am going to check her out, Joe. This evening if I can. Need to see how close to the ground she's crawling. Oh, what about Brad and the group?"

"They should arrive late tonight.

"Okay, partner, and her name is Marnee but looks exactly like Devorah." Click.

As the sun is setting, Pisces has the crew bring the *Sorridenta* into the Marina Poseidon in Milazzo. The evening is beset with beauty; the sun leaving the day and travelers behind, but all believe it will push up in the sky tomorrow and give another day of life and sunshine. And it is said in this country that Milazzo is like a beautiful woman. The saying goes, "Let's not know if she has gotten married to a good husband." It is also a historic city, laden with myth, tradition, and legend. Legends like the beautiful Helen Baele; of St. Anthony from Padua; of St. Stefano Protomartire, Patron of Milazzo and so many more, and dozens of treasures to visit and festive days to celebrate.

After docking, Estella, Chiarina and Roberto sit on the afterdeck, have a glass of wine and discuss what the evening will hold. The ladies are tired of their seafaring. They decide after finishing their drink, they all will clean up, go into town, have dinner at *Al Pescatore* ristorante. It's famous for its Swordfish Roulade stuffed with breadcrumbs, however perhaps not its service. And after, a stroll around the harbor visiting shops, perhaps stopping for an after-dinner drink before coming back aboard the *Sorridenta*. Pisces agrees. The return to the boat is the portion of the evening of most interest to him.

The evening goes as planned. The swordfish is wonderful Better, it's superb. The service is fine except the waiter staff seem to argue amongst themselves in their attempt to provide. Perhaps it's part of the ambiance. An act. Whatever, the cast of waiters have all the gestures and animation to make it believable.

The after-dinner stroll goes well and serves several purposes. It's refreshing; it works off the pasta that accompanied the swordfish; it tones the body; and it provides the time for the ladies to purchase tantalizing lingerie; and time for imaginings of the remainder of this evening.

Once back on board the *Sorridenta,* Roberto and Chiarina play together in Roberto's shower. Estella alone in hers. However, when Pisces and Chiarina enter his bedroom, Estella is lying, half-curled in the middle of the bed wearing her newly purchased sheer nightie. Her head is propped on her arm and cocked seductively to one side. She coos, "I thought we could play, perhaps one last time?"

Chiarina drops her towel, steps lively to the bed and slithers next to Estella. She pushes Stell over on her back and embraces her in a long, gasping open-mouthed kiss. Estella's legs separate, her knees raise. Chiarina looks over her own shoulder; Estella lifts her head a few inches and whispers, "Roberto, come join us."

Chiarina smiles, nods, motioning Roberto to them while Estella slips out of her shorty gown.

He drops his towel, crawls onto the bed, sighs, "Life is good," as he nestles between Estella's legs.

Estella pulls Chiarina's head to her breast and with the other hand grasps Pisces' hair. Squirms, murmurs, *"Ti piace?"*

"Mi piace davvero."

Hunter, rested, mind clear and showered sits in the hotel's Bar Svevo, fingers casually holding a glass of Carricante. The bar sets on a panoramic terrace with a poster-like, twilight view of the bay and the Calabria coast with the light houses of the small harbor in sight across the strait. He's richly dressed in leather sandals, off-white linen slacks and a silk navy blue long-sleeved shirt opened at the collar. The couple with the camera from this afternoon stop at his table to say hello as they leave for dinner. They are chatting with Hunter as Marnee enters the bar, glancing but not noticing him as she passes the table and is seated at the far end of the terrace. As the couple continues their tête-à-tête, Hunter watches the Israeli sit, order and glance around the bar. Their eyes meet for a split moment. Then she looks to the bay and settles in her seat.

Hunter keeps her under subtle observation as he tells this lovely American couple of sights they should visit tomorrow, seemingly struggling with his English from time to time, and loud enough for his voice to carry several tables. The couple leaves as the waiter returns. Hunter orders another Carricante in faultless Italian. Then adds, "And one, whatever she having, for the," pointing, "lady." The waiter nods, smiles and leaves.

Several minutes pass until the waiter returns with Hunter's glass of wine. Serves it, and with a smug grin departs with his tray and the lady's Chianti.

Hunter watches the delivery and the momentary dialogue. The woman turns enough to meet his eyes, accepts the drink from the waiter and nods to Hunter. No smile, more of a shrug.

When the waiter leaves her table, Hunter stands, drops more than enough lira on the table, and heads for Marnee's table with glass in hand. He shakes his head. *She's trouble. But, better together than tripping over one another.*

Hunter bows slightly, hand on the back of a chair at her table. Says in perfect Italian, "May I join you?"

In good, but not perfect Italian, Marnee replies, "You're here."

"Join you?"

She nods toward the chair across from her, still with one hand in her lap out of view beneath the table.

Hunter sits, clasps his hands in front of him on the table, and whispers in Hebrew, "Let's cut to the quick." He sees a glint of shock in her eyes with the language change. "I'm going to mention two names. If you nod, I stay and we talk. If you don't, I leave and you accept this as an insult or a warning." He removes his hands, putting one on the stem of his glass and the other in his lap. He hisses,

"Pisces." He stares, watching her eyes, and hands. Always watch the hands.

Marnee nods, asks in Hebrew. "Have you eaten? And we can do this in Italian or English."

Hunter responds in Italian. "Italian is best for now. English, later."

"Fine. Do we eat or watch each other's hands?"

Hunter smiles, leaves his hands where they are but says, "Eat. At The Scogliera, here. It's extraordinarily good. And an a la carte menu based on the catch of the day." He shrugs. "Not mine. I don't fish."

"For anything?"

They both laugh, remove their lingering hand from their laps and shake hands gently. She asks, "How long have you been here?"

"Before Pisa ... and before you drove past the villa this afternoon."

"Well, my name is Marnee. Yours?"

"Alfonse Battaglia."

Marnee gags on her sip of wine at his answer. Laughs. "Sure. Let's finish our wine and we'll leave for dinner but only when you tell me your name. I don't dine with strangers."

Hunter does. They finish the last of their wine as they stand and leave the bar for the restaurant as a couple, her arm on his. Both with one hand free.

CHAPTER 28

*"Two rules of unarmed combat.
First, never go unarmed. And second, bringing a
Jewish girl won't hurt."*

A special gunfighter's rule

"Yes, Mister President. I'm positive. He's gone, disappeared." Joe Zachary listens carefully while nodding and replying with the required "Yes, sirs," and "No, sirs," for the Commander-in-Chief during the telephone exchange.

Then after the silence of listening, a firm, "Yes, sir. He is on target. On site, and has sent photocopy proof. And he will bring the original papers when he completes his task." Another pause.

"Yes, sir. He's fine." Zachary listens intently.

"Yes, sir. There will be two down and the Hawk will return. I'd bet on it." A short pause, then, "I know we both are, sir. And yes, he still likes to be called Hawk." Joe listens carefully then replies, "I'll find MacBeer. He's where the money is, or will be, I'm certain."

Several moments pass, then, "Yes, sir, I will as soon as it's completed," and Joe looks at the now silent red phone in his hand. He's been in MacBeer's office and steps out into the reception area, says to the agent waiting. "Change the locks. Bring me the only key. The 'only' key." And returns to his office and calls MacBeer's secretary giving her strict instructions to follow at home and when she arrives at the headquarters building.

Then he calls home. Waits for several rings. "Ruth, has your gift arrived yet?" He listens, then, "Well, please don't leave until it does. Or until I arrive home. This is important, Ruth." There is more to her response than 'yes sir, no sir, two bags full sir'. He listens, then responds. "Yes, he is. Just fine, now do as I ask. I have to go." Click.

He leans back in this chair. Hands clasped behind his head, thoughts wandering as he thinks about all the years he worked for John MacBeer. *I'll find your traitorous ass.*

Hunter and Marnee sit on the terrace of one of the hotel's restaurants. Perhaps its finest. The Scogliera. Most gorgeous women seem to resemble someone. A Sophia Loren, a Liz Taylor, or a Gina, or a Jane or a Rita. Someone. Marnee however has a beauty all her own. An olive or perfectly tanned complexion and she is wearing soft, pink make-up. Her beige slacks and matching lightweight jacket, which is now hanging on the back of her chair, accentuate her skin tone. The sheer, white sleeveless blouse her bountifulness. Her mouth is everything. Large, full lips but not too much, and the perfection and whiteness of her teeth enhance every murmur, word, grin or full smile. And although she projects the softness of a woman, she is toned, athletic, hard. When she first walked in Hunter noted her buns. Inflated soccer balls. One could grip them but not leave even a momentary indention. May even injure the hand.

They've ordered, and are waiting for the waiter to return with their bottle of Malvosia, an amber colored local wine. Marnee has allowed Hunter to do the ordering to include the dinner. It will be Taranto Oysters in Trella, an antipasto, basically baked oysters. And for the entree it will be a Sicilian classic, Tonna Ammuttunatu which is tuna filets, delicately seasoned with mint and served with fresh peas.

The wine arrives, and the server pours a taste for Hunter. He takes a sip, savors it, and nods to Marnee. The wine waiter smiles, pours Marnee only a taste at Hunter's urging. She does the same, smiles and says to Hunter and an anticipatory waiter, "Lovely". The attendant pours for both, sets the Malvosia in a bucket and leaves, wringing his hands in delight. The Malvosia was Hunter's idea, the brand and vintage, the wine waiter's suggestion. And damn expensive.

The two chat conversationally in Italian, meandering through meaningless topics. Like a dating couple in love might or two strangers that are struggling not to fall into that abyss but feel themselves hurtling at near terminal velocity. The restaurant has a trio that plays soft, mellow dinner music throughout the evening. During the short wait between the antipasto and the entree, Hunter leans close and says, "Although it's difficult under the circumstances, perhaps for the moment we can follow a Hebrew Proverb."

"My goodness. You and your Hebrew. What next?"

"Well, the proverb says, 'when you're in a strange city, adopt its manners'. Familiar with it?"

"Yes," and Marnee gathers herself some, "and many others such as 'when a life is at stake, don't follow the majority.' It is difficult to release one's self and forget, shall we say, one's job."

"Yeah, you're right. But you see, I know that we're safe; safe here tonight. Perhaps not so tomorrow or the next day, or a lifetime. Whatever ours is to be."

Marnee now relaxes from her gathering episode and slips her hand on top of his on the table. Glances around out of habit, then smiles and says, "Music washes away from the soul the dust of everyday life. I heard that or read it somewhere. Listening to this music, and aware of our situation, brings it to mind." Hunter jerks his hand away as the waiter arrives with the tuna dish. Marnee leans back, head slightly cocked to her left, wondering.

They eat in more or less silence. A few words are exchanged about the excellence of the dish and the wine. When finished the waiter is there to whisk away the dinnerware, then begins to make a suggestion when Marnee says to Hunter. "I would like a Limoncello."

"Absolutely. Sounds great." He looks at the waiter, "A Limoncello for the lady, and I'll have an apricot brandy."

"Of course," and the server moves swiftly from the table.

Marnee looks at Hunter and murmurs, "The tuna was wonderful, but it seemed to curtail the conversation we had just started, or perhaps thought about."

"Maybe it was the last proverb?"

"Oh, and here I thought it was the hands again? Or something deeper."

Hunter tenses, then takes in a breath that is hardly perceptible but audible enough for Marnee to have a snatch of a grin begin to form at one corner of her mouth. For her, that's noticeable and Hunter catches it. He looks directly into her dark brown eyes. Glances around the terrace and the adjoining dining area and bar out of habit. Takes in a deeper breath, says, "The music is wonderful. There are a few couples dancing. Would you like to join them? I would, but only with you."

"Yes, I would love to."

Hunter gets up quickly, moves to Marnee and they leave hand in hand to the small dance floor by the piano. They ease together, take a few steps, then draw close, perhaps in the abyss now. Hunter says, "Well, I guess music does wash away the dust of life, or whatever."

"Yes, and the heart sees better than the eye." She moves her head slightly back, smiles, "And I'm going to forego the quotes and just listen to the music, take in your scent and feel your heartbeat." She places one hand on Hunter's chest, and gives him a peck on his cheek, more of a small lip bite.

"You smell wonderful. Fresh. Sweet." Hunter pulls her closer, she melts into his body, virtually one. *Wow!*

Marnee brushes her lips on his cheek once again. *Oh, Lord!*

Bradovich and the entire DeLuca family arrive at the boat landing on the Isle of Capri. They are at varied stages of being red-eyed and all are worn to a frazzle. Maria greets them with the Limousine arranged for her by the concierge. It brings them to the hotel where the Night Manager is waiting to facilitate a rapid, already arranged check-in. The children are exhausted and confused. The grandparents angry, perplexed, anxious and way overtired. The father is enraged but tired enough that he too, like the grandparents, agrees to get some sleep tonight and because of the late hour, well into the morning before any discussion with Maria. And then after a solid breakfast. And then perhaps the man Bradovich will be more open and less authoritarian.

When the family is finally settled, asleep if not restfully so, Maria and Bradovich sit in Maria's suite, adjacent to her grandparents. She offers the detective a seat, says, "Would you like a glass of wine? A DeLuca Chianti? It's all I have here in the room."

"Sure. Would be great."

Maria pours two glasses, hands one to Bradovich and sits next to him on the sofa. Takes a sip of hers, puts the glass on the coffee table and asks, "Mister Bradovich, Hunter referred to you by your last name only. What do you prefer I call you?"

"Well, Ms. DeLuca, you can continue to call me Bradovich but Eugene, Gene, or Brad will do. Whatever suits you. Some call me son-of-a-vich. My best friends, however, call me Brad."

"I'd like a chance to become one of those. Brad it is. How did everything go?

"Ahhh, okay. Well, actually ... can I take a sip first?" He does. "Wow. Good. Truly good. May I call you, Maria?"

"Oh, I'm sorry. Sure, that would be nice and I guess that truly qualifies us as best friends. Now then, Brad, my question?"

"Okay, not so good. Your dad and grandfather are fuming. They even think they know nigh on everything, and in the end, blame Hunter for Dee's death. If he hadn't taken her, or if he had been there, they believe, actually "feel", it wouldn't have happened. The kids don't know too much but enough to think that Hunter caused their mom's death. You know they're listening all the time. To everyone." He takes another sip of the Chianti, smacks his lips a tad. "Your grandmother feels the same only but for most part silent about it all. She's apprehensive. No, deeply troubled about the children and their future. No dad and no mom, and they've heard the talk about their mom having Angelo killed. Your grandmother doesn't say too much, but I believe in the bottom of her heart she knows how deceitful and ghastly Dee has been. How voracious her greed has been. But, to her, Hunter drove the stake."

"Oh, Lord. I knew that. Or, I know it. I'm beginning to have trouble with the whole process as well." She takes another sip. Looks and sees that Brad's glass is empty. She nods and points to the glass.

Brad says, "Yeah, if you don't mind. Love my wine, and this is genuinely good. And I can use it. Haven't had a drop, not a sniff, since starting this trip. Been all eyes, ears and senses. And on edge since this started." He watches her pour. Then, "You know, Hunter didn't cause this to happen. No way. Dee caused this. Dee and ... never mind, I'm talking way too much. But, Hunter is a good man. The best."

"Well, then it wasn't handled properly."

"Ms. DeLuca, this ..."

"It's Maria. Please call me Maria."

"Okay, I will. That's nice. Soft. You know, you are a dead rin ..." He flushes, drops his head. "I'm sorry, I mean you look so much like Dee. Taller, thinner, more beautiful and still have a great ...damn, I keep puttin' my big foot in my mouth."

"Dee and I look like twins except for my height, and age of course."

"You're younger. Wow. Well, you know I met, well, I mean I saw Hunter and Dee together on the Coronado Ferry not so long ago. I thought she was a knockout, but you're completely stunning." He takes another drink of the wine. More than a sip, and once again says, "This is good. I mean, the best."

"Thank you. It's our family's own."

"Oh, that's right. The winery. Yeah, beautiful place. Oh man, as much as I like wine, I'd be hard-pressed to leave the vineyards." He puts his glass on the coffee table, stands. "Well, it's late. Real late. I need to be going. Get some sleep myself."

"Yes. Yes, I understand." Maria clasps her hands in front of herself, wringing them gently. "Brad, could you stay a little longer. I'm a little stressed out, and frankly, scared out of my wits."

"Okay, but no more of this wine. I'll fall in love ... with it, I mean."

"One more, and I appreciate your remarks, but Dee is younger. And not by hours."
"Could of fooled me."
"Really?"

Back in Hunter's room and not necessarily cooled sufficiently from the dancing and the hand-holding walk back, he says, "We can speak in English here if you'd like. Be easier perhaps."
"Yes, that it will. Can I get comfortable?"
"Comfortable? How comfortable?"
"Just want to take my jacket off, and slip out of these shoes. Is that a problem?"
"No. Fine. Want something to drink? I have some *Pellegrino* and some ice, I think." He looks into the bucket. "Yep, got some. It's refreshing."
"That would be wonderful, then before you, we, get started on the background and the plans, why don't you tell me something about yourself. Perhaps starting with your full name if you have one."

Hunter laughs. Pours two glasses of the *Pellegrino* over ice, says as he hands one to her, "Be better with a twist of lime, or perhaps, lemon, but," he shrugs.

She says, "Lemon. Twist of lemon. Always. Now sit, and tell me about Hunter whoever."

Hunter sits and does. The routine stuff. Parents, school, military, and his job now. When finished, he refreshes himself with more than a sip of his drink and says, "Now you."

"Remember, lemon. It will be important." She laughs and as Hunter starts to speak, she puts her finger to her lips, "Shssss." And continues.

"My full name is Marnee Kaslar. I'm single. Are you?"

Hunter is taken back for a moment, then, "Yes. Always. And not committed."

"Nor am I married, or was, or in a relationship now or ever. But not a virgin." She pauses. Hunter starts to speak. She giggles quietly, then becomes dreadfully serious. "My mother is Italian, my father an Italian Jew. All of us were taken to Campagna concentration camp in

277

1941. We were released later and both my parents became a part of the Assisi Underground in Italy. We left for Israel in 1949. I have no siblings."

Hunter says, "Jews in Italy. I knew of course. The Assisi Underground is famous. But Italians in *Eretz Yisrael* ... the 'Land of Israel' is actually something. Wow."

"There is your Hebrew again. I am impressed. Well, certainly a minority. In fact, minority is a grossly derisory word, but we were Jews so we are part of the seventy percent or better. Most all the others are Arabs. We lived in Ein Kerem; that was within Jerusalem's municipal boundaries. Right now, as you know, the Palestinians are launching wave after wave of attacks, and have been for several years. We, the Mossad, are responding with our assassination campaign. Hence, for me, Pisces. A Palestinian paid assassin. Of my uncle. My father died a few years ago in one of their attacks. My mother has returned to her family home and family business, near the Amalfi coast. Her parents, my grandparents are old and need help. Family help. They are vastly wealthy both in life and material riches."

Hunter chokes on his sip of *Pellegrino*. He thinks. *Omens. Omens. Omens.*

Marnee raises her eyebrows with the gagging, but continues. "I stayed in Israel, in service of my country. I have been doing this for eight years, after three years in the Army. All of us are drafted at eighteen. Women are only required to do two or three years in the Army, and no reserve duty. I was chosen for the Mossad because of my service in the Army. But, I need to go home, to Italy. To help my mother and grandparents run the business and the orchards. So, it is to be hoped this is my last assignment. And that's me in a lemon twist."

"Lemon twist? Oh, yeah. Lemons. What's with the lemons?" A light bulb comes on.

Before it turns to full bright, Marnee says, "Lemon orchards. And among other things, Limoncello ... the best. And I apologize for my Italian earlier. It should be better but perhaps too, too long in Israel and elsewhere."

"Well, we have a lot in common. Italian heritage. Military. The service. And I suspect, the mission. So let's talk of it, what we know, and how we do it. As a team. Okay with that?"

"I am, but if possible, let's get it done before my help arrives, and any others. Is that possible?"

"I believe so. I know the villa. Have been inside, and I have it juiced so I have a means to do it immediately if necessary. Preferably wait for "his majesty" to return which I believe will be tomorrow morning. I believe he will have a woman, or women with him. That will be tricky and a deciding factor. Rocco is here. The help, and there are currently three, live aboard. In separate quarters. There is no security at this moment other than a casual stroll around the grounds after dark. If Pisces does return tomorrow morning, I plan to enter the villa late tomorrow night, actually early morning, and terminate both Rocco and Pisces. Pisces first. Then set the timer, and leave town, and country."

"What of the house staff?"

"They'll be in the quarters. Won't hear anything until the house blows. They'll live through some broken windows and smoke."

"What about the woman or women?"

"If we can't work out something quickly to get them out of the house beforehand, then they become collateral damage."

He leans forward, arms resting on his thighs. Stares at Marnee. The several moments of silence seems longer. Both take a long, slow drink of their iced mineral water.

Marnee asks, "Are you sure Pisces is arriving tomorrow?"

"That's my hunch."

"This is a guess!"

"No. Not really. Actually, a hunch is a guess that has certainty. And, in the morning we're going to the harbor below to watch the hunch become a reality. I'm sure that's why Rocco DeStefano came home today. And he will be at the harbor to meet and greet his boss. It will be so."

"And after, how do we leave? The ... the country you said."

"I think you'll like the idea. We sail to the Isle of Capri and nestle in with the rest of the rich and not so famous."

He stares at her for a moment. Waiting. Then adds, "I have a boat. A yacht ... launch. Purchased it the first day here. Why are you staring?" She smiles. Hunter adds, "It has more than one cabin." Her grin fades. He continues, "Well, it's a long trip ... three days or more. They'll be watchin' the planes, trains and ferries but not for a wealthy, young couple cruising on a yacht."

"Why Capri?"

"Because I have unfinished business there. You can leave immediately if you choose, or wait. Or take a chopper or ferry to Naples on from there." He grins, "That's if you can drag yourself away from me."

Marnee stands, stretches and wiggles her toes. Faces Hunter. "It's a deal. We'll do it. I want it to hurt, Pisces. Both actually."

"I understand, and I would also, but we have no time for hurting. Just a double-tap and go. I have one item to pick-up. If women are there and involved we knock 'em out and drop 'em in the garage. We will be in masks and hoods. No voice commands or chatter. Just swift and silent. If that can't be accomplished, then they are done. Then I'll set the timer. Only the house goes up. We'll be down the hill, in the harbor and gone by the time the authorities, especially here, put anything together. We'll be on the boat and long gone."

She nods, strolls to the balcony, opens the doors and steps outside. Takes in a deep breath. Says over her shoulder, "I'll have to think about the boat and Capri." Feels Hunter come up behind her. Asks over her other shoulder , "How old are you, Hunter. Thirty-eight?"

"Yeah. You?"

"A few less footsteps." She takes in a deep breath. "Not a lifetime but that's a long time on a boat together. Just the two of us." She leans back and feels Hunter inch forward. Marnee whispers, "I want a life." She sighs, "After this."

"Me too. A life. Not this nor the one before."

Marnee turns slowly into Hunter. Arms at her side. Staring into his eyes. "Maybe this is our moment. Our omen. I sense it. Feel it," and slides her arms up his chest and around his neck, and engages his lips with hers. There is no resistance. Only heightening eagerness. They release, stand staring at each other. Hunter says, "Where do people like us go, and what do we do? Is there a place in this world for us to live? Not reside. Live."

"We go to my mother's. We grow more lemons. And we make Limoncello, some apricot brandy on the side and love the remainder of the time."

Hunter leads her from the balcony. "You got a date."

"Our second, and to make sure it happens, let us go over the details of this Op, and the layout of the villa ... outside and especially inside. Weapons. Options. Okay?"

"Good, let's do it." Claps his hands and in an order sounding voice, "Then some sleep so we're fresh for tomorrow."

"If you insist but sometime between now and the boat ... and the apricots, ... and the lemons, brandy, and Limoncello ...I would like a sample."

"There are no samples. Only appetizers and entrees." She smiles, big. "But there are tastes."

CHAPTER 29

"Accuracy is relative: most combat shooting standards will be more dependent on 'pucker factor' than the inherit accuracy of the gun."

"And use a gun that works EVERY TIME!"
A gunslinger's rule

The Shanahan lads park the car at Muldoon's garage as planned and immediately hoof it to the Metro Pub so that they can report to Colin Muldoon since he's not home and can only be at the pub, as usual. Late or not. It's a good hike so when they arrive they are a bit flushed in the cheek, and more than a tad thirsty.

The elder Muldoon and his son, the Pit Bull, Conor, are waiting at their usual table at the far end of the pub. There are only a few lights on near the table and behind the bar. The Muldoons are relieving their thirst of course. Danny and Sean pull up chairs and sit at the table facing the Muldoons with their backs to the now empty pub. It's a half-hour after closing time and all the regulars and the normally few strays are gone as is the help except for the barkeep. It's open only for the Muldoons as a favor or because the elder of the two has declared it so. As soon as Danny and Sean arrive at the table, so do their pints which means there was advance word. The two lads care less and take several swigs to satisfy their thirst from the hike and the hurried trip.

When all is settled, quiet, except for the breathing of the overweight Muldoons, Colin, the old man, leans across the table and asks, "Did it get done or not, lads?"

Danny responds. "Apparently done, but not by the two of us. It was a combat zone."

"And what does 'apparently' mean, lad? I've seen the TV, you know. It mentioned an American lass and the gent with her. Was that him, the filthy bastard that done Paddy in?"

"We think."

"YOU THINK!" explodes the old man, beet colored and spitting saliva and foam from his pint.

While this exchange is going on, two men, masked and hooded, right arms hanging at their side, each clasping a well-used, nicked up, slightly rusted S&W .38 with silencer and hollow-point rounds, move into the pub unnoticed, and for damned sure unannounced. The barkeep is gone, in the back, tending the business of closing.

Then the son, Conor, also red-faced, hisses, "You two pig-shit Irishmen are worthless. You couldn't spell Irish if I spotted ya four letters." He spits on the floor over his right shoulder, and continuing while he spits, chokes, "Ya would fook-up a wet dream." He pounds his ham-like fist on the table.

Danny begins to stand and respond to the Muldoons when a hand from behind pulls him back in his seat. Another on Sean's shoulder holding him in place.

Standing on each side of the Shanahans, the two men raise their pistols. Both fire, two shots. The double-taps go into the bridge of the nose and forehead of each Muldoon. Colin and Conor, slam backward over their chairs and onto the pub floor. One of the masked men says, "Stay put until we leave or you'll get the same." The other says, "The old man ordered your brother killed. And he had the other one he sent killed as well. Now, go home. Take up a different vocation. Grow potatoes. This isn't for you or for what's left of your family, and family to be."

The two men turn and hurry, not at a run, but rather, long, quick strides, carrying them out of the pub, right arms at their side. Unnoticed they drop their weapons between tables and quietly open the pub entrance door. Close it without a sound and are gone into the darkness of the streets of Londonderry, all in less than thirty seconds.

Danny and Sean sit, stunned and following orders for what seems a millennium. Not moving. Not saying a word. Not even a whisper to one another. Then after several moments the barkeep returns and shouts, "Hey, you louts are goin' to have 'ta leave. Me ole' lady will have a chunk of me arse ... What in the name of ... Oh, Jesus, Joseph and Mary, what happened here? Did ya have to kill these two Neanderthals?"

"No, dear Jesus, no. Two men just snuck up behind us and shot 'em both dead as doornails."

"Oh, Jesus, Danny me lad. Oh, Mother of God. Saints be with ... what the Hades is ..."

Danny is on his feet, in the barkeep's face. "Listen, Donohue. Call the police. AND, we weren't here. NOT HERE. You were in the back closing and came out and found this. Understand? Do it. I tell you on my dear father's grave, and on my mum's heart, all we know is that we were here talking to the Muldoons when two men came in, shot these two, and told us to stay put or we'd be dead." Sean is now beside his brother. The complexion of their faces and the vacuity of their eyes explain the veracity of their words. "These two men were not Irishmen. Nor Brits. All you need to say is that you were in back cleaning up, didn't hear or see a thing, and came out and found this. Agreed? WE weren't here. So don't fook-up and mention how many, or that they didn't have accents. You didn't see anything but these two drinkin' late again."

"Agreed, lads. I know what's happenin' and I'm not part of the movement, and I have family. So, go and don't be seen. I'll make the call. And then someday soon, when the sun is rising bright, it might be well for all ye to move on. Londonderry may not be for you and yours. Go!"

Danny and Sean Shanahan leave quickly, out the back, down the alley and on their way to their Mum's cottage.

Donohue removes the lad's mugs, washes them clean, and rings the local constable's office.

Then he waits for all hell to break loose he supposes. *And with the constables and others, possibly a Saint will come as well and calm my soul for saving another's.*

When Hunter is done briefing Marnee in detail of the villa and their plan for tomorrow morning, afternoon, and night, he shoves his chair back from the small table in his room. Asks, "Any final questions? Any?" He pauses, "Or suggestions? Anything?"

"No, I've got it. I am ready. I did check my room for messages."

"Yeah? And?"

"Only one. My two friends are coming to visit me the day after tomorrow. Late morning."

"Well, we should be done and gone, if our luck holds. Do you need, or should you leave them a message? Tell them something? Anything?"

"Luck holds?" Her eyebrows raise, "Luck?"

Hunter smiles, "Yeah, luck is when opportunity and preparation meet. Pisces is comin' and we're prepared." He pauses, then asks, "What about the other plan, or thoughts, or dreams? Or were they just wild midnight slashes at my heart?"

"Well, if we live through all this, then on our way to Capri or wherever, I plan on finding out exactly where the two of us are in our midnight scramble. But, just so you know. So you understand. I am serious. I want to live ... a life, and I believe I found a person of the same ilk. So, no, not wild slashes, but to be more precise like the proverb says, 'I see with my heart on this'. "

"Good. Me too, dagummit. Now, we get some sleep. Rest. We've got a long day tomorrow, and after for me I hope a long life of lemons and such."

He moves around the small table and pulls Marnee's chair out. She stands and cants her head to one side. Hunter leans forward and kisses her ear, nips her lobe, then runs his tongue down her neck to her shoulder, leaning into her.

She squirms, wiggles. Warms, in fact her internal thermostat rises quickly, and she begins to get wet and sticky. Marnee turns around, and they kiss, long, wet and hungrily.

Hunter releases her and says, "Damn. Whew!" shakes his head. "Ahhh, well, I suppose the plan is right. Let's get some sleep. I'll meet you for an early breakfast, O-dark-thirty."

"This is not fair." She sighs, "At least one more before I go."

They do, and release.

The night ends, perhaps too soon but then, perhaps life begins.

The constable arrives, and not far behind is the British military. Then the entourage of investigators, and of course a coroner. Donohue sticks steadfastly to his story. The weapons are found and will be given the normal ballistic tests and of course the authorities will also find no serial numbers. Gone, filed off. And no prints. Nothing. Along with no witnesses. Just a closed pub; the utterly "ded as a dorenail" Muldoons, as the Old Irish would say; and Donohue's unshakeable story. The knowledge of who the Muldoons were and what they were about leaves no end of possibilities. Except for the PIRA, it is basically a good end for bad rubbish, and perhaps for them as well. Or by them, or somebody.

On the way, Sean tells Danny to go ahead. "I'm goin' to see Mary Kate. See if she'll have me, and if so, we'll be comin' right behind ya."

"Okay, but don't dally and don't say a word other than we just got back, and she was the first person you wanted to see."

"I hear ya."

"Good, go on your way and you can give her that kiss you've been trying to smack on me." Danny turns for home with long strides, hurrying through the dark hearing his and Sean's hearty chuckle.

Within minutes Sean is at Mary Kate's door tapping lightly but continually because of the hour, and because of the time it takes for a light to come on. Her uncle answers the door and greets Sean like a long lost son, and asks, "What do ya want at this hour as if I didn't know."

"I just got back and I need to see Mary Kate, sir. Tis urgent."

From the top of the inside flight of steps, Mary Kate shouts, "Let 'em in, and you get up here as quick as you can, Sean. Hurry now."

The uncle groggily smiles and nods, still not fully awake, nor sober. Sean brushes by him and takes the steps two at a time reaching Mary Kate who is standing at the top. Her arms outstretched in a worn, lightweight robe, open in the front, with only a short nightie beneath. Her nipples attentive already and a wet warmth is forming between her legs.

They fall into one another's arms, and immediately indulge in a homecoming kiss fitting of a knight returning to the princess. The groping and the kiss restlessly continue as her uncle brushes past grunting an approval and disappears into his room.

After several kisses and gentle, hungry clutching, Sean tenderly holds Mary Kate by her shoulders and says, "Mary Kate, I love ya. And I want to marry ya now. No waitin'. And I want for us to get away from here and live. I mean live. Not day to day, but forever. Will ya marry me?"

She shrugs off his hands and throws her arms around Sean's neck, and kisses him in a manner that leaves no doubt as to the answer. When pulling away slowly, she says, "I will indeed marry you, Sean Shanahan. And now will be fine, but I'm guessing we'll have a problem finding a priest at this hour. But, we'll do it as the sun rises, and if no one will marry us, we'll do it ourselves. And Sean darlin', we're goin' to consummate this day one way or the other before the sun gets too high in this Irish sky or me thighs will be stickin' together like a mussel."

Sean kisses her again with anticipation, and whispers, "Shouldn't I ask your uncle for permission? Again? Did I? Or something?"

"We'll be tellin' 'em, not asking, and then be off with ourselves to skip stones on the river once more and be makin' wild music and love together." She drags him by the arm toward her uncle's room.

As Hunter and Marnee walk along the dock, he says, "I've hired a crew of three for some of this venture. And, if and when necessary, I can handle her alone. I may retain them for a time, or at least one, the old crew chief. Perhaps a long time."

"Good. Now, what about breakfast, and the plan for the day? You've obviously changed it already."

"No change. Just didn't tell you one or two details. The crew is one detail and the other is we're going to have breakfast on board. On the after-deck like the rich folks do. And watch for Pisces to enter the harbor this morning, and he will. In fact, our slip will have us in position not only to see it, but up close and personal."

Marnee says, "How close and personal?"

Hunter pulls her to a stop. Says, "This is my, our, boat. The Marnie," pointing to the name on the stern, then upward to the entire craft.

She gasps, "My God. Oh, Hunter, it's so big. It's huge."

He laughs. "I hope you'll be sayin' that again."

She shoves him hard, practically off the edge of the dock. "Naughty." Then she says with a much more serious tone, "But, you've spelled my name erroneously, or someone painted it incorrectly."

He breaks into laughter. Hard enough for tears to form in his eyes. After he chokes to a halt he says, "No, it's a Marine joke, and I'll tell you about it over breakfast. But, I didn't know you when I got the boat and named it, but now it's all the more apropos."

"And the remainder of my question?"

Pointing to the next slip, he says, "This is Pisces' slip. He'll pull in right next to us. We'll see him and what he's hauling. And he won't know us from Adam and Eve."

Marnee accentuating her movement, touches her rib and says, "We are a lot alike." She chuckles and grabs Hunter's shirt at his rib cage and pulls him close and gives him a peck on the lips.

A crewman shouts in Italian from the flying bridge, "Coming on board, Skipper?"

They look up, release one another. Hunter nods, shouts, "Aye."

She murmurs, "Later."

They climb on board.

Marnee and Hunter finish eating their breakfast and pretend to relax and enjoy a morning coffee as they watch the *Sorridenta* approach. As it nears and turns its bow out, away from the slip, Hunter waves to the skipper. He waves back. Pisces is on the bridge, staring at Hunter for a moment, then returns to watching the business of backing his boat into the slip making it much easier to offload and a lesser distance to carry whatever they bring ashore.

Marnee says, "There are two women up on the bridge with him."

Hunter nods, "Yeah, see him. And the crewmen there on the after deck. But, here comes the young man from the villa to assist. And another. A much older guy and it's not Rocco."

"Have you seen him before?"

"No. You?"

"No, but then I haven't seen anyone around Rocco live exceedingly long."

"Got a point. Have to find out who this rascal is. The boy works on the cars, drives occasionally running errands, and helps maintain the property. And he's the one that's been making the nightly rounds at the villa. That won't last long."

As the *Sorridenta* gurgles to a stop, crewmen leap to the dock and tie her down, starting with the stern lines. As they do, Marnee nonchalantly waves a greeting to the two women leaving the bridge. Then she and Hunter continue their pretense of self-interest. Hunter smiles, gives Marnee a peck on the lips. She clasps one of his free hands as they gaze at each other and chat. None of this takes too much play-acting.

With the *Sorridenta* tied up, Marnee and Hunter watch as Pisces directs the young man and his elder as to what needs to be done regarding the luggage. He calls the man Benito when giving directions. As the ladies come to the afterdeck to debark, both give Benito a hug and huge smiles and talk with him for a few moments. He excuses himself, gives some directions to the boy as Pisces and the ladies debark and head down the dock toward the office and parking area. Pisces gives no more notice of his slip mates. That attitude is not being returned in kind however.

Hunter whispers, "I take it the older guy is with the ladies. I'm guessin' he works for the one that Pisces has his arm around now."

"I think you are correct. I wonder who the other one is? She doesn't look, dress or act like a domestic."

"Well, my deprived Marine mind tells me it's a threesome, or possibly he brought a concubine for Rocco. That would be a helluva gift."

Marnee gives him a playful slap on the back of his hand, "Hey, you are giving that woman more of a look than

I appreciate. And is that your 'M-a-r-i-n-e' mind, or your 'M-a-r-n-i-e' mind?"

"The former, and neither of those gals are in your class. Not even close. Now that they're close to being out of here, let's get to the bridge and get a better look-see at the parking lot." They get up and hasten to the bridge.

By the time Hunter and Marnee get to the flying bridge's starboard rail the boy and Benito have finished loading the Black Mercedes 280 sedan, not only from the boat, but also additional bags and boxes from the smaller '71 white Mercedes 280 SL Roadster. There are some more hugs. Longer ones, and then Benito gets into the white car and drives away, toward the highway, not town.

Hunter mumbles, "He's leavin' town. Good. Helleva lookin' car. Like my Vette better."

Marnee snuggles close, whispers, "I'll take the 280 SL, but let's get our minds back on business."

"Really. Yeah, right, back to business."

As they do, the young man opens and holds the front right door for the ladies, and they squeeze into the seat. Pisces gets behind the wheel while the young man fits himself in the back seat among the surplus boxes and luggage. It's a tight fit. The Mercedes is riding low in the back.

They are off quickly, no tires screeching but no time lost, and disappear out of the lot, and head in the general direction of the villa.

Hunter turns to his crew chief, the older man and most experienced of the three, and in Italian issues some instructions for the day, and this evening. Ending with, "Have this baby with a full load of fuel, and be ready to leave anytime, but most likely this evening. The two of us are taking a trip."

The old man smiles, adds a congratulatory wink and follows with, "Yes, bossa."

Marnee adds, "We are going out and about for some fun today, and when we return we will be tired and wanting to get moving as soon as possible. I am looking forward to this cruise."

Hunter says, "That's underway, not moving," and laughs.

The crew chief says, "Yessa, ma'am. And Bossa." Smiles again.

Marnee gives Hunter a more than playful punch on the arm. Smiles, and whispers out of hearing of the crew chief, "After we get 'underway', I have high hopes to get you moving, Marnie."

"Sounds like a plan. Now, let's go below and ensure we have all the provisions we need. Everything, to include your Limoncello and that *Blume Marillen Apricot Eau-De-Vie* I ordered. Even though we'll be puttin' in for fuel several times, I'd sooner it only be that. Okay?"

"Let's go," urges him forward, "and take that look around."

Hunter nods, points the way below and they leave, and as they do, he adds, "We need to be ready every time now. Weapons. Everything."

At the villa, Rocco stands, frowning, his hand resting on the cradled phone in Pisces' study. *Where the hell is MacBeer? What was all that stalling about and who the hell was that on the phone?*

He shakes his head, carries his concerned look with him as he goes onto the veranda. The look disappears as he sees his boss is back, and a young woman is staring at him as she scrambles out of the Mercedes. Halter, no bra and exceedingly short shorts. Her smile is telling. Rocco's grin starts at the corner of his mouth, then spreads rapidly to his entire jaw. *My surprise. Momma-mia!* He mentally kisses his thumb and fingertips.

He hurries toward the sedan and regardless of his fascination with Estella, he heads directly toward Pisces. Business is always business, and Pisces is always first. Foremost. All else follows.

He and Pisces hug in a mafia-like greeting. Whisper some comments to each other, then Pisces, with his arm around her, introduces Rocco to Chiarina. Then with a sweeping motion of the other hand toward Estella, he makes the grand introduction.

Estella stands with both hands on her hips, head canted to one side, gazing at the big Italian. Rocco bows, then smiles wide again with his arms stretched out, palms of his hands up. Stell nods her head several times, a grin appears, and she leaps into Rocco's arms and hugs him. Clings to him for several moments, then whispers in his ear, "I like." Then pushes away, asks, "You?"

Rocco grins. "I like. Let me show you around Mister Catalano's villa." She hooks her arm through his and they turn toward the house. Rocco stops suddenly, turns and says, "Bossa?"

Pisces nods, stares hard, says. "Yes. Go." Then smiles.

Chiarina clutches Pisces, head on his shoulder. He pulls her tight and whispers, "Whether this is the way it will be, will be up to you and Estella. Not him. He is expendable."

She lifts her head, half turns toward Pisces, says, "Roberto, what does that mean?"

"It means that all this," his free arm sweeping towards the villa, "is for the three of us. Any more is of our choosing. We are going to live." He pauses and louder exclaims, "Live!"

CHAPTER 30

"Squeeze, don't pull.
Watch, don't blink.
Move, don't wait."
A Gunslinger's rule.

Hunter and Marnee stroll past the Pisces villa. It's past noon. They pause for a moment across the street. Hunter says, "Wait 'til we walk-on, then glance up this side of the main house and you'll see a shuttered window. The only one with the shutters closed. It's an enlarged pantry of sorts off the kitchen. The shutter lock is a snap to open, and the window's lock is broken. I don't think any of the help realizes it. That's how I got in. That's our entry point tonight. Okay?"
"Yes."
"Well, take a look." Marnee gets a glance as they tramp on up the grade toward the end of a street that rivals Lombard Street in San Fran or at least Snake Alley in Burlington, Iowa. Is certainly the most crooked street in Taormina.
The two are wearing combinations of dark brown and green slacks and long sleeve shirts to blend with the terrace they are about to adopt. Each have a thin layer of neutral make-up on their faces to subdue any glare. Weapons are tucked in the rear waistbands of their slacks. Silencers already attached. Gloves jammed in pockets as are dark ski-mask covers for their heads and extra magazines for their weapons. They continue past the villa, up the hill where Hunter points out a winding path that leads to a semi-wooded portion with heavy undergrowth and rotting lemons. It's an abandoned citrus orchard. It is seventy-five yards from the Pisces villa and elevated enough so one can look down onto the villa's grounds. It looks onto the two-story side of the main house where the bedrooms are and onto the huge veranda. The patio is situated so its occupants, seated at the table, or by the pool have a view down toward the town, the beach and out

to sea to the Ionian coast. No afternoon or evening sun to contend with, and in late afternoon the house itself provides a measure of comfortable shade. Or the folks can simply move to the covered segment of the veranda. Pisces in his selection and improvements has thought of everything pleasurable to include the four-person Jacuzzi and the wood-burning oven. For pizzas probably.

Hunter leads Marnee to a spot he found on one of his previous reconnaissance's. It provides excellent cover and has an after-mission egress that will take them down and around the town and to the bay with little chance of being seen. They settle in, uncomfortably but hidden by the undergrowth. They see the four-door black Mercedes has not been put away in the garage. It's parked and they see the young man washing it with the older gentleman supervising. No roadster or Benito in sight. Nor is anyone else at the moment.

Hunter whispers, "As planned, we sit and watch. Go in tonight, late, and take 'em out."

"The women?"

"Not if we can avoid it at no risk, but we have to go in tonight. Before any chance that Pisces and Rocco institute better security. They have nothing but their belief in the serenity of this place and the covertness of their relocation at the moment. That won't last. Pisces is too paranoid."

"No witnesses."

"None. Then I go to the study, pick up what I need and I'll set the timer. We'll be long gone down the hill. Possibly on the boat and gone."

They both take a sip of water and settle.

Pisces and Rocco wander out to poolside. Drinks in hand. The chaise lounges and small tables have been arranged by the villa's staff, with Rocco's supervision, to accommodate the four of them. Rocco looks up to ensure they will have good sun to tan, or dry themselves should they swim.

Roberto Catalano eases out onto the veranda and says, "Rocco, now we start the rest of our lives. No more work."

He grins and asks before the big Italian can answer, "How was your surprise?"

"It is possible she will killa me before the day is out. She is the besta fu ... " he looks around quickly, catches himself for a few reasons. One, the ladies inside the house are about to come outside. He grins, "besta time ol' Rocco has had in longa time, and she is almost as beautiful as Signora Russo, your Chiarina." He continues, "Ahhh, Bossa, I want to thank you with all ..."

"No thanks necessary. What are friends for? Let's enjoy and speaking of that, they're about to join us."

"Finally," Rocco mutters. Then quickly adds, "Signora Russo is a classy lady. Beautiful. More so than all the others."

"Yeah, and has one helluva lot of moola and property, and a switch-hitter for a friend. Did Estella mention that while she was jumping your bones a little while ago?"

"No, Bossa. Not exactly."

"Not exactly? What the hell does that mean?"

"Well, yes. She say ... ahhh, I don't care unless ... unless ..."

"Unless it includes me? Right?"

Rocco nods his head. Pauses. "Right. Then I no interfere. Go back to Adrianna and perhaps to Rome."

"Hmmmm? Well, here we go."

The bikini clad Chiarina and Estella saunter up, sunglasses propped on their heads and with glasses of white wine in hand. Chiarina asks, "What was that you were saying?"

"Nothing important."

Pecks on the cheek for both men follow, and all four fumble around a tad to get seated properly. Sunglasses pop down, bra tops come off and lotion goes on. Roberto and Rocco remain sitting as the gals lie-out, face up. The arrangement is such that the two men face one another with the women stretched out between them. The sipping of wine and conversation begins. With a glance Pisces and Rocco can see Mount Etna in the distance and in the other direction the town and the Ionian coast. However, their fascination is focused on the four Etna's and two coves sprawled before them.

Seventy-five yards away, Hunter and Marnee watch. Gloves on. Masks on. No chance of a glint being emitted and seen. It's hot and the climb was steep. They take a sip of water. Their conversation is whispered and infrequent. It's all business. However expert and professional, their minds still drift momentarily on occasion to allow individual justifications to wander across the frontal lobe. Also at times they flicker with glimpses of the past: OSS, Assisi, CIA, and Mossad. Old world. New world. But in the end it is nothing more complex than what it is and what they are. Ambush. Hunters stalking their prey.

Chiarina moves first from the chaise lounge. She stands, tugs at her bikini bottom, steps out of it, and then drops it on the seat. She saunters to the edge of the pool, sits, then slips into the aqua blue water and breast strokes to the middle. Stands, turns and faces the group and shouts, "Roberto, come join me. Everyone. Let us have a water fight."

Pisces stands, strips off his trunks and makes a shallow dive from the edge and comes up under his woman. Stands, lifts Chiarina on his shoulders and then dumps her backwards into the water with a splash and her high-pitched scream of profanity. As is everything in his life, he sets the tone. Others follow or they ...

Estella follows, however she takes longer in depositing her bikini bottom and lingers at the edge of the pool so all see the full magnificence of her natural red hair while inhaling deeply, breasts heaving like full moons rising. Then she jumps, squealing into the cool water. Rocco waits, taking in Stel's beauty, then follows suit minus his trunks as well.

Immediately, Roberto and Rocco lift the women onto their shoulders, and the water wrestling begins. After several engagements, they change partners and continue the playful battle. Finally, Chiarina shoulders Estella and they fight Pisces lifted by Rocco. Rocco is noticeably uncomfortable with the arrangement. However, it is difficult to know who is enjoying the match more. Pisces with his groping of Estella as they wrestle or her with Chiarina's neck twisting and wrenching, tucked hard between her thighs. Or Chiarina's joy that is abundant as she grips Estella's thighs with her hands adding to the churning. It is mischievous foreplay which Pisces wins of course, and he ends the play by wrestling a flailing Estella off Chiarina's shoulders, dumping her head first into the pool. Then he dives off Rocco's shoulders in the water and on top of Estella beneath the surface pretending to dunk her. Chiarina joins them in the beneath the surface aquatics. It is what it is. The game is over. When the three surface, the women hug one another for longer than a moment in recognition of their loss, or was it a win?

The final water battle and dunking is followed with healthy laps by all, except for Rocco. He stands leaning at pool's edge with a bent arm resting on the Cool-Crete decking. Laps complete, all pull themselves up and out of the pool and return to their respective lounges. Rocco stands at his chaise, watches, wonders about what he's witnessed, as Pisces moves next to him, staring at him. Then they towel-off, step back into their trunks saying nothing and stretch out. Chiarina and Estella, finish their glasses of wine, then sit and lay-out, face up, to dry in the warm Sicilian afternoon sun. No toweling. No wet bathing suits. Pisces calls to the old woman in the house to bring more wine. She appears with two bottles. Opened. One of white, one of red. One in each hand and tries not to notice the younger, better endowed ladies stretched out, drying.

Pisces gets up and pours for the gals. It's polite. And of course provides another up-close momentary glance at Estella, and eye contact. And with Chiarina as well of course.

Rocco's head rises from his chaise lounge and catches this foreplay once again. His vibes jingle sour notes. *No MacBeer. Not a word from the master prick. Now this.*

He sits up, reaches for the bottle of red wine and offers it first to Pisces.

Pisces nods in acceptance, offering his glass, as he sits on his chaise glimpsing directly into Rocco's eyes. *He knows.*

Above the villa in the now sticky heat, Hunter whispers, "Great bods."

Marnee stares up at Hunter, says, "You keeping a close watch are you? I'm going to stay down here and rest for a short while longer. Okay?"

"Do it. Not much for you to see up here."

"But for you, it is good?"

"Yeah. The best."

"Be patient. Better is coming."

He twists around, looks down at Marnee and sees her eyes sparkling beneath the face mask which is straining from a grin as well. *She's right. They're not in her class.*

"I can see you agree," and she gives him a gentle shove back into position.

Before turning his head, he whispers, "Marnee, you are dazzling. You are the reason cavemen chiseled on walls."

Zachary answers the phone on the first ring. Responds, "Zachary."

Then hears the voice on the other end say, "I've got him. Hog-tied. What next?"

"Where?"

"The Bahamas ... Nassau. Plush, plush house."

"Good work. Now, give him a choice. He writes a note and takes the pills you hand him, or you kill him and make it look like it's self-inflicted."

"That's it?"

"That's it. Tell him what to write. As we discussed."

"Done."

Zachary orders, "I want a confirmation call."

"Yes, sir."

Joe Zachary puts the receiver down, leans back in his chair, and mutters, "Too good for the son-of-a-bitch."

Hunter tugs at Marnee as the sun begins to slip behind Etna. Motions her to raise up. Whispers to her, "The gals have gone into the house."

She scrambles to a sitting position. "The guys aren't moving."

"Nope, and look at the activity at the garage. The kid and the old woman are standing around the car. They're waiting for something. I got a hunch and possibly we get a break. Our agenda may be goin' forward a few notches."

They sip some much needed water in this heat. They are perspiring heavily in these not made for summer outfits. They continue their ambush watch. A half-hour passes and then the two women come out onto the veranda. Talk with Pisces and Rocco, give them pecks on the cheek, and go to the Mercedes. The back doors are open and waiting. They ease in, Chiarina first, both chattering excitedly it seems. Once in, Estella leans over and kisses Chiarina on the cheek as the boy closes the door.

The old woman gets in front, and the young man climbs behind the wheel. He eases the black sedan out of the parking area and onto the street heading for town.

Hunter whispers, "Everyone except the old man and those two are gone. I'd bet they'll be gone for hours, two or three. We're goin' to do it now."

"In daylight?"

"Twilight. Fitting. Those two are relaxed. Way off guard, although there was some silent shit goin' on down there. Gotta be real careful."

"What silent ... stuff?"

"Just something about the way Rocco was acting when they came out of the pool. C'mon, no one will see us. Let's get it done."

Hunter picks the shutter catch easily and finds the window lock still out of order. He peeks in first. Finds it clear, then climbs inside. Takes his weapon from his rear waistband. Goes to the door, cracks it and steals a look into the kitchen and onto the veranda. Pisces and Rocco are still outside. He eases the door closed and returns to the window, motions Marnee inside. Once she's in the interior both replace their gloves and masks they had removed moving from the hill to the house. Marnee draws her weapon as well. He whispers, "Both outside," and they move quietly to the door. Hunter cracks the door and as he does he sees a body flash across the kitchen. He holds the door ajar as it is remaining motionless, listening. He hears the outer kitchen door open and when it closes he peers from the pantry door and sees the old man on the veranda talking and gesturing to Pisces. After several moments, Rocco and Pisces stand, and all three head for the kitchen. Hunter motions to Marnee with three fingers and a gesture toward them that the threesome is coming inside. He leaves the pantry door ajar, scarcely a whisper of enough to hear the three men enter the kitchen and Pisces speak.

"Rocco, go with Carmen and see what the fuck he's jabbering about. While you're gone I'm going upstairs and take a real quick shower. Meet me in the study."

"Yes, bossa. Can I take a quickie first? Doesn't sound like much. Shabby wiring he's found."

"No, after."

"How about after and before I meet with you?"

"No, God dammit. See what this is about, and while there see if you can teach this idiot some language that we can understand when he's excited. Any language. I only hope a herd of elephants aren't charging us or that damn volcano isn't about to blow again. Besides, I want to make a call to our friend MacBeer with you present."

"Okay, bossa." Then immediately says, "Let'sa go, Carmen."

Hunter hears the shuffling of feet, and can see a flashing of bodies pass in front of the pantry door on their way. He hears the stomping of feet going up the stairs and the muffled voices of Rocco and the old man fading as they head outside.

Hunter turns to Marnee, she nods as understanding what is happening. He whispers, "We'll take 'em in the study. C'mon."

She whispers, "What about the wiring that was mentioned? Is that..."

"No. Not a problem. I put in some dummy wiring leads to be found. A wiring mistake disguise in fact."

She shakes her head in wonderment and they ease the pantry door open, whisk through the kitchen, down the tiled hall to the study, and in. It's huge. Desk facing the door, with its back to the veranda. Book lined shelves, some photos, but by and large oil paintings by the master, Pisces.

They stand inside, Hunter whispers again, "We take out the first one that comes in, then wait for the other. Quick, no time for slow kill revenge."

Hunter moves immediately to the desk, opens a drawer and pulls out the envelope he needs. Then he reaches in his pocket, removes the timer, sets it and places it behind some books on one of the shelves. Whispers to Marnee, "Got to do this on the front end. This could be close."

"Do it."

"Done."

And they wait. Not long. Minutes.

To them, their anticipatory breathing alone sounds like old steam engines climbing a grade let alone the sound of water running and shouting from the rear of the house. The passing minutes seem like a decade, a generation of operatives in ambush. Then the door bursts open and Pisces strides in to his desk, not sensing anything until he gets to the front of his mahogany display of wealth and power. He turns, reaches to his back. It's much too late a reaction. Marnee and Hunter both fire double taps. Pssffft...pssfft...pssfft...pssfft. Four hits. Two center mass, the heart. Two in the face. One at the bridge of the nose, the other in the forehead. Pisces' head snaps backward, then his body surges back to the desk. His waist hits the edge, head lurches backward again, then forward as he hits hard polished mahogany of the desk. He drops like a wet sandbag to the tile floor. Blood surging from his chest, face disfigured. Blood splattered on the desk top and the beautiful veranda windows behind. The phone receiver he had reached for in his hand, lies in his lap. The remainder of the instrument ripped from Pisces' desk, rests on the floor in front of the piece of furniture. First the drone of a dial tone, then the buzzing of the disconnect sounding loud enough for MacBeer to hear if he were listening.

Then both hear the footsteps in the hallway.

Hunter mutters, "Shit," and they turn as the door swings open.

Rocco stands in the doorway, swimming trunks and barefoot, with a snub-nosed .38 revolver in his hand. All three fire at once. All get off two shots. All within nanoseconds of one another. Four shots silenced, two not. Marnee cries out, and spins to the study floor, close to Pisces. Two shots have hit her, both high. Hunter is not hit. Four shots hit Rocco. Two in the chest, center mass, heart shots. Two in the head, his forehead like two additional eyes.

Rocco is thrown back through the study door, into the hallway, slammed against the beige plaster wall. He utters a mixture of a growl, a scream, and the gasping utterance of a huge sucking wound in the chest. Blood, brains, bone are splattered around the study door frame and on the hall wall behind. A red smear on the wall where Rocco hit, then trailing down to where he sits. Another sandbag. The snub-nosed .38, not a weapon of choice but probably necessity, unimaginably still is in his right hand. His head, face virtually gone, slumps to his left.

Hunter checks the two of them in seconds, rips his mask from his head and turns to Marnee. Sees she's bleeding profusely. He gently but hurriedly takes off her mask. Checks for a pulse. Rips off his shirt. Tears it in two. And then its sleeves from the shirt. He stuffs a piece of the shirt into each of her gunshot wounds. Then wraps the shirt sleeves as a binding around her body. Tying them tight, trying to apply as much pressure as possible. One shot high in her shoulder although serious is not deadly. The other a high chest wound is critical, probably fatal. He picks her up and cradles her in his arms, whispers, "Marnee. Marnee. Say something. C'mon darlin', hang tough. Say something. Please."

She opens her eyes, mutters, "I love you, Hunter. I love you ..." and as she reaches up with one hand, says, "Oh, Hunter ..."

She's interrupted by shouting. Hunter drops her from his arms, turns toward the door, weapon coming up.

The old man is there and shouting, "I'm coming. I'm coming. Oh my God." He stops and steps over Rocco screaming, "I told you. I told you." Then the old man turns to face Hunter, double-barreled shotgun in hand, cocked.

Hunter fires. Double tap again. Center mass. Forehead.

Carmen is thrown back on top of Rocco. The shotgun clatters to the floor and both hammers fall. Two blasts, simultaneously. A few pellets hit Pisces, a couple catch Hunter's arm, some in the desk, a few in Marnee which add to her predicament. The lamp on the desk is blown off, but most of the twelve gauge buckshot hit and shatter the veranda windows behind the desk.

Hunter surveys the scene. The carnage is complete.

He leans over, "God damn, Devorah. Gotta hurry, the timer is set. Devorah! Devorah! I'm sorry." He sucks in a gulp of air. "Gotta go."

He pauses, lays Marnee's head on the floor and puts his weapon back in his waistband. Mutters, "Mission friggin' accomplished."

EPILOGUE

*"Twenty years from now you will be more
disappointed by the things
that you didn't do than by the things you did do.
So throw off the bowlines.
Sail away from the safe harbor.
Catch the trade winds in your sails.
Explore. Dream. Discover."*
Mark Twain

    Hunter stands on the bridge with his crew chief and the two younger crewmen as they turn north and head for the Strait of Messina. The explosion itself has consumed the crew's conversation. Hunter reluctantly joins the chatter and excitement, but feels he must.

    Now, several hours later, the area is still aglow with some flames defying extinguishing. As a rule however, the glow is from spot lights and the dazzling display of emergency lights. The pandemonium from the activities can be heard through the clear night air to the sea.

    Hunter has showered, gotten rid of his clothes and weapon, everything that could tie him to the scene should they get stopped while at sea or a port along the way. He has packed and addressed the envelope with the hard evidence of Pisces' long history of treachery. It is ready to be mailed from the first port of call. He reported the mission accomplished, the deaths involved, and the condition of the villa. Suggested the bodies won't be found for hours, and when they are, it will probably take days before it is discovered that the explosion and fire were not the cause. As he sits in the lounge, he goes over the conversation in his mind. Joe also informed him that unless he chose to do so, there was no need to visit Capri, saying, "They're all leaving. Have the remains. Bradovich has everything under control. Damn good man, may try to recruit him."

    Hunter had asked, "What about the children?" He was always taught by his father, Corker Kerrigan, that kids were goats, children are children but somewhere along the line he had forgotten the lesson, until lately. "And what about the family? And of course, Maria?"

Joe laughed at his question and tried to speak, then gagged a bit on his own chuckling. Finally he said, "Maria. Yeah. Maria. Well, in Brad's words, and I quote, he started laughing again, then, "His words were ... 'Maria is in love with wine and Polish sausage. Her wine. My sausage.' As he said that I heard Maria scold him in the background. Anyway, they're all gone. On the way back home. Kids are okay or as good as can be expected. Grandparents and the father are taking it extremely hard. And you're not well liked."

I replied, "Sausage, huh? Not well liked. Well, so be it. It is what it is. What about MacBeer?"

"He committed suicide. Was found in his new home in The Bahamas. Shot himself. Anyway, I did get the photocopies you sent. Just need the original stuff. And I'm going to call the President."

"The package will be on the way tomorrow. We'll stop for fuel. To Ruth again. That's it. I'm outta here. Semper Fi ... and tell the President I said hello." And the call was over.

Hunter leans back in the lounge chair, picks up the intercom phone, calls, "Anthony."

"Yessa, sir."

"Let's run her at eleven knots, cruising speed, and head for our first fuel stop. Then head for Genoa, then Nice. We'll not be going to Capri. Keep the coast in sight."

"Yessa, sir."

"I'm going to relax." He puts down the intercom.

The Shanahan family pulls away from their mum's cottage. The moving van will follow them to Cork where the two lads hope to find work, perhaps in construction or the exploration field. A risk they are most willing to take, which is less than all the others of their lifetime. Their mum sits in the front seat of her husband's old 1962 Wolseley. It has seen many a better day as evidenced by his rusting grey painted body, fender mounted rear-view mirrors long gone as is the hood ornament. Two of four of the small, circular chrome hubcaps are missing as well. Danny is driving. Sean and Mary Kate, married by a sleepy priest, are in the back seat. Their honeymoon consisting of a few nights in Sean's bedroom where they tried hard to muffle Mary Kate's squeals and shouts, and his grunts.

They face a long journey, nearly the length of Ireland, but will live in peace, yet miss their eldest brother, Paddy, and their Pa. A stiff price, perhaps unnecessary, for independence.

Once through the Strait of Messina, and basically in the open sea, Hunter, who has gone to the bridge, is comfortable that all is under control. His crew chief, Anthony, and the two crewmen can handle the yacht throughout the night. They will shadow the Italian coast north. With its range the *Marnie,* at its easy cruising speed, can continue through the night and into tomorrow before needing to refuel. Hunter says, "Anthony, I'm goin' below again. Gonna' have some coffee and relax. Give me a holler if you need something. I'll let you know before I hit the sack."

"Yes sir, bossa. Everything is purring like a content pussy cat." He smiles. Then adds, "We will rotate the helm, but I will bunk here throughout the night. No sweata."

"Want me to bring up some coffee for you three?"

"No sir. Notta yet. We will have some later. *Grazi.*"

Hunter, as a last check, glances out at the boat's running lights, out to the calm sea, no white caps, then looks off to the northeast toward the coast line. Shrugs, then turns and leaves.

After pouring himself a mug of coffee, he puts it aside. Claps his hands, rubs them together vigorously and reaches in the cabinet for his bottle of *Blume Marillen Apricot Eau-De-Vie.* Pours a relaxing amount into his snifter, mutters, "Good stuff. From Austria. Might have to try a Baltimore Bang, or a Slope, or a Stone Fruit Sosc tomorrow."

Hunter wanders into the lounge, sits on the overstuffed, beige leather sofa, kicks his loafers off and rests his feet on the beautiful mahogany coffee table which rests on part of the throw carpet of which there are several throughout the yacht. Mostly for protection. All the decking is teakwood, except for the heads and some working spaces.

He takes a sip, murmurs, "Damn, this is good." Exhales audibly as he relaxes. Neck and shoulders lose their tenseness. He twists his neck, hearing the creaks and cracks. Takes another sip, then rests his elbow on the sofa's arm.

"And who the hell is Devorah?" says a cooing voice from behind Hunter.

Hunter stiffens, sits straight up, yanking his feet from the coffee table, and battles to keep the snifter from spilling or falling. "Damn, Marnee, you scared the B-Jesus out of me." He turns to see this beautiful creature standing behind the sofa in a sheer robe, hands on hips, and a pretense of anger on her face.

"Well?"

"What the hell are you talking about?"

"You cried out her name when you were holding me in the villa? Who is that woman? A secret love?"

"Come around here and sit." Hunter stands, holding a helping hand out to Marnee. "You actually shouldn't be up yet. You need rest. Certainly through the night. Actually, days. A week."

"I feel ... well, pretty good. Who did this?" pointing to the bandages and sling.

"Me. I'm good. Not pretty good, but damn good. Turns out no major damage, and I've loaded you up with antibiotics. Looked worse than it was. Lost some blood and you'll need time and rest." He pauses, then, "Hey, you need some food. Sit, I'll rustle something up real quick."

"My goodness, a Marine, a doctor, and a chef. How lucky."

"Yeah, well. You were lucky. We were lucky, but it's all over now. We're home free and on our way to Genoa and Nice. Stop for fuel on the way a few times. If necessary, get a doctor."

Marnee moves close to Hunter, puts one arm, the one that isn't in a sling, around his waist and pulls him close. Brushes his lips with hers, bites him on the ear lobe and whispers, "Who is Devorah, Mister?"

Hunter moves back a step, orders, "Sit." She does. Her robe slides open as she crosses her legs. The front of the robe is also open. Hunter murmurs, "Oh, geez, Marnee, don't do this to me."

"Who?"

"Oh, damn. She was a Jewish girl in a dream I had. A nightmare. She was killed. Not a real woman. Just a dream. You are my real dream. I love you. Now then, let me get you some chow, and I'll sit down and tell you about this nightmare I had. Before this mission. It was an omen. If truth be told, it was. Helleva tale."

"So, you dreamed of a Jewish girl? And now you have one. What are your plans? Your intentions?"

Hunter sits down, next to Marnee, on the edge of the cushion. "I plan to ask her to marry me. To sail away with me. To catch the trade winds. To explore one another. To dream. To discover. To love ... and to make Limoncello and apricot brandy."

She kisses him full on the lips, grimacing some as he holds her. She pulls back, pecks Hunter on the tip of the nose and whispers, "And babies."

He sits gazing at Marnee, a tear forms and runs down his cheek. He mutters, "Yes, children." He sighs, "God, I thought I lost you."

She gives him another peck on the nose, brushes the tear from his cheek with her little finger. Whispers, "Now the food. Then we'll figure out a way to get started. I can heal anytime, but I must have you all the time. All my life. We are going to live. Live."

Hunter gives her a peck on the nose and leaps up and says, "Chow's comin' up," and turns to go into the galley.

Her voice trails after him, words catching him as he enters the galley. "And we are going to keep this boat, and, keep the name. I love it." Marnee picks up his snifter and is startled by, "Put that down." Hunter stops and turns around, "I'll get you a Limoncello. Just one for now." He opens the refrigerator's door.

Joe Zachary sits at his desk. Red phone in his hand. Listening intently.

Every few minutes he says, "Yes, sir, Mister President." After a few more moments he says, "I don't know, Mister President. He says he's finished. Going to raise lemons and make Limoncello."

A moment passes, then, "It's a liqueur. From lemons of course. It's a staple in Italy and Amalfi lemons, that's where he's going to live, are known as 'Sfusato Amalfitano' and are prized as one of the best varieties in the world. They have ...

"No, Mister President. This is not going to be an agricultural lesson.

"Yes, sir. With the Hebrew woman. Marnee Kaslar.

"Yes, sir. She will be fine. Her grandparents own and operate a huge lemon orchard on the Amalfi coast. Marnee, her mother, and Hunter are going to run it.

"No, sir. But he did say to tell you that if you're ever in Italy on business or on vacation, come visit.

There is a prolonged pause before Joe speaks again. Then says, "Yes, sir, I'll tell him you asked, and that you might not visit but you might call on him again."

A pause. Joe listens some more.

"Well, sir. He did say never. He was unequivocally specific, I think ... but ... you never know. Never know. He is one patriotic son-of-a-gun."

Joe hears the click ending the call. Stares at the phone. "Good? What the devil does that mean?" He leans back once again in his chair, lets his mind drift.

He'll be back.
No he won't.
Maybe.
I hope. That's for sure, that's for danged sure.

Made in the USA
Charleston, SC
17 October 2012